"I worship at the altar of this book. Somehow Michelle has managed to write a hilarious, scorching, devastat observed novel about addiction, sex, identity, the nir ties, apocalypse, and autobiography, while also giftin us with an indispensable meditation on what it mear to write about those things—indeed, on what it mea to write at all. A keen portrait of a subculture, an ins classic in life-writing, a go-for-broke exemplar of que feminist imagination, a contribution to crucial, ongo conversations about whose stories matter, *Black Wave* is a rollicking triumph."

— **MAGGIE NELSON**, *The Argonauts*

"*Black Wave* is definitely Michelle Tea's most fearless book. Charles Dickens–sharp and attentive to the morose and glittering detail like always, yet *Black Wave* threatens to take everything and everybody down. It's Michelle Tea's apocalyptic book and I was unable to put it down for fear I no longer felt sure of what was out there beyond my reading, so destabilizing and palpable is this bad fairytale come true. It's a radically honest and scary book. And trust me, it's a bloody and wonderful place Michelle has spun, fantastic, dark, and entirely awake. It shook me up."

— **EILEEN MYLES**, *Chelsea Girls*

"With *Black Wave*, Michelle Tea has made a quantum leap, surpassing even the fearlessly fucked-up and spit-kiss vivid genius of her previous work—which is saying something. Tea renders her story with such ferocity, such soul, such shameless, wild-ass detail and weird delight, she will probably be banned from North Carolina for life. Queer, straight, fluid, or confused—if you've ever loved, ever struggled, ever felt cut off from what passes for normal on this demented hellhole of a planet, this brilliant, beautiful book will rip your heart out and put it back in a better place."

—JERRY STAHL, *Permanent Midnight*

"Michelle Tea has written an apocalypse I can get behind! I could spend my end of days with these characters. Tea is one of the most important writers of the twenty-first century. Now, go devour this book."

—ALI LIEBEGOTT, *The Beautifully Worthless*

"Michelle Tea is like no other writer. *Black Wave* amps her uniquely seductive whirl of ugliness, hilarity, and brainy, sexy, revelry to produce a work with the centripetal pull of a maelstrom. You will be sucked in."

—HEIDI JULAVITS, *The Vanishers*

"Scary, funny, and genre-bending—*Black Wave* is Michelle Tea's most ambitious, complex, and imaginative work so far. An investigation of addiction's apocalypse, it's somehow wonderfully strange, daring, and dirty, and yet completely universal and true."

—JILL SOLOWAY, creator of *Transparent*

"Listen up: it's the end of the world and Michelle Tea is the writer to be with. She's got the smarts and the laughs, the sharpness and the love, the grit and the skin and the ink she needs to see us through. I'm sticking with her until there's nothing left."

—DANIEL HANDLER, *We Are Pirates*

"Incandescent, breathtaking in its nakedness, and painfully hilarious. Every few pages, I needed to put *Black Wave* down and sigh and think and be. *Black Wave* feels so familiar and so mine, like it has always lived deep deep deep in the corners of my soul. Even if our lives could not be more different I know and have felt exactly as she has."

— **KATHRYN HAHN, actor**

"Michelle Tea is a badass, a rebel, and a marvelously dangerous artist. Whether we know it or not, many women of my generation grew up under her influence. *Black Wave* continues her unbroken pattern of kicking butt."

— **SARA BENINCASA, *Agorafabulous!* *Dispatches from My Bedroom***

"*Black Wave* . . . in which worlds end, neighborhoods transform, capitalism triumphs; Michelle leaves SF and moves to LA, gives up drugs, spots celebrities, fucks Matt Dillon, tries to write a screenplay. Tinged with dark humor and leavened by wicked insights into ambition, disappointment, celebrity, and destitution, *Black Wave* will ruin you, rescue you, and ruin you again. Think Djuna Barnes on crack, think Burroughs with balls, think feminism on fire. If you read one book before the end of the world, let it be this one."

— **JACK HALBERSTAM, *Gaga Feminism***

Also by Michelle Tea

BLACK WAVE

THE FEMINIST PRESS
AT THE CITY UNIVERSITY OF NEW YORK
NEW YORK CITY

Published in 2016 by the Feminist Press
at the City University of New York
The Graduate Center
365 Fifth Avenue, Suite 5406
New York, NY 10016

feministpress.org

First Feminist Press edition 2016

 This book was made possible thanks to a grant from New York State Council
on the Arts with the support of Governor Andrew Cuomo and the New York
State Legislature.

First printing September 2016

Cover design and text design by Suki Boynton
Cover and interior photos by Gretchen Sayers

Names: Tea, Michelle, author.
Title: Black wave / Michelle Tea.
Description: First Feminist Press edition. | New York : Feminist Press at
CUNY, 2016.
Identifiers: LCCN 2016011700 (print) | LCCN 2016018502 (ebook) | ISBN
9781558619395 (softcover) | ISBN 9781558619463 (e-book)
Subjects: LCSH: End of the world--Fiction. | Storytelling--Fiction. |
Lesbians--Fiction. | BISAC: FICTION / Literary. | FICTION / Lesbian. |
FICTION / Contemporary Women. | FICTION / Coming of Age.
Classification: LCC PS3570.E15 B58 2016 (print) | LCC PS3570.E15 (ebook) |
DDC 813/.54--dc23
LC record available at https://lccn.loc.gov/2016011700

For Beth Pickens

BLACK WAVE

SAN
FRANCISCO

1 Michelle wasn't sure when everyone started hanging out at the Albion. She had managed to pass the corner dive for years without going inside, simply noting the dank, flat-beer stink wafting from its open doors, catching the glow of the neon sign hung above the bar— SERVICE FOR THE SICK—in hot, red loops. It seemed that all the other dives had been purchased and repurposed, renovated and sold to a different clientele. The purple-lit bar where middle-aged, working-class bulldaggers nursed beers at the counter was, overnight, converted into a heterosexual martini bar where men who smoked actual cigars drank chocolate martinis and harassed the women who passed by on Valencia. It was 1999.

Aside from the neon sign glowing its sinister pronouncement, the Albion's other notable fixture was Fernando, a man who wore a mullet and a leather vest and carried a brown paper bag, the sort a mother will pack her child's lunch in. It contained cocaine heavily cut with baby laxative. Michelle and her friends would pool their resources and walk into the women's restroom with Fernando, who would tear a page from the stack of *Cosmopolitan* and *Glamour* in the corner, origami it into a little envelope, and dip it into his sack of drugs. The rumor on Fernando was that he used to work for the government, the FBI or the CIA, and was so hooked up with the most corrupt corners of the system that he was immune from being busted. Everyone felt very safe buying drugs from Fernando in the women's restroom at the Albion.

Oh, Valencia, Michelle mourned. Michelle was a poet, a writer, the author of a small book published by a small press that revealed family secrets, exposed her love life, and glamorized her recreational drug intake. Her love life and recreational drug intake had been performed up and down Valencia Street, the main drag of San Francisco's Mission neighborhood, once Irish, then Mexican, later invaded by a tribe bound not by ethnicity but by other things—desire, art, sex, poverty, politics. For six years Michelle had lived adjacent to this particular strip of gentrification and resistance, of commerce and SRO hotels and boutiques and taquerias. And, of late, it had changed. The Chameleon, a bar hung with velvet clown paintings, where Michelle had read her first poem to an audience, was no more. The poem had been awful, a melancholy love poem delivered in poetry voice, that stilted, up-toned lilt. She had compared her lover to a desert and her heart to a piece of cactus fruit busted up on the dusty ground. She had feared the poem was bad but rationalized that bad art had its fans and that her shabby offering would find its people. And at the close of the open mic a meek young lesbian had brought her shaved head over to Michelle and shyly thanked her.

Michelle had a special place in her heart for the Chameleon, its stage painted sloppily with giant orange flames. Its poetry event was famously unruly—all the poets were alcoholics, slamming each other in the head with chairs like professional wrestlers. That bar was Michelle's first home in San Francisco, when she moved there from New England. She had enjoyed playing the part of the quick-witted and enraged baby dyke, she loved to clamber up to the microphone and holler at the drunks to Shut The Fuck Up! before launching into a spoken-word diatribe against pornography and child molestation. She did it well enough that the drunks stayed quiet, gave her a grudging respect afterward. When she bound her rants into xeroxed manifestos they bought them, and Michelle traded their damp dollars at the bar for pints of beer. The Chameleon was its own ecosystem, but the owner had fallen into a crack habit and so the business went under. Some French people bought it and renamed it Amnesia, as if Michelle would forget. It was so perfect it was cruel, the new name. Amnesia. Michelle marveled at it.

It seemed to be sweeping the Mission, amnesia. Every time Michelle blinked a familiar place had shimmered into an alien establishment. The Casanova had retained its name but gotten a new crowd, people Michelle had never before seen in her neighborhood. They looked like they had jobs, and money. Restaurants she could not afford to eat in were luring people from other enclaves, people once too frightened to visit the Mission, where people sold drugs and shot at one another with guns. These new arrivals wore clothing that had never been worn by anyone but them, clothing they would tire of and donate to the Salvation Army, where Michelle would buy it and wear it on this very street a year from now. There was a chain here, a cycle, Michelle could sense its churn. Anyway, the Mexican families who had been there forever had watched Michelle and her scrappy ilk invade the streets years earlier, artists and queers, damaged white people bringing dumpy coffee shops and these poetry bars. Why did she think her world wasn't supposed to change?

Michelle pondered the question of her changing neighborhood in the darkness of the Albion, the last dive standing. A place where a cockroach once lost its grip on the ceiling and tumbled onto her notebook. A place where her checkbook was once stolen by a crackhead. Her black army bag had been slung over the back of her chair and the man was sitting behind her. Michelle had seen him and noted the scrawniness of his physique, the bug of his eyes, his cheekbones like broken glass threatening to slice through the skin of his face. Michelle played it cool. The Albion was the kind of place where one fraternized with crackheads. Go get a fucking appletini at Blondie's if you can't handle it, yuppie. Michelle could handle it. She gave the crackhead a nod of camaraderie—weren't they both high on the same substance, after all? Michelle, a white girl, took her cocaine heavily cut with the aforementioned baby laxative in an inhalable line. This gentleman, African American, bought his in the smokable rock configuration. Michelle knew there were currently people in academia writing papers about this. If the man had hung around any longer she might have even bought him a beer, depending on the bonhomie quality of that evening's cocaine, but the gentleman dipped his trembling hand into Michelle's bag, snatched her checkbook, and took off before the bartender kicked him out. The Albion did not officially condone crack smoking. They would eighty-six you for firing your pipe in the bathroom, yet the bar had a resident cocaine salesman and people brazenly cut lines atop the glass of the pinball machine. Michelle did not condone this hypocrisy. Total bullshit.

Michelle had smoked crack cocaine only once and did not find it enjoyable.

She and her friends had been playing pool at the lesbian bar when a man with a tear tattooed beneath his eye wandered in. The man had been in prison for many years, last time he'd been free the lesbian bar had been a Mexican bar. He was confused but thirsty, and so he purchased a beer and played a game of pool with Ziggy and Stitch. Ziggy's hair was orange as a traffic cone. She was an ex-junkie medicating her addiction with uppers and booze. She was a poet who enjoyed yelling her verse and a cook employed by the finer restaurants in San Francisco. When Ziggy got drunk her spatial cognition tanked and her lips got very wet. She would corner you in an intense conversation, keeping you pinned with her sharp green eyes, licking her lips. Michelle was into it, she loved intense conversations and getting drunk made the whole world feel severe and profound, teeming with wonder and pain. She enjoyed the company of others who could feel it—drunks and poets, mainly.

Stitch, Michelle's housemate, was also swapping more dangerous addictions for controlled alcoholism and the occasional cocaine indulgence. A few years back, she had transitioned from femme to butch and became everyone's project. Established butches made donations of well-worn Jack Daniel's T-shirts. Older femmes groomed her to their liking, gifting her with outsized belt buckles and other late-nineties accessories.

The two butches played pool with the ex-con while Michelle, who hated pool, hung around sipping drinks and watching the sun go down outside the bar's open door. The hue of the sky was the visual equivalent of the alcohol settling into her body—dusky blue shot with gold and darkening to navy. San Francisco, like many cities, had become a vampire town. The killer sun charged the pollution in the skies into a smoggy cocktail. By day, people darted from shelter to shelter like roaches stunned by sudden light, visors like riot gear shading their faces, SARS masks strung across their jaws, parasols arcing above their melanoma-spotted heads. Places of commerce opened later and later. Business visionaries inverted the workday. It was predicted that by 2010, nine-to-five would be fully replaced by five-to-nine. If everything lasted that long.

Michelle had arrived at the bar at sunset, still sleepy. The first rush of booze perked her up, the sugar infusing her with a pleasant mania before it released her into that darker, confused place where her mind became a sea that consciousness bobbed about on, rolling with the waves of passion and opinion.

Just then, a marauding band of already-drunk yuppies crashed into the bar and made a flamboyant fuss over the ex-convict's inky teardrop tattoo—*Oh my god were you in JAIL did you KILL someone?* As they swarmed him, Michelle and her friends were there to tell them to back the fuck off. The three of them were just drunk enough to enjoy a righteous fight, all were perpetually pissed about the changes the neighborhood was experiencing. All three knew someone who was now making thousands of dollars playing foosball and drinking energy drinks in the break room of an Internet start-up, and all three knew someone who'd been evicted from their home to make room for a foosball-playing young millionaire. Ziggy, on the verge of eviction for months now, had sabotaged the sale of her home once already by running around the apartment half-naked with a dildo strapped to her hips when a speculative realtor came calling.

What, the gang demanded of these offensive yuppies, were they even doing in the queer bar? Were they even queer? The invaders wobbled over to the corner of the bar to regroup, and Ziggy, who spoke some shitty Spanish, asked the man with the tattoo if he could find them cocaine. He could. The trio stormed out of the bar. Michelle wondered briefly if it was a good idea for the man, only just released from prison, to be sourcing illegal drugs for a passel of queer white girls, but decided to go with the flow. It would be an experience, and Michelle was a writer.

As they cruised the Mission in Ziggy's beat-up molester van—the windows blackened, the doors warped as if gangs of kidnapped children had tried to batter their way out— Michelle felt proud that she and her friends knew the proper and respectful way to hang out with a recent ex-convict with a teardrop tattooed on his face. The world was bigger than it had been ten minutes ago, a rabbit hole into which they could all tumble. The man was very good-looking, with a prison-yard physique, short hair, and a sort of humility. He hopped from the van on Capp Street and returned with his fist clenched around the drugs. He opened his palm.

No! Ziggy exclaimed. *Coca, coca!* She shook her orangey head at the substance he'd procured. *This is crack.* She laughed, a rueful snort. Ziggy wore a pair of goggles with lenses the same shade as her hair. She wore them strapped to her skull, just above her forehead, keeping her Kurt

Cobain bob out of her face. It was like a butch headband. Ziggy's teeth were so bad from her poverty and drug use they tumbled about in her mouth like a handful of chipped marbles. *I love crack*, she said sadly, and piloted the van to an empty lot in Hayes Valley, stopping briefly to purchase a special pipe off a lady crackhead on Mission. Michelle wondered for a second if there were diseases to be caught from the burned glass pipe of a career crackhead, but she had learned that fearful questions in such situations could lead to racism, to classism, to all sorts of unevolved and judgmental states of mind, and so one did not think too hard. One just accepted the chipped pipe with its charred bowl and one inhaled. And then one slid open the van door and puked onto the pavement, because crack is repulsive.

Outside the van, vines threaded themselves lushly through a chain-link fence and the parked cars sat soft, reflecting soft streetlights. It was 1999 and the earth's decline was accelerating. Most native plants and trees were gone, leaving hardier invasive species. This one had leaves like wide, flat elephant ears, their green sheened with gloss. It had no business growing in San Francisco, but Michelle, hungry for green, appreciated it. Kids growing up now wouldn't know any better, but Michelle had been raised among oak trees and maples, linden trees that perfumed summer nights. The town that had borne her was a shitty one, but back then even a shitty town had trees. Now even nice neighborhoods barely had a garden.

Michelle was too drunk to feel a single inhalation of crack. She leaned back in the van and watched Ziggy and Stitch fight over it—like, who was holding the pipe too long, who was owed their next hit, who had dropped a crumble of rock into the van's carpeted shag and needed to *fucking find it, now.* Michelle had indulged in drugs with her friends many times and never had she seen such fiendish behavior. It was disturbing to see them acting like such dopeheads. Then Ziggy and Stitch began fooling around with the ex-con. They took turns making out with him. He was cute enough, and Michelle knew how it was to be all fucked up with no one to make out with. Ziggy and Stitch weren't going to make out with each other—that would be gross. Michelle would be gross as well, maybe grosser. They were family. With his face stuck to Ziggy's, the man's hand slithered over and landed on Michelle's leg, only to be smacked off by Stitch. *Not her,* Stitch snapped.

He gave Michelle a sincere apology, the inky tear suspended beneath his hangdog eyeball, and returned to Ziggy. He had only wanted Michelle to feel included, but Michelle wasn't butch enough to mess around with men. It would be simply heterosexual, and slutty. For Ziggy and Stitch it was something else, proof of their toughness. They could tumble around with this guy and emerge from the van as queer as ever, more queer, even, and the man might now in fact be a bit queer from his time spent cracked out in Ziggy's butch bosom. Ziggy smacked the man lightly in his face and they both smiled. Radical was the order of the day and it was not radical for Michelle, with her normal girly gender, to fool around with a guy. It would be a normal, boring, sell-out thing to do. But Ziggy and Stitch, both of them looking, acting, dressing, and smelling like boys, could do anything they wanted and be radical. They brought their radicalness into every situation and radicalized it with their presence.

Michelle caught a ghost of her reflection in the dark van window—blue hair, a bit fried from the effort. Bangs fringed her forehead, uneven, hacked off at home with a dull pair of scissors. Her kelly-green pleather coat was one of Stitch's femme castoffs. She wore an orange slip as a dress, the tucks in the chest stitched for a woman more voluptuous than she. Its lacy neckline ballooned around her scrawny sternum. Alcohol bloat plumped her cheeks. A leopard scarf was knotted around her throat. She wore motorcycle boots on her feet, so heavy, every step demonstrating gravity. It was the end of the century.

Michelle stretched out on the van floor, leaning against the bench seat in the back, teetering between boredom and discomfort. As a writer, Michelle was happy to have smoked the crack. Having been unable to get it together and apply to college, she knew her literary education would happen on the streets. The streets were like the ocean—full of trash and beauty, and no one had the right to say which was which, not at this late date. Michelle would sit on the curb and illuminate what the tide pulled in.

Ziggy was an expert drunk driver. She took corners fast and loose, coming up on two wheels and returning to four with the grace of a pilot touching down on the tarmac. Soon Ziggy would tire of this escapade and drive her and Stitch home. Until that happened, Michelle knew her friends would make sure their new acquaintance didn't slide his hand up the underwear she was trying to pass off as a dress. She could relax and space out, attempt to locate the effects of the drug in her body, elusive beneath the familiar roll of liquor. She yawned and checked "smoke crack" off her to-do list. The van rumbled to her door as the rumor of morning began to glimmer in the sky. Michelle felt relief. Nights she fell asleep before the sun came up were good nights. It meant that her life was under control.

2 That afternoon Michelle woke up on her futon craving a salt bagel and an Odwalla, the inside of her mouth an apocalypse, same as always. The sun blasted her windows, the dirt on the glass more a curtain than the shreds of gauzy fabric she'd hung over the panes. A carousel of flies buzzed in drunken circles in the air above her bed. It was past noon. Stitch had left for work hours ago to teach children at a Montessori school. Ziggy, she figured, would sleep until sunset, wake up in a shame spiral, and clean her room the way men at car washes detail their sports cars—anxiously, thoroughly, washing the narrow ledges of baseboard with a vinegar-soaked rag. Color-coding her sock drawer. Superstitious cleaning, its intent to ward off demons obvious. Once Ziggy's room was clean she would roast an organic chicken or something. She would make plans to hang out with her other friends—people she knew from Minneapolis, people their age who seemed bizarrely older because they owned a house or were trying to get pregnant or managed a Starbucks in the Financial District.

They were nice people but Michelle couldn't relate to them. Whenever they got together, usually for something in Ziggy's honor, Michelle felt prickly, like she was in junior high again, eating dinner at a classmate's house, getting judged by her classmate's parents. She felt buttons become latched around her personality, she reigned herself in. Her eyes swooped down regularly to make sure her boobs weren't falling out of whatever lingerie she was pretending was a shirt. Michelle's boobs were so small they should not have been able to fall out of anything, which said much about the state of her wardrobe. Michelle would be stiff and quiet through the gathering until she began to drink, and then she would get in a fight with the woman who managed the Starbucks.

Ziggy would spend the rest of the month with these adult friends. The memory of the crack and the convict, the brutality of the hangover would all fade, and Ziggy would call Michelle, and Michelle would soon find herself in a bathroom with Ziggy, the din beyond the locked door a low roar, and they would do some drugs together and burst out into the mayhem. They would begin anew.

Stitch, too, would briefly change her ways. She would monitor her immune system nervously, feeling up her throat for lumps. She would gargle with salt water and pop supplements. She would eat niacin and flush red as it burned the toxins out from her skin. The foods she prepared would be selected for the medicinal qualities they possessed. She would eat bowls of anemic leafy greens and raw garlic smeared on toast. The pint glasses stolen from the bar would get crammed with halved lemons and cayenne pepper. Stitch would think she was getting sick for about a week and then she would be ready to drink

Budweiser, to score something powdered for her nose, to convince Michelle to let her cut a design into the skin of her arm with an X-Acto knife because they were very drunk and slightly bored and grooving on being best friends. Stitch loved carving on people when she was drunk. Michelle had a little star, an asterisk keloided on her upper shoulder from such a night. One of Stitch's ex-girlfriends, Little Becky, had what looked like the words ZOO KEG etched into her stomach, right where her sports bra ended. It actually read 2:00 KEG and was meant to be instructions for Little Becky to either return a tapped keg to the liquor store by 2:00 or a reminder for Little Becky to come to a keg party at 2:00. No one could remember. Michelle had liked Little Becky. She had an odd manner, bashfully respectful, her hands clasped behind her back, her eyes cast low. Her shaggy-dog hairdo tumbled onto her face. She was gentle. She cried very easily. But something about Stitch and Becky's relationship turned Becky into a monster. She flung Stitch's leather dildo harness out the air shaft, where it landed in an ancient pile of garbage, irretrievable. She stabbed a steak knife into Stitch's bedroom walls then burst into tears. Michelle was glad when they broke up. Her room was right beside Stitch's, she never could be sure if the rough sounds coming from her neighbor were sex or something more troubled.

Michelle got out of her crummy futon and fished around on the wooden floor of her bedroom for something to wear to the bagel shop. Every day she ordered a salt bagel with dill cucumber cream cheese, prompting one bagel worker, also a student at the Chinese medicine school, to wonder what caused her to wake each day with such a thirst for salt. Michelle just shrugged and waited for the girl to pour her giant cup of coffee and drop her bagel on the toaster's glowing conveyor belt.

Michelle lived three blocks from the bagel shop. Every morning she thought of the walk with dread, it brought her through the crossroads of Sixteenth and Mission. Crackheads, skinny and grimy and as indistinguishable as pigeons, trolled the corner, fighting with one another, spare changing or nodding off, baking where the bricks sloped up around the BART hole. That afternoon Michelle paid them special mind. At one time they were like her, they had had this day: the day after they first smoked crack. Surely none of them thought it would land them there, drooling in public, their mouths askew, shit on their pants, looking like zombies, their eyes bugged and their minds emptied. No one did drugs thinking they'd become a drug addict. Everyone was looking for fun and sure of their control, just like Michelle right then, moving past that curbside death row, heading toward Valencia where the crackheads fell away and were replaced by boutiques and bagelries. Michelle touched her cheeks, already hot from the terrible sun. She needed to buy sunscreen or one of those special global-warming visors that came down over your face and made you look like an asshole. The thought of buying anything beyond a bagel exhausted her.

What would Michelle do while her friends recovered from their drug binge? She would sit at the bagelry and try to write another book. The heartbreak of having written and published a first book is that the world then expected you to write a second. She would sit in cafés and scribble in her notebook and feel superior to the cleaner people with laptops flipped open on their nearby tables. She would write, and later she would read her efforts aloud in the remaining neighborhood bars. She would report to her job at the bookstore this week in slightly better condition for not having spent her evenings in bar bathrooms with Ziggy and Stitch. When her friends were repaired they would call for her, and she would come.

3 One remarkable thing about Michelle is that she had two mothers and zero fathers. Her mother Wendy was a psych nurse at a New England hospital and her mother Kym had been a stay-at-home, pot-smoking mom. The moms had gone through a lot to be together. They weren't big-city lesbians like Michelle and her friends, they had stayed close to the cities that birthed them, impoverished places full of xenophobia and crime. Boston was only across a bridge, but they didn't go there. Wendy and Kym had come together in a windowless gay bar that most of the city of Chelsea, Massachusetts, was not even aware existed. It sat on the very outskirts of town by an ancient rusty drawbridge that led to East Boston. In its darkened space were some gay men. Wendy and Kym were the only other lesbians in the place and so they gravitated toward one another, found one another attractive, and were grateful to have hooked up so easily so close to home. No braving Boston and all its urban treachery to find love.

They settled into each other quickly and were soon

disowned by their families. Wendy's father declared that all his children had disappointed him—Wendy's sister married a black man and her brother fathered a child at thirteen— and, declaring Wendy the final straw, cut off contact with his offspring. Wendy's siblings resented her for this and so they were gone as well. Kym should have been so lucky. Her family chose to stay in her life and torment her, vacillating between bouts of antigay rage and a weeping martyrdom where everyone phoned in on behalf of Kym's mother, who was *literally dying of heartbreak and shame* and needed Kym to get back to being straight, pronto.

But in recent years, much to her own horror, Kym had begun to think she maybe possibly perhaps wasn't totally gay. She was certainly somewhat gay—absolutely. But she was also something else. At some point in her daughter's young life, Kym had begun getting crushes on men in the neighborhood. The manager at the Salvation Army who looked the other way when she switched the price tags on furniture and appliances. The guy who worked the register at Store 24, where she bought candy when the munchies set in. The interchangeable men living unsatisfied lives with their own families up and down her dead-end street. They were the scariest. They stared at her a little too long when she pushed the stroller through the detritus-strewn neigh- borhood. They made such a big deal about being cool with lesbos that she knew they were all bigoted assholes. They winked at her and told her she was looking good. Kym was tall and lanky, her beauty sort of sunken, a tad masculine, odd the way that models were odd. Kym knew the guys in her neighborhood all thought she hadn't found the right man yet, and her heart sank into her stomach and began to rot there, for what if they were right? What if there was a man for Kym, someone who thrilled her more than Wendy? Wendy had been such a thrill back in the day, a revelation, drinking wine straight from the bottle, her stained lips coming at Kym, her voluptuous body spilling wonderfully from her clothes like a foamy head on a great glass of beer. They had both believed in their love, a love so great their families had turned against them, driving them into one another with righteousness and fury.

Kym could not be the cliché, the horror of lesbians everywhere. She could not be the woman who went gay so dramatically, who even started a lesbian family and then bailed for the straight life. She was in too deep. There were other people involved, like Michelle, for god's sake, and their other child, a fey boy named Kyle. The children had been tormented at school for having lesbo moms, and what did Kym tell them when they came home crying? She told them it was a gift to be different and that they should be proud and never buckle to the pressures of normalcy. How then could she abandon this family that was more like a political party or a grassroots nonprofit organization? How could she betray them in order to lie beneath the heaving, grunting body of some dude? She could not. She stopped leaving the house. She got really tired. Her head hurt and her appetite withered. She smoked more pot and the headache subsided, she nibbled at granola. The streets outside their small shingled home seemed to be crawling with virile men, each one a sexual fantasy, a bad porno waiting to happen. The pizza deliveryman. The plumber. A pair of fresh-faced Mormons making their conversion rounds through the neighborhood. Kym drew the blinds. Anxiety climbed her like a trellis. A doctor gave her pills and she ate them.

On the television Kym learned how the world was making people sick. People were reporting customized blends of fatigue, ache, anxiety, and depression. Their joints creaked and their blood seemed to sag in their veins. Some things throbbed while others went numb. It was suspected to be the Internet. It was suspected to be computers, generally. Probably it was chemicals, in particular the ones lodged in the air. It was the lack of water, how everyone was so dehydrated. It was time, which passed faster and, therefore, more abusively than it once had. It was the death of God. It was how meaningless everything was. It was the lack of trees and foliage, it was the animals made extinct and the sludge of the sea. It was all the wars being fought in far away places so that Kym could crank the air conditioning one more month, then another, then, *thank god*, another. It was the heat. It was the heavy rains and the black mold festering in the walls like a tormented psyche. It was Compound Environmental Malaise. No one knew how to treat it. Naturopaths recommended marijuana, so Kym kept smoking. Western medicine prescribed pills and so (to cover all bases) Kym ate them. There were support groups but Kym didn't like to leave the house. Wendy found her an online group, but using the Internet to get support for an illness rumored to be caused by the Internet felt counterintuitive and Kym declined. Only the television seemed safe. Television had been around forever and no one had gotten sick from it. Kym longed for the yesteryear of landlines, heavy phones whose cables and wires rooted into the ground like plants. Safe things, not these teeny little cell phones transmitting cancers.

Kym had the television, the couch, and some pot. She

had Wendy, who kindly pretended that everything was normal and did not force Kym to reckon with the probable psychological core of her malaise. Lesbians had long been at the forefront of environmental illnesses, shaming people for wearing scents since the 1970s. It was practically a political stance. She knew Wendy would stand by her.

4 It was the annual Youth Poetry Slam Championship. Michelle and Ziggy were invited to help score the performances and select a winner. They were shocked to be found respectable enough to be allowed around young people, and flattered that anyone thought they were so expert on poetry as to be able to form a wise opinion. But also they were sad, and confused. Did this mean they weren't youths anymore? It is so hard for a queer person to become an adult. Deprived of the markers of life's passage, they lolled about in a neverland dreamworld. They didn't get married. They didn't have children. They didn't buy homes or have job-jobs. The best that could be aimed for was an academic placement and a lover who eventually tired of pansexual sport-fucking and settled down with you to raise a rescue animal in a rent-controlled apartment. If you didn't want that—and Michelle and Ziggy didn't, not yet, anyway—you just sort of rolled through the day, not taking anything very seriously because life was a bit of a joke, a bad one.

We Are Adults, Michelle said to Ziggy. That's Why We Are Up Here And Not Down There.

Weird, Ziggy said. They sat in the risers of a dance studio and watched as teen after teen approached the microphone and delivered their wordy anthems and manifestos. Clear patterns emerged. Anger was channeled into rage against injustice. People were mad: at racism, at the cops, at teachers and parents, at the prison industrial complex and the criminalization of poverty. These kids hadn't had a glass of water in months. Their families couldn't afford meat. They were raised on ABC books featuring kangaroos and zebras, donkeys and gorillas, only to come of age and find them all gone the way of the dinosaur. The earth was totally busted and the youth were pissed.

Other poems got cosmic. Kids tranced out, imagining themselves the progeny of planets, of outer space, of mother earth. Within them the spirit of the banana tree, Douglas fir, wild avocado, and rainbow chard lived on. They proclaimed their ancestral lineage. Michelle heard shout-outs to Yemayá and Quetzalcoatl, to Thor and Nefertiti. The boys' hands reached out and rubbed the air in front of them as if they were scratching records. The girls tilted their heads to the ceiling and their tones took on a faraway wistfulness, like a bunch of little Stevie Nickses.

Michelle was bored. The two of them had considered smuggling alcohol into the event—just for the transgressive thrill, just to be outrageous, not because they were alcoholics. That they had decided against it was proof they were, in fact, not alcoholics. Their hard drinking was a sort of lifestyle performance, like the artist who wore only red for a year, then only blue, then yellow. They were playing the parts of hardened females, embodying a sort of Hunter S.

Thompson persona, a deeply feminist stance for a couple of girls to take. They were too self-aware to be alcoholics. Real alcoholics didn't know they could even be alcoholics, they just drank and drank and ruined their lives and didn't have any fun and were men. Michelle and Ziggy were not losers in this style, and so they were not alcoholics. They were living exciting, crazy, queer lives full of poetry and camaraderie and heart-seizing crushes. I mean, not that night, but generally. That night they were bored. All the teen poets sounded the same, it was sort of depressing.

They're teenagers for god's sake! Ziggy scolded Michelle when she complained. *What were you doing when you were that age?* Michelle remembered having an affair with the bisexual witch who played Frank-N-Furter at *The Rocky Horror Picture Show* in Cambridge. She had given him a blow job in the trunk of her best friend's Hyundai. He hadn't enjoyed it, he didn't like oral sex. He thought Michelle was sort of trashy for having gone there. Michelle had only been trying to do something nice for the witch, who she thought was so cute with his long, bleached hair, and such a good Frank-N-Furter with his arched, anorexic eyebrows. She relayed the story to Ziggy.

See? Ziggy said. *You were sucking dick. These kids are making art.* Teenage Ziggy had been a frustrated poet with an early drug habit, scrawling *fuck fuck fuck fuck fuck fuck fuck fuck fuck fuck fuck fuck fuck fuck fuck fuck fuck fuck fuck* in her journal, for pages and pages. She still had the books, had shown them to Michelle. They were very cool to look at, having the scrawled deliberation of a Raymond Pettibon mixed with the druggie splatter of a Ralph Steadman.

The teen poets before them were so wholesome and focused and directed, so young, with such a grasp on language and the confidence to perform in front of a crowd of strangers—they were miracles, all of them. If they managed to grow up, they would go to writing programs and summer at writers' colonies and have their fiction published in high-brow magazines, they were starting so early. It was much too late for Michelle and Ziggy. They were twenty-seven already, in no time at all they'd be thirty, terrifying. No one knew what would happen then. Michelle couldn't imagine anything more than writing zine-ish memoirs and working in bookstores. Many of her coworkers were gray-haired and elderly so she figured she really could work there for the rest of her life, engaged in the challenge of living on nine dollars an hour. Michelle thought the only thing that would change as she entered her thirties was maybe she'd want to join a gym, but it was hard to say.

Ziggy figured she'd be dead.

On the stage an adorable boy with a wild Afro that weighed more than he did spoke a jumble of new-age non-sense into the mic.

Is He Stoned? Michelle asked Ziggy. He's Not Making Any Sense.

Michelle did not enjoy pot, and often didn't recognize the signs of someone being under its influence. This kid sounded like a cat had pawed across his keyboard and he was reading the results as a poem.

It's like jazz, Ziggy explained. *It's like he's scatting. You know? Bee diddy be bop, biddy bop*, Ziggy proceeded to scat. Someone behind them hissed a shush at them. Probably the boy's parents. On stage the poet began to beatbox, con-firming Ziggy's analysis and energizing the crowd, even Michelle. He sounded like a machine! Like a robot! How was he doing it! It was amazing! The audience began to clap along. It was impossible not to be carried away on this wave of excitement. Michelle, who loathed audience participation with a panic that approached pathology, timidly smacked her palms. Ziggy was hollering and throwing her hands in the air, making the *Oo-OOOOO* noise that was like a hip-hop birding call. Others responded in kind from around the studio. The boy made a sound like a needle being pulled from a record and was done. He smiled at the audience and shuffled meekly from the stage, his cloud of hair bouncing above him.

Michelle figured they were pretty much done, and then the last poet took the stage: Lucretia. Her hair was the color of faded jeans, and choppy. Everything about her was choppy—the sleeves had been sawed from her oversized T-shirt, her pants had been cropped just below the knee, high-tops puffed out around her ankles. Her face as she moved into the light was so stony it took Michelle a moment to register her as female, a recognition that immediately bled into an understanding of the teen as queer. A queer teen! Michelle turned and clutched at Ziggy wordlessly. A queer teen! Michelle and Ziggy loved queer teens. All queers loved queer teens. Queer teens triggered so much in a grown homosexual. All the trauma of their gay youths bubbled up inside them and the earnest do-gooder gene possessed by every gay went into overdrive. They wanted to save the queer teens, make sure they weren't getting beat up at school or tossed from their homes to sleep in parks.

Nearly all the queers Michelle knew were fuckups in one way or another. Being cast out of society early on made you see civilization for the farce it was, a theater of cruelty you were free to drop out of. Instead of playing along you became a fuckup. It was a political statement and a survival skill. Everyone around Michelle drank too much, did drugs, worked harder at pulling scams than they would ever work at finding a job. Those who did have jobs underearned, quit, or got fired regularly. They vandalized and picked fights. They scratched their keys across the sides of fine automobiles, zesting the paint from the doors. Because everyone around Michelle lived like this it felt quite natural. One girl was doing an art project in which she documented herself urinating on every SUV she encountered. Everyone had bad credit or no credit, which was the worst credit. What they excelled at was *feeling*—bonding, falling into crazy love, a love that had to be bigger than the awful reality of everything else. A love bigger than failure, bigger than life. They clumped together in friendship with the loyalty of Italian mafiosi.

I Would Fucking Die For You, Michelle liked to tell Ziggy when they were wasted and sitting together on a curb, smoking.

I would fucking die for you too, Ziggy concurred. *I would take a bullet for you.* She dragged on her cigarette so powerfully the whole thing was gone in one pull. *What about Stitch, would you die for her?*

I Would. I Would Die For Stitch.

I would too, Ziggy nodded, without hesitation. Surely no one would ever be asked to take a bullet for another, but this was not the point. The world beyond them felt hostile, taking bullets was an emotional truth, it felt real.

On the stage the young queer seemed to know she was killing it. Michelle's heart tore open and wept blood at the humanity of this girl's experience. To be a butch girl in high school, to be better at masculinity than all the men around you, and to be punished for it! How everyone acts like you're a freak when really you are the hottest most amazing gorgeous together deep creative creature the school has ever housed and you know it, somehow you know it, and everyone knows it, and no one can deal with it—oh, the head fuck of that situation, sitting on the shoulders of a teenager! Michelle's hand was splayed on her chest like she was having a heart attack. Ziggy noticed.

Oh no, she said.

Michelle's eyes were like a slot machine that had come up cherries. The youth looked so bitter and fierce at the smacking, stomping close of the poem, her eyes too old to be stuck in the smooth face of a teenager. She looked like she had been sustaining the ongoing tragedy of life for longer than eighteen years. Michelle's heart had fully liquefied, was puddled somewhere else in her body.

The poet's cheekbones were high and her tired eyes had an exotic lilt. Her dusky-blue hair, cut into no discernable style, was thick, itching to spring into curls. And her poem was good enough to win the competition.

Are We Just Picking Her Because She's Queer? Michelle worried into Ziggy's ear.

Ziggy shook her head. Her orange hair, separated by grease and product into individual clumps, swung like fringe. *No, she's really, really good,* Ziggy said reverentially.

Better Than The Beatboxer? Michelle checked.

Better than the Beatboxer.

Beatboxing Isn't Poetry Anyway, Michelle pointed out.

On the stage the girl accepted her trophy and did a friendly hug slash chest thump with the Beatboxer, who had come in second. Everyone who placed was masculine, had delivered poems laced with rage and anger. None of the girls, none of the little Stevie Nickses with their yearning poems of love and self-exploration, had placed. Michelle felt the sting of injustice as she observed this, then, upon remembering she was a judge, the prick of shame. She was part of the problem! Given a bit of power Michelle was no better than anyone else. Did she hate women, too? It was true she found much of the girl poetry limp and whiny, frustratingly vague. They hadn't zeroed in on a social ill and gone to battle, they had turned their vision inward and taken the audience on a murky journey. Michelle guessed they'd all write devastating memoirs in about five years. She decided not to worry about it and went to congratulate the winner.

Mary Kay Letourneau! Ziggy shrieked, clipping her in the shoulder with their shared 40 ounce of Olde English.

What? Michelle cried. She's Eighteen! That's Legal!

Mary Kay Letourneau, Ziggy repeated, shaking her head. They moved together through the darkness of South Van Ness, passing Victorians protected from the street by wild invasive shrubbery and tall iron fences. The overhang of dying trees blotted the streetlights and the sidewalk was empty of people. In San Francisco's nicer neighborhoods people with money had converted their yardscapes to pebble and driftwood, stuck here and there with spiny succulents. In the Mission nobody could afford to uproot the giants and so they eventually would tumble, crashing through a fence and onto the street, hopefully not killing anyone, blocking the sidewalk until the city came and dragged it away.

In the coming blocks hookers would suddenly materialize, women in big shoes and cheap little outfits. Sometimes Michelle would be walking alone in a similar outfit and the women would regard her skeptically, wondering if she was working their block. Men in cars would slow their roll, also inquisitive. Michelle offered smiles of solidarity to the women and flipped off the men, masking her fear with snobbish indignation, praying for them to drive away. Once, drunk, she removed a high heel and walked toward the curb as threateningly as one can with such a gait, one pump on, one pump held menacingly above her head. The would-be predator drove away. Mostly the men were simply looking to purchase sex, not terrorize anyone. Michelle understood that to truly support a prostitute meant wishing her a successful business, which translated to streets teeming with inebriated men propositioning anyone who looked slutty from their car windows. She tried to have a good attitude about it.

Michelle wrenched the 40 from her friend's grip. She hated sharing anything with Ziggy, who bogarted the booze and whose strangely wet lips soaked cigarette filters. Once Michelle hit her Camel Light only to have Ziggy's saliva ooze from the spongy tip. Ziggy would not take a languid, gentle inhalation but a stressed-out trucker pull, one and then another, making the cigarette hot, the tip a burning cone. Michelle did not know what to do with such a cigarette. She would rather buy Ziggy a carton of Camels than share a smoke with her, but she was stuck. Ziggy was her best friend and everyone was broke.

Ziggy was both scandalized and delighted by Michelle's love-at-first-sight encounter with the teenager. Her walk when newly drunk became a sort of dance, she swiveled out from her hips as she slid down the street. Like many butches, Ziggy dealt with her feminine hips by weighing them down with a lot of junk. A heavy belt was threaded through the loops of her leather pants. The word RAGGEDY was spelled in metal studs across the back, as if you could not simply see for yourself. All the dykes had recently discovered the shop in the Castro where leather daddies got their belts, vests, caps, and chaps. A bearded fag resembling the Greek god Hephaestus would pound the word of your choice into the leather with bits of metal. It was expensive, but worth it if you had it. Ziggy went from rags to riches regularly, scoring jobs at yuppie restaurants and then slipping on a wet floor and throwing her back out. She blew her cash on leather goods and rounds of tequila for everyone, plus some cocaine and maybe a nice dinner in a five-star restaurant where service people treated her like a pig. Whatever was left over was given away to people on the street, and then it was back to bumming cigarettes off her friends.

But Ziggy's hips: a Leatherman was snapped to the belt, like a Swiss Army knife but more so. The gadget flipped open into a pair of pliers with a world of miniature tools fanning out from the handles. Screwdriver, corkscrew, scissors, tweezers. The Leatherman was a lesbian phenomenon and life ran more smoothly because of it. Ziggy had that on one hip and a Buck knife in a worn leather sheath on the other. A hankie forever tufted from her back pocket, corresponding to the infamous faggot hankie code. The hue, pattern, or even material flagging from Ziggy's ass transmitted the desire for a particular sexual activity, right or left pocket communicated whether the butch would prefer the giving or receiving end. Ziggy's tastes were varied and shifting and hankies of many sort danced between her pockets. That night a flash of lamé dangled from her right cheek, signaling her wish to be fucked by a fancy femme.

In Ziggy's other pocket sat a leather wallet, hooked to

her belt loop with a swag of silver chain. The nights Ziggy packed, yet another layer of leather and metal would be rigged across her hips, a heavy dildo curled in her underwear. The overall affect of these accessories was not unlike a woman dancing the hula in a skirt of shells and coconuts, or belly dancers draping their bellies in chain mail. The swinging, glinting hardware propelled Ziggy forward from her core, and, though your eyes were drawn to the spectacle, the flash obscured the femininity—like dazzle camouflage. A lot of butches wore this look, but Ziggy did it best.

Gay Men Fuck Younger Boys All The Time, Michelle said fiercely.

Okay, NAMBLA, Ziggy snorted. *Okay, NAMBLA Kay Letourneau.*

Not Like That, Michelle said. Just—You Know What I Mean. Older Fags And Younger Fags, Like Legally Young. Daddies. Zeus And Ganymede.

Ganymede was a child, Ziggy schooled her.

Yeah, You Were There, Michelle retorted, On Mount Olympus. You Were Working The Door. You Carded Ganymede. Michelle's joke reminded her of a true story in which Ziggy picked up a girl with hair so short there was almost nothing for her Hello Kitty barrettes to clamp onto and who wore a pink dog collar around her neck. The girl left her ID on Ziggy's bedroom floor by accident. She hadn't been old enough to get into the bar where Ziggy'd seduced her.

That's not the same thing, Ziggy defended. *That girl lied to me. Just by being in the bar she was pretending to be at least twenty-one. That was not my fault.*

So, Michelle said, If That Poet Lied To Me About Her Age It Would Be Okay?

It's too late, Ziggy said scornfully, swigging the Olde

English. *You met her at the Teen Poetry Slam. It is too late for you, NAMBLA Kay Letourneau.* Ziggy's hips swiveled as she skipped along. She sashayed down the block, nearly running into a shriveled old crackhead woman who had emerged from the mouth of an SRO hotel. At least Michelle thought she was old. She might have been thirty, but crack is such an evil potion it turns maidens to hags in a season.

You know what to do!!!! the woman croaked in a prophetic timbre. Her lips were split with dehydration and cancer. *Do it! Do! It! Do it now! Do it now!* Michelle and Ziggy looked at one another, alarmed. Lifelong city dwellers, both were accustomed to the spooky public outbursts of addicts and crazy people, but Ziggy tended to treat them as oracles dispensing coded messages.

Do what?! Ziggy asked, suddenly desperate. *Do what?! Oh god! I feel like that woman just looked into my soul!* Ziggy's eyes got the focused-unfocused look that only a drunk Pisces with eyes that color green could achieve. She retraced her steps and pulled a palmful of coins from the tight front pocket of her leather pants. She placed them in the woman's chickeny hand.

You know, she told Ziggy. A bright piece of her fabric wound around her head and her eyes stared out from the cave of her face. *You know!*

I do, Ziggy replied solemnly.

Michelle thought Ziggy was probably crazy herself, but there was a chance she wasn't and that the street people of her neighborhood were, in fact, prophets, apocalyptically wise, witches damaged from being born into a time with no respect for magic. Michelle preferred this story over the alternative of everyone having chemical imbalances and genetic predispositions toward alcoholism. She supported

Ziggy and helped her puzzle out the cryptic warning of the street oracle.

Is There Anything You Think You Should Do Right Now? Michelle asked.

Ziggy thought.

Write a novel? she mused. Ziggy stuck to poetry, but it was hard to make money as a poet and Ziggy really liked money. Another option was moving to Los Angeles to direct films but that seemed like such an intense thing to do. Apply for a grant? She dug deep. *I was thinking about doing yoga,* she said. Recently Ziggy had briefly dated a bicurious yoga instructor who kicked everyone's ass at pool. *Prana,* the girl, smiled after sinking the final ball, raising her fingers to the barroom ceiling in a spiritual gesture.

You Want To Do Some Yoga And Improve Your Pool Game? Michelle asked. One of the errant ways Ziggy brought in extra cash was pool sharking. Another was shining shoes with an old-fashioned shoeshine kit she lugged from bar to bar, a butch version of those Peachy Puff girls selling cigarettes and candy and useless light-up plastic roses. Just as the Peachy Puffs wore ridiculous and sexy costumes resembling the spangled outfits little girls tap dance in, Ziggy knew which garments would appropriately fetishize her labor. She shined shoes in a stained wifebeater and a tight pair of Levi's.

Maybe She Was Talking To Me? Michelle suggested. Do It. Like Make Out With The Poet.

The teen, Ziggy corrected.

Lucretia, Michelle insisted. But the name was such a mouthful. Was it her real name? she wondered. San Francisco was full of people who changed their names upon moving to town. Trash Bag, Spike, Monster, Machine, Scout,

Junkyard, Prairie Dog, Flipper, Oakie, Fiver, Kiki, Smalley, Rocks, Rage, Sugar, and Frog were only some of the individuals Michelle had met since coming to California. *I don't think you should do it*, Ziggy said.

The thing was, Michelle had a girlfriend. Her last name was Warhol so everyone called her Andy, though the name on her driver's license was Carlotta. Andy was on a lesbian soccer team. Michelle liked to watch her spike the ball with her head like an aggressive seal. Andy cooked meals at an AIDS hospice in the Castro. She was older than Michelle and had been doing this for many, many years and had been around for the terrible era when gay men were dying and dying and dying and dying. Michelle had assumed Andy prepared healthful, nourishing, life-prolonging foods for these men, but as they all had death sentences what she did was cook them their last meals, again and again. Pork chops, ribs, mashed potatoes, mac and cheese, fried chicken. Hamburger Helper when it was requested (and it was). Meat loaf, loafed from whatever meat could be found. Cupcakes and brownies and pies with ice cream. Andy fed Michelle, too. It was a foundation of their relationship. Without Andy there were many times when Michelle would have gone hungry, so broke and barely employable was she, so hell-bent on prioritizing liquor above food. Wasn't Beer Bread? Michelle asked in earnest. Liquid Bread? Especially Guinness, didn't they give Guinness to pregnant women in some country (Ireland she supposed), and wasn't Michelle Irish, didn't years of ethnic evolution give her a genetic gift for absorbing the nutrients in a pint of beer?

Generally, people who did not drink like Michelle—

let's call it heavily—generally, these types of people would not want to date her. It was unusual how Andy not only accepted Michelle's inebriation but encouraged it. She bought her jugs of beer beyond Michelle's normal price range. She procured pills from folks at work and urged Michelle to take them. This dynamic inspired in Michelle a variety of emotions. Sometimes she felt like a helpless princess being attended to by a handsome butch. When Andy was a little girl she prayed to unicorns to not get boobs, and it worked. Andy was white as a ghost with a head full of black, black hair. Her black hair fell into a natural Superman swirl on her forehead. Andy was attractive in the manner of an old-fashioned movie star, Michelle thought, or maybe it was her chivalry, if chivalry was what it was. Sometimes Michelle worried that Andy just wanted to knock her out so that she didn't have to deal with talking to or fucking her. Michelle tended to never shut up and she wanted big drama in bed all the time, requiring her lover to be a roller coaster or tsunami.

Michelle and Andy were not faithful to one another. Theirs was a messily open relationship, one in which the boundaries were never fully articulated so could never be fully broken. In spite of this, there was the feeling that Michelle was shitting on the rules all the time with her haphazard acquisition of lovers.

An example: She had an affair with a junkie troubadour named Penny. Penny sang Johnny Thunders songs on her acoustic guitar as they walked through the industrial wasteland of her neighborhood, Dogpatch, a place not yet gentrified, with vacant storefronts and SRO hotels, in one of which Penny lived. Penny had tangled black hair that clawed out from her head like Medusa. She wore spandex pants and clunky boots with broken zippers. The boots barely stayed on her feet so there was always the exciting possibility that Penny would wipe out. Walking down the street with her was like watching a circus acrobat. Penny's small room was padded with thrift-store clothing, mounds of it. They made out on a mattress on the floor, a muted black-and-white television strobing behind them.

In the morning, though, panic woke Michelle like an alarm clock. Who was this elegant skeleton she was curled into? This hair had a new smell, the dusty stink of Aqua Net Extra Super Hold and a drugstore perfume worn as a joke and also dirt and sweat and the tang of heroin itself, brown sugar and spoiled wine. Though Penny was who she'd wanted last night, slow kisses tasting of new intoxicants, Andy was who she wanted to wake up with, the shore she longed to beach herself upon. Michelle peered through makeup-crusted eyes at the collection of clothes making drifts up the walls—she would be smothered in an earthquake. Penny shambled out of bed, so frail in the daylight, and rutted through the base of a pile, extracting something that shimmered like the scales of a magical fish. She pulled it over the torn slip dress she'd passed out in and left to throw up in the bathroom down the hall.

Michelle fled. She wheeled about Dogpatch, an unfamiliar neighborhood. The apocalyptic times that were upon them glared from every bit of rubble, every mound of festering shit left by the packs of wild dogs she hoped she would not run into. Did buses even run out here? How had she arrived? Penny had met her on the corner, with her guitar. She had strummed "You Can't Put Your Arms around a Memory," singing it with a cracking voice. Penny really was like a girl Johnny Thunders. Someone had tattooed the lyrics to "Chinese Rock" on her shoulder with a sewing needle. It was a spidery tattoo, the lines shook crooked down her skin, but it worked with her look.

Penny was indeed amazing, but Michelle worried there was a time limit on that sort of amazing. That it was the sort of amazing that could begin to look sad with age. Michelle fought against this analysis, which seemed cruel and typical. The messed-up queers Michelle ran with tempted fate daily, were creating a new way to live, new templates for everything—life, death, beauty, aging, art. Penny would never be pathetic, she would always be daring and deep, her addiction a middle finger held up to proper society. Right? Right?

Andy had her own love intrigues, one with a shy photographer who'd grown up in Alaska. Andy insisted that this was not as glamorous as it sounded. Alaska! Michelle projected sleighs and fur coats onto the girl, who she had never met but whose name was, amazingly, Carlotta, same as Andy's. Like getting to go into the same public restroom, having a date with your exact name was a whimsical perk of lesbianism. Michelle imagined this Carlotta as a femme twin of Andy, standing on a windswept glacier wearing a fluffy hat cut from the pelt of a baby seal. No matter that the glaciers had long ago melted into floods and that baby seals were cartoony memories surviving on as stuffed animals. Unlike some of the younger people she was friends with, Michelle had remembered the hype of Alaska, had seen it on TV, had understood the state's brand. But all it had had going for it was the natural abundance thing, so when the planet started to die, Alaska had been one of the first states to tank.

Michelle was, for the most part, happy that Andy was

having affairs, unless she wasn't, and then she would demand painful information from her girlfriend.

Did You Touch Her Boobs? Michelle interrogated. Did You?

Andy bristled under these demands and the pair fought. Michelle hated when a pane of lead came down over Andy's heart, Andy who was always so ready to serve her, to bring her eggs and cider. Where had she gone? Michelle was in tears.

I Only Want To Know If You Touched Her Boobs! she cried. Andy was Michelle's girlfriend. She had a right to know.

Michelle had a second affair with a mannish girl named Captain who hosted lots of drugged-out after-parties in her bedroom above Valencia Street. Andy rarely stayed out late, but Michelle often did not make it back to her futon until the nighttime sky began to brighten with the coming day. Michelle's calculations were as anxious as a vampire's—she had to be asleep before sunrise or she would panic that her life was out of control, but the inevitable end of a party always broke her heart. She would push it to the extreme last moment, dashing down Valencia in a pair of shoes so worn-down that the nub of a nail stuck out from the heel, one step ahead of the rising sun.

In Captain's room everyone listened to Pavement and Elliott Smith and licked powdered pyramids of ecstasy from their palms. Before Michelle fell into debilitating bliss, she and Captain bonded over astrology and Captain let her pluck a card from her Salvador Dali tarot deck. Paralyzed by the drug, they made out on Captain's bed for about five hours, their friends heaped around them like the sea lions that once honked down at the piers. Latecomers brought nitrous and the crack and hiss of the slender canisters became the sound track to their slow-motion kisses. On and on this went, time made obsolete by chemicals. Captain was not an amateur—her windows were hung with black curtains, the room as immune to the passage of time as a Vegas casino.

Michelle and Captain went on a date to the bathroom of the lesbian bar. Michelle's ass, perched on the sink, bumped the cold-water faucet as she came in Captain's face, soaking her backside and wetting Captain's long bangs. She mopped up with scratchy paper towels and left to meet Andy for dinner. Rushing through the Mission, Michelle gave her hands a sniff. Captain had allowed Michelle to ransack her and Michelle's fingers stunk of her good fortune. She popped into a liquor corner store and purchased a pack of watermelon Bubblicious, chewed a piece until it was fattened and gritty with sugar and spit, and scoured her hands with it. Her hands were sticky and disgusting but they smelled like fruit, not sex, and Michelle felt better. Andy knew she was being a slut, but she didn't have to rub her girlfriend's nose in it.

Together, Andy and Michelle had an affair with a girl named Linda. Michelle had found Linda at the bookstore where she worked and was excited by the girl's willingness to consume large quantities of drugs and alcohol. Sometimes Michelle felt resentful toward Andy for being so moderate, for sipping some ridiculous fake drink like a daiquiri while Michelle got hammered on shots and cocaine. Andy would go home at a reasonable hour, abandoning Michelle at the bar, but Linda would party until her intake knocked her out. On their second date Michelle petted the girl's head as it hung out the window of a party, sending streams of barf onto the street below. When she was finished the pair found a closet in a bedroom and had sex, Linda's forearms, tattooed with rockets, shooting into Michelle's deep space. Eventually Michelle flipped Linda, working her hand inside the girl for about ten minutes before realizing she had passed out. Michelle put her clothes back on and rejoined the party, leaving Linda tucked beneath a leather coat.

Andy could recognize the threat of Linda. Unlike Penny or Captain, virtual one-night stands, Michelle kept returning to Linda. She talked about her too much, in that wistful way. Everything about Linda became sort of magical. She Wants To Own A Flower Shop, Michelle gushed. That's Her Big Dream, Isn't That Sweet? Andy thought it was actually pretty stupid, seeing as how there weren't really flowers anymore, and her concern swelled. Michelle loved the tattoos on Linda's calves, the Little Prince on one leg and Tank Girl on the other. When Andy named six other girls who had either one of those tattoos, Michelle iced her for the rest of the day. Linda wore slips as dresses, just like Michelle. She wasn't butch and wasn't femme, she was kiki, a 1960s throwback. Her hair was sort of greasy, which was right for the time. People were buying expensive hair products to make their locks hang as limply as Linda's home-cut bob. She would bundle the length of it into twin buns on her head, like animal ears. Linda's face was round, and since Michelle was so often looking up at her in darkness she began to think of it as the moon, the way it caught the light and glowed. Linda was raised in a hippie commune in Vermont. She was so obsessed with corn dogs she planned on getting one tattooed on her shoulder.

Andy conceded defeat and joined their affair, which had the desired result of squashing it. Everyone felt bad at the end. Linda had bitten Andy on the lip and given her a cold sore, so now Andy quietly held Michelle responsible for having contracted oral herpes. Michelle felt like her libido was out of control and this made her feel crazy and ashamed. Linda felt that where she perhaps should have had boundaries she in fact had none. She started hanging around with Ziggy, staying out all night and showing up for her morning shift at the bookstore looking positively greenish.

What Did You Guys Do? Michelle asked Linda after one such evening. Michelle had been home in bed with Andy, watching television and eating popcorn. She was trying to live a different life, and was worried about her ex, if that's who Linda was.

I smoked crack, Linda whispered, scandalized by herself.

Oh My God! Michelle gasped, Be Careful! She tried to talk to Ziggy about it later. Don't Smoke Crack With Linda, she begged her friend. Ziggy was tough and could handle herself in the druggie jungles of the Mission, but there was something vulnerable about Linda, something defenseless. Michelle could imagine her falling into the gutter and never coming back. She was too gentle, she'd be a goner. Michelle would find herself giving Linda spare change as she walked home from a bar five years from now.

Ziggy was annoyed at Michelle getting all nosy about Linda. *Linda's fine*, she said. *Linda's a grown-up.* Ziggy resented Michelle's suggestion that she was a bad influence on the girl, plus a little hurt that Michelle wasn't worried about her drug intake, too. She had initiated the crack adventure and consumed far more of it than Linda. What did that say about her, then? Was she already written off as a waste case, beyond help? Ziggy thought there was maybe no one in the world that worried about her.

The conversation had made her feel terribly alone, and a fracture thin as a spider web had begun to climb the surface of their friendship.

Linda wasn't all that long ago, Ziggy reminded Michelle as she pondered the teen poet Lucretia. Michelle had made many pledges to Andy, both spoken aloud and deep in her heart. I Will Never Do That Again, she had promised, referring to Linda. How many lovers did a person need, anyway? Why was she so greedy? In her heart she prayed to whatever was listening, Please Don't Let Me Forget How Much I Love This.

Later, she was lying fully wrapped around her girlfriend, her face nuzzled in the glossy sweet stink of her pomaded hair. Royal Crown, the grease came packed in such an aesthetically pleasing container, squat and round, its tin cover pin-poked into a relief of a royal crown. It was rumored to be Elvis's pomade, and even Michelle would rub some into her long, wet hair to make it fragrant and less burned-out looking. It smelled like oily flowers, like the worn pillowcases of long-ago lovers. Michelle worried as she pushed her face into her girlfriend's hair that the product would give her zits, but she did it anyway, feeling devotion surge through her: Please Don't Let Me Forget How Much I Love Andy. But she would.

5 Michelle came upon Lucretia at the Albion. This is fate! she thought. Yippee! She wanted to grab Ziggy and tell her the news—What Were The Chances?— but Ziggy was deep in a pool game with Fernando the Coke Dealer and she'd just ruin Michelle's shot at romance or whatever anyway.

Hi! she said to the teen. What Are You Doing Here? Michelle could hear the words coming out too strong, too excited. She didn't know how to play it cool.

Huh? asked the teen. She did not recognize Michelle. She had met her for two seconds after someone had thrust a trophy into her hand, all she remembered was the trophy.

I Was The Judge At The Teen Poetry Slam! Michelle gushed. I'm A Queer Poet Too! She stressed *queer* not because she walked around identifying as a queer poet but so that the youth understood she would fuck her.

Oh, Lucretia remembered, *Right, thanks for that. My name is Lace—*

Michelle! screamed Michelle. And she hadn't even had any cocaine yet. She was just buoyant, it was her nature.

Yeah, yeah, I remember. Listen though, my name is Lacey. She said the name intensely, and through gritted teeth. *Lacey.* She flashed an ID at Michelle with the photo of a blond girl who appeared to have renewed her license on the heels of a Caribbean vacation. Her hair was knit into ridiculous bead-tipped cornrows and between the braids ran little aisles of sunburned scalp. LACEY JOHNSON, it read.

You Don't Look Anything Like That, Michelle said, laughing. Are You Kidding?

Lucretia shrugged. *They don't care what I show them as long as I show them something. It's just to cover their own ass.*

Where Did You Get It? Michelle asked.

It was in a purse I stole, said the juvenile delinquent, boastful and sheepish at once, a combination Michelle found very attractive, though not nearly as irresistible as the crime itself. A flush of something billowed like steam through her body. Michelle had great admiration for criminals and crime, though only from a distance. To be so close to a purse snatcher was heady. Why should this blond girl, Lacey, have a nice purse, a safe life, when no one else did? Lacey, who vacationed in third world countries and wore culturally appropriated hairstyles. Also, Michelle could not imagine a way to get a fancy purse aside from stealing it, and if that was her option she might as well embrace it. Might as well make a religion out of it, a Robin Hood lifestyle. Michelle had read Jean Genet: *I recognize in thieves, traitors, and murderers, in the ruthless and the cunning, a deep beauty—a sunken beauty,* wrote the faggot. And Lucretia was beautiful. Her lips were full and sullen. Her eyes were almonds, the skin of her face was almond, her hair was lush, and she moved like a boy.

It was Lucretia who invited Michelle into the women's restroom for a line of Fernando's cocaine. This would be very important later, when Michelle would be charged by her friends of corrupting a youth, a queer one. Corrupting? Lucretia who spoke of spoonfuls of heroin, tiny puddles of sweetness and vinegar, Lucretia who knew where to get speed so pure it was lavender, like crushed amethyst.

It was Lucretia's high school graduation money that had purchased a supersized bindle from Fernando, Lucretia's fake ID that muddled the powder on the back of the toilet, and Lucretia's twenty that got rolled up and stuck into Michelle's nose. But it was Michelle who was unable to stand the awkwardness of being so close to the teen, her blood newly boiling with amphetamines. It was Michelle who blurted in her characteristic way, Want To Make Out? And the youth grabbed her by the chin.

Any flicker of fidelity to Andy was sucked from her throat. Lucretia kissed Michelle like she was in love with her already. She kissed her like she'd been shipwrecked on an island, notching each stranded day onto a fallen coconut, slowly losing her mind. She filled Michelle like weather, worked her mouth like a cherry stem being tongued into a knot. Michelle had nevernevernever been kissed like this. Michelle had always thought that kissing was like coming upon a golden trunk lodged in the ocean floor. She tried to tug it open but never could, and this was okay because she still beheld the luminous trunk in all its splendor. But Lucretia knocked the chest right open. With one wrenching motion Michelle's sea was full of coins and rubies, strands of pearls floating like fish in the waters. The clichés of physical love were suddenly available to her. Her knees were weak. She was seeing fireworks. She had butterflies in her stomach. It didn't occur to her that it might be the cocaine.

Michelle barely recalled phoning Andy. She had the blurriest memory of bumming coins off someone to use the pay phone. No one but yuppies had cell phones then, yuppies and, inexplicably, Ziggy, though she would often lose hers while drunk. Cradling the heavy black receiver that stank like beer breath, Michelle told Andy she'd made out with someone, a teenager. Andy's hurt was a cloud on the other end of the line, one that picked up energy, velocity, and humidity as the clock ticked on Michelle's quarter. But between the liquor and the kiss, Michelle felt anesthetized to Andy's pain.

I'm Going Home With Her, she told her girlfriend. Andy could hear the slur of Michelle's slow-mo lips forming the words.

Michelle, Andy said. Should she be angry or tragic? Manipulative or permissive? Cry, yell, guilt, act like she didn't fucking care, should she just end this relationship once and for all? The thought of getting back on the non-monogamy roller coaster sickened her, and the realization that she had never actually gotten off, that the calm between Linda and this moment had simply been a mellower part of the ride, made her feel sicker still.

You're like a butterfly, Andy had once flattered Michelle in the midst of an affair. She'd been working toward viewing Michelle as an ethereal, liberated creature, something with wings, something whose freedom she, Andy, was charged with protecting. It had worked for about five minutes.

Indeed, Michelle seemed more like some sort of compulsively rutting land mammal, a chimera of dog in heat and black widow, a sex fiend that kills its mate. Or else she was merely a sociopath. She was like the android from *Blade Runner* who didn't know it was bad to torture a tortoise. She had flipped Andy onto her belly in the Armageddon sun and left her there, fins flapping.

The quarter ran out and Andy held a dead line in her hand. She lay back in her bed but she did not sleep. She thought of the occasional feral creature that crawled into her house, a converted basement apartment cut into the side of Bernal Hill. Animals sometimes came through her open window. Once a tomcat with enormous balls rocking between his back legs and a stunned bird in his mouth sauntered in. Andy shooed the tomcat back onto the hillside and used her bedsheet to net the bird flying crookedly around the apartment. Birds were increasingly rare in the dead wildness of Bernal, the neighborhood had become a sort of petrified forest. Andy brought the bundle into her yard, feeling the bird flutter weakly inside the sheet. She unveiled the animal to the night sky with a flourish, like a magician releasing conjured doves. Andy's heart tilted in her chest as she watched the crazed thing loop and smack into the side of the house. It landed with a feathery *thwaaap!* and Andy went back into her basement. She did not want to know if it had collected itself back into the air or not. It looked like a cowbird anyway. A parasitic nonnative. The moms dumped their eggs into nests of native birds, leaving them there to be raised by the adoptive parents. The cowbirds were bigger and bossier and commanded all the food, and so the native babies starved. There was once a huge cowbird population on the hill, but even they were becoming scarce as the other birds died away, leaving no one for the invaders to con food out of. It depressed Andy.

Another time Andy came upon not one but two Jerusalem crickets in her bathroom. They were large as frogs and humanoid, with jointed appendages and heads with little eyeballs. They seemed to have skin and it seemed to be greasy. The sight of them made Andy throw up in her mouth. They looked like nothing she had ever seen before, except maybe in B movies from the sixties where space aliens were imagined as giant bugs. She stunned them with a spatula and flipped them into a Tupperware container. She wrapped the bowl in duct tape and drove it to Michelle's house.

Michelle's roommate Stitch loved insects, especially the cockroaches that infested their home. She thwarted her roommates' lazy attempts at fumigation, allowing only a nonviolent sonar gadget someone purchased on a late-night Home Shopping Network binge. You plugged the gadget into the wall and it emitted roach-repelling waves. It didn't work. In fact, Michelle found a tiny bug stuck in its vents, seemingly drawn to the sonar. Maybe it was the equivalent of heavy metal for roaches, some enjoyed it.

Stitch believed that at this late date in the history of the earth, with more species extinct than alive, humans had to drop their preferences regarding the natural world. San Francisco used to have pumas. There had been occasional whales in its waters. Now even the butterflies were gone. They had roaches and feral cats and gangs of abandoned dogs patrolling the outskirts of town, all evolving a tolerance for the rancid bay water. They had invasive species.

Burly lionfish menaced the ocean, trash speared on their venomous quills, Mad Maxes of the sea. Scavenging green crabs cannibalized the last of the natives and took out the scallops as well. Soon even these barbarians would be gone. Pirate hermit crabs with no snails to raid secreted a glue from their back and papered themselves in Snickers wrappers and sea-worn chunks of Styrofoam.

Stitch was a Taurus. She felt the damage of the natural world in some deep place inside her. She was not separate from the stinging South American ants burrowing through the backyard dirt, sculpting conical hives. Not separate from the abandoned canines living in trash caves in the Bayview. Not separate from the roaches scurrying through her kitchen each night. Their home was supporting life! That seemed crucial to Stitch, radical even, and she believed it was only a matter of time before ecopeople woke up and began championing the species they were currently scapegoating. Better invading Asian citrus beetles than no beetles at all.

Look, Stitch would point at a roach couple brazenly mating atop the microwave. *They're having sex!*

They're Making More Roaches! Michelle shrieked.

Exactly, Stitch gloated, proud that her laboratory was thriving. On a speed binge Stitch dripped globs of glow-in-the-dark paint on all the kitchen roaches and the nighttime result was breathtaking, grotesque, and psychedelic. Like a child mad scientist, Stitch had created phosphorescent cockroaches. It did work to strip the bugs of some of their ickiness and the roommates began to laugh when they came upon them, rather than shriek. Except for the time Michelle was curling up to sleep on her futon and felt something tumble from her wild, dry mane and onto her cheek. She shook it onto her pillow and screamed at the poster-paint radiance glowing atop the pillowcase.

Andy had left the Jerusalem crickets with Stitch, who had doted on them. She'd lowered their broken bodies into a terrarium and watched them die on the kitchen table— they had suffered internal damage when Andy whacked them with the spatula. Stitch kept a vigil beside them as they slowly left their bodies, a Buddhist priest ushering them to the Bardo. Their faces were uncannily human, maybe it was their wide eyes or how their heads seemed stacked on their necks. Their antennae were long and their skin seemed Caucasian. Stitch was encouraged to learn that a native bug species was apparently thriving in Bernal Hill. She hoped more would tunnel from the earth and back into Andy's home. Stitch had never seen an insect so large and strikingly grotesque and wanted another shot at domesticating them in her plastic terrarium. But Andy knew that if she ever found one inside her home again she would have to move.

In her bed Andy took an inventory of invaders. She should have thrown a net over Michelle and cast her out. She should have smacked her with a spatula and left her for her roommates to deal with. She was like one of those long, crackled bugs that had evolved to look like sticks and leaves. Michelle had evolved to look like a normal girl, one capable of love and loyalty, one able to assist in the creation of a stable relationship, one that promoted good cheer and a feeling of safety. She had seemed true. Those last weeks had been so sweet, with popcorn in bed, the television pulled close. Watching the Westminster Dog Show, listening to doll-clutching Marilyn Manson fans defend their facial piercings on *The Jenny Jones Show*, getting caught up in a lurid movie on Lifetime. Andy had thought this one thing was happening, but in fact this other thing was happening. Michelle was lying in wait like a predator. She had colonized Andy's nest and Andy had unwittingly fed her, mistook her for one of her own. Now she had found a fucking teenager? She was gross. Tears shot from the sides of Andy's eyes and slid into her ears. From her windows she could see the planes in their holding patterns above SFO. Bright lights shining in the sky, just sitting there, not moving.

In the afternoon Andy came to Michelle's house. Michelle would not let her inside because Lucretia was up there, in her bed. She stood with Andy outside on Fourteenth Street. She was barefoot on the disgusting ground, in a thrifted Garfield nightshirt that read AQUARIUS. *Why are you in your pajamas?* Andy asked skeptically. *It's like three o'clock.*

It's Healthier, Sleeping In The Day, Michelle bluffed. Then: I Was Up Late.

Up late snorting watery heroin with Lu, but she omitted that part. After the bar had closed, despairing that she had not thought ahead and run to the liquor store for after-hours alcohol, Michelle had whined, and Lucretia had suggested copping a bag off one of the gentlemen entrepreneurs who offered *Coca, Chiva, Outfits* as you passed them on the corner of Sixteenth and Mission. Michelle had never done heroin before—it seemed the time to try such an obvious and stupid drug had passed. On the other hand, it had never been offered to Michelle and so she'd never had the opportunity, and she was drunk and the night was so bright with the street lights and the shop lights and the cars shooting beams from their eyes and the cocaine was electric inside her and Lu's kiss had unhinged her and she had already broken Andy's heart again—if now wasn't the time to try heroin, then when?

Michelle made the youngster make the purchase while she waited across the street, leaning against the wrought-iron fence that kept a trailer park school protected from the daily chaos of that intersection. How terrible to go to school in a ring of trailers on the corner of Sixteenth and Mission, where homeless crackheads breeched the fence to sleep and piss and puke and screw on the patch of dead grass and trash ringing the schoolyard. Michelle wondered if it was a school for children who'd killed their parents, she hoped these kids had done something terrible enough to deserve such a bleak learning environment.

Lucretia returned with the drugs. Thanks, Michelle said, Thanks For Understanding. Michelle could not accompany the teen to buy the narcotics because she could not be seen doing such a thing. She couldn't get arrested, she was an adult.

Yeah, I'm an adult too, I'm eighteen, Lucretia said.

Yeah, But That's Hardly An Adult, They'd Let You Off, Michelle said.

The youth laughed. *What are you talking about? I have two friends in jail for drugs.*

Hmmph, Michelle said. She just didn't think a teen slam poet would be arrested. Someone would come to her aid, right? Besides, there was the matter of Michelle's reputation. She was a writer. Not many people had read her book, but all those who lived in her neighborhood had. She was given a kindly regard. Yes, she was a little messy but she couldn't be too far gone if she made it to her shift each day at the bookstore, if she'd managed to write an actual book while still in her twenties, if she managed to pen an article here and there for the local weekly. Why, that was more than some people did in their whole lifetime! Also, Michelle could not buy heroin on Mission Street, for then these drug dealers who harassed her daily would never stop, they would think they knew her, and Michelle would be mortified. The whole thing was too trashy even for her. Her attitude toward heroin was like her attitude toward hot dogs: she didn't want to see where they came from, she just wanted to eat them in the privacy of her own home while sick with PMS. And so Lu returned with the drugs, and the pair retired to Michelle's bedroom where the sticky brown nugget was dissolved in a tablespoon of water, the impurities burned away, and then sucked down the back of their throats with the tubes of hacked and gutted pens.

Unlike the barfelonius crack, Michelle liked the heroin. It made her feel princessy and submissive. It was like liquefied sex splashing down the back of her throat. Not any sort of sex, but a creepy kind Michelle liked to imagine alone at night, fantasies of kidnap and poison and molestation. The drug sluiced into that place inside her. A tuning fork was struck inside her psyche. She laid her head, swarming and sick, on Lucretia's lap, dreaming that she was a runaway thirteen-year-old and that Lu—deftly fixing her own hit with one hand while keeping the other warmly on Michelle's head—was the creep who picked her up at a bus station. It was all darkness, the drugs and the dreams they loosened, but Michelle was enchanted, suspended in a dark water. Lucretia, a teenager, a stranger, her hand on

Michelle's head, felt like a message from God. This is love. The drugs swamped her. This is love. God, all Michelle ever wanted was love, and it had been so close all along, right at Sixteenth and Mission, tucked into the grimy pockets of the Coca, Chiva, Outfits man.

In the sex they had—lazy and hard, slow-motion, invasive—Michelle found new possibilities inside her body, gasping into the teen's mouth, the drug removing all resistance to anything, everything. This is love. They did it for a while, seeing how close they could come to breaking Michelle, and then they fell into a slumberless sleep of floating images and waking hallucinations. At some point Michelle began to cry. This was not unusual—Michelle cried all the time, she had some kind of crying problem, she always had, her moms had called her Waterworks as a child. They'd had to, to not laugh about her sadness would have meant they'd have to take it seriously and to take seriously a little girl who cried all the time was too disturbing. What was Michelle feeling when she cried beside the teen, who was locked in her own dreamtime? She had opened herself so wide and now she was alone. She had felt swells of love but understood, as time spiraled around her, that it was not love. She was a chemical disaster. And what about Andy? Andy would really hate her now and Michelle would never find another girl like Andy ever again, someone who would *not* do heroin with her, someone who fed her pancakes and pork chops. Michelle could see the sun rising above the overpass outside her window and she was certain, finally, that her life was out of control. She cried.

On the sidewalk in her Garfield nightie Michelle crouched

beside a parking meter and threw up. *What is wrong with you?* Andy demanded with disgust and alarm. She noted the puff of Michelle's eyelids. It's what happened when she cried, like she was allergic to her own tears. Her face would swell up red and bulbous, she looked like a whole other girl. Michelle was terribly vain about it. She hated being ugly and she hated being weak. She hated the proof of her emotional instability sitting on her face. The swelling took forever to go down, she applied various remedies to the salted wound of her face. She kept tablespoons in the freezer, would place their rounded bottoms on her eyelids, but the cold only made them tear. She kept chamomile tea bags soaking in the fridge. She kept cucumbers handy and would layer her face in slices. At a beauty store she selected a product with raspberry extract that promised to reduce eye puffiness. Michelle was shocked at how many beauty products were marketed as balm for swollen eyes. She imagined thousands of female consumers sobbing hysterically all night and acting like there was totally no problem by day, smearing creams into their haggard faces at the bathroom mirror. She was part of a demographic.

From a drugstore once she purchased a tube of Preparation H. She had read in a fashion magazine that it was the secret weapon of models who stayed up all night partying in Ibiza, snorting premium cocaine and then arriving at 5:00 a.m. to be photographed on a beach in a sequined bikini, their lives expertly managed. Not having nervous breakdowns. Michelle smeared the Preparation H over her ballooned eyelids. The stink of fish was immediate and intense. So was the slick of the stuff, the grease clotting her fingers and her eyelids. Her tears, still so close to the surface, came again. There was fish oil in Preparation H!

Indeed, it seemed to be little more than fish oil. Michelle scrubbed and scrubbed and scrubbed the first few layers of skin from her face. The oil clung to her like lard to a frying pan. Were there different sorts of Preparation H, some with fish oil for hemorrhoids, some without for the beautiful faces of hungover supermodels? The stink of dead ocean stayed trapped in her nose all day. She raccoon-ringed her eyes in smudgy eye shadow and hoped for the best.

Andy didn't think Michelle seemed happy with her life choices. She was puffy and somnambulistic. Andy hadn't fed her in three days. Bony to start, a few meals skipped had swift and visible consequences for Michelle. She seemed to have gone around a certain bend.

Are you on drugs? Andy demanded of Michelle as they stood above the splat of fresh vomit.

What Are You Talking About? Michelle asked.

Do you think it's all the cocaine, maybe you are doing too much and that's why things are crazy again?

Michelle summoned her speech, the one about the Beat poets and their awful, reckless behavior—their outlaw heroics, their hedonistic freedom: Neal Cassady, Jack Kerouac, Allen Ginsberg. Michelle would thus begin her speech, then shift focus to Hunter S. Thompson, on pills and LSD, firing guns on a Western ranch, totally boozed up. If the situation was bad enough to invoke Bukowski, well, then she would. She totally would. Did anyone think this canon of druggie men were out of control? Only in the most admirable of ways! Out of control like a shaman or a space explorer, like a magician sawing himself in half. Out of control like a poet.

But then Andy began to cry and Michelle couldn't launch into her manifesto claiming drug and alcohol abuse as a feminist literary statement. Her heart cracked at the sight of Andy's crumpled face. She knew she had betrayed her. She had done it multiple times, and she knew now she could never return to Andy for she would only do it again. She did not have what it took to be faithful to her.

You Should Go, Andy, Michelle said, leaning on the parking meter.

Go? I'm not going to leave you like this. I'll bring you upstairs.

No, You Can't. That Person Is There.

That kid?

Yeah.

Well, wake her up and tell her to go. Or I will.

Michelle's roommate Ekundayo, who hated her, bounded down the stairs, giving Michelle a curt glance, more repulsion than concern, and tossed her a hostile head nod. To Andy she aimed a fat smile. Everyone loved Andy. Andy liked to give people rides home in her 1970-whatever Chevette. She was techie and would help everyone understand their computers. She was a great cook and sent people care packages with homemade soup when they were sick. Everybody felt bad that Andy's benevolent, caretaking energies had been so exploited by Michelle. No matter how much she appreciated it, Michelle would never be able to return the favor. It just was not in her.

I Can't Kick Her Out, Michelle protested. This Is Getting Too Dramatic. Her stomach soared up one way and down the other, like a pirate-ship ride at a traveling carnival. She clutched the meter.

Getting too dramatic? Andy demanded. *I am standing above your fucking puke on the street, Michelle.* Michelle couldn't handle Andy's voice. It was outraged, pissed off, furious. That part was okay. But tunneling through it was pain, a real hurt, a heartache, a Why? Why why why why why? Michelle couldn't handle that part. She imagined Andy's voice as a candy bar with a crunchy outside and an inside so gooey and tender it made you weep.

I'm Not Waking Her Up, Michelle said. You Have To Go.

If I go that's it. That's it, we are done. You kick her out or I'm gone.

Michelle stared down at the puddle of puke at her feet. A pale orange, like a melted Creamsicle. Soggy clots like cottage cheese. She could not drag another person into this thing, her life. Okay, she said to Andy, Okay, Go. You Should Go. She wouldn't look at her, kept her eyes trained on the vomit. That's what you make, she thought, resisting the urge to kick at it with her bare feet. That's what you get. She could hear Andy's breathing change but would not look at her.

Fuck you, Andy breathed, hyperventilating through tears. Her hard outside and the molten inside crushed together, a broken bridge. *Fuck you, you are so fucking sick, a teenager, that is so gross, that is so fucking gross, god, I can't believe you, fuck you, fuck this, fuck you.*

Michelle stayed glued to the parking meter in her turquoise Garfield nightshirt, hearing Andy go into her car, hearing her crying turn to weeping, muffled behind the glass, hearing the engine rev and purr, Andy's pride, this car, the product of so much work and money, hearing it tear away from the curb like the shriek of a nerve in pain inside the body, hearing the engine gun, standing there in the exhaust of it, like a drink thrown in her face.

Don't you ever fucking write about me! Andy hollered, and was gone.

Michelle placed her two feet squarely in the slop of her guts, feeling the liquid push warmly between her toes. She'd made her mess, she'd lie in it. She walked up the stone stairs and into her home, up another flight of wooden stairs, the years of grime sticking to the vomit on her feet. A flyer for some gay event stuck to her heels and she let it. She left a faint trail of bile down the hall and pushed open the door to her room. The teen stirred, cracked an almond-shaped eye. There was blood on the sheets from where she had pulled into Michelle like a pomegranate. The memory sent a tremor through her, but Michelle knew it was only an after-shock. You Have To Go, Michelle said, Now.

All right, the teen said. It was perhaps not uncommon for her to be tossed from a strange lover's house without fanfare. She hadn't gotten undressed for their lovemak-ing—that was Michelle's job. She stuffed her feet into her high-tops and stood awkwardly in Michelle's cluttered room, a mess of dirty clothes and papers, books and shoes and stupid knickknacks, pictures and photos rippling from the wall in the breeze from the window. One bookshelf was an altar because Michelle was spiritual. Candles and rocks, mostly. She liked to light the candles and hold the rocks in her hands and pray for something to help her out.

All Right, Michelle repeated, looking at her toes. She glanced up quickly at the teen. Thanks For All That. She allowed herself a smile. She didn't want to be a bitch.

Who was that downstairs? Lucretia asked.

My Girlfriend, Michelle lied, but it did the trick.

Oh, okay. I better get out of here, huh?

Yeah, Sorry. Michelle allowed herself a larger, more regretful smile and showed it to the youth: not my fault.

Well, that was fun, said the teen. Really, Lucretia seemed fine, totally fine after a night snorting heroin, a drug famous for being so bad and awful. She hadn't puked and she seemed really coordinated. Look at how much a person deteriorates in ten years, Michelle thought. The night had left her barfy and haggard, her life now destroyed. Lucretia gave her a swift peck on the cheek and bounded out the door. She was halfway to the stairs when she turned. *Hey, where am I?*

The Mission, Michelle said. Fourteenth Street. Michelle could see that this wasn't enough information to orient the teen, but, not wanting to seem stupid, Lucretia gave a sharp nod.

Thanks. She was down the stairs and out the door.

7 In the lesbian bar Stitch pulled her wallet from the ass of her baggy black jeans to pay for Michelle's drink. She wore a cowboy hat on her head and a faded beer T-shirt on her body. She flirted with the bartender, another butch. All the butches were seething with sexual tension for one another. They chased and dated femmes, girly-girls, keeping their clothes on in the bedroom, and then hooked up with each other like straight dudes on the DL, pushing their fists up each other's pussies.

Stitch had the word GENIUS tattooed on her stomach and the quadratic formula tattooed on her neck. Her knuckles looked like a calculator keyboard, marked with + and −, % and <. Michelle thought if Stitch hadn't been a fuckup she could've maybe been the next Einstein. She liked to imagine who her friends could have become if they hadn't been saddled with a low-grade PTSD from being queer, if they hadn't been forced into the underground, away from the world and its opportunities. Stitch would have been Einstein, Copernicus. She was obsessed with the astronomer Tycho Brahe, who had lost his nose in a duel and tied a golden prosthesis around his head with a ribbon. Stitch tagged GOLD NOSE in barroom bathrooms and bus-shelter walls with Sharpies. She would have been Jane Goodall, Jacques Cousteau. She would have been a marvelous surgeon, her urge to slice herself, her friends, and her lovers with sharp objects redirected toward healing. Stitch talked to Michelle about math the way Michelle talked about poetry, so that it became understandable, even beautiful, a natural language that was both the code and the decoder.

Michelle was scared and attracted to the strange things Stitch did to her body—the cuttings, how she once heated up the decorative edge of an antique spoon and attempted to sear the design into the skin of her arm. It didn't work, what she got was a blistered blob, but the idea had been such a good one. In the nineties in San Francisco artistic self-mutilation was not an uncommon way to pass the time. You could pay people to cut swirls into your skin, to brand you like a heifer on a ranch. Once at a lesbian dance party Michelle witnessed the spectacle of a girl sewing up her labia on the bar top. At another club a giant skewer was pushed through a girl's face, entering her cheek, sliding through her mouth, and coming out the other side. Michelle had seen crowns of pins crisscrossing a shaven skull, she had seen more needles stuck in chests and breasts and sternums. Such scenes became normal astonishingly fast, especially if you were inebriated all the time. Drunk at a party, she once allowed Ziggy to push one such needle through the place where her third eye pulsed weakly, a lighthouse stuck in fog. Michelle barely bled, just a tiny splotch of blood, dry and sticky. She figured it was because she was so dehydrated.

Outside the bathroom Ziggy chugged a pint of beer and shot pool. Who would Ziggy have been if she had been born into a different place and time, a different gender, with different desires? Ziggy would've maybe been David Lynch, maybe Charles Bukowski. Actually, Ziggy was Charles Bukowski. She was that drunk and clever and ornery, that prolific, filling up notebook after notebook with her poems and then losing them. She lost her notebooks regularly, followed by a full day of mourning and angst and then *Oh well, what the fuck* and she would get to filling up a fresh one with her words. What would it take for Ziggy, queer Ziggy, to ascend to the peak Bukowski died upon? She couldn't. She was a whiny woman, a complaining queer. In order to have your complaints listened to in this world you couldn't have that much to really complain about. Otherwise, Ziggy could have been Malcolm McLaren—someone in the shadows who had all the power, you could not see her but you could smell the smoke from her cigar, hear the rustle of dollars in her pocket. Men in suits would flock to Ziggy for her opinion, and they would pay her handsomely for it.

Stitch brought Michelle her cocktail and gave her a soft pat on the back. Michelle accepted the cocktail coldly, with a nod at her roommate. *Come on*, Stitch complained, *Stop being like this, you're being mean. You're making a really big deal about nothing.*

After Michelle had said goodbye to Lucretia she had walked down the long hallway, the soles of her feet still sticky with barf, toward the kitchen, where she intended to clear her head with a pot of Café Bustelo. It was with shock that she noticed her living room had been painted.

We did it like a week ago, Stitch shrugged. *You weren't around to talk to, you're like never here anyway. So we painted the living room. Who cares?*

Michelle cared. The living room was wide and high ceilinged. A giant, busted sofa ran the length of one wall, its cracking plastic stabbing your thighs. It had been there when Michelle moved in seven years ago and her hunch was that its origin was the streets. Along another wall ran a low bookshelf and another wall sported a glass-paned built-in cabinet also stuffed with books: *Bastard out of Carolina*, *School of Fish*, *Macho Sluts*, *Infinite Jest*. Zines, their fragile pages crimped and torn. Issues of *Love and Rockets*, not in any kind of order. *Lesbian Land*, *Girlfriend Number One*, *Hello World*, *The New Fuck You*, *Chelsea Girls*, *Trash*, *Memories that Smell Like Gasoline*, *How I Became One of the Invisible*. Tiny, precious Hanuman books. *Because You're a Girl*, *The Madame Realism Complex*, *I Love Dick*, *Go Now*, *The Basketball Diaries*, *T.A.Z.*, *Angry Women*, *Shy*, *The Letters of Mina Harker*, *The Bell Jar*, *Queer*, *Howl*, *Lunch Poems*, *Sex Work*, *Closer*, *Hell Soup*, *The Unsinkable Bambi Lake*, *Walking through Clear Water in a Pool Painted Black*, *I Married an Alien*, *Monkey Girl*, *Discontents*, *The Terrible Girls*, *Bad Behavior*. The final wall was a giant window. It looked out onto the cluster of backyards at the center of their block, a mess of dull straw, dead landscaping, fallen trees, and clotheslines tangled with those hardy apocalypse vines. Their own house had nothing out back but a foot of concrete and a foot of dirt where their trash barrels lived.

The glass window was punctured by a BB from a long-ago neighbor. When Michelle first moved in one of the straight girls had told her not to sit near the window during a sports championship or New Year's because the Mexicans in the neighborhood liked to fire off their guns in celebration. Michelle thought this was racist, but Michelle generally thought anything any white person said about a person of color was racist, so her judgment was not always sound.

Still, she pledged to not be scared of holidays or her windows or her neighbors.

Before the betrayal the living room had been a brutal purple trimmed with mango, a color combo found on cheesy velour pimp suits worn by assholes on Halloween. A bunch of lesbians shooting a lesbian film about lesbian relationships had shot a spin-the-bottle scene in the room, paying a full month's rent in exchange for constant access and the right to paint the space this horrible color combination. Michelle was glad when it was over, but she had come to love the garish new living room.

I think I died in a room like this, Ekundayo had commented darkly on the purple hue. *In a past life I mean.* Ekundayo was morose. And hot. Her long hair was clumped and woven into braids and dreadlocks, she wore only black leather pants and thick hoodies, the hood pulled up over her head. She brought a long dark stick with her when she left the house, in case anyone fucked with her. She smoked a ton of pot and was paranoid, as well as suffering the stress of having been black and female and queer her whole life. Ekundayo kept to herself, living in the back room off the kitchen. It wasn't really a bedroom, a large industrial sink hung off one wall. Michelle supposed it had been intended as a sort of washroom. A past tenant had installed a rickety loft, making the back room an exciting place to be during a minor earthquake. Seemingly tacked to the back of the building, the room trembled like a plate of Jell-O, the poorly built loft inside the trembling room trembled separately. It was like carnival ride, the kind assembled by druggie fugitives in parking lots. Ekundayo painted the entirety of her little room black, including the door that closed on the kitchen. She made trance music, sometimes layering her own poetry over the beats—spacey, mystical.

Michelle looked at what her roommates had done to the living room and thought that maybe *she* had died in such a room once, while institutionalized in a past life. It was a sickly gray green, a color selected by hospitals because it already looks sort of dirty, so any actual dirt goes unnoticed. It was the color of the sky when the sun refused to come out. It was the color of bathwater when you haven't cleaned yourself in a long time. It was like a dirty shade pulled down against the world. It was the color of her skin, that morning, after her first run-in with heroin, the greige shade of a drugged-out white person. Michelle hated it and she couldn't believe her roommates would do such a thing without asking her. She was the primary roommate. She was the one who had found the house seven years ago. Back when it had been crammed full of straight girls. A Trekkie who ate lots of meat, had a violent cat, and did Crowleyian magick, leaving cryptic phrases on the walls in marker. She had left to go back to school and study the Civil War. A girl who belly danced at the Moroccan restaurant on Valencia and also stripped at the peep show in North Beach, who had a Muslim boyfriend who didn't know she was a stripper, who walked through the house in boxers, burping—every lesbian's fear of living with a straight woman. When she moved out Michelle took her room, the best room, and found sequins from her costumes embedded in the floorboards. Michelle filled the house with a series of transient queer girls. Lara was a jolly Brit who made giant puppets and sponge-painted her bedroom so it looked like a coffee-house bathroom. She had violent fights with everyone who lived there, so eventually she left. Tia the MC and DJ who brought with her a teenage runaway girlfriend who tied up their phone line and left glass beer bottles in the shower. Ellis from Texas, who Michelle had had such a crush on, but then, seeing her with her back thrown out in bed all the time, stoned on weed, asking housemates to bring her bowls of ramen, the infatuation died. Michael, who had just gotten sober and started meditating and was always mad at everyone for smoking crystal meth in the kitchen. Karen, whose mother paid her rent. Stacy, who was totally on heroin, but, as Michelle hadn't yet met heroin, she believed the girl was simply on pills when she passed out with an ashtray of lit cigarettes on her belly, on the couch, in front of the television set. Stacy had a psychotic break on speed and, thinking there were miniature policemen shining red lights at her, wound up locked in someone's closet in a Tenderloin SRO, her parents came from South Carolina and took her to a Christian rehab. Michelle had been there forever. Michelle had moved Stitch in and now Stitch was going to go and paint the living room, defend it, and then freak out at the sight of heroin implements scattered across Michelle's desk. The truncated pen, the burned-bottomed spoon with a tangy ring of drug stuck to its curve. The little balloon the drugs had come in, one and ones, one bag of dope and another of yellowy cocaine so horrible not even Michelle would do it, both of them twisted up in bits of cellophane from a cigarette-pack wrapper.

What the fuck? Stitch had followed stomping, pouting Michelle down the hall and into her bedroom, to be shocked at the tableau. *What are you doing? You're doing heroin?*

I'm Not "Doing It," Michelle said in a voice that perhaps a teenager would use with its mother, I Did It. Once. And I Didn't Shoot It. Michelle was annoyed to have her drug intake policed by Stitch, of all people. Stitch, who she had once spied making a purchase from the Coco, Chiva, Outfits man. Stitch, who Michelle had followed home and found fuming on the front steps, having learned the Coco, Chiva, Outfits man had sold her but a crumble of peppermint candy and not an amber nub of chiva. Stitch had tried to convince her to walk back to Sixteenth and Mission and make the Coca, Chiva, Outfits guy give her her money back, which even Michelle, at that naive moment in her urban education, knew was ridiculous. This was who was going to police her drug use? Stitch who had once knocked on Michelle's door and asked, *Hey, will you check on me every so often to make sure I don't die?* Sure, Michelle had said awkwardly, not bothering to ask why her new roommate thought she might die, knowing it had something to do with drugs. Stitch, who had once shot ecstasy in the closet, then fucked her best friend's girlfriend, then crawled into bed with Michelle to cuddle because the drug had made her cold. You Shot Ecstasy? Michelle had asked, incredulous. Who Shoots Ecstasy? *It works faster,* Stitch had chattered. How impatient, Michelle had thought. This was the person monitoring her drug ingestion?

Okay fine, fine, I'm sorry, okay? Stitch had her hands in the air like it was a stickup. Michelle, in her foul and sickened mood, decided she would punish Stitch for the rest of the night. Everything was stupid. The heroin, that trickster, had made her feel actual love and then ripped it away, leaving her serotonin at low tide, her stomach nauseous, her pallor unattractive. The teen was a goofball, Michelle was embarrassed at how quickly the simplest person could fascinate her. One pretty feature—and really, who doesn't have at least one pretty feature?—and she was off, a romantic narrative spinning hay to gold, eking out a nobility, a deep sense of profundity out of your average drunk, fuckup, has-been, never-will-be. Michelle saw potential the way a psychic saw auras. It was a gift, in a way. It was like she was some sort of love Buddha. But it was dumb, too. She had blown it with Andy again and she would not go back, not even if Andy would take her, which, Michelle hoped for Andy's own self-esteem, she would not. What would she do? Hang around and wait for another date to pop up. Get drunk and etc. with Ziggy and Stitch. Work at the bookstore. Fall in love and be all yeah this person is magic, this is the one, yeah! all over again, with no sense of irony, and once again ruin the relationship—somehow, Michelle would figure out how to ruin it. She began to cry into her cocktail, salting the sweetness. Stitch (who was really a true-blue friend, really a tender heart, a sensitive, caretaking Taurus to the core, one who resented astrology and all the fake sciences), came quickly to Michelle and hugged her fiercely.

I'm so sorry, I'm so sorry. Listen, we'll paint it back. We'll paint it whatever horrible color you want, me and Ekundayo will do it.

No, No. Michelle brushed her away. Stitch's face was close to hers. It was a thin vegan face, one prematurely aged from dehydration and poor living. No matter how much powdered kelp she sprinkled into her PBR, it didn't matter. Her skin's lines were deep for a twenty-three-year-old.

I Don't Even Care About That, Michelle wept. It's Everything, Everything. It's Andy And Our House And The Cockroaches And Love And How Fucking Gentrified The Neighborhood Is Getting And The Dead Earth And My Sick Sad Moms And—

It's the heroin, Ziggy chimed in, expert. *It really is just the heroin. Let it leave your system, you'll feel better.*

Take some niacin, Stitch offered.

The thought of hot flashes on top of all her other

sensations sickened Michelle. No, she said, I Have To Get Out Of Here.

Go home and rest, Ziggy suggested.

No I Mean I Have To Get Out Of Here, San Francisco, It's Fucking Depressing. I Have To Move.

To where? Stitch asked skeptically.

Los Angeles, Michelle said.

Yeah right, her friends said in unison, and looked at each other, startled.

Weird, Ziggy said.

It's An Omen, said Michelle. It's A Sign. I'm Moving. I'm Getting Out Of Here Before It's Too Late.

8 Michelle knew people in Los Angeles. Her friend Fabian had been evicted, moved south, and was now hooked up with some movie company. He had phoned Michelle and asked for a copy of her book. Michelle had sent it along without excitement. Such things happened to books, possibility eddied around them. Michelle knew a couple writers whose books had been optioned for film, but no one whose books had been made into a film. Michelle and her ilk were not the writers whose books became movies. They were the writers who scarcely believed they'd managed to be published at all, who not very long ago were publishing themselves on Xerox machines with stolen Kinko's cards. They were writers who invaded bookstores to truffle out the shop's sole copy of their book, then scrawl their autograph on the flyleaf with bleeding Sharpies. They did this not so that a reader could have the delight of an autographed book—no one could be sure such readers existed. They did it to damage the book with their signature and render it nonreturnable. Bookstores can return books that don't sell, but not if someone draws on its pages, even the author.

Though having your book made into a film was too much to hope for, Michelle and her writer friends did yearn for a fruitless but profitable option. Sometimes a movie company bought up the film rights to bunches of books, stories they'd never in a million years make into movies, just so that some other movie company didn't get it. The studios optioned the work and let it sit on a shelf and the author collected a check and nothing more ever happened. It sounded like a good deal to Michelle. The movie company would only ruin the book anyway.

Michelle and her kin spoke proudly about how they would never let Hollywood turn their stories into watered-down, homophobic films, the musicians among them chiming in that they would never sign to a major label, never sell out. To feel the heat in these conversations one would imagine mainstream success was beating down their doors, that Starbucks wanted to sponsor their next tour, that Julia Roberts was itching to play the part of a fucked-up alcoholic baby dyke in her next film. In actuality, no one cared what these queer, low-rent San Franciscan artists were doing. No one was paying attention and that was fine. These artists didn't really fucking care about anyone outside their world, either. They wanted only to continue and survive. Michelle dreamed of a corporation paying her a thousand dollars to ensure her book was never made into a movie. A thousand dollars! Michelle had never been in possession of a thousand dollars.

Fabian emailed her when Michelle's book arrived in the mail. *Thanks,* he typed. *If you ever write a screenplay let me know*. Michelle felt the dread of expectation hit her shoulders. Is that what she would have to do? She'd pulled herself from poetry to memoir in order to have more access to the world around her, would she now have to write movies? It was a terrible thought, like needing a job. Michelle already had a job, the bookstore. Writing was the antijob, the fuck you to all jobs, her claim on her autonomy, what kept her feral and free. To hitch her liberty to a screenplay would be to kill it. She'd become an adult, a worker, a grown-up, no longer a writer, not really.

Screenplays followed prescribed arcs, adhered to formulas that forbid departure on the Tangent of No Return. Tangents were Michelle's favorite part of writing, each one a declaration of agency: I know I was going over there but now I'm going over here, don't be so uptight about it, just come along. A tangent was a fuckup, a teenage runaway. It was a road trip with a full tank of gas. You can't get lost if you don't have anywhere to be. This was writing for Michelle: rule free, glorious, sprawling. Screenplays were the death of this, and on the offhand suggestion of an acquaintance she now felt a deep pressure to write one. Because she was poor. It wasn't her fault, she was born into it and it is famously hard to climb out of. But if there was an avenue available to her, even a crapshoot like writing a screenplay, and she didn't take it and she remained poor for the rest of her life, well then it would be no one's fault but her own.

Also in Los Angeles was Michelle's gay brother, Kyle. Like everyone, Michelle had a family, though she didn't talk about them much. She had written a little bit about them, and the people around her had read what was written and then this weird thing happened. Michelle would be talking about her family and someone would pipe up, *Yeah, I read that in your book.* And Michelle would get such a tripped-out, postmodern feeling about it. She thought it poor form for the listener to morph from a person or friend into a reader, a voyeur. It made Michelle feel caught, like she'd done something wrong. Perhaps she had, perhaps it was too much to have written the book. Her mothers certainly thought so. Kym had written a full critique of the book and emailed it to Michelle as an attachment, in it her own linguistic prowess was displayed. She used words Michelle did not understand in order to eviscerate the prose, indeed *eviscerate* was one of the words, it was how Michelle learned it. Kym was the only one of their clan to have gone to college and thus occasionally felt like an intellectually superior underdog. Michelle didn't understand why, if her mother was so learned, she hadn't lifted her family out of poverty—wasn't that the whole point of higher education?

Kym's just jealous, she always thought she'd write a book of her own, Wendy had soothed Michelle, but Wendy refused to read the book at all. Instead, she would pull it off Kym's bookshelf, scan a few passages about herself, burst into tears, and phone Kyle to process.

She makes me look so ugly, she'd said to her son. *Always smoking.* But her mother was always smoking. Michelle felt that if people didn't like the way they looked in her book then they should have behaved differently. Michelle never tried to make herself look awesome, Michelle strove to portray herself as the fickle, self-righteous martyr she was. If her mother thought chain-smoking was ugly behavior for a lady, she should quit. Michelle didn't feel great about this hardness but she could see no other way.

I thought she made you look noble, Kyle had comforted his parent. *Like a hard worker, a really good worker.*

Wendy was a nurse at a state hospital for the insane.

This had really compromised Michelle's adolescent fantasy of being locked up in a sanitarium. Hers would not be the manicured lawns and curving mahogany staircases traversed by wealthy friends sent to McLean in Belmont, the prestigious asylum of Anne Sexton and *Girl, Interrupted*. No, if Michelle lost her mind it would be off to a state loony bin, horrible places run by hardened New Englanders who looked down on the mentally weak. *Get it together,* she imagined a caretaker hissing, slamming Michelle's meds down on her tray. New Englanders were more bitter and resentful than people of other regions. They couldn't fake it like a Southerner, couldn't make it passive-aggressive like a Californian.

What the fuck are you? local strangers routinely demanded from teenage Michelle, on buses and trains, in stores and in the street. Her beauty ideal then was hair erupting in a mushroom cloud around her head, bangs obscuring her face like a veil, lips blackened with the gummy Elvira-brand lipstick drugstores sold at Halloween.

You think that looks good? people she'd never met would challenge her. After a while Michelle began to think every cackle in a public place was aimed at her. If a stranger approached with an *Excuse me,* Michelle responded like she was ready to beat them with sticks. This was PTSD. Michelle was so damaged from it that when she finally arrived in the safety of San Francisco and a kindly ex-hippie looked at her hot-pink ponytail and chirped *Nice hair!* Michelle turned on the woman with a growling Fuck You! People had said *Nice hair!* to Michelle all the time in Massachusetts and never, not once, had anyone actually thought her hair was nice.

Teenage Michelle knew that everyone at the state

hospital—the doctors, the nurses, the cooks and cleaners, the receptionists, the handymen and lunch ladies—all of them thought the patients were scamming the system, faking crazy so they wouldn't have to work a day job while they were working their asses off as butlers to the pathologically lazy.

If Michelle were to give in to mental collapse she wanted to be gently caught, fed well, and given restorative craft projects. Her wealthy punk friends got to silk-screen Misfits T-shirts at McLean. At the state hospital there was only a television bolted to the rec-room wall, some board games with pieces missing, plastic furniture dotted with charred holes where patients nodded out on their meds while smoking. The room felt like the setting for a gang rape. Teenage Michelle kept it together.

The people who'd read Michelle's book, who knew about her mothers and interrupted to tell her so when she spoke of them, made Michelle clam up in hot embarrassment. They deprived her of that basic human pleasure: sharing your story. The shame she felt! Like when you're telling an anecdote and someone interjects—*Yeah, you already told us that story.* Oh, no—you are repeating yourself, you cannot stop talking, you are so checked out you cannot remember what you have said to whom, you are so self-involved. To hear a person say *Yeah, I read that in your book* is this shame times twenty. You so cannot stop talking that you actually wrote down your talk and then expected others to read it, and not even that will exorcize your narratives, you will in fact continue to talk and talk, expecting us to pretend we don't know the story, which you have performed into actual microphones in public places. Guess what, Michelle? We know your mother is a chain-smoking lesbian psych nurse. Everyone does.

Michelle didn't know how to rectify the situation. She supposed it was simply a consequence of her writing and she would have to man up to it.

So she spoke little of her family, but she had one. Two mothers, one a disabled intellectual and one an underearning caretaker of the crazy. Wendy could have gone back to school and upgraded her degree but she preferred to stay where she was and judge those with more success. Michelle was just like her, they both enjoyed scorning those who had taken steps to better their lives. Wendy felt she was too old to go back to school and Michelle understood, at twenty-seven she was also too old to attempt college. Too aged, too proud, too broke, and too hapless. They had selected their paths, Michelle and Wendy and Kym, and there was nothing to do but continue the trudge forward and see what happened.

After Kym got sick, Wendy got depressed, and the moms had been frozen in this configuration for about twenty years. *The last time I had an orgasm was when I was conceiving you,* Wendy overshared. *And Kym only did it because we knew it helped my chances of conceiving and the sperm had been so expensive.* Horrifed, Michelle urged her mother toward basic masturbation.

Do You Have A Vibrator? she cried into the phone. Do You Want Me To Get You One?

No, where would I get a vibrator, you think I go to the Combat Zone? I don't want you going into those places either, you'll get raped.

— 78 —

How, Michelle marveled, were her mothers lesbians? They were totally ignorant of feminist sex shops. They were lesbian townies.

There Is A Woman-Owned Sex Shop In JP! Michelle said. She could imagine her mother gesticulating a *no way* gesture, a wave of hand, a stink face, and a shrug.

That place is for college students, Wendy said.

Well, You Don't Need A Vibrator To Have An Orgasm, Michelle counseled.

The conversation was creepy, a sort of reverse incest that left Michelle feeling like she'd been inappropriate with her mom. Now the woman would never be able to masturbate without thinking about her daughter wielding a vibrator and interrogating her.

Wendy had carried Michelle, pregnant with sperm from a sperm bank, and Kym had carried Kyle with sperm from a penis that had actually been inside of her. They'd chosen the old-fashioned way because the likelihood of impregnation was higher, the risk of complications lower, and it was free. Kym and Wendy did not have a lot of money and they were offended, as lesbians, to be forced to pay for something straight women received gratis, something men spilled on the ground all day long. The donor had been an old community college acquaintance of Kym's. They'd selected him because he was smart and good-looking, and if he was a bit of a pompous jerk, well, that surely was not genetic, that was cultural, a man raised in a man's world, they weren't going to find a handsome, intelligent man who wasn't arrogant, they let it slide. Kym got pregnant right away, but they kept at it for another week or so, just in case. Out came Kyle. He looked exactly like his dad, only gay.

Thank god you're gay, Wendy would say. *Both of you, and I*

*would have loved you both no matter what, we had no idea we'd
be lucky enough to have two gay kids, but you, Kyle, I thank god.
You look so much like that donor, but then you look so gay, it
breaks it up.*

"That donor"? Do you mean my father? Kyle liked to dig.
But he did look gay. He was tinier than Michelle, with
impressive, compact muscles he did absolutely nothing to
earn. Living in Los Angeles, Kyle spent most of his days
on his ass in his car eating Del Taco and Burger King. The
poison California sun had blonded his hair, which he kept
in a stylish, gay haircut. His clothes were skintight and he
swished. He had that excellent and scary gay-boy humor, a
sharp, searing wit honed in the busted part of New England
where they'd grown up. He'd gotten fucked with a lot. The
same boys who messed with him in the street later sought
out complicated scenarios in which blow jobs could occur.
It had germinated in Kyle an affection for rough trade,
for macho, bicurious straight dudes, self-loathing faggoty
thugs, and Craigslist DL hookups.

It would be sweet to be close to Kyle again. Of course she
would have to hide her drug use, even some of her drinking,
her brother was bizarrely innocent about such things for
a gay man. But Michelle was thinking that in Los Angeles
she would lay off the drugs. Her drinking would also slow
down. She would become healthier away from mossy, soggy
San Francisco. Kyle hated San Francisco. He thought the
gays there had no ambition, they wanted only to fall into
an infantile orgy of suckling and self-obsession, constantly
trolling for hookups and making a big rainbow deal about
how gay they were. In Los Angeles Kyle was out because he
couldn't not be, he was such a sissy, but it was no big whoop.
San Francisco was so retro like that. Kyle was postgay and,

like his mothers, a bit of a townie. He was an assistant to one of the most powerful casting directors in Hollywood, a famously psychotic bitch. It was Kyle's dream job, he felt like Joan Crawford's personal assistant. When his boss hurled an ashtray in his general direction, he let it smash upon the wall, raised a waxed eyebrow, and made a brilliant deadpan comment. Kyle felt his purpose in life was to be witty, to perform capability with flair and style, like a secretary in a 1950s movie. To be the secret backbone of the more accomplished yet unstable figurehead, privy to the private breakdowns, the one handy with a glass of Scotch and a touch of tough love. The one, Kyle hoped, to inherit the business, to feature prominently in the will when the woman keeled over young from a stress-induced heart attack.

Kyle, too, had previously suggested Michelle move to Los Angeles and write a television pilot, but Michelle had resisted. She did not want to write television pilots, she wanted to write another memoir, something that was feeling harder to do. At twenty-seven, Michelle had already covered the bulk of her life in her one published book. She recalled Andy pulling away in her fabulous car, hollering out the window, *Don't you ever fucking write about me!* Michelle was haunted by the thought that the work she did, her art, brought pain to other people. People she cared about, whom she'd been close to. Her mothers were bummed. Kyle was uneasy, though he did his best to be supportive. Now Andy was resentful in advance. Michelle's bravado—don't act that way if you don't like to see it in print—was wearing thin. It seemed to require a certain ugliness to maintain it. She'd grown weary of herself. Perhaps she would try something new. Could she write about herself without mentioning any other people? That seemed impossible. She could fictionalize things but this ruined the point of memoir, frustrated the drive to document, to push life in through your eyes and out your fingers, the joy of describing the known, the motion of the book ready-made. It had happened! It was life! Her job was to make it beautiful or sad or horrifying, to splash around in language till she rendered it perfect. Perfect for that moment.

Michelle didn't believe in perfection, in writing or anything else. Belief in perfection was a delusion that spawned mental illness. But she could capture the essence of a moment, the moment her mind conjured the words to document the scene—yes. This was writing to Michelle, but it was no longer allowed. Poor her! She would have to write fiction—real, actual fiction. She would have to write a screenplay. She didn't want everyone hating her forever and she didn't want to be a loser. She would have to move to Los Angeles.

9 Kyle was thrilled that Michelle was finally moving to Los Angeles. In two phone calls he secured for his sister a studio apartment in Hollywood. The studio was $400.

I'm so glad you're not going to hang out in San Francisco forever, waiting to get evicted, Kyle clucked. News of the city's dot-com upset was leaking out of San Francisco and into the nation. Rents in San Francisco were now officially more expensive than in Manhattan. People were charging $2,000 to sleep in a closet. High-paid Silicon Valley execs were spending the night riding buses, unable to find a vacant apartment. Strippers were coming from all over the country to dance in Bay Area strip clubs, collecting big tips from Internet nerds. The city was coming apart.

But Michelle had paid only $200 to live in her shabby-chic room. And she was in no danger of being evicted. Her landlord lived right downstairs, a sad widower named Clovis who gave the household platters of supermarket cookies at Christmas. Michelle had learned that before the straight girls had occupied it, the flat had been a haven for fucked-up, dysfunctional lesbians. Ekundayo's room had been a practice space for Tribe 8, the dyke punk band that performed topless and pulled dildos from their pants, goaded men from the crowd to fellate them, and then castrated themselves and flung the silicone into the audience. Man-hating lesbians who couldn't cope with reality had lived there, pulling traveler's-check scams, faking insanity to get on SSI. Roommates had pooled lists of ex-boyfriends and hustled them out of money for nonexistent abortions.

When she moved in, Michelle had had no idea that the house had been a magic castle of queerness with a secret outlaw history. It was as if the Dillinger Gang had hidden out there. A lesbian porn had been filmed in her bathroom! An infamous lesbian hooker had once lived in her bedroom, had nailed hardware into her floorboards to tie down her lovers! Michelle had restored the flat to its former glory, all rooms occupied with barely functioning lesbian alcoholics. And now she would leave.

But Michelle loved her bedroom. The floors were blue and the wall behind her lousy futon was also blue, and stuck with chunky glitter. Three windows looked out on the street below, where a stolen car ring operated out of a garage. The dismantled alarms wailed all night, but Michelle was used to it. Gauzy thrift-store curtains hung in the windows, tied back with Mylar ribbons. A giant bullhorn mounted on a piece of rotting wood dangled in the center window. Michelle had found it on the street, the source of so many unexpected treasures. The ocean of poverty pulled many gifts to shore. Stolen luggage was often gutted on the sidewalk, and Michelle was not above rummaging the contents. She'd found velvety platform shoes, satiny gowns, chipped knickknacks. It was okay that she didn't have money to shop ever because the streets provided her with such hunter-gatherer thrills.

Michelle had loved her room so long, had lived inside it seven years, and now could feel herself being pushed out from it. It wasn't the economy. Clovis the Landlord had promised he would not raise the rent and he had no intention of selling the house. The man spent his lonely nights singing into his personal karaoke machine in the flat downstairs. The sound of him singing Sammy Davis Jr., his warbling voice floating up through the floorboards, broke everyone's heart. Everyone in the punk house loved their landlord. It was okay that the shower, a metal closet, was rusting through the bottom, surely harboring gangrene and soaking the house in soggy rot—Clovis's second-floor apartment was in no better shape. If he had the money he'd fix their shower, but to get the money he would have to raise their rent, and so they put a milk crate in the shower to stand above the jagged rust and wore flip-flops while they bathed, just in case.

When the word got out that Michelle was moving everyone assumed she was getting evicted. When she told them she was not, she was just vacating her $200-a-month room in the Mission by choice, everyone was baffled. Why would anyone do such a thing? To move to Los Angeles, that shit hole? Hers was surely the last room in town renting for under $800. Once she left the Bay Area she could never come back. She could never afford it. She was evicting herself, it was crazy. But the city had bad vibes and they'd infected her. Michelle hardly ever saw the sun anymore, sleeping until her evening shift at the bookstore loomed. Her boss had asked her if she had lost weight or if she had just started to wear tighter clothes. The answer was both. Michelle was beginning to look like a Ramone. At night she began to dream that her room was haunted and the spirits wanted her dead. She had gone as far as she could in San Francisco. She would move to Los Angeles and write screenplays.

10

A problem with Michelle's plan to move to Los Angeles was that technically she did not drive. She'd been taught, briefly, years ago, by an old girlfriend and she hadn't felt incompetent. She'd enjoyed tooling around in the car under supervision, getting praised for how well she drove. She'd intended to make it legal, go to the DMV and get a license, but Michelle was so lazy and there were always other things to do, like drink and sleep and go to the bookstore. The DMV was in the Panhandle, wherever that was. Michelle didn't really leave the Mission. In a burst of can-do responsibility, she figured out the bus route to the office and arrived early one morning, prepared to spend the afternoon. But the woman at the counter turned her away quickly.

No more, she shook her head. *No more driver's licenses.*

What? Michelle had expected bureaucracy, hassles, annoyances—it was the DMV. A person didn't have to drive to know that—but she hadn't anticipated this.

No more licenses till 2000. January and July there will be a lottery if you want to enter your name.

You Stopped Giving Driver's Licenses? Since When?

January this year. The lady was bored.

How Was I Supposed To Know That? Michelle felt outraged. Driving was a right, right? So she put it off for about a decade, so what? It was still her right, wasn't it?

It was in the news. The woman spoke to Michelle as if she were a dummy. *It went into effect in San Francisco on January first, and in the state of California last month. No new driver's licenses. Not enough gas, you know?*

The woman looked tired. She was Latina, her hair was in a claw at the nape of her neck, she wore gold hoop earrings and a little cross on her clavicle. *I'm lucky to still be here, they laid off half the office.* It was creepily quiet. A few people were renewing their licenses. Outside the windows was a patch of barren soil. The natives had died and the landscapers had tugged out all the invasive species and so there was just dirt.

Michelle left. She didn't take the bus, she walked. The Panhandle, the long park that ran into the frying pan of Golden Gate Park, was lined with trees in various death states. Some had been eaten from the inside out by invading beetles and some of those had been burned to stumps in an attempt to stop the outbreak. Some were starved of water by the drought and some of those were so shriveled they had toppled over and smashed like plaster. Others were strangled by kudzu and Michelle at least appreciated the green gloss of their leaves. She hurried back to the Mission, which never had much wildlife in the first place and so was not as depressing as these doomed, once-green neighborhoods.

Did You Know This? Michelle was outraged. This Thing With There Being No More Driver's Licenses?

Ziggy nodded. *Yeah, everyone knows that.*

How Did I Not Know?

I don't know, you don't watch the news or anything, read papers?

Michelle didn't. When she watched TV it was to view marathons of *Unsolved Mysteries* and when she read the paper it was for the horoscope and sex-advice columns.

Is There Really No Gas?

I mean, not a lot. Ziggy shrugged. They were sitting on the stoop on the side of the queer bar, smoking. They had smuggled their pint glasses of beer out with them and if the dyke who owned the bar, who was their friend, caught them she would tell them that they were compromising her liquor license and make them feel guilty, like they were bad friends. They kept the beer low, sneaking glugs behind their army bags. It was too much to expect people not to smoke and drink at the same time. It was almost cruel. Michelle imagined it was like the mythical blue-balls syndrome men experience. To have the compulsive glow of a wonderful buzz and not be able to eat half a pack of cigarettes while quenching your smoke-parched throat with beer? It was inhuman. No smoking in bars, no more driver's licenses.

The World Is Ending, Michelle said grimly.

You know how to drive, who cares? Ziggy said.

I Can't Rent A Truck, she said, Without A License. I Can't Rent A Car Or A U-Haul Or Anything.

Ziggy sighed deeply, took an even deeper pull of her squishy cigarette, and sighed out all the smoke. *Look, you want the van, just ask for it. Take it. You'd be doing me a favor.*

What? Michelle yelped, surprised. Did You Think I Was Being, What, Passive Aggressive? I Don't Want The Van! I'm Just Complaining About My Life!

Really, you'd be doing me a favor. There are so many tickets on it, next time I get one they're going to tow it. And if I don't start paying them off they're going to boot it. And it won't pass smog. It's doomed. Just take it.

Are You Serious?

Yeah. You can drive a van?

Yes! Michelle cheered, having no idea whether or not she could drive a van. Oh My God! She flung herself at her friend in a fat hug, knocking over her drink, sending beer everywhere and the pint glass rolling into the gutter.

You guys! Their friend the bar owner came over, grabbing the glass from the street. *That's it! Really! You guys can't drink here anymore!*

Michelle stood abruptly, knocking over her own.

Really, their friend the bar owner said. She was not an unkind person. She was deeply disappointed in Michelle and Ziggy. She had given them many opportunities to change their behaviors and they refused to be different.

Sorry, they mumbled in sheepish, busted unison and shuffled off to the Albion, where somehow you were permitted to smoke inside despite the ordinance and where cocaine was freely for sale despite the illegality. It was where they belonged, anyway.

Ziggy dumped the van on Michelle the very next day.

But I'm Not Leaving For A Month, she protested.

You want it, take it now or else I'm torching it.

Ziggy had once made a little bit of money helping some

skaters she drank with torch their car for insurance money. According to the poem she wrote about it, in which she compares the flaming hunk to the burning, ruined earth, it was an awe-inspiring experience.

It was awkward for Michelle, driving the van around the Mission. It was enormous and it shuddered. The plastic case that locked over the engine, the doghouse, grew so hot that Michelle's foot burned. Her blind spot was too big. It was a relic, people gave her dirty looks when she drove it, which was not often. Mostly just from parking space to parking space as she waited for the day she would leave the city.

Michelle was withdrawing from her life in preparation for the strange pain of leaving. She slacked off at the bookstore, not even pretending to work, just openly reading magazines or talking to Kyle on the phone long distance. She was pulling away from Ziggy and Stitch, staying in her room when she heard Stitch making smoothies in the kitchen, not coming out until she heard her friend tromp down the stairs. Mostly she stayed in her room anyway, sleeping off whatever she had done the night before. (Increasingly, this was heroin with strangers.)

Michelle had a few rules about the heroin to keep her safe from the worst-case scenarios everyone knew so well. Never shoot it, duh. Take one day off in between, at least! Never do it alone. That would be extremely addict-y. And why would she want to? The best part of the drug was bonding with another person about what clandestine idiot badasses you were. To have your clandestine idiotic badassery witnessed by another. To have bad-kid bonding and to have sex all doped up on a dirty fluid that gave each coupling the illusion of love.

It was surprisingly easy to find people to do heroin with

her. After Stitch told Ziggy, Ziggy told Linda, and her old crush showed up at her house. People always showed up at Michelle's house. Despite the violence of their neighborhood the door was rarely locked. Michelle had once come home to a party in her living room, lines of cocaine on the table, and a Kenneth Anger video in the busted VCR. No one who actually lived in the house was there. The house had ceased being a home and had become a sort of bar, a public space where anyone could show up and get a drink.

No, Michelle said to Linda, who had come for heroin. You'll Get Addicted.

No I won't, Linda said, sounding unconvinced. *And even if I did it wouldn't be your fault.*

Michelle didn't believe this. It would totally be her fault if she gave Linda heroin and the girl got strung out. Was this the kind of influence she wanted to have on the people in her life? It was a question of karma, which was complicated, subtle, and real. And anyway, she just didn't want to see Linda become a heroin addict. But she would.

Another person Michelle turned on to the drug was an androgynous person she'd spotted at the Albion. Michelle couldn't tell if the person was a boy or a girl or someone born male who was dressed like a girl or a dyke who was somewhat transgender or what. All Michelle knew was that the person was tall, like almost six feet, with a sweet, hard face and strange, smudgy makeup and odd leather clothes from the thrift store. The lipstick on their face was too dark. It was an interesting look, sort of Lou Reed circa *Rock 'n' Roll Animal*, only taller, and a girl. Right?

You Look Like Lou Reed, Michelle told the being, who took that as a compliment. Michelle was perfect, she was perfect inside, she had the perfect balance of beer and also vodka plus some of Fernando's stash and she felt loose and daring, she could talk, she could talk to anyone, she could talk to this person who she was thinking of as a being, whose gender, come to think of it, she had no desire to know, why should she care, this person's gender was Lou Reed. All she needed to know was: A. Does the being like girls of Michelle's particular sloppy, down-on-her-luck femininity? and B. Did the being want to do heroin?

My name is Quinn, said the being, and Michelle almost smacked her hand to her forehead, it was just too much, it was too perfect. Quinn was like a noun that meant Androgyny, Lou Reed, Drugs. It was a synonym for New York City, 1983, red leather. Quinn had blocky black glasses on their face and a rattail snaking down the back of their neck.

I'm Michelle, said Michelle. I Don't Even Want To Know What Your Gender Is, Okay? Don't Tell Me. It's Just Lou Reed, All Right?

Quinn nodded, excited. *You mean you really don't know?*

I Don't!

That's pretty cool, Quinn said, and a slight shyness came about them like a vapor.

I'll Pay For The Heroin But You Have To Buy It, Michelle instructed. I'll Show You Where, I'll Show You Who.

What do I say? How do I ask for it? The being seemed delighted by this turn of events. Michelle could tell they'd be a true adventurer.

I'll Tell You Everything, Michelle said. She left with the being, not even bothering to say goodbye to Ziggy or Stitch.

At home at her desk Michelle chopped pens and dribbled water into a spoon and played PJ Harvey on her boom box. The being watched with muted interest, inhaled the liquid obediently, and followed Michelle to her futon. They had an intelligent face, something Virginia Woolf–ish about it, perhaps in the nose.

You know, they said, *I met Lou Reed once and he told me I looked like a poet. So that's so weird that you said that.*

It's Weird, Michelle said, And It's Not. She was high enough to be in the space where all things are so deeply one, so nothing was really a surprise. And You Are A Poet, Right?

Of course, said Quinn.

Of Course. Michelle would have nodded if she could have moved her head, which was perfectly sunken into a perfect pillow. Of course Quinn was a poet, wrote by hand in a notebook forever tucked into a messenger bag, had the sort of literary vibrations Lou Reed would pick out of the air on a New York City street. Michelle felt proud of herself. Whatever Lou had seen in the being, she'd seen too. They shared a certain wavelength.

Why doesn't everyone do it this way? Quinn asked, blissed out on their back on Michelle's futon. *Why even shoot it, this is so perfect, you couldn't get it more perfect than this.*

I Know, Michelle breathed. It seemed so desperate to shoot it, sort of American. Greedy. Vulgar. This way, you simply breathed. You inhaled water, like a mermaid. Michelle rolled over in such a way that if the being found her alluring it would be easy to take advantage of her.

I'm seeing things, Quinn said, their eyes gently shut. The poet's face looked chiseled from a fine European marble. The eyes gently rolled the eyelids.

What, What? begged Michelle, who believed drugs were holy, connected you to the divine. This belief fell apart if you traced the drugs' route to her bedroom—from poverty-stricken people to violent, bloody-handed drug lords, up the butts of people desperate enough to shove drugs up their butt and risk prison for the money, into the hands of more desperate or ruthless people here in her own country, finally making it into the streets of her city, cut with who knows what chemicals, sold by individuals trapped in the throes of their own addictions, individuals who had an arm, a leg, a chunk of their ass eaten away with abscesses and various flesh-eating bacteria. No matter! In the hands of lesser people drugs were a menace, but Michelle was a lover, a spiritual seeker. The drug's moody wave washed over her as Quinn detailed their gentle hallucinations— violet, flashes of color.

It's you, Quinn explained to Michelle, *You are the violet.* This delighted Michelle, who felt crucially seen for the first time in her life. Not seen by dates who'd known she was cute or liked her writing, or by girlfriends who saw her lack of fidelity, her shallowness, her mania. Seen by a stranger whose drug-addled mind beheld her mystical reality. She was violet! She always knew she was special. The drug dropped her down a well of deep love for this genderless, many-gendered being, this Quinn.

Who Are You? she asked. How Come I've Never Seen You Before?

I'm married, said the being. *I don't come out much. I stay inside watching* The X-Files *with my husband.*

You're Married To A Man? Michelle asked, and Quinn nodded before realizing she had revealed her gender.

Oh! she cried, and brought a hand up to her face weakly. Her hands were carved from ivory tusks, glorious animals had died so that Quinn could have those hands, elegantly enormous, veined like cocks, slender and powerful and promising of thrall.

Fearing that the being would lie there blissing out on her

violet visions forever, Michelle completed her roll, butting up against Quinn like an animal brought to shore by a persistent current. She brought her lips over and Quinn kissed her back and it was soft soft soft like a dreamtime enchanted forest and they were two children dropped down into a fairy ring. Oh my god, Michelle thought, I think we're making love. It was a term everyone barfed at. No one wanted to make love, people wanted to fuck, to rake each other's skin apart with knives and pin it back together with needles. But the tenderness thrilled Michelle and she reconsidered the phrase: making love. It so repulsed Stitch that when forced to she used the abbreviated ML. But Michelle loved love. Heroin was love, the generic of love, what you got if you couldn't afford the original. The approximation was fine by Michelle. It was a wonderful mimic. Michelle and this being were in love and when they brought their bodies together they made even more love. It was pretty awesome. And then Quinn took the formidable length of her body and used it to subdue Michelle, easily, for Michelle was such a shrimp and so deliciously weakened by the drug. Powerless beneath her lover's crushing physique she struggled lightly, enough to rouse the being, who stilled her with her jaw like a mother cat hushing a kitten. Michelle's wiggles calmed and from her mouth came teasing, doped-up whimpers. The being slid her hand deftly into Michelle's underwear and asked, *You like to get fucked, huh?* and it was on.

11

Then the van got stolen. There was a dizzying minute when Michelle spun around the empty parking spot, discombobulated. She'd moved it, hadn't she? She had left it right there, yes, yes. She reeled, looking at the landmarks. Near the free clinic where she had gotten her most recent HIV test. Near the discount grocery store with the intense lighting, where that food riot had happened a few months ago. Right there. And it wasn't. It wasn't there. Michelle stood hapless and blinking, waiting for it to tool around the corner, a cartoon van with winking eyes where its headlights should be. Just kidding! It would honk its weak little honk. That didn't happen.

The sun skulked lower in the sky, then lower still. The bastard sun had shone upon the thievery, done nothing to stop it. Stolen in broad daylight! The insult of it. As if she had been doubly tricked, as if she should have been able to stop it simply because she had been awake. But Michelle had been at work, at the bookstore. Hanging out in the Self-Help section. She liked to read books about alcoholism and personality disorders to assure herself that neither was a problem in her life. When she finished pretending to organize Self-Help she moved over to New Age and consoled herself with astrology books. Aquarians weren't really prone to addiction, that was more Scorpio's jam. Sagittarians could also get out of hand, *Cuidado*, Ziggy! Michelle felt better already.

That afternoon Michelle walked sadly through the Mission. The day's smog was a thin gas in the air, growing weaker with the sun's disappearance. There was that smell in the air all the time, the tinny stink of environmental collapse. The fog clung to Michelle's glasses and wouldn't come off, her view of life perpetually smeared. She decided to get sushi. We Be was empty, she sat in the window and gazed out the mucky glass. What will I do? Michelle thought. Police report. She remembered when carrots were more plentiful, how they would be gratis in a little glass cup on the tables. Michelle didn't care about vegetables but missed the orange cheer of them. The walls of the sushi restaurant were marked with broad Xs over fish that had gone extinct. Michelle ordered a cucumber roll and a bowl of rice.

Okay, a police report. Then what? Rent a moving truck. But Michelle couldn't get a moving truck, she didn't have a driver's license. Or, she realized, a credit card. Did you need a credit card? Michelle had a debit card from the credit union. It only worked at the ATM machine at the co-op grocery store. Maybe Michelle wasn't equipped for life outside her immediate vicinity. Too Bad, she told herself darkly. Her room was already rented out, she'd been swiftly replaced. Ekundayo couldn't wait for her to leave, and Stitch—Stitch was hurt by Michelle's move. She felt abandoned. She wasn't going to beg Michelle to stay in their rotting home, notching off the days with knife marks in their arms. Fine, go, see if I care. It had been Stitch who had sourced Michelle's replacement. A girl from Olympia, Washington. Olympia still had living trees, why would this girl come to busted San Francisco? Michelle thought scornfully. But she was leaving for Los Angeles. You can't let the apocalypse rule your life.

Michelle would find someone to drive her to Los Angeles. Maybe her new friend, Quinn. Could Quinn get permission from her husband to go on a road trip with her lesbian, heroin-snorting new friend? That's not what I am, Michelle scolded herself.

Once in Los Angeles Michelle would have no car. She thought about this and gave an internal shrug. So what, she'd be another carless loser in Los Angeles. Michelle was used to being various sorts of losers. You weren't a loser if you didn't drive in San Francisco, though. You were sort of a hero. Even more so if you biked, which Michelle didn't. She tried to once, when an ex had given her an old mountain bike, and within five days she had almost been run over by a fire truck and had wiped out hugely on the corner of Sixteenth and Mission, directly in front of the bus shelter, trying to drink coffee and ride at the same time. She'd been wearing a plaid skirt that had once belonged to a Catholic schoolgirl when she bailed. Her knees were raw and everyone at the bus stop just stared. Michelle had laughed grandly, to make them feel more comfortable with her accident, but they all just continued to stare.

Michelle would not be riding any bikes in Los Angeles but she'd figure it out. She loved taking buses and trains, it gave her time to read books. Everything was going to be just fine, Michelle assured herself, as her sushi was delivered.

12 Some mornings later the doorbell rang at Michelle's house. The noise of it gave her bad flashbacks of the days of Andy loitering outside her house, leaning against her amazing car, her tattooed arms folded protectively around her heart, looking at Michelle with kill eyes. No one ever rang the bell at Michelle's house. Cautiously, Michelle edged to the window. She was hungover but not too bad—her body was becoming accustomed to the heroin, her mornings weren't ruined with the residual poison, she had learned to metabolize it. She was proud of her mysterious body and its strange wisdoms, its hardiness and strength. Was there nothing she couldn't endure?

She slid up to the windows, concerned about her nudity. The gauzy curtains hid nothing from the street, they were but decorative pink ponytails framing the face of her bedroom. She edged against the wall and craned her head toward the glass. A cop car was double parked outside, taking up space with an air of entitlement, its angle on the street jaunty, careless.

It's The Police! Michelle gasped, terrified. What had she done? Michelle looked at her desk. Small and rickety and scarred with chipped black paint, it held the remains of last night's indulgence. The spoon and the lighter and the gutted ballpoint pen. The yellowy bag of cocaine that came with one and ones, the worst cocaine you had ever seen. For a while she'd been snorting it, hoping it would take the nauseous edge off her high, but now that her tolerance had improved she didn't really need it. It sat there, packaged inside a twisted shred of Saran Wrap. Evidence.

Hey, Lou Reed, Michelle poked at Quinn's broad shoulder. Quinn had shoulders like a football player. Michelle's poke did little to disturb her. Quinn seemed like a giant in Michelle's bed, a whale beached upon her futon. A lovely beluga, long and white. Tall people were sort of alien to Michelle, whose growth was likely stunted by her time spent in Wendy's smoky womb. How had this strange creature landed in Michelle's bed? Surely it was the ocean. Michelle's sinuses felt waterlogged from kissing her. She was proud of how little she cared if they were girlfriends or not. The part of her heart that usually roiled with longing had been sated by the heroin. Michelle felt more functional for it.

Quinn's eyes cracked open as Michelle nudged her in the gut with the heel of her foot. Hey, Quinn, Would You Please Answer The Door? Michelle asked, running her hands anxiously over her nakedness. It's The Cops. I'll Hide The Drugs.

Quinn watched Michelle open a desk drawer stuffed with flyers for long-ago poetry readings and black-and-white strips of photo-booth pictures. With a sweep of her hand she knocked the drugs, the spoon, and the chopped-up pens, the lighter and the wrappers, into the drawer and banged it shut it with the side of her hip, mumbling a rising chant of alarm. The doorbell honked again.

Get It! Michelle cried, anxious. Please! Quinn sat up in bed, her rarely seen giant breasts exposed to the day. She felt around Michelle's bedding for her T-shirt. It was a magic T-shirt—when she put it on, her breasts disappeared. Quinn wondered how many times this week she had purchased their drugs in full sight of the cameras the city had mounted on street lights to dissuade drug dealing. They'd been hard for Quinn to take seriously—was there really someone somewhere eating donuts in front of a screen, watching it all go down? No way. But what if she was wrong?

Um, I'd rather you answer it, Quinn said, thinking, Who is this bitch? First Michelle made her buy the heroin, so as to not risk this "reputation" she thought she had. Quinn had a hard time saying no—like most females, she was codependent—so she approached the dealers and made the purchase, and surely it helped that she looked like a guy, even a weird one. If Michelle made the purchase in her teeter-totter heels and the slip she was failing to pass off as a dress, it was possible that the dealer might harass her and Michelle would not roll with it, she would get into a scream-fight with the dealer, she would whap him with her heavy plastic purse, who knows what would happen. So, fine, Quinn bought the drugs, but fuck if she was going to answer the door to Michelle's house, this person who— let's be real—was still a stranger to her.

Quinn was proud of herself for this rational and self-protective train of thought. It quelled her fears that her life was out of control. The doorbell shrilled the air around them.

Oh! Michelle yelped, suddenly lucid. It Could Be About The Van! She pulled a pair of black skinny jeans from the floor and wrestled on a clingy long-sleeved shirt that made her skin look like a rattlesnake's. She slapped her bare feet down the front staircase. She was suddenly grateful for the cops' diligence, doggedly ringing the bell, ringing the bell. She flung the door open with a swoosh that scattered the nest of junk mail padding the landing. Grocery store circulars, a local BDSM group's social calendar, and a postcard announcing Ani DiFranco's upcoming tour dates washed up around her ankles.

Are you Michelle Le-Dus-ki? the cop carefully sounded the syllables.

Yes! Michelle cried. Did You Find My Van? He had found her van. It had been abandoned in a bus zone across from UCSF Medical Center. Let Me Get—Someone, Michelle spluttered, and dashed back up the stairs. They Found The Van They Found The Van They Found The Van! Michelle danced around the room. Quinn felt saturated with relief, a relief that swept through her body like drugs. That was scary. Maybe she would stop being such a miscreant. For years she had been happy with a bottle of wine and whatever pills she could bum off friends with bad backs and anxiety disorders. But she wondered if she could be happy with such chemicals now that she'd seen the bliss abyss.

Michelle and Quinn left the bedroom, moved past the trash pile and down the stairs. A gigantic heap of garbage sat at the very top of Michelle's staircase, where feng shui tradition suggested you place an altar to welcome guests and purify outside energies. It had been accumulating there for nearly a year. At first it had been a couple items too cumbersome to place into the trash cans, objects waiting to be left by the curb on Big Trash Night. But no one knew when Big Trash Night was scheduled and no one took up the task of finding out, and so the junk lingered, was joined by more junk, growing until it looked like an art installation, a pyramid of bulging, shiny trash bags, alien pods cocooning new life. In a perverse way Michelle supposed it was a feng shui altar for their era. If nature had mostly been replaced by garbage, then wouldn't a "natural" altar be sort of phony, nostalgic even? The trash pile evoked the shores of Ocean Beach, where the tide brought industrial wreckage on the sand with the blind generosity of a pet cat leaving a kill on your pillow. The ocean wanted only to give and had been wrecked of its ability to bring anything but regurgitated garbage. Michelle thought everyone should live with a giant trash heap in their homes. They deserved it.

Quinn gave a short glance at the cop and felt her empty belly rumble with hunger and dread. She'd thrown up some pizza last night after the drugs had hit her, that was the hunger. The dread was, well, the cop was bound to mistake her for a boy. Quinn would either have to correct his mistake or sit there, anxiously waiting for the dude to figure it out. The anticipation would be agonizing. If the cop caught his blunder he'd feel played and betrayed and it would be left to Quinn to comfort him. The cop would resent Quinn for being so gender ambiguous—it wasn't his fault, anyone would mistake her for a man, look at her, why does she look like that if she doesn't want to be a man anyway, this fucking city, I'm getting transferred to Vallejo.

Quinn's gender confusion studded each day with potential land mines. Who knew what would happen? Public bathrooms were famously traumatizing, even in San Francisco. Queers stuck to their bubbles for a reason, the outside world was hostile. But the cop hadn't paid her much attention since the initial bro-down head-nod. Quinn was passing. She settled into a morning of maleness.

Without even looking at Quinn, Michelle knew what was happening. Like all females Michelle was codependent, but in femmes codependency could become so sharp, so intense, that it reached psychic proportions. She could feel the atmospheric conditions that produced a gender meltdown, the currents spun her like a weather vane. She hoped her normative gender could somehow smooth the spiky vibrations. She would fill the small space of the squad car with classic female cheer. She would twinkle like a little star. A little, scrawny, strung-out rattlesnake star.

Michelle wished the public understood the extent gender deviation was punished in their culture. Her wish was naive, Aquarian—who did she think was punishing gender deviation, if not the public? Still, she dreamed of a *Black Like Me* experiment, something like the MTV show that put a bunch of skinny morons in fat suits and sent them out into the world to cry. People are so mean to fat people! was the tearful conclusion. Michelle loved reality shows that punked the ignorant into feeling compassion. It affirmed her belief that humanity was inherently kind. It just sometimes took a production crew and public humiliation to shock the heart into opening. She wondered if there was a way to enlighten the people to the struggle of her friends. Maybe if they shopped more they'd be more relatable, but you need money to shop and you need jobs for money and it was hard to get a job when people didn't know what gender you were, hence the need for an illuminating television show. Michelle sighed. Maybe she would find meaningful work in Los Angeles after all.

So, there's some blood on the passenger seat, the cop announced as the police cruiser rolled out of the Mission. Michelle had had her face pressed to the glass of the cop car, dying to see someone she knew. How hilarious would that be! Think of the rumors! But it was so early, like eight o'clock in the morning. Michelle didn't know anyone who got up that early. Maybe she'd see someone stumbling back from one of Captain's after-parties or something.

Blood! Michelle gasped. Had the van been used in a crime?

Not a lot, the cop said. *Maybe none at all. But there's something on that seat. We'll have to open it up.* Michelle and Quinn stared at one another in excited horror. What if there was like a dead body in the van? Both watched a lot of *Unsolved Mysteries* and had bonded over a mutual obsession with Robert Stack, his suits and his hair and his grim delivery. They liked when he delivered his mournful epilogues before a blue screen no one had bothered to project an image onto. It was so low-rent—the sordid vanishings, the bad reenactments, the alarming sound track.

If There Is A Dead Body In The Van I Could End Up On *Unsolved Mysteries*, Michelle whispered, but the cop heard her. He played down the likelihood of murder.

It's not like a blood bath in there, he said, glancing at them in the rearview mirror a little too long. Michelle grew nervous. If there was a murder the lovers would be immediate suspects. Warrants to search Michelle's home would be issued swiftly. Drugs would be discovered and nobody likes a druggie. People kill for drugs, everyone knows that. Drugs are a gateway crime for murder. Quinn was already passively lying to the cop, allowing him to think she was a man even though no one had said anything. It didn't matter. None of it would look good on paper. Michelle forsook her *Unsolved Mysteries* aspirations and hoped there were no dead bodies in the van.

The van—a Dodge, fat and blue—had been brought to

the curb at a hectic angle and abandoned. No windows were smashed. The vehicle was laughably easy to break into, you jiggled the handle and the locks practically popped themselves open for you. The pair looked for the blood the cop had mentioned. They found it on the cracked front seat, a few dark red sprinkles on the pleather. A bizarrely familiar sticky nub of heroin clung there as well. A plastic bag of syringes on the floor. The van had been stolen by junkies! A Big Gulp from the 7-Eleven sat on the dash, the ice melted, condensation sweating through the waxy cup. Everywhere were cookie crumbs, as if the joyriding dopeheads had grabbed great fistfuls of animal crackers and crushed them in their palms, flinging the sweet debris around the vehicle like confetti. Someone had had a great time in that van. Michelle walked around the side of it and slid open the door for the cop. It was empty.

All right, the cop said, *I got a tow truck coming, you can pick it up at 850 Bryant.*

What? Michelle asked. Can't I Just Take It?

It got a ticket for being parked in a bus zone, the cop explained, *and on top of that you have a bunch of outstanding parking tickets. You like to park on the sidewalk, it looks like?*

Fucking Ziggy! Drunk driving home from the bar and leaving the van on the sidewalk in front of her house. The arrogance! Those Weren't My Tickets, Michelle began.

This vehicle has too many tickets. You pay them at 850 Bryant and we'll release the van to you. And, here. The cop grabbed the bag of needles and flung them at Michelle. *Take care of these please.*

The cop's work was done. He gave them a nod of dismissal. Michelle was aghast. She'd been pulled out of her narcotic slumber for this? To be abandoned on top of some godforsaken hilly part of San Francisco she had never been to? Where was the Mission? Aren't You Going To Drive Us Back?

I'm not a taxi, the cop said. He went back to his squad car to wait for the tow truck.

What Am I Supposed To Do With These? Michelle shook the bag at Quinn. Never mind what she would do now that the van had been impounded. She couldn't afford to bail it out, no way. It would rot there. How would Michelle get off this sinking ship of a city? Michelle had to get out of there. The energetic walls of San Francisco were closing in on her. Of course the van had been stolen, her plan ruined, by druggies. How desperate do you have to be to actually inject something into your bloodstream? You did not have control of your life if you were unable to wait two minutes for the drugs to work through your sinuses.

I Cannot Bring These Home, Michelle said intensely, rattling the bag.

Of course not, Quinn shrugged.

No Really, Michelle said.

Throw them away, Quinn nodded at a trash can on the curb.

Someone Could Get Stuck. A Sanitation Worker.

So? They're clean.

Yeah, But Imagine How Scared They'd Be. They Wouldn't Know They're Clean. They'd Have To Get Tested And Everything.

There are actual dirty needles in the trash in San Francisco, Quinn said. *There's like toxic waste. I'm sure they wear gloves and stuff.*

Michelle's mother Wendy had once been stuck with a questionable needle at the psych hospital. She was dosed with precautionary AIDS meds that made her terribly sick. For a week she writhed in bed, sweating from fever dreams of sawing her own lip off or having bullets lodged in her brain. She was certain she had AIDS, punished by God, but for what? Being gay? Did Wendy really believe that? She supposed, in some dark corner of her brain, she did. And the AIDS medication had turned her brain into one big dark corner.

Michelle and Kyle learned of their mother's hardship like they always did, long after the fact, when the opportunity to help had come and gone.

Why Didn't You Tell Us? Michelle wailed, though what could she have done? Her mothers were so far away, and plane rides were pricey.

If Michelle thought about putting the needles in the trash can on the sidewalk she thought of her mother's hand, laden with Claddagh rings and shaded with nicotine, reaching in and getting pricked.

I'll Take Them To The Hospital, she said.

Walking through the lobby, searching for a biohazard bin, Michelle couldn't stop thinking of her moms. She hadn't told them she was moving. Michelle's life made her moms nervous and Michelle hated the feeling of it—sort of monstrous, always bad all the time. They were happy she was gay, of course, but she was a weird sort of gay, a degenerate gay. She didn't want to sue the government for the right to marry, she wasn't interested in gays in the military, she was queerly promiscuous and thought that this was enough, that this was activism. Wendy and Kym hated to say it but it was Michelle and her generation that were holding back the gay rights movement. When Fox News wanted to show gay people, did they bring a camera crew to Wendy and Kym's to show two middle-aged, out-of-shape lesbians smoking cigarettes in front of the television like the rest of their audience? No. They went to people like Michelle and her friends, who seemed to only want to scar their bodies and strap rubber phalluses to their crotch.

Wendy and Kym checked in on Michelle and Kyle, and Michelle and Kyle checked in on their moms, and then the siblings checked in with each other about their moms—epic conversations wherein Michelle and Kyle detailed all the ways in which their mothers' lives were sad and stunted, all the ways they could be better if they would just do something to improve their circumstances. They clucked and marveled at Wendy's unwillingness to become a different person, not this chain-smoking, codependent caretaker of crazy people by day and Kym by night. Working too much overtime, getting bleary with sleep deprivation and then jabbing herself with a needle. Michelle and Kyle talked about the needle incident forever. Was it a cry for help? How ironic it would be for their mother of all people to get AIDS.

And what about Kym? Was she really sick? Had Michelle seen the movie *Safe*? Kyle wanted to know. Was their other mother really physically ill or was she profoundly depressed, mentally ill, or, even worse, was she simply a lazy bitch? The options were all so terrible to consider. They found themselves oddly hoping that their mom was in fact struck down by a diabolical, new environmental illness.

Everyone hung up their phones upset and grim. Everyone's hearts were clogged with love for one other—inexpressible, jammed-up love, love that leached like a toxin into the bloodstream, one it would take a surgery to release. This was a family.

Sometimes Michelle tripped out on her deep and painful love for her mothers. If they weren't related, Wendy would just be one of those trashy lesbians she couldn't relate to. Kym would be one of those people you see on the bus, sick and stoned. It seemed everything had gone wrong for these people—if there was a social injustice it had happened to them, if there was a malaise they suffered from it, if there was bad luck they'd been stroked by it. Michelle felt repelled by these people, as if their condition, the whole of it, was contagious. She felt bad about this but it was true. And her own mother was one of them. Sickly and paranoid, a drain on those around her. Michelle loved her with a love that had nowhere to go, a bird flying into a window.

Michelle couldn't save her mothers and that was all her love was meant to do. And so the love was useless and exhausting. It turned to rage inside Michelle and so she also hated them. Why was she supposed to help them? Michelle could barely help herself. She lived below the poverty level in a city rapidly filling with rich people. At least Wendy had a career. She could go back to school and better her earning power, she could stop smoking. Kym had gone to community college, she could stop smoking pot, go to therapy, get on an antidepressant, leave the house, make some friends, maybe teach a fucking class or something. Why did Michelle feel like she had to do such things for these women, register Wendy for classes or find a homeopath for Kym?

Michelle felt responsible for her moms' happiness. She felt she owed them something, something big. The families that had disowned them were full of older women whose go-getter daughters had married up or gotten into antiques and took their mothers gambling in Atlantic City or on Caribbean cruises. Was that what Michelle was supposed to do? Was that what her moms were waiting for? Another perk that their lesbianism had robbed them of.

And so it was in this dark space that Michelle entered the hospital on the hill, a bag of needles in her hand, thinking that by saving a hypothetical sanitation worker she was somehow helping her moms. Deep in the throes of her emotional bender, Michelle was oblivious to her appearance. She looked like a wild drug addict, face bloated and splotchy, hair a blue tangle, malnourished in her skinny jeans, braless in her thin shirt, the twin pyramids of her tits poking around, her nipples staring out from the worn rattlesnake fabric. The secretary showed alarm at the bag of needles in her hand. *Can I help you?*

My Van Was Stolen And Whoever Did It Left These—*rattle, rattle*—In The Back Seat. They're Clean But Maybe You Have A Biohazard Container I Can Leave These In?

The woman's face twitched. *You can't bring those in here.*

You Don't Have A Biohazard Container? I Don't Think They're Dirty But—

You can't just bring a bunch of needles into a hospital trying to dump them. There are laws, we can't even—

I'm Not Just Bringing Them, My Van Was Stolen And They Dumped It Outside And Left These—Michelle cut herself off as the reality of her appearance dawned on her. She felt embarrassed, then mad at her embarrassment. She was telling the truth! She was the victim of a crime! Though perhaps she was what the woman thought she was, those weren't her fucking needles. Fine, she spat, I Was Just Trying To Make Sure Some Poor Sanitation Worker Didn't Get Stuck, But I'll Go Throw Them In The Trash Out Front Then.

You can't, the woman said nervously. *You can't just leave them in a public trash can. And you can't leave them on our property.* The two stared each other down. What was one supposed to do with a bag of fucking needles then? *Oh, hold on,* the woman's annoyance broke and she punched some numbers into her phone. Eventually a man showed up, a doctor looking harried and a little nervous, possibly scared of Michelle.

Can I help you? he asked at a distance. *Rattle, rattle.* Michelle shook the bag.

I'm Just Looking To Get Rid Of These. They're Not Mine. I Found Them. If I Was Shooting Drugs Why Would I Be Throwing Away A Perfectly Good Bag Of Needles?

The phrase *a perfectly good bag of needles* rang in Michelle's head. Why was she throwing them away? The dealers on her corner sold rigs as well as drugs, they whispered *outfits, outfits* under their breath at passersby. Maybe she could have gotten her new friend Quinn to barter with them, trade the needles for some balloons. Too late now. The doctor moved toward Michelle to receive the bag. A clear plastic bag jumbled with clear plastic syringes, clear plastic syringes with bright orange caps.

Thanks, Michelle said. She'd been ready to fight the doctor and now had to readjust herself internally. The doctor seemed kind. He had white hair and white clothes and clear spectacles on his eyes.

Are you okay? he asked her. *Do you need anything?* His voice was heavy with subtext but Michelle didn't want to know what he was getting at. She hated how shifty she must've seemed, hungover, talking about a stolen van, wielding a bag of drug needles.

No, she said, her voice extra cheery like she was

interviewing for a job. Just Happy To Have My Van Back! Never Had To Handle A Bag Of Needles Before, Didn't Really Know What To Do With Them! She laughed a big laugh and shook her head at how crazy life was. She was an average citizen having a really weird day. She waved good-bye at the doctor, at the receptionist who still wasn't convinced Michelle was not a drug fiend, that she hadn't stolen her own van, if there even was a van at all. She left the hospital. The light was so bright it rammed into her eyes and shot up her brain. Michelle couldn't wear sunglasses. She was so blind she'd have to get prescription sunglasses and those were really expensive, so in the sun she just squinted a lot and held her hand to her forehead.

The doctor's kindness had left her shaken. Why couldn't her mother work for a nice guy like that? Maybe Michelle should start to look for nursing positions on the Internet, print them out, and send them to her mother, maybe her mothers would have a better quality of life in San Francisco. Wasn't San Francisco full of sick lesbians, too? They had art shows and gatherings, Kym could be part of a vibrant sick community rather than wasting away on the couch. Why did some people get excellent lives while other people's lives were so shitty? She couldn't bear the thought that her mothers' lives sucked. It filled Michelle with heartbreak and panic. By the time she got back to Quinn she was in tears.

What happened? Quinn was alarmed.

The Doctor—Nothing. He Took Them. It Just Made Me Sad About My Mothers. Michelle burst into tears.

Oh! Quinn panicked at the sight of Michelle in tears. Partly she wanted to pet her new friend, but she was also aware that her new friend was sort of crazy. She didn't want to get in too deep. She couldn't tell if having a drug bond with someone was a light bond or a deep bond. It felt deep when they were high but so did everything. By the light of day, there by a bus stop in a random part of the city with this crying, trembling wreck of a girl, the sort of girl a person sees and says, *Give her a cheeseburger!*—scrawny and alive with wild emotion—Quinn wondered what the fuck she was doing. What, if anything, did she owe this person?

The bus came and the pair climbed aboard. At the back of the vehicle Michelle quietly wept. Her emotions were now almost 100 percent chemically regulated. She felt happy when high, nervous and tragic while crashing, peaceful as the intensity faded, optimistic as she planned her evening's chemical intake—just alcohol tonight, just one beer, just a cocktail, maybe one line, the rest of the leftover nub of heroin and then no more until next week, no cocaine until the weekend, okay okay okay.

Quinn was not heartless. Her hand came to rest upon Michelle's neck and stayed there, bouncing with the jumble of the bus. It felt nice. Michelle appreciated it. She didn't think things were going anywhere with Quinn, but that was fine. Where was *anywhere*, anyway? All anyone had was this moment. Michelle was in the moment. She liked the way she was. People adopted lifelong courses of religious study to try to achieve a state that came naturally to her.

Quinn's heart leaped when she realized this random bus skirted her neighborhood. Strangely, Quinn did not live in the Mission. She lived in some other neighborhood where, like the Mission, the streets were numbered, but they were not streets, they were avenues. People called that part of town the Avenues. It seemed sinister to Michelle, like the Mission's evil twin. What did people do out there? Apparently, they watched *The X-Files* with their husbands. Michelle still could not understand that Quinn had such a thing.

What's Your Husband Like? Michelle asked Quinn suddenly, realizing she had never inquired.

He's really nice. He's stable. I was having a lot of panic attacks when I married him. She paused. *He takes glassblowing classes.*

Is He Taller Than You? Michelle asked. Quinn nodded.

Is He Going To Let You Come To My Going-Away Party? Michelle asked. Quinn lifted her hand and bopped Michelle in the head.

It's not the 1800s, Quinn laughed. *I don't have to ask him for permission to go to a party.*

What About Sleep Over At My House? Michelle asked. Do You Have To Ask Him? Does He Care?

Quinn shrugged. *He doesn't love it.*

What About Drugs, Does He Do Drugs?

No. I do drugs.

Michelle nodded. It didn't actually sound like a bad arrangement. Sort of like a parent. Michelle would like someone to take care of her, too. But she'd had that with Andy. Something was always expected in return. It wasn't worth it.

What About Driving Me To Los Angeles? Michelle asked. Is He Going To Be Okay With You Driving Me To Los Angeles Now That My Van Is Gone?

I'm not driving you to Los Angeles! Quinn laughed a nervous laugh and hit Michelle in the head once more.

You Have To, Michelle whined. How Else Will I Get There?

Can't someone else drive you? Quinn asked.

No. You're My Only Friend. She laid her head on Quinn's

shoulder and began to weep anew. She had meant it as a joke but it was too real. Stitch and Ziggy and Linda and Andy all felt variously betrayed by her, and she by them.

Oh, come on. Quinn shook Michelle from her shoulder.

You Kind Of Are. Michelle looked deeply, tearfully, into Quinn's eyes, which meant into her eyeglasses, which reflected herself back to her. She looked like a wreck. It was not helping her situation. She would not be able to seduce Quinn, she was too grotesque. She would have to draw on the girl's pity and her inability to say no.

How? I don't have a car.

Your Husband Doesn't Have A Car?

No, he rides a bike.

Oh, one of those. Does He Have A Credit Card? Michelle asked. Can One Of You Rent Me A U-Haul?

This is insane, Quinn said in a brief moment of clarity before she capitulated to Michelle's tears and agreed to rent a U-Haul and drive her to Los Angeles in the morning.

13 Michelle's going-away party began at the Eagle, a bar Michelle did not particularly like. The outside was so dark and the heat lamps made her hot and sleepy and occasionally ignited a clump of dead twigs and leaves. She could never find who she was looking for, and there was no place to sit unless you pulled yourself up on the tables and then your dangling legs made your feet fall asleep. But it was big enough to accommodate a large gathering and you could smoke outside, and if you hadn't eaten all day you could feed yourself from the wooden barrel of peanuts by the door, so that was good. The after-party would be at Michelle's.

Stitch was excited about this, as Stitch was generally amenable to an after-party. Ekundayo hated after-parties. She had to breathe down the violence she felt whenever Michelle and Stitch brought one home. But this one was different. Michelle was finally leaving. It was a true celebration. Ekundayo was not joyful enough to join the festivities but she would not bust them up, would not drag her stick through the living room on her way to piss in the water closet, glaring at the little doped-up fools snorting lines off the dumpstered coffee table. Michelle had dragged that coffee table back from the Marina, a nice neighborhood. Andy had arranged a couple's counseling session for them there during the Linda era. The counseling had gone poorly. They'd spent most of the hour unpacking why Andy didn't like going to the movies. *What's wrong with the movies?* the therapist, who'd had a lot of plastic surgery, had asked in a slightly shaming voice.

I don't know, Andy shrugged, uneasy. *I just don't like going to the movies.*

Well, maybe Michelle would like to go to the movies? the therapist suggested in a more playful yet still scornful tone.

Yeah! Michelle chimed in. The therapist liked her! The therapist was on her side, would understand why Michelle had to look elsewhere to get her needs met. Andy wouldn't even go to the movies with her! What was that about? But when the focus shifted to Michelle, she bristled. I Don't Think Long-Term Relationships Are Inherently More Important Than Short Relationships, she said airily. We Learn All Sorts Of Lessons From All Sorts Of People, Who's To Say Which Relationships Are More Meaningful? Michelle was busting out the big hippie guns.

So, the therapist began, *do you not want a long-term relationship with Carlotta?*

I Want The Relationship To Be What It Is In The Moment, Michelle said. I Don't Want To Label It. I Want It To Be Free. I Just Want To Go To The Movies Sometimes. She tried bringing it back around to the movies, she'd liked that part. The rest of the conversation felt so stressful. Why were they even there? What did Andy want from her? It must have been so expensive, the therapist, and Michelle wasn't paying for it, not even a little.

We'll talk more about this next week. The therapist leveled her surgically lifted eyes at Michelle. *I think there is a lot to discover here.* But Michelle knew there would be no next week. She felt confused and surly as they left the therapist's office, on the verge of lashing out at Andy. And then she found the coffee table, sleek and black, a higher quality of trash than the stuff left curbside in the Mission. Andy drove it home for her in the back of her classic car.

But the party! Many people came. Not as many as would have come if Michelle had packed up and left town about a year or so earlier, before becoming such a druggie that some began avoiding her. A certain demographic was present. Those who had shared bindles of cocaine with Michelle, key bumps in the queer bar bathroom, or lines on the pinball machine at the Albion. People she had popped open tiny ziplock baggies of crystal meth with. Michelle's speed dealer came, though she would not have ever called him that, no way, that made it seem like their relationship was based on, well, drugs, when it wasn't, it was based on a shared enthusiasm for *The Gossip*, an enduring affection for Courtney Love no matter how fucking crazy she was, a nostalgia for old San Francisco, before the yuppies and the dot-commers had come, when the good old drag queens were still alive. Michelle's speed dealer DJ'd at some of the better—meaning seedier—fag bars in town, ones where leathermen hung out totally naked but for their caps and boots, sucking each other off in the corner.

Michelle would miss San Francisco. She couldn't think about it too much lest it give her a panic attack. Her bedroom, that blue and sparkly place, was all but empty of her now. She'd packed herself up and loaded it into the truck Quinn had parked on the corner. Her futon was the only thing left in the room. Michelle and Quinn would sleep one more night on it, then drag it down the stairs and leave it by the parking meter for some desperate person to take home. Until then Michelle would drink with the last of her friends. She would accept drugs from the tips of proffered house keys. She would play Truth or Dare.

Michelle dared a girl she didn't know to stuff her ass crack full of leftover rice from a bowl in the fridge. Michelle then poured soy sauce onto it and dared Quinn to eat it. Michelle had seen Quinn watching the girl, who had long dyed black hair and the eyes of a crazy person. The party was thick with uninhibited druggie sex vibes. Quinn knelt before the strange girl, stuffed with food and spread across the Marina coffee table like a human buffet. She dug her mouth into the soft, cold pile of rice and swallowed. People cheered.

The two of them were visibly enjoying the attention. Michelle watched along with the others, her feelings swirling into violent focus. She had given the dare to let Quinn know she was on to her. Michelle had bitch's intuition, she always knew when someone was vibing her date—if that's what Quinn was—or when her date was even thinking about thinking about vibing someone else. That Michelle could detect the vibrations before the vibers were even sure of what they were feeling gave her a sensation of superiority and power. Michelle was of some other, rarefied realm, so above the mundane sexual tensions of commoners like Quinn and this girl with the rice up her ass, their flirtations as blatant and tacky as tabloids.

Michelle was disappointed in Quinn. The girl was a two-bit stripper who couldn't wait to tell everyone about what a stripper she was, as if everyone in the room hadn't already been a stripper for a million years. The girl was tedious. Michelle looked around for someone to get a crush on, but there was no one left. She knew everyone already, had known them for so long she was bored of their friendship, even. The cocaine was crashing Michelle before she was even off the ground with it. Michelle hated cocaine. Her mood darkened. Why did people bother when speed was so much stronger, cheaper, and kept you high so much longer? *Well, maybe some people want to fall asleep eventually*, a partygoer defended her shitty cocaine in the face of Michelle's tirade.

It's Like Watching TV With No Cable, Michelle said scornfully. It's Like Playing Atari When You Could Be Playing Nintendo. Michelle's reference points were whack.

Have another line, someone gently shaped a tuft of drugs into a stream and Michelle inhaled it. She felt okay for one minute, excellent for five, then promptly suicidal. She looked for Quinn. She was helping Rice Ass wipe soy sauce from her thighs with a dirty dishrag. There were probably roaches on the rag, it had come from the kitchen. Michelle hoped the girl found one on her pussy. Better yet, she hoped Quinn found it there for her. Wait, did she really hope that? She thought about it. She walked over to where Quinn was rubbing the edge of the dish towel under the elastic of the girl's shiny underwear. All around them it was a melee of make-outs and more. Two people were showily fucking on the dirty armchair in the corner by the window. Outside the window Michelle could see the Filipino metalheads next door sitting on their back stairs and watching the spectacle. They sat out there most nights, drinking beer poured over ice and listening to Metallica cassettes on a pink boom box shaped like the grill of a Cadillac. They were pretty cool boys, one rode a dirt bike and was cute like a butch girl. Michelle wondered if she should invite them over. She'd miss them more than half the people currently celebrating her departure. She gave them a little wave and they waved back. She was at Quinn's side.

I Want To Kill Myself, Michelle said.

What happened? Quinn smiled. Rice Ass hadn't heard anything. She just sat there with her legs spread, smelling like Chinese leftovers. Liquid eyeliner flicked out from the edges of her eyelids and red lipstick had etched her mouth into a perfect heart-shaped pout. Michelle tried not to look at her and leaned in closer to Quinn.

I Want To Kill Myself, she repeated.

Are you serious? Quinn asked, bewildered. *What are you talking about?*

You Know What I Mean, Michelle snapped, sick of repeating herself, sick of hunching over because Quinn couldn't pull herself away from Rice Ass's crotch, sick of Rice Ass's flawlessly made-up face staring at her with those sociopathic blue eyes, sick of feeling like indeed, yes, she had become the psychotically jealous person at the party, at her own party, her own going-away party, this was how she would be leaving San Francisco, in ruin, humiliated, staging a suicidal cry for help because she could not deal with the attentions of her casual and married drug and sex acquaintance being pulled from her for five minutes.

You Know What I Mean, she said again, choking on tears now, and dashed down the long hallway into her empty bedroom.

I Didn't Really Want To Kill Myself, Michelle insisted a little later. It Was A Feeling Of Wanting To Kill Myself. It Was How I Felt. But I Would Never Do That.

Well, Jesus, Quinn huffed. Michelle was snotty with tears, her face was already swelling. Her emotions were a feral animal that she could not get her arms around.

I Was Just Upset, she said. I Feel So Emotional About Leaving San Francisco And I Look Over And You're Giving The Poor Man's Bettie Page A Rim Job.

But you dared me to! Now Quinn was mad. *We were playing a game!*

I Saw You Looking At Her, Michelle seethed. Vibing Her. And I Just Felt Like You Like Her So Much Why Don't You Just Eat Rice From Her Ass Then? Michelle knew in her gut that cocaine was to blame for this harsh scene. If the cocaine had been better she wouldn't have crashed so hard so fast, felt so crazy. If the cocaine had been good she would have felt powerful and sexy and she would have eaten the rice from the stripper's ass, or had the girl eat the rice from her ass. She would have done something lunatic and memorable and very, very sexy. With better cocaine she could have left San Francisco like that, high on the wave of her own reputation. Not like this, with people down the hall gossiping about her in her own living room. With Rice Ass, smug in her beauty, thinking Michelle an unhinged bitch. With poor Quinn rethinking her decision to slum it outside matrimony with a hysterical and aging femme who could not handle her cocaine—oh no, was that Michelle? That was Michelle. She wept into her futon. There was a slight knocking. It was Ziggy, calling into the bedroom. She cracked open the door.

I'm going home. You're leaving in the morning, right? I'll come say goodbye. Rice Ass flew up suddenly behind her. Her face, undeniably striking, gorgeous even, pushed through Ziggy's orange hair as if through a fringed curtain. She rested her chin on Ziggy's shoulder.

Thanks for the party! she cried cheerily. She shot a wink at Quinn. *Let's go*, she pulled Ziggy by her studded belt backward out the door. Michelle listened to them clatter down the stairs, their voices rising giddily from the sidewalk below the window.

Ugh, I can't believe she'd go home with that person! Quinn spat.

Ugh, I Can't Believe You Care! Michelle raged, a fresh batch of tears exploding from her eyes. She's Like A Trashy Fucking Dime-A-Dozen Stripper! Gross! And If I Had A Best Friend, Which I Do Not, It Would Be Ziggy, So Shut Up!

Quinn put her hands up to ward off Michelle's charging emotions. *Sorry, sorry.* She reached out and actually petted Michelle's head. Quinn was a Libra, she couldn't bear for the upset to linger. *She's actually a sex-work activist, that girl,* Quinn said. *She does really cool work. She's unionizing the club she works at. She read your book, she really likes you. She couldn't believe she was at your party.*

Ugh! Michelle cried. She didn't know what to say to all of this, so she made unattractive animal noises instead. Ugh! Ack! Ech! She slammed her head back down on the futon and cried. She cried for her room, which was not hers anymore. She cried for the bookstore, which had employed her in spite of her being so unemployable, just because they thought it was cool that she'd written a book. Now who would employ her? She cried for the friends who had come to her party, who she had all but ignored in the face of Quinn's flirtations. She cried for the friends who hadn't come to her party because they weren't really her friends anymore, just people she used to be friends with, how had that happened, how had Michelle allowed them to drift away? She cried because Quinn's giant palm was resting on her thigh and it didn't mean anything.

Quinn was thinking the exact same thoughts as Michelle: that their whole connection was a mistake born of drugs, that if not for Quinn's weakness of will she would be back with her husband where she belonged, plucking tender pops from a warm bowl of popcorn, snuggling. *You know,* she began, *I think I'm going to head home.*

What? Michelle was alarmed.

Don't worry, I'll still drive you to Los Angeles, okay?

You Have To, Michelle begged desperately. You Really, Really Have To.

I don't actually have to, Quinn corrected her. She was glad this person was leaving. When Michelle was gone Quinn would go to Kabuki hot springs and spend all day in the sauna. She would find kale, somewhere she would find it, and she would eat it. She had had her dalliance with heroin, maybe she'd write some poems about it. It had been crazy and Quinn had been looking for crazy. But she was done. She craved feeling her husband beside her, the sleeping bulk of him, like snuggling down with a bear in the woods. She found her jacket on Michelle's floor, red leather with extreme snaps and lapels. No one looking at Quinn would ever think she had a husband and you know what? Quinn thought that was cool.

See you in the morning. Get some sleep. Quinn crouched beside her crying friend and gave her hair a ruffle. Michelle shrugged it off. Sometimes Michelle felt like everyone else was a poser and she was the only authentic person in the whole world. She was 100 percent on this. There was nowhere else for her to be, no husband to return to, nothing safe, nothing anywhere. It was a lonely thought. She fell asleep trying to make it feel triumphant.

14

Michelle woke in the morning to the noise of Ziggy hip-chucking the bedroom door open. Layers of paint kept it stuck to the jamb, it required a bit of violence to pop open. The punch of it giving way stirred Michelle, alone on her futon. Her sinuses, clogged with snot and cocaine, had drained into the left side of her head as she slept, and so her face looked lopsided, puffier on that end, like a fun-house mirror or the boy from *Mask*. Ziggy walked into the room with two coffees steaming from their paper cups. *Rise and shine, LA woman.* It was incredible how well Ziggy functioned. Her neck was spotted with hickeys as if with leprosy. Her goggles held her unwashed hair back from her face, which was scrubbed clean. Ziggy used fancy face wash that heated up as it lathered. She smelled like the inside of an Aveda salon. Michelle did not know how she did it. She had been up all night fucking that girl and had arrived exactly on time to awaken Michelle, with coffee. Michelle lowered her face into the steaming cup and let the bitter cloud rouse her.

Your married woman's outside and ready to go, Ziggy said. *You excited?*

Michelle shrugged. Do I Look Like *Mask*? she asked, touching the swollen roll of her face. Like Eric Stoltz In The Movie *Mask*? Where He Has That Disease, You Know, It Makes His Face All Bumpy?

And Cher is his mom? Ziggy asked. *And she's like a biker and gets him a hooker for his birthday?*

Yeah!

I fucking love that movie. Ziggy pulled a pack of Camels from the ass of her white jeans and lit up in the empty room.

But Do I Look Like That?

Ziggy squinted at her friend. *I don't know,* she said slowly. *I don't think you look like Cher.*

No, Do I Look Like The Boy, The Boy In *Mask*!

Oh god! Ziggy snorted a cloud of smoke from her nose. *No, you don't look like the boy in* Mask. *Why? Because you were crying?*

You Can Tell?

Ziggy nodded. Michelle drank her coffee.

You didn't have a great going-away party?

Michelle's finger shot out and poked the mottled skin of Ziggy's neck. You Did.

That girl's crazy, Ziggy said with a grin. She rubbed her neck and winced. *She bit my fucking throat off.* She drew on her cigarette like an asthmatic sucking on an inhaler and tossed the butt out the window. *I should get back there, I left her outside in her car.*

Who? That Girl?

Lelrine, yeah. She's out front with Quinn.

That Girl! That Girl!

Yeah. Ziggy shrugged.

God, I Fucking Hate That Girl!

Ziggy looked unfazed. *She likes you. She brought your book, she wants you to sign it.*

Ugh! Michelle cried and reinserted herself into the futon, sinking her face into the pillow. Ack! Ech! Ziggy kicked her gently with the toe of her motorcycle boot.

Get up, she said. *Get off that and I'll drag this downstairs for you.*

Outside, Lelrine clambered off the hood of her purple Datsun, where she had been perched, flirting with Quinn. She charged toward Michelle bearing a copy of Michelle's book. Michelle autographed it. She inscribed, *To Lelrine, On the day of my departure. I will never forget you.* Lelrine looked different in the daylight, with no makeup on her face or rice in her ass. She was in her walk-of-shame ensemble of satin hot pants, a ratty T-shirt stretched like skin across her intense tits. Michelle would have to find out from Ziggy if they were real. Michelle sort of loved fake tits. It was her favorite part of any strip bar, the girls with the boobs that looked like someone had hurled them onto their chests from across the room, strong as muscles with a little wobble. They fascinated Michelle.

She waved to the pair as they drove off in the little purple car. She sat on her front stoop and thought nostalgically how she would never sit there again. So much had happened on that stoop. She'd cried, of course, over girls who had stopped loving her, and she had smoked many cigarettes, she had drunk beers. She'd written part of her book here, her back against her front door, pen in a notebook, crying over a girl who had stopped loving her while smoking and drinking beer. She wanted to nail a plaque to it, the stoop. There was that one sweet crackhead related to the woman who lived on the first floor. Michelle would often come down and see the lady sitting on the stairs, nodded out. Michelle would startle her and the lady would swiftly begin sweeping the stoop with her hands, brushing debris into her palm with her fingers.

I'm Susie's cousin, she'd say in a stuffed-up voice. *Susie said I could sit here.* She'd dust a little path for Michelle to pass through.

It's Fine, Michelle assured her. Generally Michelle didn't mind if people sat on her stairs. Sometimes gangs of boys with bottles of beer would be intimidating, but they weren't shitty to her and once even helped her upstairs with her laundry. Susie's cousin was very tender and had such a strange, froggy voice. Stitch enjoyed imitating her.

I'm Sooseez cousin, Stitch would roll her eyes back and pantomime sweeping with her hands. *Sooseee said I could sit here.* Stitch did really good impressions. She did the Susie's cousin imitation to Ekundayo once and it made her hostile. Ekundayo acted like drug addicts were holy and became defensive if you laughed at them, like you were being racist or poking fun at a disabled person.

It's not funny, she said.

It Actually Is, Michelle said. It's Actually Quite Funny. Stitch also did a killer imitation of a junkie they'd seen nodding off with a bag of chips in his hand at the gas station, but she only did it privately, to Michelle, to make her laugh. People could be really sensitive about drug addicts.

Michelle thought about Stitch, upstairs in her bedroom, her choppy haircut asleep on some strange pillow filled with barley or natural husks. The pillow was horribly uncomfortable but Stitch swore it was good for your neck. Stitch. Michelle's eyes teared. She wasn't going to wake her friend up, Stitch knew she was leaving. She could have come down and said goodbye. Whatever. This city was stupid. Michelle lifted herself off the stairs and walked slowly toward the U-Haul, where Quinn sat resentfully in the driver's seat.

15 The heat in the truck's cab was grisly. California was on fire and once out of San Francisco the highway shimmered in the windshield like a mirage. The land on the margins was dry, even charred. The farmland decreased as they drove. The water was too ruined for effective farming and the animals were out of whack, the bugs and the birds, the pests and pollinators. They drove past wide plowed fields whose sickly crops had been abandoned. What Do You Think That Was? Michelle asked, staring at the mangled stalks, everything hay colored beneath the brutal sun. Quinn shrugged and kept her eyes on the road.

Michelle hadn't left San Francisco in eight years and Quinn, a native, never had. The ocean was a giant toilet lapping at San Francisco's edges, but mainly things were functioning. On the highway Michelle felt alarmed at all the dead land. These towns were abandoned. A gas station had been torched, blackening everything around it in a wide, ruined circle. Michelle leaned back against the leather seat, her skin stuck hotly to it, suctioned with sweat. She watched the wasteland glide by on the 405.

Then, the cows. The cities of cows stretched out into the trashed landscape for miles, a pixilated black and white, their spotted backs blurring together until the sight of them all became something else entirely, a surrealist landscape, an M. C. Escher drawing referencing infinity.

The smell was something to complain about for the first twenty minutes. It was as if their faces were being cruelly mashed into a vat of wet shit. The humidity rose as they entered the cow cities, the steam of the animals' sweat and breath and farts, the water systems churning to douse them, all of it changed the air, saturating it, carrying the stench. The sounds, too, the dull bleats and moos. The cows continued alongside them forever. *Cowshwitz*, Quinn spoke. She had heard of this part of the drive. Her husband had warned her of it, gambled she'd become vegetarian by the time they drove out of it.

The lovers tried various things to save them from the smell, such as cupping their hands over their faces and inhaling instead their own rank breath. Michelle lit cigarettes. She held a carton of chocolate milk over her mouth and nose like an oxygen mask, smelled sweetly sour candy before the stink of shit rushed back in. They breathed through their mouths, giving them the disgusting feeling of eating the smell. Their tongues rooted their gums, searching for the taste of cow dung. Eventually they could no longer smell it, despite the bovine landscape shifting toward the horizon, their collective motion like the swells of a gentle tide. It was creepy to know the horrible shit cloud was still with them, entering their bodies. They would try to locate it, pulling air through their noses the way Ziggy smoked her cigarettes, but they smelled nothing, nothing at all. And so they relaxed, succumbing to their bodies' merciful denial.

Michelle allowed the incomprehensible landscape to fuck with her mind. The round-backed cows became a sort of sea, she then allowed the sea, emerging beneath the cliffs, to become a menagerie, the lumps of trash beneath the pudding waves taking the shapes of animals she'd seen in books and magazines—a thick gorilla, a wide-eared elephant, the spindly neck of a giraffe. The waves drew back and heaved forward, the nauseated contractions of someone poisoned. Michelle saw real buses and airplanes, shopping carts and the roof of a home. An old telephone pole strung with gunk. She unfocused her eyes and they became dinosaurs, sea monsters. Broken boats bobbed, abandoned, looking like ghostly pirate ships. Perhaps some of them were. Across it all a web of oil stretched, like ebony lace or fishnet stockings.

1 I just can't open my screenplay with a scene of myself
smoking crack in Ziggy's van, Michelle thought, and
deleted twenty pages of text from her desktop. It felt
like she'd deleted her stomach, something vanished
in her body—well, that was rash. Too bad. The computer
glared at her with its vacant cyclops eye, daring her to try
again, to tell a universal story.

Michelle wracked her brain for successful books with
prominent crack smokers. The A. M. Homes story where
the suburban straight couple smokes it after the kids go
away. *Permanent Midnight*, where the guy wrote for *ALF* but
was really a total crackhead the whole time—that one got
made into a movie, even.

What made those crack stories work? What made
them, um, universal? Michelle suspected class. The suburbanites wanted to shake off the strangling yoke of
prosperity and good behavior. Michelle imagined if the
characters were black or gay the story wouldn't work

as well. The characters wouldn't be able to risk it, their foothold on suburbia tenuous as it was. The reader was having a hard enough time trying to relate to a black person or a gay person without then having to relate to a crackhead. It was too much. Though black and gay suburbanites surely deserved a relaxing hit of crack cocaine more than the couple in the Homes story, they would have to settle for a glass of wine with dinner.

What about the television writer? Well, he was successful, that was crucial. People seemed to enjoy stories in which someone who Has It All almost Throws It All Away, but doesn't. Redemption. For the crack narrative to succeed, the character has to be starting out on top, with a place to fall from. It can begin in suburbia or in the glass-walled office of a television executive. Readers anticipate the rungs descended. Crack wouldn't work for Michelle's character. She's already sort of a loser, really broke, born that way. What the fuck is she doing smoking crack, the reader would want to know. Is she retarded? This is boring. I can read the newspaper for this. For Michelle's story to be universal, it can only go in one direction, and crack does not further that trajectory.

All the writing had exhausted Michelle. She recalled Andy's parting words, a curse, really—*You better not ever write about me!*—is that what she said? Michelle felt bound to it, though she had never agreed, never made such a promise. Still, it would be lousy of her to break Andy's heart and then tell her secrets. It made Michelle's stomach lump. She began a screenplay based on Quinn's relationship with her husband. That was better—a lot of women had husbands. Very relatable. It could be a modern *Belle de Jour*, where the wife sneaks around with a downwardly spiraling lesbian, snorting heroin. She would have to make Quinn's hair longer. She'd have to be girly for it to work. Otherwise she just seemed like some closeted lesbian married to a man who is maybe a closeted gay himself for having married such a manly woman. People would just be weirded out by that story. Not universal at all.

Michelle opened the film treatment with a shot of Quinn and her husband on the couch watching *The X-Files*. The husband idly played with Quinn's long, luxurious hair. They fed each other popcorn. Michelle tried to imagine what they would say to one another and quickly became bored. Behind her, her knees on the scabby carpet, Quinn glanced at the screen as she packed her duffel bag.

I'd rather you didn't write that, Quinn said. *The story of my marriage.* Her hands went up to her head and felt around her mop of messy curls, making sure they hadn't morphed into ponytails. *And why would you give me long hair? I have never had long hair. Not even when I was a kid.*

Sorry! Michelle was a little defensive. I Was Trying To Make You More Universal. And Plus It's Not Really You. She's Based On You, But She's Different.

I see she's different, Quinn said. *She has long hair. But that's it. She has a husband who's a glass blower, she works at an art museum, she's having a heroin affair with a lesbian writer. The changed hair doesn't do anything. It's like you just wanted to humiliate me or something. If you're going to write about me at least give me good hair.*

Michelle turned back to her computer, feeling like a petulant child. Okay, she said. Fine. I Won't Write About You. I Won't Write About My Life Because No One Wants To Be In

My Story. I Won't Write About My Family Because They're Fucking Over It. I Should Just Give Up And Get A Job At Taco Bell Then 'Cause This Is It, This Is All I Know How To Do, Write These Glorified Diary Entries And Now I Can't Even Do That Because Everyone Is So Fucking Sensitive.

There was perhaps no way out for Michelle, not at this point. She had taken up documenting her own life with such vengeance, back when it seemed that vengeance was necessary. When she was angry at her moms for not having raised her better, noticed her genius or something, put her in a good school for chrissakes or at least an art program, anything to nurture her creativity, to acknowledge that she was creative at all, that they saw her. What good was having lesbian parents if they didn't bring you to a goddamn art show?

While she railed against the women who birthed her, she decided, of course, to also rail against everyone who had ever slighted her as she trudged the landmine of childhood, adolescence. So many bullies and squares! So many heartbreakers! The heartbreakers continued into adulthood, and writing was a wonderful place to even the score. Michelle could express herself so wonderfully, her pain, their insensitivity. They would read her words and know that they had had this special, smart person in their arms and they had tossed them away, and they would forever regret it. They would never stop being sad.

There had never been a girl like Michelle in literature, of this she was sure. It tinged her writing with a bit of cosmic justice, which assuaged the icky feeling of self-obsession nicely. Someday she would be dead—as would all the people in her books, their petty problems evaporated—but this *book* would exist, the most holy object in the world, a book. All their dumb lives were elevated for it. Even a book like Michelle's, a small book read by few. It didn't matter. She had rendered them cinematic in their small lives. Really everyone should be grateful.

Except they weren't. Quinn was only the latest to protest her inclusion in Michelle's story—which, basically, felt like protesting their inclusion in Michelle's *life*, which didn't feel great, honestly, and besides, what were they doing there, then? But even this tantrum was but the last gasp of Michelle's bravado. She'd grown weary of feeling like her writing hurt the people closest to her. She'd become more attuned to their feelings. She'd grown older and read wider and had begun to question how singular and important her story even was. Was she a war orphan, a refugee? No. She was a skinny, white, marginally attractive female living in the United States, where even poor people have MTV. What did she think was so important about her pain?

In reality, Quinn and Michelle weren't scheduled to meet one another for over a decade, when a series of flirtatious Gchats led to a brief affair involving diners, karaoke bars, and blanket forts. It was sweet for about five minutes, but then Michelle found herself in possession of a bottle of Vicodin from a bout of oral surgery. Believe it or not, Michelle hadn't ingested drugs or alcohol in eight years. But, being a drug addict, Michelle swiftly began abusing the Vicodin. By the second day on painkillers she had stopped eating in order to increase the chemical's effect.

Michelle wound up sickened with a panic attack outside an In-N-Out Burger in Hercules, California, sending Quinn inside to get her a cheeseburger, animal style, with fries.

When Quinn returned, Michelle was sobbing, terrified she would have to change her sobriety date, awestruck by how quickly she'd become insane. Sober for nearly a decade, all it took was one day on pain pills for Michelle to become obsessed and scheming, starving herself to plump her high.

Quinn didn't believe in the rhetoric of addiction and thus consoled Michelle, *You're just a girl who forgot to eat. You're upsetting yourself by seeing it all through this lens of addiction and AA.*

Michelle thought that only people who went to AA understood the true nature of addiction. She didn't hold Quinn's ignorance against her, but she wondered how safe it was for her to date a person who didn't believe in alcoholism. Michelle was nothing if not an alcoholic. More than being queer or a writer, Polish, or even female, it was what had shaped her life.

Quinn couldn't believe that this might be a deal breaker. *Let me get this straight,* Quinn said. They were heaped moodily in a large curving booth in an Italian restaurant in North Beach. The Mafia Booth, the bartender who had seated them called it. *You would break up with me because I don't agree with your definition of alcoholism.* They ate pizza and salad. Michelle still felt off from her pill binge. She'd forgotten how immediate and epic her hangovers were. People talked about this in AA—how your alcoholism continues to worsen even as you abstain, and if you do use again the effect is far worse than it was the last time.

My disease is in the basement, doing push-ups, Michelle had heard addicts say. And it was true. Two days taking Vicodin as directed, only altering her diet for maximum high, and she was still fragile and teary a week later. She shared her insight with Quinn.

Alcoholism is not a disease, Quinn argued.

It's Been Proven, Michelle said. By Science. A Million Times Over.

Really? Quinn asked skeptically. *Really? Because I don't think that is true. I don't think science has all the answers.* Quinn was also against therapy and the entire concept of *healing*. It was ridiculous for Michelle—whose days were divided between AA meetings, Al-Anon meetings, meditation at the Zen Center, the elliptical machine at 24-Hour Fitness, and sessions with a therapist—to date this person.

Wait, I'm really confused. Quinn felt a rising panic as she sat there on the carpet of Michelle's studio apartment. *What do you mean we haven't met?* An existential chill ran through the girl. It felt true. Something about this whole connection had felt otherworldly, like Quinn was experiencing everything through a shallow pool of water. Life wavered. She'd thought it was the drugs.

This Is A Story, Michelle gestured at the studio apartment. It was a bleak place enlivened by the brutal constancy of the Southern California sunshine. Michelle had decided against wearing a visor or carrying a sun umbrella. No matter how deadly its rays, the sun always cheered Michelle. It made the spotty white walls of her new studio less depressing. The hard plank of carpet. The sag of the futon on the floor. The strange parade of end-time insects doing their last waltz underneath the kitchen sink.

This, Michelle told Quinn, Is My Memoir.

Memoirs are true, Quinn, also a writer, pointed out.

This One Is Part True And Part False. All That Stuff I Just Said, About When We Dated, Is True.

God, Quinn said. *It doesn't make me look very good. Did I tell you you could write about me?*

No, Michelle said, But You Didn't Tell Me I Couldn't. The Person I Really Came To Los Angeles With Is Lucretia. I Actually Wrote The Whole Book With Her In It. Our Whole Story. Eight Years, Five Hundred Pages.

Quinn whistled through her teeth. *Eight years! The slam poet from the first part of the book? You were with her for eight years?*

I Know, Michelle said. It Was Really Complicated. She Didn't Want Me To Write About Her But Our Breakup Was So Shitty And Awful I Just Really Needed To Tell The Story. You Know How A Story Needs To Get Told?

Quinn did. It was one of the reasons Michelle brought her into the book. Quinn was a poet and knew the feeling of writing bubbling up inside her, like a pot coming to boil. You lunge for a pen before it goes away. You have to capture it. If you let it come, it just pours out. Five hundred pages.

At a bookstore in New York City in the year 2011, more than a decade after the world ends in *Black Wave*, Michelle stood before a microphone and read from that five-hundred-page memoir novel. She read about being there in that very apartment. How it had smelled strongly of the dish soap they used, yellow, purchased at the dollar store. Michelle and Lu had both been delighted to find that all items in the dollar store really were only a dollar. Dollar dinner plates painted with tulips. Dollar juice glasses with elephants and bumble bees. They brought these items back to this little kitchen in Los Angeles and placed them inside the built-in cabinets, at least in the ones that weren't painted shut with gobs of white paint.

In the story she read, Michelle tries to make Lu a bowl of beans. She adds corn and grates cheese into it, she seasons it with cumin and chili powder. All the while Lu is terribly mean to her. Lu has very low blood sugar. She can't find a job because she looks like both a boy and a girl and this makes people uncomfortable, so they tell her they are not hiring even though there are NOW HIRING signs hung all over the place. This makes Lu feel insane. She fights with Michelle, who is only trying to help, until Michelle collapses on the linoleum floor.

Like This, Michelle shows Quinn. They're in the kitchen in Los Angeles. Michelle beats her fists against the floor, then lets her forehead come to rest upon it. Her shoulders shake and heave as if she is sobbing. She raises her head.

Imagine There Are Little Bits Of Saucy Beans Splattered Around Me, Michelle guides her. Because I Just Threw The Wooden Spoon.

Eventually, Lu takes over and cooks the beans and they eat together. Michelle sobs through dinner. She is not yet on psychiatric medication and so once she starts to cry she cannot stop until she retires for the night. She is also not yet sober, so she spends almost every night getting drunk in the kitchen, alone, while Lu tries to sleep, the kitchen light shining on her head. Michelle fills the kitchen with cigarette smoke. Lu is nineteen and Michelle is twenty-eight.

After the New York reading, Michelle and Lu had a tremendous fight in front of the beverage table at a party. At the end of the fight, Michelle agreed to remove Lu from the book. It just wasn't worth it. It kept Lu close to her, she realized, when they had been separate for so long, four years. If the book was ever published she'd have to talk about Lu all the time, what a horror. And it was bad for their respective romantic lives, keeping them linked in this way. At the end of the fight they felt closer, like comrades, and Michelle realized with a sick feeling that this was the same mechanism that had kept them together as lovers all those years. She returned from her trip and deleted Lucretia from the manuscript.

Sometimes It Feels Like A Mental Illness, Michelle said to Quinn. They were seated on the kitchen floor, relaxing against the cabinets. Their knees bumped together in a friendly fashion. Being A Writer. Being This Kind Of Writer. It Feels Compulsive. I Get Sweaty. I Wish I Was A Painter. I Wish The Story Came Out In An Image Of Like A Rotting Eggplant. A Dark, Swirly Rotting Eggplant With Really Thick Ridges Of Oil Paint That Take Months To Dry. And I Could Point At It And Say—That Is Lucretia. That Was Our Relationship. I Could Paint A Cigarette-Smoking Corgi In A Visor And Name The Painting *Mother*. That Would Be Awesome. But It's Not What I Do. I Write Five-Hundred-Page Books About My Life And Then Have To Remove The Main Story Line So People Don't Think Someone Was A Jerk For Being A Jerk.

Well, I bet you were a jerk too, Quinn said. *I mean, so far in this story you've been pretty unsympathetic.*

Thanks, Michelle said. I've Really Tried. I Just Wanted To Write About What Happens To Your Heart And Your Mind When You're In An Oppressive Relationship. I Wanted To Try To Understand How People Stay In Shitty Situations, The Weird Head Fuck Of Love And Anxiety. It's Like Being Electrocuted, It Makes You Cling To The Very Thing Hurting You.

Ooh, that's a good metaphor, Quinn said. *Why don't you just write a poem about it? No one ever really understands what a poem is about. You could hide all kinds of complaints in there.*

It Just Isn't Coming Out That Way.

Quinn understood. *Well, what are you going to do?*

I Have To Get Back Into My Story, Michelle said sadly. It was hard being such a mess. She knew what had happened to her in Los Angeles and she was not looking forward to reliving it. I Can't Wait For This Book To Be Over So I Can Be Sober Again.

What's the book even about? Quinn asked. *If you've removed the main story.*

Michelle wasn't sure. Couldn't a book just be about life? Me, My Alcoholism, I Think. The Nineties. Being Poor. The Feeling Of It All.

The nineties, Quinn said in a dreamy voice, and shook her head with longing. Like everyone, Quinn was younger than Michelle and had rosy feelings about 1990s San Francisco. A place that Quinn would never get to go, and Michelle had lived there. Quinn wasn't alone—lots of younger queers held the decade in this reverent light. It was funny to Michelle. The nineties had been so ugly in so many ways. No one's clothes fit them right. Everyone wearing men's leather jackets, all boxy and awkward. Dog collars as necklaces. So much sexual acting out, like the whole community had been sexually abused and had agreed to purge the trauma by having lots of violent public sex. In fact, just last night, not in this book but in real life, someone had asked Michelle, *Remember that Thanksgiving when I went to your house and wound up getting pierced by Cooper in your bathroom?*

Michelle remembered. She'd had to go into the bathroom to retrieve her coat, which for some reason was in the bathtub. She remembered the precision of the pins and the beads of blood shimmering on the girl's solar plexus, the latex-gloved hands of her friend holding the needle. The nineties. Like a folie à deux shared by an entire community. A sort of sexual mass hysteria.

I Think I Should Make You Go, Michelle told Quinn.

Okay, Quinn said. *When do we get to hang out again?*

Not In This Book, Michelle shook her head sadly. The World Is Going To End In About A Year, Before We Ever Meet Each Other.

Oh. Quinn nodded. *It's like a metaphor for the end of love.*

Breakups Alter Your Brain Chemistry, Michelle said. Everything Is Doomed And Ruined And Horrible. You Used To Be This Beautiful Trusting Thing And You Just Get Used By Thoughtless, Shitty People And Then You're Irreparably Damaged.

Quinn sighed. *Bummer.*

Also I Couldn't Figure Out How To End The Book, Michelle explained. With Memoirs The Story Just Keeps Going. You're Supposed To Wrap It Up All Nicely But It's Real Life. It's Hard. So I Think I'm Just Going To Have The World Explode.

Quinn nodded. *Okay, so—what should I do? To leave?*

You Don't Have To Do Anything, Michelle said. I'll Do It. She hit save and closed her computer.

2 Where did your own story end and other people's begin? Michelle wrestled with this question. After her first book came out she'd been invited to give some lectures and teach some workshops, and always the people who came were females, females who wanted to tell their stories. Their stories being female stories, there was a lot of hurt inside them—abuse, betrayals, injustices, feelings. They were all worried about getting in trouble for writing the truth. They didn't want people to be mad at them. It's Your Story, Michelle would insist.

She wanted to free them all, all the girl writers. Girls needed to tell the truth about what the fuck was going on in this world. It was bad. It was brave of the girls to let themselves stay so raw, though Michelle worried that some of them had had to conjure personality disorders in order to cope. Sometimes the girls were too much even for her, Michelle wondered if she could handle another piece of writing about sexual abuse or sex work. But it seemed that this was to be her job upon the earth. If you don't tell your story, who will? It was important. Our stories are important.

Then Michelle started hanging out at the Zen Center too much. What was a story if you didn't even exist? Michelle observed the way she told the same stories about herself, thereby cementing this false idea of self harder and harder in her psyche. It was all ego. There was no Michelle, so how could there be her memoir? It seemed to Michelle, sitting on a straw floor in a wide room, her legs folded atop each other, eyes half-mast, that being a writer of memoir was one of the most violent and anti-Buddhist things a person could do with their life. She thought of her fight with Lu. It was her story fighting with Lu's story. If neither of them even existed, why bother fighting? No self, no story. Michelle felt the ache and burn of her ego hurling itself against such thoughts as she sat down at her computer in Los Angeles.

Michelle would begin the story with her nonexistent self smoking crack in a van in San Francisco. Alone, so as not to stomp on anyone's right to privacy: Her friends' right to smoke crack with a recent ex-con, the ex-con's right to procure crack cocaine for a bunch of dykes and then play with their tits. Everyone's inalienable rights would be upheld within the text of her book. She would write only about herself, and she would make it Buddhist and universal.

The more Michelle stared at the glow of the screen the more she noticed it had its own pulse, seemed strangely alive. She recalled that people who'd done certain psychedelic drugs claimed that in their heightened state they'd understood that electricity was alive. Michelle thought about it, this invisible force that strung her world together. What was electricity? Maybe it was God, the universe she prayed to. She prayed to God, the universe, electricity, and her computer to please help her write another book. She had written one already, why was it still so hard? In most occupations the tasks become easier with practice, the worker grows confident. Michelle thought of her mother Wendy, able to insert a catheter, administer a shot, execute her nursely duties with a swiftness and élan her patients were grateful for. *I had to push a woman's rectum in,* she told Michelle on a recent phone call.

What Are You Talking About? Michelle asked, terrified to learn. Each woman was in her respective kitchen, smoking her respective cigarettes. Michelle's kitchen was awash with carcinogenic sunlight, making the kitschy yellow table she'd thrifted in North Hollywood look especially cheerful. Michelle thought the table had magical properties, was a shade of yellow that corresponded to positive neural pathways in her brain. Daily she awoke in the dingy gray of her bedroom and pulled herself to the kitchen to stare down at the table like meditating. After a minute of flooding her eyes with that hue she was able to smoke, make coffee, kill the cockroaches scurrying along her countertops.

Her rectum fell out and I pushed it back in, Michelle's mother repeated. There was a stiff pride in her voice. She knew she had been brave, had accepted an experience few would be able to handle. Michelle could hear her take a dry drag off her cigarette and it inspired Michelle to do the same.

I Still Don't Understand What You're Talking About, Michelle said, fearing her mother was trying to dramatically draw the story out. Michelle hated when people did that. She feared she actually did it all the time, was possibly doing it right now, as she typed the story of her mother and the fallen rectum onto her computer. She stubbed out her Camel in the empty ashtray then flung it out the window.

She strained and it fell out, Wendy said. *She's an old lady. She's been living there since she was, I don't know, before I started. I don't even think she was crazy when they brought her in but she's crazy now. Thirty, forty years she's been there.*

I Still Don't Understand How Her Rectum Fell Out, Michelle maintained. How A Rectum Falls Out. A Rectum Is A Hole, How Does A Hole Fall Out Of Something, A Hole Is Nothing, It's Negative, It's Like—Michelle waved away her initial comparison of her vagina—It's Like You're Telling Me Someone's Nostril Fell Out And You Pushed It Back In. It's Negative Space, Please Tell Me What You Mean. Michelle shook her pack of cigarettes on the table and lit up a fresh one. Her mother heard the click of the lighter, the familiar crackle.

You smokin'? Wendy asked, alarmed. *When did you start smokin' again, I thought you quit? Are you stressed out, am I stressing you out?* Wendy's voice was thick with the accent of her region. There were no *R*s and words banged into each other awkwardly, like people not paying attention to their movements on a crowded street.

You Know, Michelle said airily, I Smoke, I Stop, I Smoke, I Stop.

You're lucky, Wendy said wistfully. *Your mother is like that too. I wish I could pick 'em up and put 'em down.* She heard the familiar click and crackle, a smoker lighting up on the other side of the country. They each exhaled into their telephones.

Anyway. The Rectum.

You don't understand biology, Wendy said. *The rectum, the muscle around the hole, you strain it from, you know, pushing too hard, it can fall out of the body.*

Michelle was glad to have a strong mind, one not prone

to hypochondria, germ-phobia, or anxiety in general. Being raised by a nurse meant you were privy to all the tragedies that could befall a body. As a girl, Michelle would pour through her mother's nursing-school textbooks. Terrible rashes sprawling across skin like a map. Parasites, slender monsters that could live inside your body. Athlete's foot taken to extremes, cleft palates, birth defects. Diseases of the eyeballs and the gums. Mouth cancer. Elephantiasis of the gonads. Hemorrhoids the size of apricots, hung from the anus as if from a tree. Her brother, Kyle, couldn't look at them—he had an anxiety disorder—but young Michelle enjoyed them, much as she enjoyed the B-grade horror movies shown on cable late at night. There was something so unreal about them, so extreme. But the older one becomes, the more it occurs to you that perhaps all these things are inevitable. Michelle felt less welcoming to the idea that one can lose one's rectum. Your body is destined to fall apart, why not in this manner? Why not your rectum falling out? Does the rectum fall out of itself? Michelle still couldn't wrap her mind around it. She imagined a long pink tube with a winking hole at the end sliding from a body, like a grisly penis or one of those water-snake balloon toys kids give hand jobs to. She shuddered.

The CNAs were freaking out about it, Wendy said. *Oh, call the doctor, call the doctor. I said, for what, that? I'll do it. I just put on some gloves and pushed it back inside. She was fine, the poor thing.*

That's Amazing, Michelle said. You Are Amazing. I Hope You Get A Raise For That.

Mom snorted. Michelle imagined dragon gusts of smoke blowing from her nostrils. Oh, don't write that, she thought. Wendy hates looking so smoky in these stories. Michelle questioned her desire to make her mom look rough. But the woman spent her days returning fallen rectums and smoking cigarettes. I'm not making this up, Michelle pouted.

A raise? Not likely, Wendy said bitterly. *Not in that shit hole. They give the manager raise after raise and they're hiring these RNs with no experience, these kids.*

Why Don't You Go Back To School, Ma?

I'm too old, I can't deal with that. Plus, I don't want to be like them.

Like Who?

The RNs. They all think they're hot shit. My supervisor likes me though. He's nice. Young. Reminds me of your brother.

He's Gay?

Flaming.

Okay, Can You Tell Me What I Have To Do To Make Sure My Rectum Never Falls Out? she asked.

Oh, it only really happens to old people.

Well, I'll Be Old Someday, What Should I Do?

Don't strain. You should never strain anyway, it gives you hemorrhoids.

Didn't Elvis Die From Straining?

He had a heart attack. He was on dope, don't be a dopehead and you'll be fine. How's Los Angeles?

It's Good.

Michelle looked around the apartment. The apartment was too small and smelled weird. The wall-to-wall carpeting was suspiciously stiff, like something had been spilled across it, mashed into the fibers, and allowed to dry into a crunchy board. It felt creepy on her bare feet. It was a charcoal-colored carpet that Michelle feared was supposed to be some other color. Like, white.

How's your friend? Michelle's mother extended the

conversation. Michelle couldn't tell if it was cute or made her crazy that her lesbian moms referred to her dates as *friends*. They referred to one another that way, too. Michelle chalked it up to their place and time. It was hard to be mad at her parents for their homophobia when they were gay, too.

My Friend? Michelle asked. Do You Mean Quinn Or Lu?

I don't know, Wendy laughed nervously. *Not for nothin' I can't keep them straight with you.*

Michelle couldn't remember which version of the story she was in. Was It A Teenager Or A Married Woman?

Oh Jesus, Wendy said. *Are you kiddin' me? Don't you want a real relationship with someone? What are you doing, a teenager? How old? You can get arrested, you know. That's statutory rape and they won't care that you're a lesbian. Lesbians can be rapists too.*

She Was Nineteen, Michelle said.

And a married woman! Marriage is a sacrament. You have to think about a person who is not true to her word like that, what kind of character she has.

Ma, Michelle said, You Know You Were Excommunicated From The Church Like A Million Times Over For Being Gay.

It's between me and my god, Wendy said staunchly. *God doesn't care who we love, only that we keep our promises. What makes you think that woman will keep a promise to you when she didn't keep her promise to her husband?*

They're Both Gone Anyway, Michelle said. I Took Them Out Of The Story. I'm Just Going To Be Alone. It's Easier.

Wendy exhaled a worried cloud of smoke. *I don't like you living alone in that city.*

Kyle's Here, Michelle said.

Why don't you live with him? Wendy suggested.

Michelle thought about it on the level of a plot twist. It would be interesting. But having Michelle move in with Kyle would require Michelle to rewrite the last two hundred pages, rather than just edit extensively, and writing was exhausting.

I Don't Think So, Michelle said. I'm Already Here. Paid My First And Last And My Security. The Building Is Fine, People Are Nice, The World Is Going To End In Like A Year Anyway. I Won't Make Anything Bad Happen To Me Before Then, Michelle promised.

The world's gonna end, Wendy chuckled. *You sound like Kym. That's all she talks about, she's paranoid.*

Really? Michelle perked up.

Yes. I told her I can't listen to it anymore, she sounds like a crazy person.

Can I Talk To Her? Michelle asked.

She's sleeping, Wendy said. *Her illness. You find a job yet?*

No.

How come you can't find one, aren't there any jobs in Los Angeles? Can't Kyle get you a job?

No, Ma, Michelle said. People Can't Just Give People Jobs.

Well, why can't you find one? You went to UMass Boston for that year, that should make a difference.

College Only Helps If You Finish, Ma. Otherwise It Doesn't Count.

It still cost you like five thousand dollars, that should count for something.

Well, It Doesn't.

The conversation had entered the danger zone. Wendy's insistence to be helpful coupled with her total inability to help plus Michelle's reluctance to ask her mother to back off times her determination to endure the conversation equaled the probability of Michelle being cast into a dark mood.

I Basically Have A High School Education, Michelle said with gritted teeth. High School Means Nothing, Nobody Cares About High School, Everyone Goes, It's Meaningless.

You know, your grandfather never went to high school, Wendy said. *He dropped out and went right into the Navy.*

I Know, Ma, Michelle said. She lit a new cigarette from the crushed tip of the old. I Can't Talk About It Anymore.

Oh, I'm stressing you out. I can hear it in your voice. I don't want to stress you out. You know about the stress hormone? When you're stressed out your body makes this hormone and it makes you fat. Watch out.

Okay I Will.

And watch it with the smoking.

Okay, Ma. I Will.

A pause. *You okay?*

Yeah, Ma, Of Course. I'm Fine.

Michelle took the bus out to the beach, just to see if the ocean was as bad as in San Francisco. It was both worse and better. The water was clotted, a vast dumpster, but an eerie fog came off it like something out of a Stephen King story. Michelle was sure a chemical reaction was occurring, like when you dump bleach into ammonia and create a murderous steam. Whatever was deadly in the waters had merged with the low-slung Los Angeles smog and a new fatal compound was born. Michelle was afraid to linger by the wreck of it too long, even though artists had built the shore into a trashed fun house. Whimsical sculptures rose from the mucked sand. Michelle fell in love with a mermaid fashioned from oil drums and rust, her hair a wreath of burned plastic. The mystery mist crawled from the waves to the shore and slipped around the statuary like ghosts.

Michelle had actually not gone to the beach alone, but with Lu. They had driven there together. They had had a car, a terrible source of stress. Something from the seventies, a Continental, bigger than half a city bus. They fought about the car a lot, but Michelle didn't want to think about fights right now. She wanted to think about how they had played in the sand. It was a sweet time, when they had first arrived. Before they had to get jobs, and so jobs weren't a problem and Lu's gender wasn't a problem and money wasn't a problem. They had made the mermaid on the beach. They had done it together, sand on their hands.

Michelle felt sad at all the sweet moments she would not be able to write about. The sweet parts were important, without them Michelle just looked insane. Lu was storm clouds and eggshells but she was also goofy sweetness and tender love. Funny dances with a dog-faced underbite and low, dangling arms. Fingers that were kissing bird beaks. Their own language: *Bummerino, Vinnie Barbarino!* was one stage of disappointment, *Bummerino, Grand Torino!* another. Life with another person was built on such things.

Back in the story, Michelle walked to the bus stop and began the arduous return trip to Hollywood. The ride took Sunset all the way, past the street that turned off into the gay center. She looked over at it with mixed emotions, wondering if she should check it out. She missed her friends back in San Francisco, who had completely forgotten about her. She'd seen people leave town, she knew how it went. No one ever spoke about them again. Life moved too fast.

There was too much in front of your face to concern yourself with what wasn't there anymore.

Michelle wondered how she would find new friends, she wasn't the kind of gay who hung out at a gay center. Michelle supposed she was a postgay. It was an offensive term, how could anyone be postgay when queers were still getting beaten and strung to fences and shot at and raped? But it would be a lie for Michelle to pretend her environment had been hostile. She'd lived in West Coast cities, she was gender normative. She was kind of postgay. And as a postgay in Los Angeles, she figured she would not really have any friends. Fabian was busy like LA people were busy, each day a succession of meetings. Michelle didn't quite understand what Fabian did, it had something to do with the Spanish film industry, like in Spain, but also with Brad Pitt. Kyle was in the clutches of his psychotic boss, working twelve-hour days and then managing the woman's social calendar, keeping up with her Match.com profile, and fast-tracking her adoption of a third world baby. Michelle got a membership at a Hollywood Video within walking distance from her apartment and rented so many movies the simpleton behind the counter whistled through her teeth at her. *You watch a lot of movies,* she said, shaking her head.

So? Michelle snapped defensively, then wondered if she should ask if they were hiring. The dull cashier seemed vaguely dykey. But Michelle was too proud.

Back at the computer, Michelle strove to universalize herself. But the more she thought about it, the less universal she became. She had tried to write herself straight, but she was so low-rent. She tried to write herself male, but then

there was her pussy and her PMS, the blood that dribbled out from her on its own erratic schedule, ruining her
underwear again and again, never mind that she had been
menstruating off and on for fifteen years, it didn't matter,
she could not keep up with her tampons. Until the cotton
overflowed it did not occur to her to change it. The stain of
her femaleness bled through her attempts to write herself
male. She struggled.

Page after page she built a straight, male, middle-class
Michelle who did not drink and did not do drugs. Oh, wait—
could she do that now? As a straight, male, middle-class man
could she now shoot literary heroin and go on a literary crack
bender? It depended, she suspected, on where straight, male,
middle-class Michelle worked and how many dependents
depended on him. Michelle realized that this was what they
called raising the stakes. Sometimes the fact that she had
not gone to college really did seem to have a negative effect
on her life. If Michelle had gone to college she was certain
she'd have been taught how to write from the perspective of
a straight, white, middle-class man. She would have to teach
herself how to be universal. She could do it, it would just take
time. Meanwhile, she found a job around the corner, at the
used book and record store.

Michelle lived in a neighborhood, a rarity in Hollywood.
It had a name: the Franklin Strip. It was a strip of Franklin Avenue, just one block long, but that was enough. The
block was packed with merchants. A coffee shop called—
no, really—the Bourgeois Pig. Michelle was aghast. She
knew that Los Angeles embraced wealth in a manner she
was unaccustomed to but this was unreal. The Bourgeois
Pig? Their coffees were four dollars and Michelle once
spied Christina Ricci sitting at an outdoor table. Next to

the Bourgeois Pig was a magazine store that sold a severely edited selection of about five different magazines. It was a very minimalist shop, and the girl working the counter looked bored and superior as she flipped through a copy of *Index*. Michelle envied her employment, she was right to vibe superior. Michelle could think of nothing better than being paid to flip through magazines all day. She thought about asking if the magazine store was hiring but knew instinctively that it was the kind of place where you were invited to work, like a beautiful young girl discovered by a modeling agency at a soda fountain.

There was a small theater run by second-rate soap-opera actors trying to do something serious while clambering out from the daytime TV ghetto. There was a bar and grill where the soap-opera actors would get tanked and pick each other up. Michelle once saw the actor who played Lex Luthor on *Smallville*, looking handsome and gay with his shiny bald head. Michelle thought all men looked gay, it was an effect of having lived in San Francisco so long, where all the men actually were.

Fancy boutiques sold feathered mules and bejeweled purses, guides to foreign lands and candles that smelled like leather. These were lifestyle boutiques, their inventory was random but had a certain logic. If you didn't understand, it wasn't your lifestyle. There was a French restaurant with DJs and fistfights on the weekends, well-dressed men tumbling through the glass doors in a violent clutch.

Then there was the used book and record store, an eyesore on the block. Michelle peered in the window. The interior was nothing but dust and wood and books, books everywhere, more than the shelves could hold, books in tumbled piles, books invading the space reserved for records, heaped atop stacks of rare opera albums, books blocking the aisles and sliding off wooden carts. The shelves were hand-built with unfinished wood, the apparent creation of hippie gnomes. Inside Michelle could hear hip-hop playing, recognized the obscene lyrics of a Lil' Kim song. A tall, skinny, gay boy, his head wrapped in a red bandana, leaned idly at the register, mouthing the lyrics into the air.

Michelle had a deep feeling of magnetic purpose while peering into the bookstore as if into an aquarium, or perhaps a crystal ball. She turned away from the shop and faced the Scientology Celebrity Centre across the street. It was a Disneyesque compound, all peaks and turrets, lit with soft, glowing lights. The sun had set, the HOLLYWOOD sign was dark, someone had turned out the lights so the city's desperate weren't called to hurl themselves from the letters in the suicidal night. In the daytime the Scientologists blared classical music from their landscaped gardens, loud enough to envelop the Franklin Strip and make it feel like a sort of Main Street USA to the Scientologists' Cinderella Castle.

Michelle turned back to the bookstore. She had a résumé stuffed in her army bag and a psychic understanding that if she walked into the bookstore and handed that boy the piece of paper she would be hired immediately. She regarded this uncanny knowledge with dread. Maybe she didn't want a job. The dread was ridiculous, a toddler's tantrum—Michelle could not *not* have a job. She'd been working since she was fourteen, had had to get a special card from City Hall to be signed by her mothers and brought to the grocery store that had hired her. With the exception of one terrifying month when she could not get herself employed and lived off the generosity of Andy, Michelle always worked. But if she got a job in LA it would mean she really lived there.

She regarded the grimy used bookstore. She belonged there. If it were an animal it would be her power animal, if it were a spirit it would be her guide. If Michelle were a bookstore she would be that bookstore. If she waited and brought in the résumé tomorrow, or even later that day, the universe wasn't making any promises. But if she walked through the doors right then, employment was guaranteed.

Michelle's psychic impulses were rare and useless. Once she had a precognitive wave that Linda would start brushing her teeth at work, and the very next day the girl shuffled in, hungover with a toothbrush and a fresh tube of toothpaste. I Knew You Were Going To Do That, Michelle said. Otherwise it alerted her to potential romantic threats. Finally her sixth sense was offering her some practical direction. She pushed open the doors and inhaled the cool scent of gently rotting paper.

I don't want dick tonight, Lil' Kim chanted over the sound system. *Treat my pussy right.* The boy behind the register shook his ass, bony inside his cargo shorts. Michelle passed him her résumé and felt herself become hired, energetically. Two days later she had a job.

3 *How's LA?* Ziggy asked. Her cell phone crackled, Michelle could hear air whooshing over the receiver.

What Are You Doing? Michelle asked. Are You Riding A Bike? The thought was hilarious. Michelle imagined Ziggy pedaling a ten speed, her hip accoutrements chiming and swinging, a cigarette clamped in her mouth, one hand steering the bike while the other pressed her cell to her head.

I'm driving a car. I got a grant and bought a bitch bucket.

You Got A Grant? Michelle gasped. Who got grants? People who wrote about long-ago trees, about ye olde beavers gnawing down long-ago trees in an extinct autumnal landscape, patting homes together with their flat, muddy tails. People who conjured the lost beauty of the natural world and made the reader feel bad about the state of things in a nostalgic, gentle way—that's who got grants. Not Ziggy. Ziggy screamed her poetry. She had such ADD she couldn't sit still long enough to type them into computers, she committed them to memory or else read them from the little wrinkled notebooks stuffed in the ass of her pants. Ziggy's poetry was about the horror of men, about racists and fascists. The poems were graphic and mean and made everyone in the audience feel awful, complicit somehow, recalling every time they didn't do the right thing, didn't yell at the man punching the woman in the street, didn't flip off the cops as they harangued a row of Latino teenagers on Mission Street. There were many such instances in a life, and listening to Ziggy, a warrior in her belts of metal, people resolved to have more courage, to fight harder for more freedoms. Ziggy's work was thick with *fucks* and *cunts* and the defamation of the Christian God, and San Francisco had given her a grant.

What's A Bitch Bucket? Michelle asked, jealous.

A Cabriolet. It's a car. A little convertible. A Volkswagen.

You're Talking To Me Now In A Convertible? On Your Cell Phone?

Yep. Ziggy's breathing revealed that she was also smoking.

You Should Move Here, You'd Fit In Perfect.

How are you fitting in? Are you partying with celebrities or what?

I Saw Gwen Stefani At A Breakfast Place, Michelle reported. I Used The Bathroom After Her And My Wallet Fell Out Of My Back Pocket And Into The Toilet.

It's like she christened it, Ziggy said.

For Real. She Hadn't Flushed.

If it's yellow, let it mellow, Ziggy said. *There's no more water. I donated the van to a water preservation organization. It would be a tax write-off if I did my taxes.*

I Saw Marilyn Manson Walking Into A Bookstore With His Girlfriend, Michelle remembered. She Looks Like A Suicide Girl. They Were Holding Hands.

Was he hot? Ziggy probed. *Did you say hi to him or get his autograph or give him your book or something?*

He Was Tall, Michelle said, But I Think He Was Wearing Platform Boots. His Hair Is Really Long. I Only Saw Him From Behind. He Looked Like A Swamp Monster, Just Sort Of Lumbering And Leathery And Dark.

Hot, Ziggy declared. *He was hot?*

I Suppose.

What's your problem? Ziggy asked. *Remember when we saw him at the Cow Palace? When he came out from the stage crucified on a cross of television sets that burst into flames? And then he came out later like a four-legged beast on those stilts and then he stood up and put his arms in the air and he was like twenty feet tall and the strobe lights were going through him? Remember how good that ecstasy was, you almost didn't take it and then it was so amazing, remember?*

I Can't Believe You Got A Grant, Michelle said. I Want To Come Back To San Francisco And Get A Grant. I'm Going To Kick That Olympia Girl Out Of My Room And Come Back.

You can't, Ziggy said. *You can't come back. Didn't you hear?*

Hear What?

About your house? About Clovis? He got hit by a soda truck the morning you moved. Like minutes after you left, I swear. If you had left any later you would have fucking seen it happen. It happened right outside your house. Your old house.

Oh, Michelle said, Oh No. Sweet Clovis, a humble, bent landlord. He had nursed his cancer-stricken wife until death there inside that second-floor apartment, and so he could never leave it. Her spirit could be lingering, Clovis could not risk abandoning it. He sang to it on the karaoke machine. He had pledged not to raise their rent to profit from the housing-mad dot-com millionaires. He had promised not to sell and he hadn't. He died as broke as anyone, owning a piece of property suddenly worth millions. Michelle cried for how hard his life had been. There was no redemption for Clovis. If there was no redemption for Clovis, why should there be any redemption for anyone? Why, Michelle fumed, did the people demand redemption from their literature? She vowed to make the straight, male version of herself get whacked by a soda truck in the first chapter, after smoking crack with a vanful of lesbians to try to get over his dead wife.

What Will Happen To The House? Michelle asked. That old house was a monument, the city should have bolted a plaque to its doors. Every queer female artist to have a drug problem in San Francisco within the last twenty years had lived in it.

It already happened, Ziggy said. New owners, the place looks totally different, they painted it and put these ugly doors on it and a gate on the stoop so no one can sit there. Everyone got money, they all got paid to get evicted. A couple thousand each, I think.

Bile burned in Michelle's belly, giving her an instantaneous ulcer. Seven years she'd suffered there—suffered the roaches, the gangrenous shower, the criminal neighborhood, the fuses that blew every time she plugged in a hair dryer. And when the big payout came she was gone. In Los Angeles. Broke as ever, alone. Michelle thought of Ekundayo getting thousands of dollars, moody Ekundayo who had made her feel like a trespasser in her own home, a bother, an interloper, though she'd lived there a hundred times longer than anyone. Ekundayo who'd spearheaded the effort to paint the living room psych-ward green. Cursed Ekundayo! And that Oly girl! There but a month or two and paid cash money to evacuate! Only Stitch deserved it, Michelle thought. Stitch who'd lived there nearly as long as she had, caretaking the cockroaches. Why hadn't Stitch called her and told her this had happened? Michelle and Stitch loved Clovis, they'd talked endlessly about having him up for dinner but never got around to cleaning the kitchen.

How's Stitch? Michelle asked. What's Stitch Doing?

Stitch went to Prague, Ziggy reported. *She's gone.*

Prague? Prague? Why Prague? What The Fuck's In Prague?

Beer. Her ancestors. She's Praguian. She's got cousins there.

No Way.

She had a big party about a month ago.

She's Been Gone That Long?

Uh-huh.

The crackle in Ziggy's cell flared and became deafening. Michelle hollered into the receiver, trying to locate her friend, but the call had been dropped. She flung her landline into its base and dropped herself onto the futon. Michelle cried. It was like she had climbed out of a hole and the hole had closed itself behind her. She felt profoundly cut off from herself. That room in that house was the last affordable room in San Francisco. Her studio apartment, a cozy place, grew creepily cozier as the walls closed in on her. She'd left her heart in San Francisco, in that shabby Victorian with the haunted bathroom and the cigarettes ground into the floor, her glittered, moldy bedroom and the beer bottles rolled against the walls. She had only wanted a change of scenery, a strange vacation to clear her head. But without that house to return to, Michelle was trapped in Los Angeles.

She had seen the exiled try to come back. They wore out their welcome sleeping on couches until, truly homeless, they were forced into unfathomable situations, returning home to live with their parents. Michelle checked the digital alarm clock plugged into the wall by the bed. She could cry for twenty minutes and then she was due at the bookstore. She stuffed her face into a pillow and wept, then climbed from her futon and into her new life.

4 Michelle's bookstore was owned by a husband-and-wife team. Beatrice was thin and wan and visibly repressed. She spoke in a hushed tone and seemed perpetually on the verge of tears. Sometimes Michelle wondered if Beatrice was in fact crying, the way her voice creaked and croaked and her eyes grew red and teary. Perhaps Beatrice had been so depressed for so long she had mastered the art of continuously weeping in public, a subtle sobbing that friends and customers chalked up to allergies or simply the state of her face. She was prone to migraines, and when her headaches came on she left Michelle alone in the vast bookstore. That was the best. Michelle would drift dreamily from pile to pile, lifting the grimy, sneezy books, reading a bit from this and a bit from that, Basquiat and Bukowski, lesbian anthologies from the 1970s, Margaret Mead and Carl Jung and *Hollywood Babylon*.

Beatrice's husband was sick with an esophageal disorder that sent acidic bile and undigested food rolling up his throat whenever he bent over. He would come to work in spite of his distress to remind everyone of his kingly role. He would trail Michelle through the store, pointing to various things on the floor, having her bend and lift them. He was a bulky man and liked to linger in the kiosk behind the register. Michelle would be there too, and Beatrice, and mounds of books—books that had arrived that day in the arms of hopeful strangers, quality books, rare or antiquated, out-of-print or cult classics that the couple sold on eBay. No one in the kiosk could move. Michelle practically gave the husband a lap dance each time she came behind the register. It was hectic at the bookstore. Though it should have had the sleepy, cozy feel of a library, when the owners were around it felt like an ER, like a single detail might be being overlooked that would cause this empire of used paperbacks to crumble.

In thirty years of owning the store, the husband had never learned how to operate the cash register. Michelle felt this was all she needed to know in order to understand Beatrice and the source of her headaches. The husband possessed a vast knowledge of classical music recordings and that was his role in the operation, judging the quality of the classical records people came to sell and cultivating a community of classical music nuts to purchase them. Otherwise, he condescended and lorded over them and complained about his esophagus. His irritation was oddly exuberant, like he was an actor playing the part of the cranky bookstore jerk, long white hair cascading from his head and face. Sometimes he and Beatrice would fight and Michelle would be trapped there, hemmed in by the books, caught inside their dysfunctional relationship.

If Michelle hated working with the owners, she adored working with Joey, the gay manager who wore a do-rag and had the lyrics to Lil' Kim's entire oeuvre memorized. Together they bided their time until the owners left, then swapped out the acceptable bookstore jams— Norah Jones, Aimee Mann—for Lil' Kim, Tupac, and Marilyn Manson. Working with Joey was fun, the most social activity Michelle was getting in Los Angeles, but she still preferred working alone, the time careening by as she lounged on a ladder with her nose in a book: Violette Leduc, Phoebe Gloeckner, Monique Wittig. The bookstore was a treasure chest, stuffed with books by publishers and writers who long ago had failed. This was the last place left to find them, a cemetery of sorts. It was her favorite place in all Los Angeles.

5 Michelle had placed her futon along the back wall of the studio's main room, flush against windows that overlooked the alley below. Cops routinely ousted homeless youth from the alley, barking at them in the night, waving their flashlights like kids at a rave. The windows looked directly into the apartment next door, occupied by a man with long gray dreadlocks who shopped at the bookstore. Joey claimed to see him picking up the rent boys who worked the ho stroll by the gay center. Joey knew all about the gay center and shared with Michelle its secrets—by day all the rich Hollywood A-gays had meetings and fundraisers inside the compound, but when the sun began to set the neighborhood seethed with rent boys and tweaker transgender women selling their ass. It was the first time Michelle felt interested in going there.

The man across the alley was roommates with a dog with a meaty head, a rottweiler. Drool came rainily from its lips. The dog would come to the window, slap his paws on the sill, and crane his head, barking at Michelle as if seeking revenge. It was scary. Scarier still was when he propped himself in the window and simply watched her. He was like a monster or a man—a serial killer, a Peeping Tom. A large, intelligent animal considering you. Michelle would close the blinds, robbing the apartment of sunlight.

Michelle knew the placement of the futon was energetically wrong. She suffered nightmares of Kym and Wendy dying, of being stabbed in her sleep by killers who crept in through the rotting bathroom window. The position of the bed was wrong but there was nowhere else to put it. She had copied the layout of the woman who lived across the hall, after glimpsing her studio as she unlocked her door. In her apartment the sun felt soft, gentle, not murderous. The place was clean. It did not seem to have the pall of gloom that hung over Michelle's studio. Her neighbor's bed was backed up against wide, bright windows, inviting sunlight to pour over homey patchwork quilts, over ruffled throw pillows, over her cat—a cat that sprawled in the delicious glow, its tail twitching lazily. Wow, Michelle said, shamelessly peering through the door.

The woman smiled sheepishly and shrugged. *Yeah,* she said. Her cat was named Freedom and every so often the thing would escape and the woman would chase it down the halls yelling, *Freedom, no! No, Freedom! No, Freedom!*

Everyone in the building seemed to be thriving in Los Angeles. A guy downstairs was a computer programmer who drove a VW Bug he'd painted to look like that Mondrian painting: blue and red and yellow. Upstairs was an aspiring actor with shiny hair who had helped Michelle and Quinn carry a couple of boxes upstairs the night they arrived, then generously offered them a line of cocaine. A golf punker named Tommy lived down the hall. His hair was a torture chamber of perfectly straight spikes around his head, like a porcupine. He had created the ultimate styling gel for golf punkers, the Krazy Glue of hair products. Michelle hadn't been aware of golf punkers before moving to Los Angeles, but apparently it was a thing—there was even a store called Golf Punk. Golf punkers were rich kids who didn't think it paradoxical to enjoy their riches and familiar traditions of, say, golf, while also jamming out to punk music and adopting the aesthetic.

Michelle's next-door neighbor hung seasonal decorations on her front door, above a chirpy perennial sign reading Think Pink! As time wore on, Michelle watched the ornaments on the front door shift from summertime ladybug to goofy-toothed jack-o'-lantern to glittering plastic snowflake. Passing her door gave Michelle the sinking feeling of living in a college dormitory. Why did this woman feel the need to hang a sign instructing everyone to Think Pink? What did it even mean to Think Pink? Michelle came upon her once as she unlocked her accessorized door. Her Chiclet teeth stretched into a newscaster smile and her hair was a maroon color, a fake reddish purple that swung above her shoulders in a perky bob.

Boy, am I glad you moved in! She greeted Michelle as if she knew her. *The last guy who lived in your place—ugh!* She flicked her hand around to ward off the evil past of Michelle's apartment.

What Do You Mean? Michelle inquired.

Oh, he was an alcoholic, she said, *but a bad one. Real bad. And PCP too. They brought him out of here one night on a stretcher and there was blood everywhere. I don't know what he did. I don't know how they got it out of your carpet!* She chortled. Her door swung open, revealing a pale-pink temple of single girlishness. *We'll have a drink sometime,* she promised. *I'll tell you all about it.* The door clicked shut behind her. Think Pink!

Michelle moped into her gruesome apartment. Had someone actually died here? Was that the vibe of wrongness she felt, the bad feng shui? Was the ghost of this man hunkered in the corner, drifting above the suspicious spots and stains, blotches that Michelle now knew to be blood, was he watching Michelle like the rottweiler across the alley, did he recognize her as a kindred spirit, another addict who had come to die, alone, in this miserable little piece of Hollywood?

6 What is this guy's problem? Michelle wondered, staring at a character outline of man-Michelle on her computer screen. He's got a great job and this house and stuff, and his wife is nice and his kids aren't deformed. Why is he so angsty? Is it just the human condition to be angsty? If so, why couldn't Michelle just be her queer feminist fuckup angsty self and be universal that way?

Don't be reactionary, Michelle scolded herself. The human experience is male. Okay. Does he have a problem with his father, aren't men always competing with their father or something? Michelle didn't have a father so she didn't know how to pursue that narrative. She cursed her lousy imagination. The real problem here was she just wasn't a very good writer. Okay. If this guy is going to do a bunch of drugs, what is it that he's trying to escape? The prison of masculinity? How sexism hurts men, too? Maybe he just wants to cry. Maybe he becomes a massive drug addict because the patriarchy won't let him cry, they'll call him a fag and throw shit in his hair. He'd get fired from his job if he cried and would be forced into a life of crime and he'd get busted because nothing in his protected, middle-class existence prepared him for that. He'd end up in prison getting gang-raped till he shanked himself in the throat with a shiv made from a burned toothbrush.

Michelle could intuit the clear narrative trajectory of a man crying to his suicide in prison. This seemed promising. Maybe Michelle could actually keep the ideas that obsessed her—injustice, struggle, gender, feminism—but put them onto a man, thereby making them universal! Women have been trying to make feminism universal forever but had anyone ever thought of this? She would be such a hero! Michelle felt all fired up but it was probably just coffee. She felt herself sag as the caffeine peaked in her bloodstream and began its retreat.

All anyone would have to do is look at her, Michelle, the author, and her ulterior motives would become clear. The book would be deemed suspect, have an intention other than literary, be branded propaganda. For such a novel to succeed a man would have to write it.

Every female Michelle knew was writing memoirs, excavating dark childhoods and heartache. Michelle didn't know any men writing memoirs, but she also didn't know any men. Maybe she could write a memoir under a pen name, a man's name, infuse it with all the molestation and tragedy found in a common female memoir, and bam! a best seller, maybe. She could write a novel about a girl pretending to be a guy in order to write a successful book. Or a girl pretending to be a guy pretending to be a girl to stir up a sensational literary scandal. This was the terrible thing about fiction, Michelle could write about whatever she wanted.

She could write about dinosaurs mating with unicorns in the lost city Atlantis and some fool would read it. In the face of so many options she spun, paralyzed, overthunk. She just wanted to write a humble novella about a girl in love with a petulant genderqueer teenager, both trying to get their lives together in Los Angeles, but even if she were to convince Lu to let her do it, even if she fashioned a different Lu who never got low blood sugar or did drugs, who hadn't been raised in a household where everyone yelled at the mother, thereby learning that yelling at women was a great thing to do—even if Michelle worked all of this out, such a book would never cross over. She deleted the man-story she'd written.

Michelle closed her laptop. Maybe something was germinating inside her and she was fucking it up with all this obsessing over the perfect universal male narrator. She had an inkling of inspiration—maybe she could take her life and sort of superimpose it onto Wendy. Maybe an aging, crack-smoking, Bostonian psych nurse in a lousy relationship would be compelling to readers, maybe they would sympathize with her and not judge her drug use. That was the thing—people tended to judge drug abuse unless you were an imposing or hardy man and then they sort of reluctantly envied your daring. Still, the tragedy of Wendy was so compelling to Michelle, perhaps she could find a way to articulate it to a large audience and cross over and really be a writer then, be safe, have a future. Michelle thought about it. She sat in her kitchen late at night listening to the Smiths.

And when you want to live,
how do you start?

Where do you go?
Who do you need to know?
Oh . . .

Well, Wendy would have to be straight, for starters.

7 Michelle was drinking from a great big jug of wine. When the jug ran dry she would lie upon her futon and sleep. Except for the nights when she craved, really craved, another jug of wine. If she had emptied that first jug by a reasonable hour the Pink Dot would still be open and she could order herself another. Oh, the Pink Dot was so marvelous! Michelle didn't understand why all cities didn't have them, it had convinced her of Los Angeles's superiority—sorry, San Francisco. Yes, the earth is deader here than anywhere else on the planet, but facts are facts: in Los Angeles you could make a phone call, read the numbers from your ATM card, and forty minutes later a man would be at your door with liquor, cigarettes, and a dish of pasta in a takeout container. Los Angeles wins.

Michelle liked to order champagne. Though she might actually want another jug of Carlo Rossi Paisano, a sturdy bottle, wide and round, low-slung, like a lady pregnant with a belly full of wine, she ordered instead champagne. Champagne was less alcoholic. It was more celebratory, performative. Michelle was taking on the persona of a slightly lunatic female drinking champagne at her kitchen table at three o'clock in the morning. There was a strength inside the tragedy of it, if you regarded it from the right angle and depending on what you wore. Drinking and smoking in a pair of sweats and a stained T-shirt was an obvious cry for help, but if Michelle teetered around her kitchen in a fluffy nightgown made in the 1950s, something pink and polyester with bits of lace and flowers, and over that wore a cover-up of sheer pink chiffon that floated out behind her when she clicked around in her golden mules, yes, mules, stuck with wavering bits of marabou—if you were wearing this and drinking champagne right from the bottle, well, something fabulous was happening! No matter that no one was there to see it. In such a getup, late-night binge drinking was acceptable.

Also, in addition to what you wore (finery) and what you drank (champagne, preferably pink, to match your finery), what you did while drinking alone late at night made the difference between alcoholic and artistic. Like if you sat at the window and cried because you had moved miles away from home and friendship and had nothing, if you were left only with the dregs of your personality, replaying everything that you had done wrong in your relationships, psychoanalyzing yourself, alternately blaming your parents and then feeling terrible and weak for blaming your parents—that would be really alcoholic.

But if you sat at your kitschy 1950s kitchen table and made a gigantic scrapbook out of your life's ephemera, turning your regret and sadness into a craft project, that was artistic. That was what Michelle did, in a thrifted nightgown, finishing off a bottle of wine she'd found on sale at the Rite Aid earlier that day. The Rite Aid was at Hollywood and Gower, in a part of Hollywood called Gower Gulch. In days of yore, aspiring actors would hang out on the corner in cowboy gear, hoping to be picked up to work as an extra in a spaghetti western. The front of the drugstore was painted with murals of cowboys swinging lassos and pointing shotguns. Inside, Michelle bought ice cream. She loved Rite Aid's rocky road in a dense, square scoop on a cone. She also liked the discount red wine. She went to Rite Aid often.

Every photograph Michelle ever snapped went into her scrapbook. Photos of her singing karaoke with Andy one Christmas Eve, hours before becoming alcohol poisoned. Photos of Ziggy on New Year's Eve, topless at the queer bar, a metallic paper hat on her head, piercing needles and glitter stuck to her skin. A photo of Michelle outside her old house in a fake leopard fur coat—snow leopard—her clunky motorcycle boots, a cloth flower in her hair, looking at the camera with love in her eyes. Andy had been behind the lens. She pasted them into the scrapbook. Flyers for every event Michelle had gone to in the past ten years—benefits for sick dogs and bunnies, for Model Mugging, to save a failing queer business, to put a band on tour. Letters from people Michelle would never see again because she moved to Los Angeles. She would sit and drink and smoke out the kitchen window, her fingers growing gummy with glue stick, and when the glue stick went dry she moved to Scotch tape and when the roll spun out she switched to duct tape and then she was really drunk, about a half hour away from putting in a call to the Pink Dot—Think Pink!—for a bottle of celebratory champagne and another pack of blackout cigarettes. The scrapbook was a massacre of torn pages and fibrous slabs of industrial tape.

I'm making a scrapbook! Michelle thought. Michelle's mother Kym made scrapbooks. Michelle felt oddly close to her mother in those late hours, imagining Kym crafting through the heat of the New England night, also unable to sleep, smoking joints and pasting pictures of the past into tidy albums.

Michelle had moved to Los Angeles with three little suitcases packed with her personal memorabilia. She lifted piles of paper from the luggage onto the table and worked through the heap methodically. Smoke gusted from her mouth and fruit flies dive-bombed her glass of wine and died there, Michelle fished them out with a spoon. After a certain point she was too drunk and too obsessed with the scrapbook to remember to push the plastic cork back into the cheap jug of wine and the flies would invade the bottle, swiftly drinking themselves to death, becoming a raft of bodies floating on the surface. Michelle poured herself a fresh glass, straining the wine through a paper towel, making a bit of a mess, but the table was already so grimy with glue. Bits of snipped paper blew around like confetti. Michelle looked up and caught her reflection in the darkened kitchen window.

Is This Gross? she asked herself, wrinkling her nose at the paper towel full of dead flies.

In San Francisco Michelle had drunk nightly and long into the morning, but she did so among a community of drinkers and so nothing looked amiss. It was social, it was lively, it was what everyone did. In Los Angeles, cleaved from her drinking buddies, Michelle continued solo in her habits and found them to look a little different. Maybe a little pathetic

It's Not Any Different, she said grandly, raising a dollar-store juice glass painted with a happy elephant. Wine and a stray dead fruit fly sloshed inside. It Is No Different Than Before.

Michelle pasted another smiling picture of herself into a notebook. She wondered, drunkenly, if she were perhaps dying, if she had lugged herself to the edge of the state to die like a dog alone on a cliff. Maybe she should dry out, go on a health kick. She had cut her drug intake drastically, no more heroin, no more cocaine. It had seemed fine for Michelle to keep drinking, but the scrapbook carnage before her on the table, the paper towel lurid with wine and the bodies of a hundred fruit flies, it looked worrisome, like a metaphor for a situation too awful to consider. Michelle vowed to put it away. She would learn to grill fish. Too late, no more fish left. She would learn what the healthy thing to grill was now and she would get it and she would grill it. She would wear moisturizer on her face and clean the house, put traps out for the roaches so she would not be forced to kill them with her fists each morning—that wasn't sexy, Michelle was letting herself go. This was how women got ruined. In the darkened bedroom the telephone rang. It was the Pink Dot. Michelle buzzed the delivery person into the building. She returned to the kitchen, the foiled neck of a champagne bottle golden in her hand.

8 Michelle's morning hangover and subsequent posthangover plan that afternoon was no different than any other hungover day in Los Angeles. She woke up on the futon, her head stuck to the pillow with sleep, her body dampened with a mild sweat, cooked with heat, the sunlight like lasers shooting through the venetian slats, burning her skin in stripes. She was underslept. Her body had metabolized the wine to sugar and she'd woken high from it, bouncy, her heart racing, dehydrated. Michelle woke up craving pineapple juice, rounded triangles of watermelon, long salted slices of cucumbers. She thought of San Francisco, of its dampness and mold, right then she did not miss it. She enjoyed the "tan" she was getting just snoozing, naked, in her bed at home. Sleepily she drifted away from herself, gazed down at her somewhat tragic life and found it looked good, like a Tennessee Williams play. Hangovers made Michelle tender, made her nostalgic—not for her past but for the life she was living right now, the moment passing through her fingers. She was not deep enough inside it, she had to live harder somehow, write it out, or maybe she just really needed to get laid. She should make Joey take her to a gay bar, or maybe start flirting with some customers at the bookstore. In that sleepy, sentimental moment Michelle pledged to lay off the alcohol for a while. At work she would seek out poetry books to augment her contemplative mood. She would read philosophy and self-help. She would cut down on her drinking, maybe take a break for a month. She would feel on the verge of changing her life.

By the end of her shift Michelle would feel normal—stronger, caffeinated, fortified. She'd think about how gloomy she'd been all day, how dramatic. She would laugh at herself, quietly, inside her head—how silly, how histrionic! She would stop at the Mayfair Market on the way home and purchase a bottle of wine. Why was she so extreme all the time? Get too drunk and it's all, Oh, I have to stop drinking! Why so hysterical? She would have a glass of wine with dinner—civilized, European. She would fill tortillas with honey and cheese and let the blue flames of the stovetop singe them. Maybe Michelle would work on her scrapbook afterward, just for like an hour, then go to sleep. No calling the Pink Dot. No need to, she would just be having a glass of wine with dinner.

Michelle lay in bed teetering between her plan for the day (the same aspirational plan as every day) and her understanding of what would actually happen (the same drunken ending as the many nights before). Her hangover beat like a heart inside her head. If Beatrice and the husband came in today her hangover would be painful. If it was just her and Joey she could make her hangover funny, a sophisticated gag. She would tell Joey all about calling the Pink Dot, the flies dive-bombing the wine, and it would be funny, really funny, funny in a way it couldn't be alone. Joey understood tragicomic lifestyles like only faggots do. Michelle would give him all the details of her nightgown and Joey would die, Joey would love it.

Joey didn't drink anymore, not after almost dying of a heroin overdose while working retail back in New York City. He'd worked at a couture boutique and everyone who worked there was really hot and had a problem with heroin. They would go downstairs to the basement, shoot up, clamber back upstairs to collapse on a couch and stare at the customers. He got fired for dropping his bagel in front of the designer. He'd been nodding out early in his shift, standing in the middle of the boutique, swaying, an egg bagel in his palm. It landed all over the floor. *You're dropping your bagel,* hissed the manager, and sent him home forever. Dropping the bagel was Joey-speak for not maintaining, for losing control, dysfunctioning. Michelle felt proud that she had never dropped the bagel at work, never, not ever.

There was another new employee at the bookstore, an unemployable rocker chick whose parents were friends of Beatrice. Beatrice was doing the parents a favor, paying the rocker chick minimum wage to alphabetize a crate of CDs in the back room. The girl was very twitchy and wore a stormtrooper doll on a cord around her neck. She'd been there for three days and had already passed out and been sent home twice.

She keeps dropping the bagel, Joey clucked.

Amateur, Michelle said.

One morning the telephone rang and rang. It rang and rang and rang and rang. Who the fuck is calling? Michelle wondered uselessly, unable to answer the phone. She wasn't ready to be in the world yet. The digital beep trilled, the phone's red light flickered. Maybe Joey had a celebrity sighting at the bookstore. Michelle had had her best celebrity sighting about one week ago, a life-changing experience. So far the celebs at the bookstore had been impressive but minor. Alan Quartermaine from *General Hospital* came in with his boyfriend, oh yes, Michelle was sure, that was his boyfriend, Alan Quartermaine was gay! Michelle couldn't believe she hadn't realized that, all those years watching *General Hospital* in the 1980s! She had much more respect for the actor. He played straight so convincingly.

Many shoppers had faces that nagged at Michelle. That was life in LA. She had seen them in commercials, speaking a single line on a sitcom, the silent villain in every movie ever, but she could not place them. She stared, but they probably liked that. All actors were narcissists. Kyle told her this. Kyle said that many nonnarcissistic actors were completely talented, but it took a narcissist's particular and terrible skill set to make it in the industry. Michelle stared at a customer with unruly black curly hair. She was on the verge of giving up when it came to her: Booger from *Revenge of the Nerds*! She phoned Joey at home to tell him.

That actor was on Moonlighting *too!* he added.

Oh, Right!

Then Matt Dillon came in. Apparently Matt Dillon came in all the time. He collected old rockabilly records. Beatrice kept a stack for him in the back room. Michelle had become obsessed with Matt Dillon at a young age, after watching him die in a hail of bullets in *Over the Edge*, a great seventies movie about disaffected youth shooting guns, having sex in unfinished suburban tract homes, and lighting their school on fire. The obsession was stoked when he fucked Kristy

McNichol in *Little Darlings*, and went totally haywire when he embodied all Michelle's favorite characters in all her favorite S. E. Hinton books: *The Outsiders, Tex, Rumble Fish*. Michelle was crazed with him in *Drugstore Cowboy*. Any movie where Matt Dillon got shot was an amazing movie. He was the number-one influence on her sexuality, a bigger influence than queerness itself, as everyone Michelle had ever been hot for resembled, in some vague way detectable only to her, Matt Dillon. And now he was in her store. And he wanted to talk to her. He had brought to the counter an ancient rockabilly record and asked her to play it on the turntable in the kiosk.

It looks good, no scratches, I just wanna make sure, he said in that lackadaisical voice, the voice of Dallas Winston in *The Outsiders*. Michelle's hands were trembling. She got the record on the turntable without smashing it, though the needle was dropped into the groove a bit sloppily. She turned back to the register. Matt Dillon was leaning against the counter listening to the scratchy record, an old man's voice and a shaky guitar. It sounded good, it sounded very old and unknown. Matt Dillon liked it. He smiled.

Let me see your tattoos, he commanded.

Like all tattooed females, Michelle went through the world dodging the grabby fingers of men. People reached out and stroked Michelle's arms in ways they would never touch another stranger. The bounds of common courtesy and basic privacy were breached daily. *Lemme see your ink,* douchebags would mumble, their hands already wrapped around her forearm. *Nice tat. Nice ink.* Or the grossest, *Nice body art.* It filled Michelle with rage. But this was Matt Dillon.

Michelle extended her arms and the actor seized them.

Matt Dillon's hands were upon her. He manhandled her limbs, twisting them to get better looks at each piece, flattering them with his attentions, studying even the crappiest among them—the faded word *doubt* scripted blurry on her wrist, the poky tattoo a friend had given her with a needle and India ink. He particularly enjoyed the illustration of a young devil child peddling a Big Wheel up her shoulder.

That makes me think of that band, Gaye Bykers on Acid, Matt Dillon smiled up at her. *You know them?* Michelle nodded, mute. Her personality, thoughts, and charisma had shrunk up inside her body like testicles dropped into cold water. Here was Matt Dillon, fondling her tattoos, making small talk, and she could not respond. *Gaye Bykers on Acid,* he repeated. He swallowed, staring at her, his Adam's apple dancing in his throat. *There's Lesbian Dopeheads on Mopeds too, you heard of them?* Michelle nodded. She had heard of them.

Michelle had the word *Lezzie* tattooed on her shoulder, right above the devil child he'd been admiring. Michelle wanted to disclaim the Lezzie tattoo to Matt Dillon. Or maybe she should flaunt it. You never knew with a guy. It didn't matter anyway, Michelle was so unable to converse with Matt Dillon that he eventually dropped her arms and returned to the record bins in search of more obscure rockabilly, leaving Michelle alone at the kiosk to sink into a shame spiral about her clothes. She was wearing a pair of cutoff camouflaged pants for god's sake, like a man, like a butch. Her T-shirt—armless, thank god—had the Nike swoosh with the directive RIOT above it. She had gotten it at an anarchist book fair. It was impressively punk, expressed an admirable impulse, but was it sexy? No. It was enormous on Michelle. She wore combat boots on her feet, boots she had idly scrawled stars over with a paint pen one night, bored and drunk in Stitch's room. Her hair was crunchy and blue. She had given herself bangs during a recent bout of PMS. The only time Michelle felt deep regret at not having a lover with her in her studio apartment was when she gave herself this haircut. A lover would have stopped her. The bangs of course looked awful. Michelle could look forward to the hair poking her in the eyeballs until she gave in and pinned them back like a small dog humiliated with hair accessories.

Michelle was powerfully hungover, as she was every morning, and she had picked her outfit blindly. She wore no makeup. What was she thinking? She lived in Hollywood. The most beautiful people in the entire world lived in Hollywood. People whose good looks commanded millions of dollars, people who then used those millions to become more beautiful still. Michelle had learned a valuable lesson: do not leave the house unless you look ready to meet Matt Dillon.

If she had looked cuter perhaps she would have had the confidence to speak to him. From then on, each morning Michelle would look into the broken full-length mirror, found curbside in the Mission and lugged to Los Angeles. She would stare into its glass and ask herself: Am I ready to meet Matt Dillon? She would take the time to ring her eyes in kohl or stick a pair of earrings through the holes in her lobes, but it hardly mattered. She figured Matt Dillon would never return during one of her shifts. These sorts of things rarely happened twice.

Michelle stumbled from bed and answered the telephone. The curved gray screen of her little television mirrored the gray of the apartment, warped it like a fish-eye security mirror in a convenience store. Michelle caught her reflection. The bloat of her tiny booze-belly pooched out, her face was drawn and haggard, needed watering. She had untangled the dreadlocks that stubbornly overtook her head, and now her hair frizzed out around her skull, damaged and staticky. She did not look ready to meet Matt Dillon. She looked ready to meet Krusty the Clown. She looked like Sideshow Bob.

I Have To Go Back To Bed, Michelle said. I'm Sick. She was. Her reflection had hurt her stomach. I Feel Awful.

You have to listen to me. Kyle's voice sounded strung tight, vibrating with controlled anxiety, but Kyle often sounded anxious. Twice in high school Michelle had come home to find an ambulance out front, summoned by her brother who was sure he was having first a stroke, then a heart attack. His face felt numb and his hands tingled. His heart was racing out of control, his thin body shook with its gallop. Once inside the ambulance, his vitals being collected, he calmed. He flirted with the EMTs, charmed himself out of a bill, thank god. Kym was furious. *Do you know what a ride in an ambulance costs? A thousand dollars! Are you going to pay for that?*

Fine, I'll just let myself die next time, Kyle replied. *You have like three minutes to respond to a stroke before the brain starts losing oxygen. I'll be a vegetable. You can pull the plug on me.* He slammed the door to his bedroom.

Is this a gay boy thing? Kym looked to Michelle. *The drama?*

Maybe, Michelle admitted. She thought having been raised by a Scorpio nurse who talked constantly about infection and malaise and also a Libra stricken with an endless illness might also have exacerbated her brother's condition.

The grisly medical books that filled Michelle with a detached fascination gave her brother anxiety attacks. He didn't like hearing about falling rectums or South American parasites that swim up men's penises or junkies accidentally injecting a flesh-eating bacteria into their bodies.

You don't do that, do you? Kyle had once focused his nerves on his sister.

Inject Flesh-Eating Bacteria Into My Body? Michelle tried to joke herself out of the conversation. Nope.

No, you know, you don't do, um . . . Kyle ransacked his brain for its scant drug file. Michelle held her breath. *Morphine? You don't do morphine, do you?*

Morphine! Her brother was such an innocent. Who did morphine? Civil War amputees? *All the doctors at Ma's work have secret morphine addictions,* Kyle said. *You and your girl-friends don't do that, do you?*

No, Michelle was happy to tell him. I Don't Do Morphine.

You don't shoot drugs?

No, she was pleased to assure him. I Don't Shoot Drugs.

Swear to god?

Swear To God.

You don't believe in god, though.

It's True, I Don't. Not A Fearsome And Punishing Christian God Who Would Strike Me Down For Lying To You. What Do You Want Me To Do?

Swear on something you love.

I Swear On You.

That morning Kyle's anxiety was insistent. *Michelle, you've got to get up. You're still in bed? Get up, please. There's a state of emergency. They're grounding planes.*

What, Why? Michelle said. She stood up. The blood drained from her head, dizzying her, then filled her back up. On a recent morning Michelle had passed out on the toilet bowl shortly after waking up. She'd been hunched over, in her normal amount of hangover pain, clutching a glass of water, and when she sat upright it was like her blood swirled down some drain in her body and her vision got sprinkled with black confetti. The glass slipped from her hand and for a moment she was not there. It had scared her.

People are jumping from the buildings in New York City. People are jumping from the World Trade Center, the Empire State, the Chrysler Building. I can't get through to anywhere, I've been calling New York, I've been calling Boston, calling the moms, everything is a mess. I'm so glad I got through to you.

What Is Happening?

The world is ending. It's such a mess. Scientists can't reverse anything. The problems, the oceans, we've passed some point where it's going to accelerate and become like some sort of horrible like sci-fi movie where we all start eating each other and bands of crazed rapists roam around murdering each other and no one will be able to go into the sun or they'll explode like vampires, it's going to get so hot. The levees in all the cities are cracking under the sea, they can't keep up with how fast it's rising and all the shit in it, it's going to be like that crazy molasses factory in New England that Wendy likes to talk about, the one that exploded and everyone in the town drowned in molasses. There is some tsunami that is big enough to take out the entire West Coast of North America. They're tracking it. It's just a baby now, a baby wave, but it's going to grow big enough to do that, and once it does all the waves will be like that, like all waves just become tsunamis and the ocean eats the land.

Really? Michelle said. Are You Serious? Do You Have

Xanax For Yourself Right Now? Kyle's words were so fast and crazed, they sickened Michelle like a carnival ride.

I'm fine, Kyle snapped. *Stop projecting. I think I'm having a normal reaction to learning I'm going to be dead at twenty-six. But yes, I took a Xanax.*

Can I Have Some Xanax?

I don't know, Kyle said. *I'll have to see how many I have. I don't know what's going to happen to the pharmaceutical industry. I don't want to be without antianxieties if the world is ending.*

I Don't Understand. Michelle wrestled with the information. Can't Someone Do . . . Something? What If They're Wrong? What If They Kill The Planet And They're Fucking Wrong And The Tsunamis Never Come And We're All Dead?

How do I know? I'm not a scientist. I cast movies and stroke the ego of a crazy person. Do you want to know what I'm casting right now?

What? Michelle asked.

This movie about a Nordic boy who is lost on the coast of North America and raised by Native Americans and then grows up to save their tribe.

That's So Racist! Michelle exclaimed. Why All These Movies About White People Saving Brown People?

I know, Kyle said. *I'm casting that, plus a film about a really mean mother-in-law.*

Oh, Kyle.

And now the world is ending. I wonder if I'll have a job?

People Will Want To Go To The Movies, Michelle predicted.

But what if everyone loses their minds? Kyle worried. *My boss is already so unstable. Things might just fall apart. People are killing themselves in New York City.*

People Aren't Killing Themselves Everywhere?

Not like there. They got the news first. And they'll be one of the epicenters of the waves, one of the impact sites. It's just hitting people there harder.

Michelle looked out her window, peeking through the shades. The rottweiler's panting breath hit her in the face. Michelle was experiencing a disconnect, or perhaps her environment was. If the world were really ending, would the rottweiler remain at the window? Would cars keep cruising the freeway behind her building? Michelle could hear the smooth sweep of them, like rain.

Promise You're Not Fucking With Me? Michelle demanded. Your Psychobitch Boss Didn't Ask You To Try Out A Premise On Me? This Isn't A Treatment For A Film You're Casting?

No, I wish. Bruce Willis is not coming to save us. Turn on the TV, see for yourself.

Michelle knew once she turned on her television it would remain on for a very long time. She considered people leaping from buildings. She didn't want to see that. Michelle just wanted to get back into her futon for the slightest bit longer. Just drink some water, let her headache subside.

I want you to know that I love you, Kyle said. *I love you and I'm glad you're in Los Angeles and that we can be close. You should come to my house today.* Kyle lived out in North Hollywood, in a suburban neighborhood ten degrees hotter than any other part of the sprawl.

I Have Work, Michelle said.

No, Kyle said. *You won't work today. They're closing everything. In case of attacks or riots or mass suicides or looting. Everything is closed but the In-N-Out Burger. Just come over.*

Kyle! Really? Michelle thought of her mother: *Is this a gay boy thing, this drama?*

Girl, Kyle sighed. *Just turn on your TV.*

— 199 —

9 In the kitchen Michelle killed cockroaches with her bare hands. She'd become immune to it. Every morning they were there, scuttling across the counter, seeking refuge in the slats of the plastic dish rack. The only weapons handy were the dollar-store glasses prone to shattering, and so Michelle began bringing her hands down on them with a slap so hard it pulverized them, it juiced them. Her hand would go warm and tingle, vibrations rising up her shoulder. She would turn on the faucet and rinse the tiny carcasses from her palm. The big ones, the baby ones they called tweedlebugs—she smacked them all to death.

I Am Killing Roaches! Michelle hollered. With My Bare Hands! Michelle needed a witness. To both her bravery and the mundane horror of her life.

Michelle's studio was full of bugs. Michelle thought perhaps the government should visit her apartment and investigate, maybe there was something they could learn about sustaining life, because the bugs had learned to work it out. Invaders, but still. Jungle bugs, stowaways on ships, on trucks driven up from the tropics. They would emerge from nowhere, alarming Michelle. One looked like a feather, it had a million wispy legs floating its slinky body across the linoleum. It was almost beautiful, except it made her throat close and her eyes water. When Michelle killed it, its legs shriveled away and it became just another stain on the kitchen floor.

Beetles fat as tanks waddled from cracks in the walls, sturdy, shiny beetles that looked fake, like a gag beetle you'd scare a coworker with. Or a robot bug plodding toward you by remote control. Michelle screamed. If she killed the beetle she would hear its body crunch. Her arms rolled with goose bumps.

Michelle grabbed a glass and captured the formidable beetle. She released it in the alley below, knowing that it would only find its way back inside.

On the first day of the end of the world, Michelle got out of bed, walked into the kitchen, and smacked some roaches. She dumped a half-empty champagne flute swampy with dead fruit flies into the drain. She made coffee. Michelle made her coffee camp-style, tucking a filter into a plastic cone and hovering it over a mug. She knew she needed to buy a coffee machine or a French press or something, but she'd been scared to spend the money. Michelle wondered if things would perhaps become free now that the world was going to end. Would people become very greedy or very generous? Michelle could imagine manufacturers succumbing to an insanity of scarcity, raising their prices and padding their mortality with profit. She could also imagine them shrugging a cosmic oh-fucking-well and releasing their inventory, allowing the world to take whatever it wanted.

If Michelle had only a bit more time left to be in the

world, she wanted to stop worrying about money. The relief of that possibility, never before considered, shone over her head like a new sun. Imagine, to stop worrying about money! Michelle was born into such anxiety, it had been her placenta, the water breaking between her mother's legs, dollars and coins scattered on the ground. *They'll nickel and dime ya to death* was a phrase Michelle was acquainted with. No heirlooms, no property or fortune to be passed on to her. Michelle received bitter chips of wisdom from her mothers instead. *Money goes to money,* like cash was a carousel and Michelle's people did not have a ticket to ride. *Just as easy to marry a rich man as a poor man.* The advice seemed to contradict. If money went to money, then a poor girl would find it difficult to find a moneyed man to marry, no? There were no rich men in Chelsea. Indeed, in Chelsea, Massachusetts, it was just as easy to become an unwed teenage mother with a jobless baby daddy as it was to marry anyone, period. Anyway, if rich people sucked so bad, why was Michelle being encouraged to marry one?

Here at the end of the world, Michelle was suddenly over poverty. The shield she had welded around her heart to protect herself from the pain of it was corroding like rust in the rain. It had felt so strong, but there in the apocalypse kitchen Michelle felt it flimsy as a floppy disk—so much philosophy, political analysis, rebellious identity, and liquored intoxication just to stave off the simple scary sadness of being broke. Michelle began to cry. The anxiety of being poor and not understanding how to not be. Learning she would die so soon had cracked Michelle's bravado. Her hand holding the plastic coffee thing over a mug, she fed slow gulps of boiling water to the grounds. Still hungover, spacey, tired, not caffeinated, in that honest pocket, a tender, beaten place, not yet inflated with the day's efforts, Michelle felt the broken reality of her life. She was not her mothers, but she was in fact her mothers' daughter, valorizing a struggle that was breaking her down.

A decade spent in the downtrodden underground had warped Michelle's ambitions. In a place where powerless people fought over who had the least amount of power, Michelle had applied herself to the acquisition of hardship. People bragged about and competed for who had it the worst. Whose parents were brokest, whose PTSD the most damaging. "Calling people out on their shit" was a worthwhile way to pass the time. Michelle wanted her last days to be of a higher quality. She knew that she would likely leave the world as broke—*broker*—than she had entered it, but she was through pretending she was somehow the better for it, had chosen a superior mode of existence rather than been assigned a losing lotto ticket of economics and genetics at birth and then written a love story about it. She also thought she would think about trying to stop drinking.

Michelle took a shower. The news of the coming calamity had not impacted water purification, the plumbing that snaked through her building and out beneath the street, tubing off—where? Where did Michelle's water come from? Where did it go when it spiraled down the drain? The world would end before Michelle had the chance to understand how it had ever worked. Outside the rotted bathroom window the freeway whizzed with cars. Tiny cars, zippy electric things propelled by their batteries, plus some older ones buzzing on compost and then, every so often, a lumbering antique wheezed by, gargling gasoline.

Michelle often read news articles that explored how the poor, in their ignorance, destroyed their own environments, be they Los Angelenos torching their neighborhood grocery stores or South Americans slashing their rain forests. The poor inherited the archaic systems of the rich as the rich moved on to better ways of life the poor could not afford. And so the poor drove their gasoline hand-me-downs, sold away their corner of the earth and ate the last endangered sea turtle. Michelle imagined the poor would be blamed for the earth's catastrophe, the way gay people and artists got blamed for gentrification when people in suits came to town and the landlords jacked up the rent.

A crash happened on the freeway below, a battery car driven straight into the wall. It looked like a television show. Michelle realized she only ever saw cars crash on television. After the one car crashed, another car, gas powered, crashed beside it. It didn't need to crash, it's like it was inspired. It simply followed suit, swirling the wheel and aiming itself into the wall. It took three cars crashed on the bank of the freeway, accordioned and steaming, for Michelle to realize she was witnessing suicides. She turned off her shower and climbed out of the tub. Michelle felt the urge to return to the window, to gawk at the spectacle of the fire, but also to convince herself of what was happening because it felt unreal. The smoke streamed down her nose and clutched at her throat, choking her. She did not return to the window. She would probably begin seeing lots of car crashes, she thought.

Michelle moved through her bathroom gingerly, as if through a haunted house. It felt like she could trip an unseen wire and cause the roof to collapse or a car to burst through her walls. The wail of fire trucks and ambulances pierced the air. She zipped herself into a dress perhaps originally worn by a stewardess for an airline that went bankrupt in 1971. It was Creamsicle orange and woven from polyester so dense it could stop a bullet. It had a weird mock-turtle-neck neckline, golden buttons angling down the torso, and box pleats. The second she zipped herself into it Michelle's armpits began to stink. She pulled her hair into a bun atop her head. She looked like a waitress on *Star Trek: Enterprise*.

Michelle boiled a pot of pasta and plopped a chunk of margarine into the tangled noodles. She walked the food into the bedroom, something she normally avoided lest the roaches follow and climb through her hair as she slept. She settled onto the floor with her pasta and coffee, her back against the bed. On the television, planes smacked into buildings in an unrecognizable country, perhaps some-where in Eastern Europe. The planes on the television dropped burning to the ground, the image synced with the smell of smoking automobiles coming in through the rot-ted bathroom window. All over the world, wherever there were streets, people were running through them. Wherever there were buildings, people were leaping from them. Or blowing them up. The world was a sandcastle doomed to the tide. Why not experience the release of demolition? Buildings vaporized, became a rolling cloud of debris, curl-ing through the streets like a sideways mushroom cloud. It looked like a monster approaching, the shockwave foot-steps of a giant lizard. The people who survived it stood stunned and dusted in the street, shit in their hair, speak-ing to news cameras with the glaze of shock upon them.

Michelle thought it was irresponsible of the journalists to speak to these victims. They needed medical attention, ambulances, all of them. Michelle did not want to watch these people. They looked like they'd had strokes, how they could hardly speak, their twitching faces and their stammer. Michelle chewed her pasta. The TV was so staticky she could barely see the footage of people suiciding from bridges and towers. They were pixels merging into pixels. Michelle began to cry. At the idea of their fear, the moment when they understood they were about to die, even though they had chosen it, that moment when they were both alive and dead, there had to be a split second of instinctive regret, it made Michelle weep with spooky grief. The mock turtleneck of her polyester dress absorbed her tears like a parched landscape. Her hangover was powerful, she was all jangled nerves. She lay down on the floor and cried, the bowl of pasta on her stomach. The phone rang, and it was one of her mothers.

Have you seen the planes? Kym wanted to know. No one ever wanted to talk to Kym about television but today all anyone could do was watch and comment. It was her time to shine. *The one in Ukraine? The one in Ohio?*

Not The One In Ohio.

Oh my god. And the people, did you see them jumping in New York and in London?

I Saw New York, Not London.

Kym had been tuned in for hours. The carnage filled her with fear, yes, and sadness, of course, but also with an odd satisfaction. She knew something like this would happen. She knew it would get too bad, was getting too bad, had gotten too bad. People could not become incapacitated from their food and water, from the rays conjured to enliven cell phones and tiny gadgets, from computers. Think of all the computers, the dead computers piled upon each other, leaching poison into the earth and the water table. Think of all the new computers, millions and millions being birthed each day by third world women wearing gloves and masks to keep the deathiness of the machines off them, good luck, fat chance. People could not be gasping for air in the very air of their time and not have a solution dealt out to them eventually. A terrible solution for a terrible problem. It was a cancer. People were a cancer on their very own body and like a cancer they would band together and kill, cell after cell. Kym expressed this into her telephone, a true landline, a thick wire curling from a heavy receiver. The phone had been manufactured in the 1980s, it was safe.

Michelle thought Kym's metaphors were a little off, but her mom was stoned and Michelle got the general gist.

It's True, Michelle said simply. You Were Right. Michelle was prone on the floor, the phone jammed into her ear, the television rolling its loop of destruction. There's A Lot I Don't Understand, Michelle began, I Don't Know If It's Because I Actually Have A Bit Of A Hangover, I'm Not Going To Lie—

You out late last night?

No, I Don't Go Out. I Stay In And Watch *Friends*. I Rent Movies. I Sleep A Lot. I'm Working On A Scrapbook Project That Is Taking Up A Lot Of My Time.

You writing another book?

Yeah, Michelle lied. It's Just In My Head Right Now. I Have To Write It There First And Then Put It On The Computer.

You should write a screenplay, Kym suggested. *Being in Los Angeles and everything.*

Yeah, Michelle said. Well, Being In Los Angeles And Everything There Are Already A Lot Of People Writing Screenplays.

What's the book about?

Um, It's About A Crack-Smoking, Aging Psych Nurse In New England.

Whoa, Kym said. *I'm not going to tell your mother that. What happens to her?*

I'm Still Sorting It Out, Michelle said, distracted by a woman on the television. Her face was smeared with probably blood. On the black-and-white television it looked like chocolate, like fake blood, Karo Syrup and food coloring. But Michelle presumed it was, in fact, real blood. The woman's mouth was open in a scream.

You might not get to finish it now, Kym said practically. *I mean, how long does it take to write a book?*

I Don't Know, A Year? It Depends?

Kym was quiet, considering. *You could do it. There's that National Book Writing Month, right? Where everyone writes a book in thirty days? You might do it. I'd forget about publishing, though. It might not be worth it to go through the trouble of putting out a book if we're all going to die the day after it comes out, you know?* Kym's voice had a certain crushed quality to it. She kept the phone jammed between her head and a throw pillow, her throat bent around the receiver.

Will You Explain What Is Happening? Michelle asked. Because I'm Confused.

The planet's dead, Kym said, cheerfully. *You know, the ocean keeps rising and it's so awful, it's full of computers. And the weather patterns have changed and the hurricanes are getting so much worse, there's a chain of tsunamis somewhere out in the middle of the ocean and they're just going to take out most of Southeast Asia sometime this year, and the drinkable water is all but gone, there are all those water riots, we had some this year, not New England we but America we, I think maybe you had some down in Los Angeles—*

Michelle bristled at being lumped into Los Angeles we, but bit her tongue. On the television screen the news guy cried so hard his face was wet.

—and basically, you know, there's no food, everyone has cancer, right, there's no clean power so every time you turn on your lights you're killing something that hasn't already been killed while most things have already been killed, right, there's the food shortage because there's a land shortage because the land, the soil, is so dirty, dirty dirt, right, you know what I mean, and the nukes that got exploded last year I mean that whole region is just gone now and then there are all the nukes underneath everything and in the actual ocean, there are nukes getting exploded in the sea, can you imagine, that would make a big wave, right, and the chemical compounds being created in the ocean, these totally new, really bad chemicals are being manufactured sort of organically, well not organically because it's not organic, what's in the ocean, but the chemicals we dumped there are coming together and creating these totally new chemical compounds no one understands—

I Saw It! Michelle gasped. I Saw The Ocean, Here In LA, With This Smoke Coming Off It—

Yeah, it'll kill you, stay away from it, not that you can, really, I mean, not in California right, you live right on the ocean, we do too, we'll probably all keel over before the month is up, but the idea is that we're all doomed, really doomed, and you know human nature is so terrible, once things get worse they're going to really get worse, like science-fiction worse, people eating each other and I don't know, looting, yeah, but looting who cares about looting it's going to be total anarchy, just very abusive, a very abusive environment on earth once everything gets so bad, no gas no water no food, just total collapse. Kym laughed. *We finally have something that all the world's governments can agree on. Everyone wants to die. This whole world has a death wish, it's always had a death wish, it makes sense, it does, it's just sad. It was a nice place. When I was young we still had animals, we had, you know, land, with trees and grass, that wasn't so long ago. It's stunning how quickly things went bad. We had zoos. You and Kyle never even got to go to a zoo.*

No? Michelle asked. When I Was Very Little? She had a memory of animals in a pen, small beige furred things, but she couldn't be sure if it was a memory or a wish or a dream.

There were still some around but they were really pathetic. I mean, zoos have always been pathetic I think, but they got so bad when the animals began getting sick. Animals know, Kym said. *Animals know. Watch. I bet the cats will start to die off. The domestic animals, the pets. They know.*

Her conversation with Kym was growing wider and more tiring. She arranged for Wendy to call her when she returned from work. Michelle killed the telephone and returned to the TV. The plane crashes were beginning to run together, swoop crash explode, swoop crash explode. Michelle wondered how it felt to steer the planes into the buildings. The planes entered as if into water, a liquid column, smooth. Then the blooming fire, a flaring burst against the sky. Again and again they ran it, until it looked beautiful. Michelle turned the sound off. It was a ballet. It was stop-motion photography of a milk drop or a bullet coring an apple.

Beatrice phoned next. *I don't think I'm going to stay open today,* she said simply. *It doesn't feel safe. Or respectful, selling things.* Michelle felt a bolt of love for Beatrice. For being such a high-strung hippie, for keeping a junkyard of books open on that slick strip of commerce. For crying all the time. *It's a day for us to be with other people,* she said sniffily. Michelle hung up. She was thrilled to not have to go to work.

Kyle picked her up in his Honda Civic, which made creaking, tweeting bird noises as it drove. *Squeak, Squeak,* Michelle made puppet noises at Kyle, pushing her chirping hands at him as he aimed the car into the sole In-N-Out Burger that had remained open all day. A giant American flag had been draped across the dead trees that ringed the drive-through. What did America have to do with it? Michelle wondered. Were people going to die as Americans rather than as earthlings? Michelle braced herself for a surge of nationalism. Suicide and patriotism, people feeding themselves to the lions with the stars and stripes clenched in their teeth? Michelle realized the end of the world might actually be profoundly tedious. That story hadn't occurred to her.

Michelle knew that the In-N-Out Burger workers made more than minimum wage and, thus, were making more per hour than she was making at the bookstore, with benefits. Perhaps it was time to investigate the fast-food industry. It was stable, she noted, she'd just gone through Cowshwitz and had seen the gears churning. Unless the cows started dying off before they could be slaughtered, Michelle figured the burger shacks would stay in business longest of all. And even if the cows did begin dying in the mysterious mass deaths that had claimed all the other species, Michelle bet the companies would still sell the meat. People needed food and everyone was going to die now anyway. Michelle anticipated a severe drop in safety standards.

I Wonder If I Should Get A Job At In-N-Out, Michelle wondered aloud.

You've got to write a screenplay, Kyle said robustly. Kyle was wicked optimistic. Not even the pending apocalypse could challenge the fantasy he'd concocted for his sister. Michelle would write a screenplay and he would inherit his crazed boss's successful casting agency. No longer bullied by his narcissistic overlord, he would proudly reject projects that dealt in stereotypes. No more Latina maids and gay hairdressers. The fat best friend would get the man unless the man in fact wanted another man. Kyle dreamed of these future days while being abused by his boss, vacuuming up the chipped glass of another ashtray shattered against the wall in a fit of rage. Kyle's boss didn't even smoke. She kept ashtrays around to express her anger.

The previous day, before everything changed, Kyle had been auditioning a roomful of young African American actresses vying for the role of a crack whore in a fake independent—meaning, a film with the aesthetic of an independent but with the content and budget of the studio producing it. Kyle's stomach twisted tighter each time a woman entered his office wearing ridiculous, humiliating clothing—mismatched platform shoes, shirts stained with food, the poky outlines of their braless nipples. They had given it their all, every one of them, and this depressed Kyle even more because the part was awful, they were all too good for the shitty little film, but that was life, that was the life they had all signed up for, there in Los Angeles. Kyle had signed up to cast shitty, offensive films and these actresses had signed up to embody them and they were all in it together. Kyle adopted the persona of a weary faggot who knew their plight well, yet also knew better than to presume he could know what it was to walk in their shoes, the mismatched Lucite stilettos of a brilliant black actress fated to spend the end-times portraying stumbling crack whores in crappy movies.

Michelle didn't know how she and her brother would make this leap from the assistant and the barely employable to Hollywood sibling power duo before the world ended, but Michelle loved what her brother saw in her. Had they been born into a life of privilege, if Michelle had been able to identify and then believe in all the options that were out there, then yes, maybe she would be able to clamber out of the ghetto that her brokenness and queerness and political affiliations had kept her in. But deep in her heart Michelle did not believe that the world was so open to her, and so she sniffed out jobs that paid single digits an hour and every job she scored felt like a huge scam, like she had tricked the employers into thinking she was someone else—a college graduate perhaps, a clean person, a person with a rich wardrobe who did not kill cockroaches with her bare hands.

Michelle and Kyle sat on the sectional sofa in his North Hollywood one bedroom, packages from In-N-Out Burger nestled in their arms, the greasy steam opening the pores in their faces like a trash facial. They put french fries into their mouths and watched the world fall apart. Kyle had cable and a better TV and Michelle could now see how blue the skies were, how brightly the flames curled out from buildings, like solar flares shooting off the surface of the sun. The people leaping from high dark windows were people, not pixels. They sat and watched and watched. Eventually, they shut it off. They agreed that it was too much, it had been on for hours and the networks were just milking everyone's anxiety, it was sick—there was nothing new to show but they were desperate to keep us there, watching.

Michelle was hooked. One newscaster, stationed in Geneva, kept promising that some buildings were about to blow up and Michelle wanted to see it happen. She knew that there was something really wrong with her desire to keep watching. She was in the grips of a detached fascination. She wanted the images on the television to wear her down so she could truly feel whatever it felt like to truly feel what was happening. Surely this alarmed, rubbernecking interest was not what she should be feeling. She was supposed to be feeling something a few layers down, something authentic and meaningful. Michelle feared she was not having an authentic experience of the beginning of the end of the world. She was having a deeply authentic experience of inauthenticity.

The shots of New York City had rattled her the most. It was hard matching up the city she'd visited so many times with this chaotic landscape of rolling debris clouds and screaming, scorched humans. It was like watching *Blade Runner* and looking for Los Angeles. New York was like one of those asteroid-hits-earth films. Kyle poked at the remote, finally settling on a film about a plucky lady alcoholic who gets sent to rehab and eventually comes to understand that she truly is an alcoholic, and then she finds love—real, sober-person love—and she dumps her British party-man boyfriend to be with her new recovery soul mate. When it was very late, Michelle was scared to go to sleep, to leave Kyle awake on the sectional. He had such problems with anxiety and Michelle was sure he would sit up all night in front of the plasma television, watching suicides and having panic attacks. Which is exactly what he did.

10

Michelle slept deeply the night she learned the world was ending. She'd feared long hours tossing and turning, humming with disbelief, the news shows rolling through her mind, images of buildings already tumbling. She was sure her fear of a nearby, immediate catastrophe would keep her uselessly alert. What would prevent anyone from beginning the inevitable destruction of Los Angeles tonight? She considered lunatics, the barely hinged madmen and madwomen clutching at their slipping sanity with sweat-greased fingers. Why should they hold on any longer? Maybe the earth itself would awaken to the diabolical plotting of the human race and shake them off its back. Anything seemed possible that night, and Michelle felt herself an impotent sentry on the lookout for nothing she could control, fretting away the darkened hours. She worried about Kyle and his nerves, his mind lit with horror, anxious thoughts careening like pinballs—metallic, smacked with flippers, a panic multiball, image after image zooming out from a consciousness cramped with the effort of flinging them away.

But Michelle slept. She'd waited for her mind to engage the gears of panic, but instead she began to dream.

Michelle dreamed of a boy. In the dream she walked alongside him in a great garden. His arm was wound around her waist and with each step they took her hip rubbed against his. In sync, they curved around a path that brought them by tall, wiry stalks of echinacea, their purple petals peeled back in submission to the sun. Their ankles rolled as they navigated the cobblestones in fancy shoes: hers bright as a child's toy with plastic chains and shining strips of leather, his delicately soled, the leather a carpaccio, slippers really, to be worn climbing in and out of fairy-tale carriages. Michelle enjoyed the sight of their shoes shuffling in unison through the garden. They paused beside a bush of angel's-trumpets and huffed the waxy horn of each dangling blossom. They rubbed the fuzz of the kangaroo paw, were dazzled by the new-wavy hue of the sticks on fire, Euphorbia tirucalli. The boy spoke and Michelle thought, I'm Euphorbic!—so blissed out and goofy her observing self wondered what she was on.

In her dream the boy knew the name of every plant. In her dream Michelle understood Latin, the noble, ancient music of it making sense. A receptor in her mind was activated and in an instant she felt an understanding of all languages! Understood that she had always known them! Her mind was a hive of words. A rush of excitement washed over her. She turned back to the boy, who was more beautiful than all the flowers, more aesthetically pleasing than the water fountain with its patinous bronze, than the curve of the cobblestones, the stitching of their fancy shoes. His voice, speaking Latin, was sweeter than the water's splash and trickle, the patter of their feet upon the stone.

Oh, Michelle felt so romantic! The boy pulled her closer and together they made fun of the docent leading the tour, a woman who didn't know the Latin words for anything, who hadn't discovered that she could speak Latin or Spanish or Swahili if only she flexed that part of her brain. Michelle and the boy whispered to each other in a succession of languages, their minds' potential illuminated. The boy's shirt was slashed as if it had survived a knife fight and Michelle's pants were too tight. The energy between them flashed from pure to sleazy, they pecked each other's cheeks and restrained themselves from groping. Michelle bit back her desire to slip her hand through the gash in his shirt, to press her ass against him. *I'm your Eurotrash boyfriend,* he murmured in Castilian Spanish. Their love expanded as they expressed it in Norwegian, German, Italian. So many nuanced words! Different kinds of words for different kinds of love and Michelle felt them all—sad love, inspired love, hopeless love, affectionate love, friendly love, desperate love, passionate love, murderous love, respectful love, platonic love, forbidden love, trashy love, sacred love, holy love. Michelle's heart felt full and drooping as the blowsiest rose in the garden. The boy's attentions buzzed inside it. She was so open to him, she shed pollen on the cobblestones.

The boy did not like how the designer of this garden had deliberately starved certain plants of water so that their stressed-out leaves would turn a more pleasing color. Neither of them liked how the designer had employed a worker to pluck every other leaf from the canopy of trees arcing above them so that the light filtering through the branches would be dappled just so. What A Control Freak, Michelle said, in French, just to hear the chic sound of it sliding from her mouth. She was concerned for the worker charged with this duty, imagined him a Mexican man struggling on a ladder, earning minimum wage, slowly losing his mind as he scanned the boughs—pluck a leaf, leave a leaf, pluck a leaf, leave a leaf—the cancerous sun mutating his body. His body, Michelle imagined, would be heavy, would wear coveralls, a navy blue jumpsuit sewn from stiff fabric. She thought she would maybe write a story about him, this man who plucked leaves in service to a megalomaniacal garden designer. She shared her inspiration with the boy, who gave her waist a squeeze.

I want to know your work, he told her in Armenian. *I want to become familiar with your praxis.* His hands, tipped with slender fingers, gestured out from his chest as he spoke, as if his desire were a gift he offered from his heart. Michelle didn't know what praxis was, but she felt elated that the boy believed she had it, was dizzy with his desire to become familiar with it.

The boy's work was flowers, plants. He believed it was people like the mad garden designer, with his need to manipulate nature like plastic putty, who brought problems into their world. The designer's artificial aesthetic was a poison in the garden. The boy wanted to feed the thirsty plants water, to restore them to their native, less flamboyant color. He wanted to return the missing leaves to the anemic branches that rustled above them. Michelle wanted that, too. She imagined how damp and green the air would feel beneath a lush canopy, how shaded, how the boy would kiss her, brushing the animal fur of his cheeks against her skin, his gentle mustache. With every step Michelle could feel the pressure of a ghost hand between her legs and knew that the imprint was his, the boy had been there, had worked her like a puzzle box. With each step she savored the sweet, dull pain of how he'd solved her.

In her dream Michelle pulled a cell phone from her purse to check the time. Dreaming Michelle had a cell phone— Observing Michelle noted this absurdity. Michelle didn't want to be late to meet Kyle, Kyle was in the garden, too, strolling alongside a row of succulents with a man, his boyfriend. Kyle was in love, too! I'm In Love, Michelle said happily, for *in love* was her favorite place to be. I'm In Love, she blissed, Just Like Kyle. The thoughts came to her in Mandarin and she enjoyed the choppy, chunky noise of it inside her head, words beginning in a call and ending in a trill, squeezed, almost sung. She wanted to tell the boy how special it was that everyone she loved was in love, but her cell phone melted away into a Salvador Dali jumble of floating nonsense and Michelle realized then that she was in a dream.

Swiftly, reality slammed down on the part of her mind that could comprehend Latin, Armenian, Mandarin. With great sadness she understood it had all been gibberish, gobbledygook, she could not speak Cantonese or Tagalog or Portuguese. She was in Kyle's bed, a single damp sheet knotted around her, the Los Angeles smog coming through the open window like the exhalations of a chain-smoking god. Michelle lay on the mattress feeling the dream evaporate from her body. In the next room she could hear the low chatter of the television broadcasting the apocalypse and hoped her brother had at least fallen asleep out there.

I Dreamed Of You, Michelle told her brother. We Were In A Garden And We Both Had Boyfriends. We Were In Love.

You had a boyfriend? Kyle asked skeptically.

Yeah Who Cares, Michelle shrugged. He Was Pretty, Like Johnny Depp. He Spoke Very Pretentiously And Seemed Well Educated.

Wait! Kyle winced. His neck was tangled and sore from sleeping on the sectional. The television had infiltrated his dreams all night, but he had dreamed, and where had he been? In a great garden, with his sister. *We were in the Getty!* he said. *I did have a boyfriend! Oh my god . . .* He turned and stared at Michelle. *Not only did you have a boyfriend,* Kyle said, *you had a cell phone. That's how I know it was a dream!*

Kyle's dream boyfriend was a terribly handsome interior decorator who was not promiscuous and had glittering blue eyes. He was gentle with Kyle and in the dream Kyle had enjoyed it! They had strolled hand in hand, discussing the health of their surrogate, a college student who had agreed to carry their baby. Their surrogate was robust and loved the feeling of her body morphing in pregnancy. Having babies and giving them to gay men was her greatest joy. The dream had been a good dream. Kyle would have liked to contort himself back onto the sectional, finding the exact terrible pose he'd slumbered in and call for the dream to return, but he'd promised Michelle he'd drive her back to Hollywood.

11 On the second day of the end of the world, Michelle changed into something worthy of a run-in with Matt Dillon and left for work through the back door, passing through a small, sad square of concrete that functioned as a sort of pathetic backyard. Little green shoots came up through the rocky gaps in the pavement. Seasons of dead leaves moldered along the perimeter. Sometimes homeless kids slept there in the afternoons, protected by the building's constant shade.

Turning the corner, Michelle walked along a stretch of sidewalk owned by the Scientologists. They had landscaped the walkway with those expensive fake plants, they trusted that the scant foot traffic of Los Angeles would prevent them from being messed with but Michelle couldn't resist. She would pluck a single yellow orchid blossom from its stalk and vivisect it as she strolled, wondering at the plasticky fibers, the cool gloss of the petals. They felt so real but they weren't. She kept the stolen flower low, they were as protected as endangered plants had once been. She couldn't afford to replace even a bud and didn't need to get hauled into court by a bunch of Hollywood Scientologists.

Michelle stuffed the shredded flower in the pocket of her cutoffs and watched the Scientologists dash in and out of their compound. She especially appreciated the maids, who wore real, old-fashioned maid uniforms, black and white with little aprons and nursing shoes. Michelle longed to get a job at the Scientology Celebrity Centre, cleaning the rooms of visiting celebrities while wearing such an adorable costume, but she knew they would never hire her. The Hollywood sign sat wearily on the dead grass, a wavering mirage in the smog. Michelle entered her bookstore.

Beatrice was already there. Every day Michelle had to tell some customer that Beatrice was not a Scientologist, that their store was not a Scientologist bookstore, though they did keep a lot of dictionaries on hand because new Scientology recruits came in daily, having been instructed to go out and buy themselves a dictionary. The customers remained skeptical about Beatrice's affiliations. Really, Michelle would insist, She's Just An Old Hippie. In San Francisco there were a million ladies like Beatrice, but here in Los Angeles she was such a rare breed people thought she belonged to a cult.

Beatrice had written a poem about the wonders of the world and had hung it in the front window. Michelle's project that day would not be her regular Sisyphean task of finding space on the buckling bookshelves for yet more books, but to find art books containing photos of some of the planet's high points. Waterfalls, canyons, mountain peaks swathed in mystical clouds. Beaches with gentle, curling waves—nothing too awesome, we didn't want to make people think about the coming tsunami. Just lush canopies of glossy leaves and flowers as big as your head. Jungles and fields of flowers, forests and the tiny bear cubs that clawed honey from the beehives that dangled from branches.

Never mind that most of these things had been gone for some time. Beatrice was in the grip of an anxious nostalgia and she was paying Michelle an hourly rate to indulge it. She also had a migraine. And her husband's esophagus wasn't operating right. She left the shop soon after installing the poem behind the glass. Michelle got to work culling books from the cramped Art section.

Joey stopped by briefly to place a copy of Metallica's *Kill 'Em All* in the window beside the poem. She's Not Going To Think That's Funny, Michelle said. She Has Me Looking For Pictures Of Rainbows And Pine Forests. She'll Take It Out.

Yeah, well, Joey said sadly, with a small smile and a smaller shrug. The more Michelle worked with Joey the more he revealed and the more she enjoyed him. He was intensely mystical, new age, belonged to some faggoty men's group that gathered in the desert and did man-witch activities. He had the important retail skill of being able to make fun of a customer to their face without them knowing it. He had a knotty, gnarled scar running up his torso from his big New York City drug overdose. *Someone was in here earlier and said there was nothing to stop him from going out and killing a bunch of, um, "faggots and niggers" is what he said. That he'd just be beating the government to it.*

Oh My God, Michelle said. Who? Who Said That?

Ted, Joey said.

Ted, a regular bookseller, a white guy in his forties who didn't brush his hair, who wore a track suit into the store every day to try to unload old paperbacks and cassette tapes. Though his offerings sucked, he acted like he was offering them a first edition of *Catcher in the Rye*.

I Can't Buy This, Michelle recently wagged a busted mass-market paperback at him, the pages yellowed as if urinated upon, the whole book looking sort of exploded.

How about this? The man loaded a dingy hardcover photography book about Australia onto the counter, followed by a Chuck Palahniuk with a torn front cover.

We Have Three Copies Of That Already, Michelle shook her head. Sorry. It was like the "sorry" you gave to a person spare-changing you on the street, only worse because Ted felt like he was working for it, really working, and you were withholding his rightful pay. He dumped a small bag of cassette tapes onto the rejected books. Red Hot Chili Peppers, Journey, Mariah Carey. The Mariah Carey was a cassingle. We're Not Really Buying Cassettes, Michelle said uneasily. The man was glowering at her. His face was speckled with a five o'clock shadow, like a snickerdoodle that had been rolled in cinnamon sugar. He glowered at Michelle with a face she realized was desperate. Not a pleading desperate but a harder, resentful desperate. A desperation that knew itself to be pathetic and hated you for seeing it, for refusing to do the little you could to relieve it, buy the fucking Red Hot Chili Peppers cassette, what the fuck do you care anyway? It was a standoff. Michelle decided the best way to deal with the situation was to pretend she didn't notice how completely unhinged Ted was. She shrugged, allowed a goofball grin to hit her face. She would not recognize his desperation. She would give him the dignity of her feigned obliviousness.

She wished someone, anyone, was in the store. Beatrice,

her useless husband, Matt Dillon. The store took up half the block, the building was not only the gigantic shop with its many miniforts of books and rolling carts stacked with slowly warping opera albums, beyond that cavernous room smelling of the slow rot of pages and glue was a side room stuffed with more books, books too good for the store, to be sold on eBay or at antiquarian book fairs. And the side room had its own little side room with more hoarded crap, maybe a bathroom. There was the break room at the far end of the store with a staircase leading to an upstairs room containing every cassette ever recorded. Michelle was confident they had multiple copies of that Red Hot Chili Peppers cassette stashed in the upstairs room.

The wide store was empty of people, ringing with the bad vibes of this one customer. There were a million places he could stuff her body after he raged on her. He could jam her into a bookshelf, wall her up with *Star Trek* paperbacks and no one would ever find her. The guy ran a pork-chop hand through his dark hair. His hair was black and sleek and shiny except for the textured gray hairs that sprung in a tough fuzz of swirls across the top. He ran his hand through his hair and slammed it on the pile, cracking a cassette case. Michelle had wished desperately for Joey and, miraculously, he appeared.

Ted, Joey sang in a bored tone, clapping the psychopath on the back. Joey was so good at the casual bro-down, half the customers didn't even get that he was gay, despite his intense nellyness.

Hey man, can you buy some of this shit?

Joey flipped the merchandise around on the table, landing on the blasted paperback. *Two bucks.*

Dude. Just give me five and I'll give you everything. Michelle rolled her eyes. Like the asshole was doing the shop a favor, dumping a pile of garbage on the counter and charging them five bucks for it. Michelle didn't know why she cared so much. It wasn't her money. She realized that she'd become identified with the bookstore.

Joey dug five bucks out of the register. The dude thanked him with a fist-bump, stuffed the bill in his tracksuit, and strode out the door, his plasticky clothing making an airy noise. The bell roped to the door clanged as he left. He'd begun ignoring Michelle the minute Joey had arrived and had never looked at her again.

I'm Sorry, Michelle said to Joey, motioning to the pile of crap on the counter. She was shaken by the whole thing and didn't know where to project her riled energy. I Didn't Think I Should Buy Any Of It.

You shouldn't, Joey affirmed. *It's shit. But whatever. I wanted to get rid of him. He's a writer and he's got a heroin problem and he'll stick around haggling forever. I just felt like I would rather pay him five dollars than deal with him.*

The guy was a junkie. A writer with a heroin problem. In Los Angeles Michelle had learned of the sources of other drugs. There was a meth trade near the gay center, a trans woman sold it or you could get it from the taco truck or from a deadbeat donut shop, all within a one-block radius. Michelle suspected Tommy the golf punk sold club drugs, and Joey, who treated his heroin addiction with weed, could hook her up if she desired. But this was the first sign of the availability of heroin, this surly asshole Ted. Many times Michelle had longed for the vinegar sting of the stuff as it tunneled through her nose, the strange drowning sensation as it hit her sinuses. Michelle knew she had run out of San Francisco three steps ahead of a physical habit—that was the point of Los Angeles, sort of. She'd wanted to stop doing so many drugs, and she had.

Michelle didn't want to put Ted in a mental Rolodex of people who could get her heroin, but she did anyway. She couldn't not. Her brain, it seemed, had its own secretary and she did her job diligently. Ted. Heroin. Never mind that Michelle had only just feared him smacking her across the jaw with the staple gun and burying her alive in a pile of old jazz records. Ted. Heroin. Michelle thought that the next time he came in she would tell him that she, too, was a writer. That she had written a book. She would ask him what he was working on. Michelle hadn't met any writers in Los Angeles—no writers working on books, anyway, if that is what this Ted character did. Michelle bet he was writing a novel. Maybe even poetry. A junkie writer desperately selling a battered copy of *Fight Club* was probably not writing a movie. He was starring in it. Ted. Heroin.

Ted Threatened To Kill You? Michelle marveled.

Ted threatened to kill faggots. Apparently he has no idea that I am one.

What Did You Do?

I kicked him out.

Michelle gazed at the glass front door, half expecting Ted to be out there, crazed, dope sick, sweating hate, a monster. Joey swished his hand.

Whatever.

Do We Have A Gun? Michelle asked out loud. Is There One Of Those Panic Buttons You Can Hit To Sound An Alarm If We Get Robbed?

You think Beatrice is stashing guns around here? Joey waved his lanky arms around his head. *You want a gun to protect you from Ted? Ted is fine. He's a fucking racist homophobe drug addict and he'll probably kill himself off before the world actually ends. Certainly before he gets around to killing anyone else.*

Michelle wasn't sure. She was spooked at Junkie Ted's pronouncement, even if Joey had decided to not take it too seriously. Joey had other problems. One of his roommates wanted to hang an American flag out the window and the other roommates didn't. The proflag roommate was working-class and the others were upper-middle-class academics and it had turned into a class war.

Oh God, Michelle groaned, Flags. She had noticed them, too, suddenly everywhere, as if a national holiday had been declared, as if the country had triumphed in a sporting event. As if it were America that would die within a year and not the world. On her way to work she'd seen the sheet someone had hung out their front window, GOD BLESS THE USA gusted across it in spray paint. The other shops on the strip had obediently taped little flags in their windows. Beatrice, bless her heart, had refused, had placed her poem there instead, and a little peace flag, a cartoon image of a healthy planet, all blues and greens, with the hippie peace symbol on top of it. Michelle walked Junkie Ted's book about Australia over to the window, torn between displaying its cover of the triumphant Sydney Opera House or the centerfold shot of an archaic white beach. She removed the Metallica album and handed it to Joey. He took it and swiped the peace flag, too.

Maybe I can get my housemates to compromise with this. He gave it a sad little wag.

It's So Awful, Michelle said. The Planet Does Not Look Like That.

They might as well put a smiley face on it too, Joey agreed. He lifted his face into a stupid grin and marched in place, shaking the wistful flag on its little stick. The door jangled and a small, gray-haired woman walked in.

Judy, Joey greeted the woman, bowing at the waist, the peace flag held high.

Hold on to that flag, Judy said. *We're going to have a neighborhood vigil. That's the flag we want. Peace on earth. Peace for the earth.*

You want the flag? Joey asked. He thrust it at the woman. *Take it. Beatrice would love for it to be in a parade.*

A vigil, not a parade, she corrected sternly. *A parade! There is nothing to celebrate. But we've got to get out there. We've got to let them know we're watching.*

Judy ran the Franklin Strip neighborhood group. She was real hustle-bustle. Michelle hated her. Judy always ignored her. When Beatrice had introduced them Judy had only glanced at Michelle impatiently, as if her presence was preventing an important conversation about permit parking from happening. Michelle had nodded awkwardly and retreated back to her project, organizing the messy Gay Fiction section in the far corner of the store.

Amazingly, Michelle had found a copy of her own book sitting there on the shelf, its orange spine familiar. PLAYLAND, the bold black letters read. Then, LEDUSKI. Michelle pulled it from the shelf. The inside had been signed, inscribed to someone named Betty. *Thanks, Betty!* She read her own familiar, cheerful scrawl. *Great glasses! Enjoy the book!* Michelle was at a loss when signing books. She always wanted to write something profound but wound up bursting with nervousness and etching a slight compliment about the reader's appearance: Great glasses. I like your hair. Cool boots. She felt shallow and ashamed each time she closed the book and passed it back to the reader. Michelle tried to remember a Betty with glasses. Had she enjoyed the book as Michelle commanded? Perhaps not. Michelle turned the book in her hand, looking at the cover photo, a girl in a plastic miniskirt and combat boots clutching an upturned wine glass by its stem, the wine dribbling out, caught in droplets by the camera. Michelle couldn't remember the girl's name, only that Ziggy had been sleeping with her. *Playland* was about leaving your crazy East Coast family and coming to San Francisco to drink a lot and have sex in queer-bar bathrooms. It was about being young and experimenting with drugs and having lousy jobs. It was about Michelle's life. Finding a copy lodged in the bookstore filled her with complicated feelings. She was proud of herself for being on the shelves, but she was only there because someone had read the book and not cared to keep it. Still, someone, Beatrice or Joey, had thought the cramped, overstuffed bookstore would benefit from the addition of it and they had acquired it. Maybe Betty with the great glasses had been an annoying junkie Joey had tossed a quarter at to get rid of her. Michelle was beginning to understand that a lot of the people peddling used books were, in fact, annoying junkies.

Michelle gave in to the specialness of discovering herself on a bookshelf and trotted up to Beatrice, still engaged in conversation with Neighborhood Judy. I Wrote This, she chirped happily.

Beatrice looked at her with her teary, reddened eyes. Allergies? Michelle wondered. The store was the dustiest place in the world. Motes swirled like a thin snowfall in the light coming through the windows. *Really? Wow.* She gave a little smile, returned to Judy who seemed to be holding her breath until Beatrice's attention returned. Clearly, if the book had been any good Michelle would not be working in a bookstore.

Michelle could not adjust to the lowly status ascribed to bookstore workers in Los Angeles. In San Francisco, bookstore positions were coveted, *highly* competitive. Michelle had been rejected by bookstores for years, she had to actually publish a book before one would hire her. In San Francisco it was totally cool to work in a bookstore. You would starve to death because they only paid seven dollars an hour, but you would die cool. In Los Angeles you were not cool. You were a stupid counter person making little more than minimum wage in a town where people made millions of dollars a day. There was something seriously wrong with you. You were completely invisible. Michelle retreated to Gay Fiction, so far from the counter she could not hear Judy's rantings, only watch the woman's jerky gesticulations, like a marionette being operated by a fool.

Neighborhood Judy accepted the peace flag from Joey and trotted out the door, flyers advertising that night's vigil fluttering in her wake. Joey kindly stuck one in the window, next to a Nostradamus book he'd slid in when Michelle wasn't looking. Michelle watched Judy bounce purposefully up the strip in her bright white Keds.

She Is So Psyched The World Is Ending, Michelle observed. She Is So Psyched To Have Something Other Than Permit Parking To Get All Worked Up About.

Joey nodded thoughtfully. *A lot of people's lives are going to get a lot more meaningful—fast.*

I Don't Know What To Feel About It, Michelle admitted. It Doesn't Feel Real.

Have you seen anybody die yet?

Michelle shook her head. Not Close Up. Just Television. And The Freeway, I Saw Some Crashes. Suicides, Michelle thought, but didn't say it.

You ever see anyone die, ever?

Michelle shook her head.

My boyfriend OD'd when I lived in New York, Joey said, both of them lingering by the front window. *We did all these things to try to save him. We threw him in the tub, we put ice on him, smacked him, shot him up with salt.*

Salt?

*Yeah, but none of it worked and he died. I watched him. It was crazy. One minute he was there, he wasn't conscious but he was there, I knew he was there, and then, I could see it, he was gone. It fucking freaked me out so much. That it is that easy to leave like, just—*Joey's fingers twitched around in front of his face, as if casting some sort of spell, the spell of a person leaving themselves—*like that,* he said, insistent. He shook out his hands like they'd fallen asleep. *Like that. Whatever keeps us here is hardly anything. We can all go like that, just like that.* Joey looked about to cry. He stretched his eyes extra wide to prevent tears from spilling out. It was the same surprised expression he made to make fun of the women with too much plastic surgery who occasionally browsed the bookstore.

Oh, Joey. Michelle looked at her friend. The tears spilled despite his stricken expression. She put her hand on his bony wrist, but he lifted his hand away to pull the bandanna from his head and daub his eyes. Joey was beginning to go bald and didn't quite know what to do about it, hence the bandanna. Michelle wouldn't have known what to do about it either and felt grateful to never have to deal with such a thing. She supposed some women went nearly bald later in life, but Michelle wouldn't be having a later life.

After Charley died I left. That exact night, I left. He died in the bathtub and I went back to my parents' in Connecticut and I never went back to New York again, I have not been back since. I left him in that house, this girl's house, Heidi, she didn't know where to find me, no one knew where to find me, only Charley would have known, and I left him in the tub, ugh. He shivered, tied his bandanna back around his head, knotting it tight at the base of his skull. *But it's okay. He would have been okay with it. We both knew what we were doing. He'd left me at the hospital when I had my OD and didn't get in touch with me till they released me, you know? That's how it is with junkies.*

Is That When You Stopped Doing It?

Joey shook his head. *No, I did it for longer, sneaking around in my mother's house. Can you imagine? I stopped when I came out here.*

Me Too, Michelle said carefully.

You had a habit? Joey asked.

Michelle blushed, halted. Not Really, she said. Not Like That. We Never Shot. We Just Were Doing It Too Much. Not Enough To Get A Habit. I Don't Think. Michelle couldn't be sure. She always felt like shit in her body, even that day she was so nauseous from bad wine she didn't know how she was going to ingest the apple and cottage cheese she had packed for lunch.

It's so bad. Joey shook his head. *So bad, so bad, so bad. But sooooo good.* He looked out the window, like there was a giant boulder of heroin sitting on the sidewalk waiting for him to come and chip a chunk of it. *I'm going to spend that last day so high,* he said. *I can't fucking wait.* He stood up and ruffled Michelle's hair, his hand briefly catching on the total snarl of it. *You're in shock, babe.*

I Am?

Totally. What are you going to do on the day it's all over?

Michelle drew a blank. She shrugged. I Don't Know.

Shock, Joey confirmed. *You don't really believe it's happening.*

Totally, Michelle affirmed. But if she knew she was in shock, was she still in shock? Was it like being crazy, how if you knew you were crazy you were somehow less crazy? I Don't Know How To Believe It.

It will sink in, Joey promised. *Once people start dying you'll get it. Once you start seeing dead people. My upstairs neighbor jumped off the roof yesterday. It took her fifteen fucking hours to die. She just lay there in the back lot sort of wailing, like an animal. She's wailing and my fucking housemates are fighting about flags. Your shock will wear off.*

Michelle could feel a pull in the thinnest, gauziest layer of her denial, like a run in a pair of panty hose. Michelle stayed still for it, then shook it away. There was a vast, flat coldness underneath her denial. I Don't Want The Shock To Wear Off, she told Joey.

Maybe it won't. He shrugged. *Maybe it's up to you.* He pushed through the door with a jangle, leaving Michelle alone in the dust and light and walls of books.

Every day the same sequence of events occurred within Michelle. She woke up hungover, totally sick inside her body. An alcohol hangover was normal, had been normal for years and years, but something had changed recently and the alcohol hangovers had become more brutal. Michelle trudged through intense nausea on her walk to work, the rise and fall of potential vomit mimicking the motion of her legs as she plodded sturdily onward. She never puked, but she always wondered if perhaps she should.

Arriving at the bookstore she opened the door with her key and did what she was paid to do. She flicked on all the lights. She turned on the cash register. She positioned herself behind the wheeled wooden cart holding the ten-cent paperbacks, the books bought against your better judgment when you could no longer endure the performance of a haggling junkie. You bought the thing for a quarter then sold it out front for a dime. Michelle wondered how the store even stayed in business with such practices, she presumed the trade of first-edition Norman Mailers on the Internet was what paid her paltry paycheck.

The dime cart was terribly heavy, especially with Michelle so weakened from drinking. It would take her forever to push it out the door, books tumbling to the sidewalk—the sun, insistent and deadly, the torturing dictator of a third world country, shining on her, turning her cells against her with its radiation. Michelle would feel faint by the end of it. She would retreat into the kiosk and stick her head between her knees, her entire body whirling beyond her control, dizziness and nausea and intense dehydration, the dew of her sweat coating her skin clammily while her throat, so dry, caught on itself like Velcro, choking her. Weak from not eating, her nerves jagged with coffee, her eyes blurred, dulled from the brightness outside, tearing from allergies or something, who knows, who knows what was wrong with Michelle. Maybe she was dying. Everyone had cancer. Michelle had had little spots removed from her body years ago, a recipient of the free health care San Francisco gave to the poor. A doctor at the charity clinic had frozen the moles scattered across her skin and sliced them off with a sharp little tool. Michelle felt like a dumpstered vegetable, good enough if you just cut the rot away. She thought of Stitch, how Stitch should get it together and go to medical school, get paid for cutting people with sharp little razors. Mornings in the bookstore, her body gone psychedelic with sickness, Michelle wished someone would come and cut away the problem within her, whatever it was.

Sometimes she knew it was the alcohol. In the morning a thought competed with the distracting illness of Michelle's body and the blare of the alarm clock—Stop drinking. The thought throbbed at her temples as she plodded through the studio. Stop drinking stop drinking stop drinking. The chant bubbled up to her consciousness. Hmmmmmm, maybe she should stop drinking? It was an extreme thought, it gripped Michelle. It seemed sort of fun, like accepting a dare, like the clean slate of potential, a new school year begun, and Michelle, tricked out with a new pencil case clattering with Number 2s, is inspired to be the best student ever, ready to understand mathematics for the first time in her life.

That was one way to approach the thought Stop drinking stop drinking stop drinking. But if Michelle stopped drinking, what would she do? That's what Michelle did, she drank. She wrote, too—not so much right now but that was okay, that's what happened to writers, you had periods where you were just living. Michelle preferred to see her whole life as art, she liked to think that she was always a writer, always writing, even when she wasn't, even when she was just trying to get out the door in the morning without puking. Stop drinking stop drinking stop drinking. Okay, fine, Michelle placated the voice. She would not drink tonight, whatever night that was. She would not stop at the market on the way home. The Mayfair Market. Joey called it the Unfair Market. Then he started calling it the Unfair to Gays Market, even though they weren't, it was just funny. *Want anything from Unfair to Gays?* Michelle liked the succotash, corn and beans, light and fresh, that was usually something she could eat without getting sick. Cold food was more soothing than warm food. Warm food was like vomit. Once Michelle had seen Jon Cryer shopping in the dairy aisle at Unfair to Gays. Duckie from *Pretty in Pink*! Michelle had stared openly at the man as he moved past the yogurt and butter with a woman and a child, his family. Duckie! Hollywood was so magical.

By the time Michelle's shift at work ended she would inevitably feel better. She would feel better and she would be embarrassed at how dramatic she had felt earlier, with the stop drinking stop drinking stop drinking. Why was she so extreme all the time, Jesus. So hysterical. A little hangover and it's, Oh, don't ever drink again. A glass of wine sounded amazing, why would she deprive herself of a glass of wine after a day of work, people in Europe drank wine all day, their children drank wine, Michelle was screwed up from being an American, Americans didn't know how to do anything properly, Michelle would have a European glass of wine and everything would be fine. Tonight she would not stay up all night, finishing the bottle, calling in another from the Pink Dot, no way would she do that. She would not be sick again in the morning, she would stroll into work strong and healthy, her heart in better shape, actually, from the antioxidant benefits culled from a glass of natural wine, from grapes, fruit, something that still managed to grow in the toxic soil of their planet, Michelle saluted the grape and its hardy, twirling vines. Nothing seemed as alcoholic as quitting drinking. That was one thing that alcoholics did for sure.

Michelle stopped at the Unfair and picked up a bloated jug of wine, one meant for a large Italian family to sip over a Sunday dinner. She brought it home and consumed the entirety of it. Each time she considered stopping—That's it, that was the last glass, time to go to bed—a feeling like heartbreak washed through her body. It was the saddest feeling in the world, the feeling of going to bed, of ending the drinking. You can drink again tomorrow, Michelle promised herself. Go to bed. But she couldn't.

In the morning she trod to work, stop drinking stop drinking stop drinking. The black wave of vomit stirring inside her commanded she pause in the middle of the sidewalk to lean against a street sign. The metal pole burned her bare arm but it didn't even register. Michelle felt crazy. How was she sick like this again? How had she stayed up until four in the morning—again—when she had not wanted to do such a thing? She did not want to stop at the Unfair to Gays after work, but she felt scared. She knew that she would. She knew that she would forget how she felt right then, dizzy and trembling on a burning street sign, she would forget all about it, and the lure of the wine would somehow seem the only sane impulse. Michelle fished in her army bag for a pen. She pulled out a receipt from the bottom of the sack and kneeling on the ground she wrote, *YOU WILL WANT TO BUY WINE DO NOT BUY WINE REMEMBER HOW YOU FEEL RIGHT NOW DO NOT BUY WINE DO NOT BUY WINE.* She folded the note and put it in the front pocket of her bag, where important things like house keys and Chap-Stick were stored. Then she took the pen and wrote *NOTE* on her knuckles, a letter on each finger.

Michelle thought of a Dean Koontz paperback, the kind she purchased from junkies for a quarter. It had been in Michelle's house growing up, Wendy was a voracious consumer of the sort of mass-market horror novels you could buy at Walgreens. Stephen King, Dean Koontz, and books by women in which the protagonist's handsome new husband turned out to be a serial killer. In this Dean Koontz book, teenagers were being diabolically controlled via waves that were broadcast through their town. The teenagers would band together outside the reach of the waves and make plans to save themselves, but once they got home the power of the waves lulled them and they did nothing. It was such a creepy story. It was Michelle's story. One of the teens wrote themselves a note in a moment of lucidity, only to destroy it once under the influence of the brainwashing waves again. At the bookstore that day, Michelle flushed her note down the toilet. It had made her feel crazy to see it, the desperate, capitalized handwriting, how the force of the pen had torn through the receipt, the word *NOTE* inked on her fingers that all the annoying junkies kept asking about. In the bathroom she rubbed the word from her skin with antibacterial soap, then ripped up the note and sprinkled it into the toilet. After work she bought a bottle of wine.

If I take Lu out of the story, how does Michelle get sober? Michelle wondered. If there is no Lu to witness Michelle's degradation, to watch Michelle jump out of the car at the red light by the freeway, run onto the freeway's shrubby shoulder, and sit there under a bush, smoking, gazing down at the red lights of the passing cars blurred with her tears. Michelle couldn't even remember what they were fighting about, she never could, and this put Michelle at a terrible disadvantage. As long as she was drunk she would lose every fight with Lu, she had no comeback for *You were drunk*. Did Michelle get sober in order to win their arguments?

If I take Lu out of the story there is no one to chase Michelle down when she runs away to the Frolic Room. You wouldn't even be able to call it running away because there'd be no one to run away from. Michelle would just be another alcoholic warming a barstool in one of Bukowski's old haunts, staring at a mural of dead Hollywood stars, trying to figure out who was who, but it was such a bad mural. Only Marilyn in her famous white dress was for certain. If Michelle couldn't run away then she couldn't be found. The bartender would never look at Michelle and say, *Someone on the phone wants to talk to the girl with blue hair. Are you here or not?*

If not Lu, then who would have come to find Michelle in the bar where she drank wine with some new friends? Who would have yelled, *Do these people even know that you have a problem? That you are trying not to drink?* Who would have convinced her to go home, still in the grip of fine, she was fine, it was fine for her to drink some wine—only to wake up in the morning full of despair. How had she gone and drunk again when she had sworn she wouldn't? She must be crazy. If Lu wasn't there to show her this insanity, how would she ever know something was wrong? How would Michelle ever get better?

12

You really can't tell half the story. People wrap around each other like trees planted so close that they fuse together. If something happens they both fall. Then you're just this busted tree walking around. Learning how to think again, learning how to be. It's like you had a stroke. In an AA meeting where Michelle had shared that she was exiting an eight-year relationship, an old woman had held her hand and said, *It's like a death*, and contorted her face in understanding. Because the woman was old Michelle presumed she had known death personally and was grateful for her condolences. Michelle felt like a part of her *had* died, the part that believed in love.

Michelle had always felt annoyance at the dramatics of jilted people claiming to have given up on love. It sounded so silly. No one gave up on love. Who could resist its pull? But now Michelle got it. It wasn't a pose. She had pulled back the curtain and found nothing. No forever, no loyalty, nothing to stake a life on. She supposed this is what it had been like for Andy. Andy had really loved her, and Michelle had shat upon that devotion. Understanding for the first time Andy's pain, wondering if she was perhaps a sociopath for it having taken so long, Michelle guessed she deserved it. She deserved to have the illusion of love ripped from her heart. Everyone did.

13 Most days at the bookstore Michelle worked alone, but Beatrice or her husband could pop in at any minute, so she could never really relax into slacking off the way she would have liked to. She would select a book that looked interesting, sit on a ladder, and try to look like she was just checking what shelf it should be placed on. This prevented her from really being consumed by the story the way she liked, but the husband especially was always looking for proof that Michelle was not earning her seven dollars an hour, and so she had to be vigilant. It also made it hard to steal books. Michelle had no qualms about stealing from the bookstore. Indeed she felt like she was doing them a favor by taking some of the dead weight of inventory off their hands. She never stole money and she didn't steal first editions or anything bound for eBay. She just clipped titles she wanted to read but would never be able to really get into while balancing on a ladder at work. Besides reading and stealing, Michelle also enjoyed masturbating in the bathroom and talking on the telephone long-distance to her moms—but all these activities were risky. On that day, the second day of the end of the world, the husband came in unannounced. He was furious about permit parking.

You know what will happen? he raged, stuffed in the kiosk behind the counter, making it impossible for Michelle to retain her post there. *The businesses will die. All of them will die. People won't come here if they can't park.*

Well, The Businesses Are Going To Die, Michelle said. Right? She said this for herself more than the husband. It seemed she should be making an attempt to lift herself out of shock, but it was hard because so many other people were also in shock, and Michelle was finding it creepily easy to just carry through her day, ringing up records and purchasing paperbacks from junkies as if they hadn't just officially entered the End Times.

The husband looked at her, first blank and then offended. *We cannot lose our humanity because of what has happened*, he proclaimed. *We cannot aid in the unraveling of civilization. Do you want to spend the next year living like a dog? Because people will. People will die like dogs, you can go join them.* The husband pointed to the door with such a fierce look on his face Michelle wondered if she was being fired. *I refuse to die like a dog. I refuse to allow my world to go to hell because of this. We have built this neighborhood into the thriving commercial strip it is today through hard work and cooperation and I am not going to let permit parking destroy it, even if we're all going to be dead in a year.* He clutched at his heart as acidic bile rose inside him like molten lava. *Especially if we are going to be dead. How do you want to spend your next twelve months, Rochelle?*

Michelle, Michelle corrected him. She wasn't mad, she didn't know his name either. He was her boss. How did

Michelle want to spend the next twelve months? She hated questions like that. She hated having to have a plan, ever. She knew that any plan she came up with would be a little pathetic. She'd rather keep it open, invite the randomness of the universe to toy with her. I'll See Where Life Takes Me, she said airily.

The boss snorted. *That's imbecilic. You should know what you want. If this turn of events has a silver lining it is that people will have to know what they want. Why don't you know what you want?*

What Do You Want? Michelle asked, defensive. She had never talked to this man for more than two minutes and now they were having a deep, existential fight. And Michelle had started it.

I am living the life of my dreams, he said grandly, stretching his arms out toward the store. *I built this place, every little shelf. I filled it with books and records. I make my living transferring works of art between people who love art, who love to read books and hear music. I help recycle. I have my woman.* Michelle blanched. *We have no children, nothing bringing us down, no drain on our resources. This is everything I've ever wanted. And I won't let permit parking suck the vitality out of what I've created.* He brought his fist down on the counter, jostling some office supplies and a copy of Jayne Anne Phillips's *Black Tickets*.

Michelle wrote a book. Beatrice had crept into the store and hovered off to the side, listening to her husband's grand pronouncements. The skin beneath her eyes was so pale Michelle could see tiny veins ferrying blue blood around her face. The husband turned.

Oh yeah? Maybe you want to do that, then. Maybe you want to write another book? Or maybe a screenplay?

I Was Going To, Michelle said slowly, But Now I'm Not

Sure It Would Be Worth It. It's Hard To Write A Book. It Might Take Me A While And Then You Have To Find A Publisher—

Your agent does that, doesn't he? He does all that for you?

I Don't Have An Agent, Michelle said.

Well, there's one thing you can do, find an agent. This town's crawling with them. They come in here all the time, I'll introduce you.

Michelle shrugged. She hated when people acted like there were simple solutions to the huge problems of her life. The husband wasn't just going to introduce her to an agent. And even if he did she'd still have to write the book, which would take her forever, and then it took so long for books to come out once they're finished, by the time the thing got published the world would have been pulped. It was useless.

Don't you want to write for the joy of it, the joy of writing?

Michelle used to. Back when she had first moved to San Francisco, when she'd had no friends. She was so grateful to have something that felt meaningful and filled up her nights. She would sit alone in bars and coffee shops writing, writing. But things were different now. There were stakes at stake. Getting published changed things. Her writing wasn't a fuck you to her job, it had become her job, one that paid even worse than her day job but was somehow more important. Michelle tried to explain this to the husband but felt embarrassed. It made her sound like she thought she was so important, and she wasn't. She wasn't important *at all*.

I'm a writer, the husband proclaimed. He sounded like he was trying on the declaration and liked how it fit. It brought a smile to his bearded face. *I wrote a letter to the editor, about permit parking. And when I wrote it, I'll tell you, honestly—I did not think they would publish it. I wasn't thinking of it being good, I wasn't thinking like that at all, I was just in that place of flow. I was expressing my feelings and it felt right. And I think that came through because the editor published it. He even asked me to write an op-ed about it! You just have to find that flow and do the work for the joy of it. That's another silver lining.* He stroked his beard meditatively. *There won't be any time for things to pay off so you'll have to only do things because you love them. Here.* He pulled a scrap of scratch paper from under the register. *Here, make a list. I love lists. They're so helpful. Make a list of five things you want to do in the next year. Think about it.*

Michelle allowed the pen to be shoved into her fingers. She stared at the red piece of paper. She procrastinated by scratching out the numbers one through five.

1. Have sex with Matt Dillon.

The husband looked at her with raised eyebrows. His eyebrows were wild, the hairs looked like they were having a party.

You're serious? I want you to take this seriously.

Mmm-hmmm. Michelle chewed the pen.

We can help you with that, he comes in here—Beatrice, doesn't Matt come in here all the time?

Oh, yes.

Michelle wants to have sex with him. He studied Michelle. *I thought you were a lesbian?* Michelle shrugged. *Okay, okay, continue,* the husband prodded.

2. Stop drinking.

3. Leave the country.
4. Meditate.
5. Write something good.

The husband analyzed Michelle's list. *I see you have a negative,* he observed. *"Stop" drinking. Try to reframe that in a positive way.*

Nearby, Beatrice leaned on a pile of books, her elbows jammed into the top paperback, the whole stack trembling with her breath. She looked at her husband adoringly. Michelle realized they were in love. She had assumed they were just resigned to each other.

Paul used to be a counselor, Beatrice said dreamily, brushing moisture from her cheek.

Paul winked at his wife, a twitch that brought the unruly tuft of his eyebrow in contact with the brush of his mustache. *I did. But then I had an acid trip and realized that people need to find their own way. It isn't for me to say what experiences are healthy or not healthy. Maybe it's beneficial for a soul to, for instance, sink into depression and end their life. They could take that experience into their next life and become a healer, how do I know? The picture is much, much bigger than we think it is. Anyway, back to you.*

This game, or whatever it was, made Michelle uneasy. It was absolutely the opposite of how she lived her life. Michelle didn't have goals or plans or wants or needs. The chances of them coming her way were slim, and then what? Then you were a loser. If you just stayed open and rolled with things you could be a champ. Plans led to disappointment, to regret, to chain-smoking and sadness. Michelle refused to be tragic. She would resist having plans.

Paul pointed at number two. *How about "I want to be sober"?*

I Don't Want That, Michelle gulped and shuddered. That's Not What I Wrote.

You wrote you want to stop drinking, it's a negative. What's the positive? I want to be sober. You want to be sober.

No, No, No Way, Michelle said. I Just Want To Stop Drinking The Way That I Do. I Want To Drink Differently.

Like how?

I Want To Not Get Drunk? Michelle said.

Okay, well, why do you drink, when you drink?

To Get Drunk, Michelle said.

Hmmm, you want to stop drinking to get drunk. But you drink to become drunk. So you want to continue to drink why?

You Know, Just To Be Able To Drink.

For what reason? How often do you drink? Do you drink every night?

Yeah.

And do you get drunk every night?

Yeah.

And how often would you like to drink, ideally?

Michelle shrugged in a full-body jerk, like Paul's hands were clamped onto her shoulders and she was trying to throw him off. I Don't Know. I Don't Want It To Be Such A Big Deal. I Want To Drink Whenever I Want To Drink And Not Have It Be Such A Big Deal. I Don't Want To Be Sober.

And the store became full with the shrill sounds of alarms then, of ambulances and fire engines tearing down the street, coming to a halt outside the gates of the Scientology Celebrity Centre. The gates were long and iron and very majestic, the trio could see it through the front window. More vehicles came, and then more and more again. Ambulances, mostly. Their sirens were unbearable. *Oh,* Beatrice expressed pain in her face, clamping her thin, spotted hands to her ears. Michelle took her list and crumpled it in her fist, tossed it in the basket. She didn't like seeing it there, red in the otherwise empty bin. She wanted it to not have ever existed. Outside in the street a maid was hysterical. She was waving her hands and screaming and crying, her body racked with sobs as if her crying were vomit, a deep heaving. EMTs took her to the side. Gurneys were being relayed from the compound. The street filled with clogged traffic. Cars honked. Ambulances pulled away only to be replaced by more. Smaller cars managed to scoot around the flashing spectacle, driving up onto the sidewalk and peeling off. One woman, her car too large, climbed out of it. She was crying too, not as terribly as the maid, more like Beatrice, her expression calm below the tears, her face wet as if she'd lifted her face from the sink while washing it. She threw her keys to the street and left her car. She walked away from the traffic, back in the direction she'd come. The car behind her couldn't accept this. It rammed into the abandoned vehicle, rammed it again.

Oh no, Beatrice said.

Not good, Paul agreed. *Not good, not good.*

The bookstore shook with the impact of the abandoned car being rammed through the French restaurant next door. The breaking glass sounded the way fireworks looked—a sparkling, bright explosion, slivers and shards pushed brilliantly into the air, a rain of tinkles growing lighter and fainter, a wind chime. Piles of books throughout the shop tumbled and slid, paperbacks and LPs skidding down the aisles. The shelves, crammed as they were, held together. Michelle and her bosses were ducked into themselves, as fetal as a person can go and still remain standing. In the silence left by the fall of glass, close enough to be heard above the constant ambulatory wail, a man yelled, *Fuck this! Fuck this!*

Oh, please don't let anyone be hurt, Beatrice prayed.

They don't open till dinner, Paul said. *How often do I complain about that, huh? How many times have I told Allan to start opening for lunch? What do I know. They could be dead now. I could be dead, I could have been sitting there eating a croque monsieur.*

They're so bad for your condition, Beatrice said.

You get my point, though. You can't listen to other people. *Remember that, Rochelle.*

Poor Judy, Beatrice sighed. *This is going to ruin her vigil.*

14 That night Judy spoke to Michelle for the first time. She came into the store as the sun was setting, the sky streaked with orange and purple, glowing down on the silhouetted neighborhood, the Scientology Celebrity Centre a haunted mansion in the darkness. The ambulances outside the gates had been replaced by news vans. Dishes of light angled at news people, stylists stood by with blotting papers and aluminum cans of hair spray.

Michelle had been collecting bits of gossip from shoppers and junkies as the sun sank. Tom Cruise had killed himself. Michelle's childhood love, John Travolta— Vinnie Barbarino and Danny Zuko, gone bulky and grotesque with the onset of manhood—he too had offed himself, right across the street from where she had stood, leafing through photo books of natural wonders. Michelle thought back to playing *Grease* with Kyle as children, both of them fighting over who got to be Sandy, tugging the neckline of their T-shirts over their shoulders, *Tell me about it . . . stud,* mashing an invisible cigarette into the ground with the tip of their invisible stiletto sandals, their bony hips swinging. Each sibling was in love with John Travolta. Michelle could never have imagined that the man's life would come to its terminus across the street from where she stood, twenty-eight years old, the world beginning its ending around her.

Giovanni Ribisi and Jason Lee, dead. Kirstie Alley and Juliette Lewis. Karen Black! The Presley women! Michelle started to feel an antsy excitement, as if these famous people were just chilling in the garden across the street, not getting rolled out on stretchers. She wanted to see. But did she? Did she want to see Linda Blair dead from poison, a corpse on a cot? This was not how Michelle had wanted her celebrity sightings to happen. She regretted frittering away her brief glimpses of Gwen Stefani and Marilyn Manson.

Julia Migenes. Judy shook her head as she entered the shop, upset.

Who Is That? Michelle asked.

An opera singer. Marvelous, just marvelous. The paramedics rolled her out a moment ago. It is awful over there, awful. Judy shuddered. *But all the more reason to keep our vigil,* she said, determined. She heaved her tote from her shoulder onto the counter, obscuring a paperback, *Baby Driver* by Jan Kerouac, Jack Kerouac's junkie, hooker, memoir-writing daughter. Like her father she was already dead and would be spared this time of celebrity mass suicides. Judy dug from her tote a bunch of waxy white candles and a stack of shiny paper ashtrays. She laid them before Michelle.

So, you have scissors? Michelle nodded. *Well, let me see, then.* Michelle pulled a pair of scissors from under the register. Judy took them up, snipped a slit into the ashtray and jammed a candle through it. *Voila! Catches the wax. Won't burn your hands. Do as many as you can.* She lifted her tote back onto her shoulder. *I'll be back in a half hour or so. Want to check in on La Bébête. Allan was crying.* Judy's voice grew hushed. *Crying! European men are just different. More sensitive. He sat inside that car and just cried. No one has come to help him, not with the suicides across the street. There's only so many resources. I'm going to help him sweep up some of the glass so he can try to open tonight.*

They're Going To Open? Michelle asked. With All This? She waved a blunt candle at the carnage across the street.

Oh, well, he'll get a lot of business tonight I think, between the vigil and the suicides. That car that got knocked through the window was a convertible, I told him he should just pull the top back and let people sit there. Won't that be a hoot? She nodded at the craft supplies. *Half hour. Do what you can.*

Judy, I'm Working.

Judy waved her hand. *I spoke to Beatrice, she told me I could leave it with you. Just pitch in, why don't you?*

Michelle lifted the scissors and petulantly stabbed a hole into an ashtray. *Oh!* Judy dug a roll of ribbon from her tote. She flung the wheel of it to Michelle, red, white, and blue stripes. *And then you tie a bit of ribbon at the base, like so. Sweet, right? One half hour.* Judy jingled out of the shop. Michelle rammed a candle through the gouged ashtray.

15 First there were only a few people at the vigil, but soon there were many. Michelle watched the sidewalk clog outside the bookstore. People held cameras, took pictures of the car lodged in the French bistro's facade. Diners reclined inside the vehicle, the top cranked down per Judy's suggestion. They held heavy-bottomed glasses of wine in their hands, their fingers lacing the stem, they raised the sloshing goblets at the cameras and smiled, their lips purple. Candles flickered everywhere, each one ornamented with red, white, and blue bows tied by Michelle's nimble fingers.

The strip's restaurants emptied onto the sidewalk and diners hoisted their drinks into the air, like it was New Orleans and a great procession was passing by. Someone held a poster-board globe with HONK FOR EARTH painted on it, cars rode by, honking. When cars honked, everyone cheered. Judy dashed up and down the strip, weaving through the people, handing out the candles. Beatrice stopped by the bookstore, holding a glass Coke bottle plugged with a candle. She and Paul had gotten good seats—not at the French bistro, whose tragedy had lent it novelty, but at the Italian joint down the street. They kept checking in to make sure the bookshop hadn't been set upon by looters. Beatrice placed the Coke bottle on the dime paperback cart, the melting wax blobbing around the ribbon.

Michelle, keep an eye on that? Make sure it doesn't get knocked over and set the books on fire.

The bookstore was empty. Michelle lingered in the doorway, by the dime cart and its burning candle, observing the strip. A man dressed as Uncle Sam was jogging in the gutter, pumping his hands in the air like a mascot at a sporting event, inciting the crowd to cheers. Everyone seemed drunk. A young kid, good-looking, no shirt on, held a large cloth peace flag above his head as he ran laps around the block, the fabric rippling in the wind above his rippled torso. The crowd loved it. A Boy Scout troop arrived and stood across the street from the drunkards, singing patriotic songs paces away from the news crews still covering the celebrity suicides. A couple of news cameras crossed the street, shifting their focus to the vigil. Was the vigil for the fallen celebrities? *No, no,* Judy said, offended. She did not want her event getting appropriated.

Inconsolable Tom Cruise fans had arrived and attempted to assemble an altar at the Celebrity Centre's gates, arranging candles and photos and iconic relics—a pair of Ray Bans, a cocktail shaker. They were quickly brushed away. It had not yet been announced that Tom Cruise was dead, it was all rumor and speculation. The fans were grief maddened, holding above their heads homemade collages of the actor in his many roles—*Jerry Maguire, Top Gun, Legend.*

The cops guarding the Celebrity Centre pushed the

stricken fans across the street to the vigil, where Judy pushed them back toward the Celebrity Centre. *This is not a vigil for Tom Cruise!* Judy shouted at the fans, the news cameras trained on her. *This is a vigil for the planet! Our planet! Planet earth!* Michelle's hand flew to her mouth as she watched Judy rip a *Vanilla Sky* poster from someone's hands and dip the edge of it into her vigil candle. She tossed the flaming effigy into the gutter.

Whoa, uh-oh! yelled the topless boy with the peace flag. There was no way around the conflagration but into oncoming traffic. He jogged in place, the flag sinking limply onto his head. Judy flung her candle onto the poster and stormed down the street, enraged.

A rebel Boy Scout climbed onto the bus shelter across the street and began chanting, *USA! USA!* The crowd roared its approval. A fire truck cruised by and the crowd howled anew, as if the truck were but the latest float in a parade. The fireman, confused, honked his horn in acknowledgment of the salute, and the crowd howled once more, hoisting their drinks to the noise. Michelle noticed many people crying. Women and men. Insensitive American men, in tears. People waved flags, American flags and peace flags.

Revelers asked Michelle where they could get candles. A Little Gray Lady. Michelle craned her neck to search for Judy. I Think She Lost Her Mind And Left. She gave away the Coke bottle candle.

A blond girl walked by on a cell phone. *Yeah, it's really awesome, you should come down, it's awesome . . .* A young golf punk from her apartment building approached, his pristine spikes standing full mast atop his head.

We were up on the roof, you should see it from there! he crowed. *You should come up with us, drink some beers.*

Can't, Michelle thumbed back toward the bookstore. *Working.*

Oh. The punk looked uncomfortable, turned away as if Michelle had revealed a great shame. *You work here? Well, see ya.* He moved into the crowd. Michelle felt a sudden embarrassment at her lack of embarrassment at having this job. She didn't even know enough to know what she should be ashamed about in life. She was starting at subzero, she would never scramble out in a year.

The same pickup truck kept circling the block until finally the topless boy with the peace flag hopped onto the bed and a cheer rang through the crowd. Bystanders leaped from the curb and joined him. Now it truly was a parade. The strangers clutched at each other in the back of the pickup, unbalanced from the beers they still carried or the bumpy motion of the truck or both. They arranged themselves around flag boy, smack in the middle, his flag lifted above him like a kite hoping to catch some wind. *It looks like* Les Misérables, Michelle overheard the comment of a passing gay man.

Beatrice stopped by again, asking if Michelle would like to take a walk down the block.

I'm Okay, Michelle assured her boss.

Go have a look, Beatrice insisted. *There's nothing to do here.*

Michelle made it as far as the bar and grill a few doors down, the crowd growing thicker and yeastier around her as she cleaved into the heart of it. She turned and shoved her way back to the bookstore, dodging open flames and sloshing pint glasses. *Too Overwhelming,* she told Beatrice, and resumed her post in the kiosk. A tall, red-faced man burst through the glass doors.

How much is that book? he demanded. *The Australia book? You know they just blew up the Sydney Opera House?* He shook a handheld communication device at Michelle. *It just hap-pened. How much for the book? Australia is being decimated. You know the whole country was founded by criminals, it's like some time-coded genetic switch got flipped on and they're blow-ing everything up! How much for it?*

It's Not For Sale, Michelle said. She hated the man. It's Not For Sale. It's A Memorial.

Oh. He deflated. His lower lip sagged down in a pout. *But I want it,* he whined.

Michelle shrugged. I Just Work Here.

No, really, he pushed. *I want to buy it and then walk around and have everyone out there sign it, to commemorate the evening.*

You're Kidding, Michelle said, wishing Joey were there. Where was Joey? Joey would love this. Like A Yearbook?

Exactly! The man brightened, hopeful. *Like a souvenir.*

You Got To Talk To The Boss, Michelle said. I Can't Help You.

The man squinted his bloodshot eyes at her. *You just could've had a really great sale,* he snapped, and stormed away from the kiosk. He paused at the door and dunked his hand into the display window, grabbing the Australia book and pushing back into the throng, the volume held tightly to his chest. Michelle scanned the kiosk for a replacement for the window display. A book of black-and-white photo-graphs from the punk years, *No Future,* the title like a blast of spray paint across the cover. She slid it into the plastic book prop where the Australia book once sat.

That's what's wrong with this country, a voice shot out of nowhere. *Maybe the whole planet.* Michelle craned her head around. There was a longhair crouched down in the sci-fi stack, sitting on the floor by the pile of *Star Trek* paperbacks. Long hair and oversized pervert eyeglasses. *They think it's a goddamn sporting event out there,* he grumbled. *This is precisely why everyone hates us. America. What's with the flags, already?*

Yes, Michelle said, grateful for the sudden presence of someone she agreed with. She shook her head up and down, her fried blue hair bobbing in stiff waves around her head. She wanted to tell him he could pocket a few of the *Star Trek* books and she would look the other way, but he seemed so moral she wasn't sure how he'd take it, so she just gave him a lot of room instead.

16 In the morning a terrible sound woke Michelle up on her futon. A blast and a howl and another blast and a thump. Michelle lay in bed, a warm dread moving through her body. The noises were so loud Michelle could still feel their echoes clotting her ears like cotton. She kneeled on her futon and tugged the worn string that lifted the blinds. Behold the rottweiler. Behold the mess of it, flung around the apartment. Behind him sprawled the man, behold his dreads fanned across the floor, his face gone. There was his gun. Michelle immediately wanted it.

Uh-oh. Is this how shit went nuts? When people start hoarding the guns of the suicided? Michelle had once read the phrase *The way you do anything is the way you do everything* inside a Buddhism book on the Self-Help shelves of the bookstore back in San Francisco. It had resonated with her. The way she did anything was the way she did everything. She did everything sloppily, thoughtlessly, with anxiety. She did everything alcoholically, selfishly. The desire for the gun, the man's still-warm fingers draped across it on the floor, made Michelle ask herself questions. How did she want to spend the next year of her life? Did she want to live in fear? In fear of her neighbors, of other people, of humanity?

She did not want to live in fear. A gun could help her accomplish this. With a gun, she could afford to risk being kind to people. If she had misjudged their intentions she could simply kill them. Could she? Could she kill someone? Michelle's heart said yes. She could totally kill someone. Michelle had always known this about herself. Still, she was a good person. And she'd be a better person if she had a gun.

In the supply closet out in the hallway Michelle grabbed a ladder and dragged it back to her apartment. It was a new world, one in which extreme acts of bravery and self-protection should not be shrunk from. She hoisted the ladder between the two windows. Michelle had always known her apartment was much too close to her neighbor's, but it was still a surprise to see the ladder bridge the distance so easily. She began to climb onto it, but the slight wobble brought her gaze down to the darkened alley and she felt dizzy. She paused for a moment and breathed, her eyes closed. In every apocalypse movie she had ever seen, people needed guns. She began again her crawling and was soon at the window, puzzling how to leap into the apartment without landing on the dog. Michelle aimed for a square of linoleum sticky with blood and placed her bare foot upon it. She was in.

Michelle was fine. Fine with a pulse of sadness, with a hint of the unreal, but she was fine. Michelle recognized it to be, not the denial Joey had diagnosed her with, but a sort of fast-acting acceptance. Michelle was resilient and adaptable. Once again she was in the moment. A place people paid money to try to get to, people sat in silence for days at a time, people fasted to achieve a state that came naturally to Michelle. She was fortunate. She felt internally equipped for the end of the world. She would be one of the lucky ones.

Michelle lifted the warm gun from the linoleum, the faceless man's fingers sliding off it smoothly. Chekhov's gun, Michelle thought. What was that famous bit of writerly advice? If in the first act there is a pistol upon the wall then by the second act it should be fired? Was she going to have to use this thing? And also, was the safety on? Of course not, it had just killed its master. The man's face looked like strawberry rhubarb pie, chunky and reddish purple. Michelle did not know where the safety was, she would have to search guns on AOL. She would find an instructional video and learn how not to kill herself.

Bringing the gun back over the ladder was a challenge. She needed a backpack or something. The man's rickety cabinets were held shut with bungee cords, and in a fit of inspiration Michelle went for one. The cabinets flung open, spilling dog treats everywhere, a variety. The man had loved his dog. Michelle felt regret and respect for the both of them and wished they could each have a proper burial, but supposed such things weren't possible. The paramedics were busy carting off dead celebrities and the cops were all stationed outside the shops on Rodeo Drive, Melrose Avenue, and Hollywood Boulevard. Michelle had seen the pictures of them in full riot gear, guns drawn, looking ready to fight off zombies. Probably the man and his dog would begin to molder, and Michelle would become as accustomed to the smell of it as she had the stink of the cows on the highway.

Michelle looped Chekhov's gun through the bungee cord and hung it around her neck. It would be awful if she shot herself in the face as she crawled. Don't think don't think don't think. She thought that maybe guns were harder to shoot than you'd imagine. A friend in San Francisco had once gone to a shooting range with that gay self-defense group, the Pink Pistols. She'd returned with a sore, cramped finger, complaining how hard it had been to pull the trigger. Michelle crawled gingerly across the ladder and made it through her window. She removed her strange jewelry and laid it upon her kitchen table.

Immediately Michelle regretted not ransacking the man's apartment. What was she thinking? She could have picked his pocket. She could have walked around and checked if there was anything she needed. The man was dead, nothing was of any use to him. What were the ethics of the apocalypse? If Michelle was dead and some nice queer girls came upon her she hoped they would help themselves to whatever they needed. She supposed that even if they ate her, why should she care if she was dead already?

17 Michelle surfed the Internet. She'd learned everything she needed to learn about Chekhov's gun, which she had deduced was a .44 Magnum, which sounded like a a condom or brand of malt liquor. Michelle taught herself how to keep the thing locked. She practiced holding it in front of the bathroom mirror, aiming it at her reflection, squinting through the sight. After a bit the novelty of the gun wore off. Maybe she'd go shoot bottles with it, really learn how to handle it. But then, she didn't want to waste the bullets, either. The gun was not a toy.

On the Interweb, Michelle read about a new global phenomenon. Since the end of the world began, everyone had been having intensely sensory dreams of love affairs. Michelle was always a fan of such articles—dreams, the afterlife, hauntings. Anything supernatural fascinated her. And she had had one of these dreams, hadn't she? The boy in the garden. It wasn't often that Michelle found her own experience reflected in the media. She read on. Some nutjobs were beginning to believe that the dreams were real. That the people in them were real people, alive on the earth right now. The article showed a picture of a couple smiling together, they lived a city or two away and had run into each other at a Chili's. They couldn't believe it. They recognized one another and they recognized their love, and had gotten married right away and were psyched to spend the End Times together.

And there were more couples like this. People began posting ads in papers and on Craigslist. Dreamtime missed connections. People found one another. Sometimes they liked each other and sometimes they didn't. They hooked up or else were totally repulsed by the person, who looked nothing like they had in the dream. It left some people bitter and some people obsessed. Michelle opened a new tab and went over to Craigslist.

There were many In Search Of Dream Lover postings. Just reading them was like cracking open a book of psychedelic poetry. *The ceiling was spinning, we were on top of it and you had three eyes,* read one. *We were on a soap opera set and we were being filmed by Princess Diana,* another offered. *Leaves flew from a tree like butterflies and carried us over a hole in the ground.* Michelle really liked that one. Michelle wondered why no one had thought to use their dreams as personal ads before. Back when the world wasn't ending and dreams were just dreams. It would have been a great way to get a vibe on someone.

That night Michelle dreamed she was having sex with a boy inside a painting. The paint was not yet dry and their sex tossed them against oily dunes of it, it got all over their skin but they liked it. Michelle was on top and the boy was shuddering beneath her. The ends of the boy's long, greasy hair were clumped with wet color that slid across his cheeks and made him look wild. He was drunk but Michelle was not. Her body in the dream was a miracle, felt like a balsa-wood plane flung into the air. She rode him in a pool of paint glittered with sugar, the sprinkles clumped and hardened into little caverns, like the inside of a geode. The sparkle of it called to Michelle and she begged the boy to take her there, but no, the boy told her it would crumble, it was very delicate. Someday it was meant to be broken, but not by her. Michelle woke up.

The entire planet was dreaming of the lovers they would have had if only they had lived. In the dreams everyone was their highest self, everyone was present and their hearts were wide-open. It was a gift and a plea, from the planet perhaps, or from the universe, from the essence of life—no one knew enough about such things to be certain.

The planet is showing us how beautiful our lives will be if we stay here and work together to heal it, pleaded mystical people and ecologists on television. Psychologists deemed it an episode of mass hysteria on a scale previously unknown and commentators blamed the Internet and globalization for allowing it to spread so rapidly. Christians blamed the devil and deemed sleeping a sin, other religious people insisted it was God and that what was happening was a miracle.

Michelle found that it was possible to achieve a sort of lucidity in her dreams, causing the more fantastical elements to fall away in order to get closer to the truth of the affair. Dreaming that a creature had implanted a device in Michelle's head, causing dark thoughts and spontaneous orgasms, Michelle became lucid and found herself holding a cell phone, masturbating on a pillow while a girl on the other end told her filthy stories. Dreaming that her junk was an endless supply of pastries, a cornucopia of tiny cupcakes and fat croissants and cream puffs, Michelle became lucid and found herself in bed with a boy so skinny Michelle forced him to eat baked goods off her own naked tailbone. Dreaming her face was a popped balloon, bits of rubber and ribbon dangling from her mouth, she became lucid and found herself with a girl who had kissed her so passionately Michelle's lip had split against her tooth.

Michelle inspected shyly the bustling Internet world of dream missed connections. She found the anorexic pastry boy but he lived in Stockholm and his English was poor, and he was not even a boy but a girl, a fifteen-year-old girl who cut herself with razors and whose parents were poised to send her off to boarding school. The one who had busted her lip with a kiss, she too was a troubled teenager, with a bristling jet-black Mohawk and a Joy Division shirt hung on her slouched shoulders. The painter was a girl as well, also quite young. She emailed a photo of herself atop a horse, in a pair of jodhpurs and a velvet helmet, leaping over a small white fence. Michelle stopped emailing these children. She felt like a creep.

18 In the bookstore Michelle rang up a customer, a woman buying old feminist books from the 1970s, herbal healing and witchery. A book about periods. So many women didn't even get periods anymore, hadn't for years. Michelle's were spotty. The doctor at the free clinic in San Francisco had told them everything was fine, no growths, no cancers, that's just what was happening to some women. Michelle had had a dim concern about it, like what if she maybe wanted to have a baby someday, was she no longer able? But now that the world was ending it wasn't an issue. Michelle felt a sad kind of relief. She'd always felt torn about having a kid and wished the decision could somehow be made for her—that the people she slept with could accidentally knock her up or that she would become infertile, anything to cancel the seesaw of indecision in her mind. And now it was done. No babies, no planet, no future. Most everyone who had become pregnant was having an abortion and those who weren't looked disturbed. Michelle had glimpsed women too far along, committed to the things inside their giant bellies. They looked like animals at the pound, stuffed into too-small cages. A lot of pregnant women were killing themselves, but then a lot of people were killing themselves. Michelle didn't know if the percentage was any higher.

The lady left and Junkie Ted came in, the doorbell jangling with his entrance. Michelle reached into the waistband of the cutoff camouflage pants she'd sworn never again to wear in case she ran into Matt Dillon. Chekhov's gun was tucked into her underwear, little boy's briefs that sat snug on her body. She unclicked the safety and pointed.

Get The Fuck Out Of Here.

One of Michelle's unexpected talents in the world was appearing totally detached and together when really she was practically shitting herself with fear. She could be very, very inebriated and hardly anyone around her would gather that she was more than a bit tipsy. Her vision would be split into a blurry triad but her voice would leave her mouth clear and concise, not a slur to her words. And she could fake it even better sober, freeze the surge of adrenaline, becoming as cold as a gun-toting avatar in a video game.

Junkie Ted put his arms in the air as if Michelle was a cop busting him for possession. *What'd I ever do to you?* He kept coming toward her, in a ratty flannel and a pair of sweats.

Get The Fuck Out Of Here. I Am Not Buying Your Fucking Mariah Carey Cassingles, You Got No Money To Shop, You Got No Business In Here, Get The Fuck Out.

Ted's arms flopped to his sides. *Come on, now,* he whined. *You work in a fucking bookstore, what do you need a gun for? You gonna kill someone to protect a fucking roomful of used books? Huh? That's how you want to go out?*

Michelle honestly believed that she could shoot and

kill Ted and feel no remorse. She doubted the cops would care enough to come after her or that anyone's life would be ruined by his subtraction. That's not right—a little thought, her conscience she supposed, nagged at her. It wasn't, it wasn't right, and yet Michelle would be lying to herself if she acted like she couldn't do it. Or that doing it would traumatize her somehow. Didn't Ted threaten to kill black people and faggots?

I'm A Fucking Dyke, Michelle said. You Want To Fucking Kill Me? You Want To Fucking Kill Black People? You're Not Allowed In Here. You Know Who I Want To Fucking Kill? Junkies In Sweatpants. Get Out!

The door jangled open and Matt Dillon walked in. Fuck! Michelle said out loud. She looked down at her shitty camouflage pants. She could not believe it. Her camisole top was at least okay and the chains she had around her neck were tough and cute. Also, she hadn't drunk wine last night and couldn't underestimate the effect of a night of abstinence on her system. Her skin was brighter and the overall puff of her body had come down, like a molested soufflé.

Whoa, Matt Dillon said in that voice, that gruff voice, classic Matt Dillon, Dallas Winston, Rusty James. *What's going on in here?*

She's a fucking crazy dyke, Ted spat. *I just want to sell some fucking books, she pulls a gun on me. I know the owners, you know. I'll get you fired, good luck finding a job in the apocalypse, no one's hiring.*

I Will Fucking Shoot You. Michelle tried to stay on track with Ted, which was hard with Matt Dillon watching her. She blew her bangs, an indigo fringe of split ends, out of her face so she could see clearly. If You Don't Want To Die, Get The Fuck Out Of My Store And Don't Come Back.

Why don't you leave, man? Matt clapped sweaty Ted on the back. *C'mon. And don't be calling girls dykes, it's rude. C'mon.* Matt held the glass door open with a tinkle. *Here, guy.* Matt pulled out his wallet, a leather billfold tucked in the ass of his jeans. He pulled out some money and pushed it into Ted's hand. Ted took it.

I'm not scared of you! he spat at Michelle as he left the bookstore. Matt Dillon released the door and it swung shut with another tinkle. Michelle laid Chekhov's gun down, gently, on the counter. Her hands were shaking, which was embarrassing. A gun was a heavy thing to hold in front of you like that. Those minutes she had considered, really considered, killing Junkie Ted had felt like hours. She was grateful to Matt Dillon. She didn't think she really wanted to shoot anyone, no matter how cold and determined she could feel when she got scared. All the pent-up nerves threatened to burst through her eyes in the form of tears. Please God don't let me cry in front of Matt Dillon. Michelle believed in no such God, but had to clutch at something lest her face turn blotchy and snotty. She took a deep, rattling breath. She felt like there were two people inside her, regular Michelle and then the Michelle she was capable of becoming under extreme provocation. She wondered which was true. Matt lifted the gun.

You know how to use this thing? He clicked the safety back into place and turned it in his giant Matt Dillon hands.

I Haven't Shot It Yet, Michelle admitted.

You got a good stance, Matt admired. *I found you very believable. I would not have argued with you if you had pointed that thing at me.* He grinned a Matt Dillon grin at her. His mouth twitched up at the corners but something in his eyes stayed dark and hard, out of reach. He looks like a dog, Michelle thought, but in a good way. There was something of the puppy in his face. It was the sort of hot he was, dog hot.

You really a dyke? Matt Dillon asked. *Or was he just being an asshole?*

Michelle was torn. If she said she was a dyke would Matt Dillon like that? A lot of guys liked that. A lot of guys thought it was cool. This pissed off many of Michelle's queer female friends, but she always felt a sad sort of sympathy, a kinship with these guys. Michelle thought dykes were cool, too. Matt Dillon seemed like the sort of guy that thought dykes were cool. He was also the sort of guy that a lot of dykes would take a boycation with.

I Date Girls, Michelle said vaguely. I Date Guys Too.

Matt nodded. *Bisexual,* he said. *Cool. What's your name?*

Michelle.

Matt.

Michelle nodded. She didn't tell him that she fell in love with him as he took Kristy McNichol's virginity in *Little Darlings*, how the love was so real that when he died in a rain of bullets in *Over the Edge* she had cried, and when in *The Outsiders* he stabbed the pillow and was cruel to the nurse she had swooned, at both his stabbing and his cruelty, and how she had loved him in *Rumble Fish*, and how she would have gladly swum headlong into an IV drug habit alongside him in *Drugstore Cowboy*, how his squint had haunted her psyche all these years, that squint and that voice, and here he was squinting at her in the bright sun that came in through the bookshop windows, speaking to her in that voice, holding a gun, her gun, and the day took on the sharp focus of an apocalypse dream as she asked Matt Dillon if he wanted to make out with her. He shrugged, his grin deepening. *Sure. You want me to put the gun down?*

Making out with Matt Dillon was weird, because he was Matt Dillon and also because he was a man, and so tall he was able to lift Michelle with one of his famous arms and hug her to him there in the kiosk where he had joined her with two strides of his long man-legs. Michelle felt like Fay Wray in the palm of a monster, swaying with vertigo on a skyscraper's peak. Matt Dillon's face was so much bigger than hers, his mouth was bigger, she was lost in his kisses, the wet from his mouth smearing her cheeks, his tongue unruly, she tamed it a little and his kisses grew softer and Michelle's grew wilder until they were in sync, and he pushed himself against her there at the bookstore wall and she could feel him insistent against her baggy camo cutoffs, and Michelle marveled at how it should feel softer than a dildo, being flesh and all, but it didn't, it didn't feel softer at all. Matt held the gun against Michelle's temple as he fucked her, and Michelle felt like she was a dying little girl granted one last wish by a benevolent organization, and her wish had been to be in a movie with Matt Dillon and here they were in a sex scene, his prop pistol against her head. Michelle swooned so hard her head knocked over a pile of books. As he began his denouement, Matt lifted the gun above Michelle's head and fired it into a wall of books. Singed paper exploded around them as the recoil jerked Matt backward and then forward into Michelle's body. She sucked gluey shreds of binding into her mouth as she gasped. Matt placed the gun down gently atop a copy of *Portnoy's Complaint*.

There, he said. *Act Two.*

Michelle was straightening the mess of books behind the counter when Joey came in. The fact of her having just fucked Matt Dillon right there in the bookstore, the electric gossip of it clacked against her teeth, she wanted to spit it out. How her head had been on the pile of books she was currently stacking, how the pages of *Atlas Shrugged* had fluttered against her cheek as the actor heaved above her. Maybe it was too personal, though.

Joey started at the sight of the gun on the counter, bringing his hands to his cheeks like Macaulay Culkin.

Mary! he exclaimed. *What is with the firearms? Peace on earth! Good will toward men!*

Michelle stood upright and lifted the weapon. She considered tucking it back into her waistband where it felt so good, but not with all the bending and lifting. She slid it into her army bag beneath the counter.

I Pulled A Gun On Junkie Ted, she said. I Fucking Hate Him. I Am Not Dealing With Assholes Like Him Anymore. I'm Not Going To Walk Around Scared For The Rest Of The Year.

Mary! Joey repeated and shook his head, stunned.

What? Really, Though. Don't You Want A Gun?

Slippery slope, girl. Joey shook his head. *I want my soul. That is my Armageddon resolution. Hold on to your soul.*

I Don't Think This Compromises My Soul, Michelle lied.

Uh-huh. Joey looked at the disaster of books littering the kiosk. *What happened back here? I just straightened this out yesterday.*

I'm Sorry, Michelle said.

No, no, it's like the greatest thing ever. I am having so much anxiety today, cleaning really helps. Shoo, he flipped his wrist at Michelle, brushing her out from the cubicle. *Give me*

*space. Entertain me or something. Do you have any good apoc-
alypse anecdotes? Besides pulling a gun on Ted? Where did you
get a gun, even?*

I Stole It From My Neighbor After He Killed Himself.

Joey poked his head above the counter like Kilroy, visible
from the nose up. *You saw someone die?*

No. He Was Already Dead. He Killed Himself. But I Saw
His Body. And I Took His Gun.

Did you take anything else? Joey's voice had a lilt to it, like
there was actually only one right answer to this question.

No, Just The Gun. But Really, Do You Think It Would
Have Been Bad If I Had Taken His Wallet Or Something?

Yes, I do.

But Why? He's Dead. I Wouldn't Care If Someone Picked
My Pocket If I Died.

When you die, Joey said briskly, *it's all about the soul, girl.
The care of your soul. That's all that's gonna count. If there is
a bigger picture—and millions of cultures for millions of years
have seemed to think there is—your soul is all you're going to
have, so you better work on keeping it right, you know? I would
refrain from pickpocketing corpses.*

Michelle mulled it over. I Just Don't Think It Would Sully
My Soul, she maintained.

I don't know, Joey singsonged. A tower of books was
rising into view behind the counter. *Who's to say, who's to
say.* A pause in his movements, and the hollow rattle of the
aluminum trash bin. *Holy Mary, Mary,* Joey said. *What do
you make of this?* He aimed the barrel of the bin at Michelle,
pointing to Matt Dillon's condom, slumped in a nest of
receipts and the browned core of an apple.

19 Remember When I Was A Lesbian? Observing Michelle recalled as she watched herself slip into a bathroom with a boy in a sideways baseball hat. Where did all these men come from? This one was young, twenty two, though he had told her he was twenty-three, as if it made a difference. She slipped into the dream with ease. She was always lucid now, crossing over as if into another life, one as solidly real as the other.

Michelle and the boy were inside a brick building in the summertime on the East Coast of the United States of America. When Michelle looked out the window she could see dirty water—not apocalyptically dirty, just the regular soiled and oily water people had become accustomed to in the years before things became irreversible. Michelle saw a greasy harbor and clouds gone pink in the sky. The light was golden and she took a picture of it with her cell phone. It looked like an oil painting on the little screen. There was a long green bridge and beyond that a water tower sat upon a hill. That's where I'm from, Michelle thought. Michelle felt a great swell of nostalgia for her life—it had been hard and strange to belong to such a place, but looking out at the piers rotting in the scummy water she knew it to be beautiful, the sort of beauty an ugly place will teach you to appreciate.

Michelle was dreaming of an art party. The old brick building housed a gallery that was having an inappropriate-themed costume party, though from what Michelle could see no one had really bothered with a costume. Michelle had bought a pair of cheap white stretch pants at Target and created a very realistic blood stain on her ass, dripping deep-red paint into the crotch, truly striving to replicate the Rorschach patterns of menstrual blood. At the party everyone thought she had really gotten her period and was bleeding all over herself.

And You Didn't Try To Help Me Out? Thanks A Lot, Sisters, she scolded the lady artists gathered shamefaced around the inappropriate snack table, where tropical punch bobbed with plastic tampon applicators and a giant rubber rat sat in the center of the cheese plate.

The twenty-two-year-old was named Reinaldo. He was an artist and a break-dancer. His break-dancer name was Fly. Michelle wondered if he was the verb, the noun, or the adjective, but he was too drunk to ask. Reinaldo had been sampling the tampon punch bowl, plus drinking cans of Mexican beer. His pinned and reddened eyes were evidence of having smoked a blunt before even arriving at the party. Like everyone else, Reinaldo had thought Michelle's ass a sad catastrophe, missing the joke. He hung out with her anyway. His hair beneath the baseball hat was a Medusa of curls, his cheekbones could peel the skin from an apple. He gave Michelle flyers for a show of his artwork, at a café in Chelsea. Now Michelle knew she was dreaming. Chelsea, the city that had birthed her, hazed her, and chased her out did not have cafés or art of any sort. Well, someone had bronzed the garbage lying around the city square but that seemed more a cynical prank than art. What Artists Do You Like? she asked the boy, and he blushed and shrugged, looking extra stoned.

You know. Picasso, Dali . . . He trailed off. *All those Spanish cats. And, what's his name. M. C. Escher.*

Oh, said Michelle.

Reinaldo was special because he was from the same place she was from, and so few people were. The City of Chelsea was filled with people from the City of Chelsea, but Chelsea is where they stayed. Michelle had not encountered any since running away, and now here was this boy. His accent was Latin and New England at the same time. It dizzied her, made her feel like she'd been sipping from the tampon punch bowl.

Michelle had invited Reinaldo into the bathroom for a kiss, but soon they were naked on the floor, having sex like frenzied animals. This is so excellent! Michelle thought. Reinaldo the break-dancer was smacking her ass, grabbing her hair, and pulling her face down to his junk, which was surprisingly pretty. I'm so not grossed out by guys anymore, she dreamed wonderingly, taking it into her mouth. Nothing about Reinaldo's body bothered her. He was petite, his chest hairless, his muscles like the caramel ropes of a candy bar. She couldn't wait to text message all her friends and tell them how she'd gotten it on with a twenty-two-year-old break-dancer named Fly.

Outside, women were banging on the bathroom door. Bleed through your tampons, bitches, Michelle thought.

See if I care. Under the ruckus of their impatience was Reinaldo, calling her *girl*. As in, *C'mon, girl. C'mon, girl.* She felt like a gorgeous horse—enormous, magnificent, potentially unbroken. Reinaldo wanted to be slapped. *Harder*, he said, but Michelle couldn't get the angle, her hand on his ass. She hit him in the face, but that was too much. He liked when she bit him on his shoulder—*Leave a mark*. He was trying to make his ex-girlfriend jealous. They still lived together, neither knew what to do, who should move out. He would come home tonight with his shoulder chewed off. His penis, too, apparently. He had to move Michelle's mouth from his crotch, she was too rough. Michelle turned red and felt sick to her stomach—she gave bad head! It was because she was a lesbian, used to sucking silicone cock for show, just getting crazy with it, gnawing on it, gazing up at her lover with the wide-eyed stare of a pornographic Keane painting. But Reinaldo's cock was attached to his body forever, and she was hurting it.

I'm So Sorry, she said, I'm Usually A Lesbian. This did the double trick of honestly explaining her sexual deficiency and letting Reinaldo think he was King Casanova of the known universe, scoring with a lesbian, who cares if she can't suck cock, she was a lesbian, that is so hot, he couldn't wait to text message all his friends and tell them how he'd gotten it on with a thirty-seven-year-old lesbian in the gallery bathroom.

Thirty-Seven? Observing Michelle gasped in her sleep. Is That How Old I Am? That was really old. Michelle was faintly concerned about her white leggings and plastic stilettos and fucking young boys in bathrooms at the age of thirty-seven. Observing Michelle peered closely at her dream face, saw the marionette lines parenthesizing her mouth, her mouth which was clamped around her wrist in an effort not to yelp as Reinaldo tunneled his hand into her. Her entire face was furrowed with sex, but those lines between her eyebrows would remain.

Michelle and Reinaldo went up to the roof to smoke a cigarette and kiss some more. Reinaldo pointed at a pile of bricks on the shore and told her that's where his uncle died, he was a drunko. That's what he called the man, a drunko. Michelle thought, Oh no, Reinaldo's a drunko too, if he doesn't stop drinking he'll die like his uncle, I've got to save him, I've got to send him books of paintings by real artists—Balthus, Egon Schiele, Frida Fucking Kahlo, Takashi Murakami! Michelle realized her knowledge of art rivaled her knowledge of fellatio, but Reinaldo desperately needed help and no one was stepping up to give the break-dancer the education he required to get out of Chelsea. She resolved to send him packages. They kissed more and Reinaldo pulled more beer from his backpack, and downstairs in the art gallery the women were aghast at how strongly the bathroom smelled like pussy.

Reinaldo said, *You should write a story about me,* and Michelle laughed.

Okay.

I'll paint a picture of you. He paused, thought about his art studio in the back closet of the house he shared with his ex-girlfriend who was still pretty much his girlfriend, really, I mean, pretty much they were still together, even though it had been so slutty of her to text those photos—it wasn't like he hadn't wanted to hook up with people, too, he'd had opportunities, he was so cute, he knew he was cute, but he just wasn't a dog like that, and though he didn't know how he could keep her as a girlfriend when she'd been such a slut, Reinaldo knew he would, probably, and so Reinaldo knew he would not be able to paint a picture of Michelle, fifteen years older than him, splayed out naked on the bathroom floor. And he would not be able to paint the angry, annoyed fists smacking at the door or the way the bathroom became fogged with their sex, because he just wasn't that good of an artist. Michelle watched Reinaldo flick his cigarette down into the water where his uncle had died. She thought, I can't write this story. How could I write it? I don't write erotica.

What if I stayed in this dream forever? Michelle wondered. If the world exploded while she smoked a cigarette with Reinaldo, would she remain here, alive? Michelle could feel the pull of the other world upon her, and for a moment Reinaldo was gone and Michelle was alert to the reality of her lumpy futon, her smushed pillow that stank like scalp, the sun searing through the venetian blinds that couldn't ever be opened, not anymore, not with the dog and the man rotting in the heat right there. Michelle didn't want any of it, she wanted the summery New England warmth, the way the air was thick with water, and the dark harbor, the way it lay calm and flat against itself, not giving off clouds of poison, not scummed over with oil so clotted you could float on it, not bumpy with the trash of history. Michelle longed to see it more and so she entered the dream as though walking into a room and she found herself walking in sandals and a flirty dress, beside Reinaldo.

Reinaldo was stoned and drinking a purple Vitamin Water. He wore an enormous T-shirt stamped with the image of Che Guevara and his hair was disheveled. Reinaldo seemed disturbed and his problems swiftly became hers, the problem of having a live-in girlfriend and no place to bring a thirty-seven-year-old lesbian to have sex with. I'm not a lesbian, Observing Michelle thought. If she would live to become thirty-seven years old, Michelle would no longer be a lesbian. What, then, would happen to this twenty-seven-year-old lesbian Michelle, the one back in Los Angeles, drooling on her futon? How did that Michelle become this Michelle? Both Michelles were baffled. The ease and comfort Dreaming Michelle had with her desire for Reinaldo was remarkable. Isn't she afraid she won't be gay anymore? Observing Michelle wondered. Isn't she afraid that her friends will be upset, that people will feel betrayed, that they'll call her a straight girl and act like she'd been faking it for the past ten years, will they not like her book anymore, will they call her a phony, will she be abandoned, will lesbians try to make her feel gross for liking a man, men, will they try to make her feel stupid? Observing Michelle observed Dreaming Michelle's complete lack of anxiety in the situation and decided she would feel it for both of them. Her slumbering body twitched with worry.

We can go to this dude's house, but he's kind of crazy, Reinaldo halfheartedly suggested. Part of Michelle wanted to see the crazy dude and have sex in his run-down apartment, and she was proud of herself for overriding that part. She was so mature in her dream! Instead they hid from his girlfriend by climbing chain-link fences and navigating piers so rotten Reinaldo's sneaker pushed straight through the wood. The terrain—a landscape of soggy piers and crumbled buildings and wild, weedy trees—was off-limits, which made it beautiful and sexy. Standing in grass that sprung up to her neck, Reinaldo told Michelle she looked pretty. She paused to consider the tiled foundation of the bulldozed building they stood upon. Michelle could tell from how the tiles turned smaller and pink that they were in what used to be a bathroom.

Reinaldo put down his Che T-shirt to protect Michelle's back from the broken glass that scattered the tile, but they were too out in the open, anyone could see them—people hanging out the windows of the housing projects on the other side of the fence, bored, people on the booze cruise toodling around the harbor, drunk. They found a slab of stone hidden by collapsed piers, the wood soaked with seawater and furred with neon algae. Sober and armed with a condom, Reinaldo was a disappointment, his creative mania gone. He seemed to have forgotten that Michelle possessed a clitoris.

Arch your back, girl, arch your back, he kept saying in that wonderful voice, but Michelle found it as frustrating as yoga instruction—did arch your back mean she should round her spine or dip it? Michelle missed having sex with someone whose penis was store-bought, possessed no nerve endings, required nothing from her but the frenzied bucking of her own wild pleasure. When Reinaldo's cell phone rang he answered it, spoke Spanish, said *Puta.* Michelle wished she could understand him fully, but she was not in love in this dream and so could expect no magic from her mind. Reinaldo dropped the condom to the shore with all the other condoms, that slab beneath the fallen piers was something of a love hotel. Michelle pulled her dress back over her head.

Getting out of the place they'd snuck into was a challenge, the sun setting at their back a real threat. Michelle considered simply waking up. Would dreaming Reinaldo—presently a twelve-year-old boy asleep in Chelsea—awake suddenly from his first wet dream? Michelle stayed in the dream. Reinaldo was telling her how his family had escaped the war, how running from war was in his blood and he could feel it when he hopped a fence or trampled a jungle of weeds in his sneakers. Sometimes he wished for the apocalypse so he could experience that part of himself, surviving. They scaled a shaking wall of chain link and dropped onto the backside of the housing projects. Michelle found climbing the fence more physically exhilarating than the sex, but she didn't regret meeting Reinaldo or staying inside the dream with him. It was all one experience—the particular smell of the rotting wood, Boston like an enchanted city across the harbor, the spires of its office buildings flaunting themselves against the dusky sky, the smashed and ruined waterfront, the weeds run riot. It was a good dream. Reinaldo walked Michelle to the subway and went on to meet his friends at a street festival. Michelle was not invited. His girlfriend/not-girlfriend would be there.

I'll tell her I was eating oysters, Reinaldo smiled, and sniffed his fingers. Michelle slipped a token into a turnstile.

You're Twelve Years Old, she told him. You're A Boy. Wake Up. Reinaldo's face held confusion, then a swirl of recognition even more confusing, and then it shimmered like the harbor waters and was gone.

20 The bookstore shelves emptied as Michelle allowed shoplifters to shoplift. At first she had tried to stop them, even waved her gun at one but the woman had called her bluff and began hurling paperbacks at her. Michelle tucked the gun back into the waist of her cutoffs and allowed the woman to ransack the place. She was disappointed in herself for caring but sometimes the chaos bugged her out. She appreciated Joey, who ran an ever-tighter ship in the shadow of the world's end. The bookstore was cleaner than it had ever been.

Beatrice and Paul hardly came in anymore, preferring instead to sleep. Apparently the couple had found a way to sync their dreams and experience, together, adventures in a wonderful world. They hiked into pine forests and sat side by side on the edge of a smoking Hawaiian volcano, eating shave ice. They experimented with herbal sleeping remedies, testing for a dosage that allowed them to sleep long hours without degrading the quality of the dreams. They were like drug addicts, Michelle thought resentfully. She shared her analogy with Joey.

It's Like They're On Heroin, she snipped. On The Nod, Having Visions. It's Fucking Weird. It's Sad.

Joey considered. *No*, he said, *They're just dreams. You know, like the ones everyone's having. You're having them, right?*

Michelle nodded. She shared with Joey the story of the painter, the boy in the garden.

Girl! Joey high-fived her. *The imagination you got! I just keep sucking dick, sucking dick, sucking dick. I swear.* He fanned himself with a copy of *Howl. It's a good time, though.*

Joey hasn't figured it out, Michelle thought. Nor had she. Apparently, he'd been destined to a lifetime of fellatio. Michelle had been destined to a lifetime of casual sex with teenage girls who grew up to become transgender men. And Beatrice and Paul, their love was real and lasting. They were destined to a lifetime with each other. Michelle burned with a quiet jealousy. It really was like her employers were on heroin, which made Michelle wish she were on heroin, too. Michelle remembered the feel of it inside her body, side by side with Lu. She didn't care if the love had been real or fake, the chemical reaction synthetic opiates or organic dopamine, she wanted those feelings again. She thought about Andy and the softer feelings of safety she inspired—that was oxytocin, wasn't it? The cuddle hormone that makes moms love their babies. Michelle wanted a dopamine/oxytocin IV drip, or, at the very least, another visit from Matt Dillon. With fresh certainty Michelle realized there was no such thing as love. It was all a quilt of sexual compulsion, unmet childhood needs, and brain chemistry. For the first time, Michelle felt glad that the world was ending. Without the illusion of love, it was no good place to be.

This is my mother's favorite song. Michelle hadn't heard the jingle of the door opening. Patti Smith blared on the stereo behind her and Diane di Prima's *Loba* was clutched in her hands, a good combination. She pulled herself out from the world of vessels and prostitutes and wolf-ladies. A young girl, barely teenage, stood at the counter, a sweet smile on her face. Her brown hair fluffed past her shoulders, held back from her freckled cheeks with a wide headband. Little earrings sparkled in her earlobes. Patti Smith crooned around them, *Little sister, the sky is falling. I don't mind, I don't mind.*

Your Mother Must Be Cool, Michelle said.

She's not, the girl said. Her lips were pushed together as if biting back impatience. Something lumped beside her on the floor, a giant duffle bag. A runaway. What must it be like to be a runaway at the start of the apocalypse? Michelle felt the impulse to help—if the girl was tough enough to clean away the rotting body of the neighbor and his rottweiler, maybe she could have that apartment. But helping a runaway had to be like helping any stray, but worse. Once helped, they would return again and again, your charge. Michelle couldn't handle it. She didn't want to be this girl's apocalypse mom. She felt the hard moon inside her rising to eclipse her heart.

What Do You Want? she asked.

I'm here to see Michelle, she said primly, the smile growing wider. *My name is Ashley.*

Ashley had found Michelle on the dreamtime missed connections site. Michelle had dreamed she was on a boat with a boy and the boat was sailing through a beautiful cemetery. The etched marble mausoleums were hung with pictures of the dead in their prime, many were mustachioed young men with feathery hair who had passed. Michelle knew they had been gay men with AIDS. The lushness of the dream was thick with melancholy. Michelle and the boy leaned against the rail, a slight salt spray dusting their faces, and they kissed with the understanding that they would die. It was a nice dream, it had gravitas. A person named Ashley, located in Alaska, had identified herself as that boy and emailed a request to visit with Michelle while passing through Los Angeles. Michelle wasn't holding her breath. She wasn't sure she wanted to meet anyone from these dreams. She wasn't sure what the point would be. Also, there were so many dreamtime lovers for Michelle they made her feel slutty and embarrassed.

Now here was Ashley. Her bouncy hair was product-free. Her skirt was tiered and fell down her legs. Her face was sweet cheeked and innocent, she could be paid to sell hope and purity. Hers was the smiling face on a box of dryer sheets or maybe advertising an HMO. Ashley. Very different than the boy who'd stood beside her on the boat.

Michelle's stare lingered until she became aware of the girl's expression of dismay. Ashley had recognized Michelle as the puffier, splotchier doppelgänger of her dream lover and her face bloomed a grimace. Ashley thought Michelle's clothes were crappy, she had the roughed-up vibe of someone who'd been pushed from a speeding car. Her hair was a blue mess. She smelled of cigarettes. Michelle had thought she looked nice that morning, ready to meet Matt Dillon again, but nice is relative. In Ashley's dreams Michelle had looked much nicer.

Oh, Ashley said. She did not attempt to mask her disappointment. *You're Michelle.*

Yeah, Michelle nodded. Hello.

Hi.

Michelle tried to recover from the blow of the girl's rejection and found she could not. She grew defensive. Well, You're Twelve, she snapped, And A Girl, So Don't Look At Me Like That.

I'm thirteen, Ashley corrected. Michelle laughed.

It's The Same. Twelve Is The Same As Thirteen. Only A Thirteen-Year-Old Would Think A Year Made Any Difference.

Well, you're . . . Ashley tripped, halted, bit her tongue.

Old? Michelle said, daringly.

No, Ashley said. *You're not that old. But you look like you are. That's what's weird.*

I Was So Great In The Dream? Michelle asked.

Better than this. Ashely shrugged. She looked at Michelle with a level expression. *You're an alcoholic.*

How Do You Know?

Well, you can kind of just tell. But I've figured out a lot. Ashley felt a pulse of sympathy for this Michelle, whose hair was not curling and glossed with heath, as in the dreams, but stained a dull blue, scraggly as kelp. She didn't know she was also another, better Michelle. Ashley hoped to show her.

The youth bent down and unzipped her duffle bag. A terrible spongy smell filled the shop. *Sorry,* Ashley acknowledged the odor. *It's my uniform.* Michelle peered over the counter at the clatter of hockey gear.

You Play Hockey, Michelle said numbly.

Yes, Ashley said. *I'm here for a game.* Ashley slapped a folder on the counter and began pulling pages from it. Her movements were calm but Michelle could feel the underlying energy pulsing the stillness. The teenager's strong vibes and her ability to rein them in felt to Michelle like a sort of authority, a skill beyond the average thirteen-year-old.

What Sign Are You? she asked curiously.

Aries. Capricorn rising. Virgo moon.

You Know Astrology? Michelle was impressed.

I don't believe in it, Ashley said. *But I know you do. You're a Pisces, Aries rising, Cancer moon.*

How Do You Know That? Michelle asked.

Ashley showed her a sheet of paper printed with Michelle's statistics, her name, her medical information, job history, a timeline of major events in her life: her move to San Francisco, the publication of her book, the relocation to Los Angeles. The timeline rose toward the world's predicted end and kept going. Michelle writes another book. She stops drinking. She writes another book and then another. She continues writing books, the world gone, long exploded. Six years after the end of the world she breaks up with Lu. Michelle looked at Ashley, confused.

You Know Lu? Michelle asked. I've Barely Written About Her.

Ashley shook her head. *Not really. I did some dream hacking.*

Michelle stared at the girl, waiting. Come On, Don't Be One Of Those People That Makes Me Beg You To Tell Me Everything. You Walk In Here With A File About Me Like A Fucking FBI Agent, Tell Me What Is Happening.

Everything that exists can be found, somehow. The teen shrugged. *I know how to break into places. Into dreams. For instance, I can be in a dream and find your computer and just look at your files, your writing, your browsing history, all that. And the story comes together.* She shook her file folder, her eyes bright. *I'm actually really excited to be telling you this. The only other people I've been able to tell are my other girlfriends.*

Your Other Girlfriends?

Ashley waved her hand. *I'll get to that. Anyway, you can actually figure out how to watch other people's dreams,* she continued. *And then enter them. After a while it's really just another world. And it's nicer than this one. There are still problems but everything isn't so ruined. It's like some alternative life, a second-chance world.*

Michelle liked that, a second-chance world. As a writer she liked it. It had a ring. How Are You Able To Do All This? Michelle asked. Are You A Genius?

Ashley shrugged. *You could do it too,* she said.

Michelle fiddled nervously with her poky blue bangs. She pushed them out of her face. In This Other World, she said, I've Written More Books?

Ashley nodded.

Am I Famous? she asked. Am I A Famous Writer?

The girl shrugged. *It's relative,* she said. *Don't get too excited. But, you're happy. You're sober. You look better.*

The girl had successfully blown Michelle's mind. I Just Can't Imagine How My Life Gets From Here—Michelle gestured to the bookshop, noticing a tweaker in the Theology section trying to shove a hardcover down his pants. Just Take It! Michelle shouted at him. Take It And Get Out Of Here! The man shuffled out the door, startled. She returned her attention to Ashley. I Just Can't Imagine How My Life Gets From This To That, she said, wiping sudden tears from her face. She couldn't believe she was going to die before her life got cool.

I've found two other girls that I have significant relationships with, Ashley said. *One is my girlfriend right now, in this world, and one is who I would fall in love with if I lived to go to college. And you're . . . well, I want you to come with me, too, to the other life where the world doesn't end.* Ashley leaned over the counter and took Michelle by her chin, kissed her.

Michelle pulled back. You're Thirteen, she said.

I am and I'm not. I'm pretty much as mature as you. You're an alcoholic and I'm an overachiever. It evens us out.

Can I Keep These? Michelle asked, her hand on the folder. I Just Need To Look At All This.

Ashley nodded. *Of course. I brought them for you.* She lifted her wrist and looked at her watch. *I've got a tournament tonight. I know you won't come, but you should know you're invited.*

What About Your Other Girlfriends? Michelle asked. She tried to imagine the harem of tweenage girls Ashley was keeping in her parents' muddy, rustic home in Alaska. The slumber party of it. Michelle, pushing thirty, trying to will herself into an alternate dimension each night. She thought about the UFO cult that had recently drunk poison to somehow hop aboard a passing comet. How was this any saner? She imagined the parents that would arrest her as a pedophile the moment she crossed their threshold. Never mind her tweenage love rivals. Won't Your Girlfriends Hate Me?

Ashley shrugged. *They're pretty cool,* she said. *They know about you. Our relationship won't really happen until the future, so it doesn't interfere with their love. We all just have to be really adult about it.*

And If I Don't Come What Happens?

You die, Ashley said.

I Could Die Anyway, Michelle said. Even If I Came. Your Plan Doesn't Make A Lot Of Technical Sense. It Sounds Like A Wish.

It's true, I might not figure it out. It does seem unlikely right now, but it's definitely the only chance.

Can We Stay In Touch If I Don't Go? Michelle asked. Can I Email You?

Ashley shook her head, her thin lips disappearing. *No,* she said. *I'll have to move on.*

Michelle opened the folder, rustling through pages of her life. Her trip across the country, leaving her mothers for a life in San Francisco. Her eight years with Lu, what it looked like, the ways it changed her, for better and for worse. Their breakup. In one passage Michelle wails long into the night like a shot animal. She feels stripped of her dignity to have such a private moment known by Ashley— Ashley who seemed so dignified, despite her meager age. She shut the folder, ashamed at how quickly she'd become obsessed with the details of her life.

Sorry, she said. This Is Just—I Write Memoir. It's Weird To Read My Story Before I've Lived It.

Ashley nodded. *I've got to go. My number is in the folder.* She leaned over the counter one more time, and as they kissed Michelle could feel a glimmer of the person she was with Ashley. How good it felt, that version of herself, what a gift it was to feel some dormant part of herself enlivened. Ashley caught a glimpse of her own future self, felt older, tougher, more of a boy than the girl she was then. They pushed their different selves between them until the door jingled open and Michelle jumped away from the kiss.

Ashley smiled. *Please call me and I will take you. I know you don't have any money, it doesn't matter.*

Michelle didn't bother trying to defend her financial state, the girl knew everything. And if she knew everything, she had to have known that Michelle could never go with her.

21 Michelle enjoyed matching music to writings. Much of the music for sale in the shop was obscure to her, so she took a lot of chances with album covers. She played gospel as she read Dorothy Allison, and with Eileen Myles skipped between opera and Sonic Youth. Peter Plate and the Clash. Charles Bukowski and Tom Waits seemed too obvious. She tried Leonard Cohen instead, but went back to Tom Waits. Dodie Bellamy and Nico. Kevin Killian and Kylie Minogue. What would the sound track be to this folder in front of her, notes for a memoir of a life never lived? She found not an album but a busted cassette of Morrissey's *Viva Hate*, slid it into the tape player, and opened the folder. This was where she was when Paul stumbled into the bookshop.

Michelle had not seen her boss in weeks. He'd grown larger, his hair longer, more matted. If she hadn't known him she'd presume he was another drug addict looking to pawn a Danielle Steel paperback. When he spoke his voice croaked, as if he hadn't spoken out loud for a very long time. He moved the phlegm around his throat with some coughs and gurgles.

Melissa, he addressed her. *Excuse me. I haven't spoken out loud in a while.*

His eyes, Michelle noted, were crusted with sleep, as if he'd been lying facedown in a sandbox. The corners of his mouth looked sticky above his beard.

It's Michelle, Michelle said. She observed her boss, who leaned on the counter, taking a breath. He was a mess. Do You Need Water Or Anything? Are You Okay?

He brushed away her kindnesses impatiently. *I'm fine, I'm fine.* He turned his face to the windows, looking out onto the Strip. *The world is really deteriorating. Have you noticed?*

Michelle shrugged. I Thought It Would Be Worse Actually, she said.

You're just accustomed to the pace of its unraveling. Go to sleep for a couple weeks and then take a look at it. It's much, much worse. You can hardly use the freeway now even if you wanted to, there are just busted cars and bodies—dead bodies, Rochelle—all over the road. It is a sight. People are considerably more unhinged, people in the streets. He heaved a breath. *I'm going back to bed, ASAP. I just wanted to talk to you about the store.*

You're Having Good Dreams? Michelle asked cautiously. Paul's appearance suggested that her suspicions that her bosses were using the dreamtime like drugs were correct.

Beatrice and I have synced ourselves up and figured out how to go anywhere we want, not just places we were destined to go on vacation. Truthfully, if the world were to continue, we wouldn't have traveled very far. I don't like vacations. Too much work, they're very stressful. But this dreaming thing is wonderful. We just link up and poof, we're wherever we want to be. You should try it with someone. You've got to really love them though. It's gotta be the real thing.

Well, I Don't Have The Real Thing. I Don't Believe In It.

What, you haven't met your soul mate on one of those websites? I thought that was working out for everyone.

Michelle tried to think of something tough and cynical to say, but nothing came. She shrugged. Not For Me, I Guess.

You seem sad about it, Paul squinted at her, his face cramped in a wince. *Don't waste your time, you're almost dead. Listen, I can tell you want to talk about this, so I'm going to get out of here. I don't want to be weighed down with your problems.*

Michelle was taken aback by the man's bluntness. She *had* wanted to talk to him. Paul was very annoying but he was also sort of wise.

Do You Love Beatrice? she blurted. Do You Really, Really Love Her For Real?

Of course, Paul said.

No—Really, Really Love Her? Or Are You Just Resigned To Her? Is She Your Habit? And Speaking Of Habits, Should You Really Be Spending All Your Time Dreaming?

One world is the same as the next, go to the world you like best, Melissa. He sighed. *Are you afraid love is not actually real because you're experiencing romantic sadness?*

Michelle nodded. I Think It Might Just Be Like Sexual Attraction Plus Codependency. Desire Plus Your Own Personal Damage Melding You To Another.

Interesting, Paul stroked his grimy beard. *I do think we have an interesting relationship with personal damage in this culture. The ways our lives, our families, and our childhoods ruin us is exactly what makes it possible to be in relationships with other people. If I hadn't been raised by such a depressed mother, could I tolerate Beatrice's constant weeping? I think it would creep me out.*

It Is Disturbing, Michelle confirmed.

I'm sure it is. But it feels familiar to me and I accept it and I don't try to make Beatrice change, you know. She can cry all she wants. I buy her hankies.

Why Is She Always Crying?

She's just sad, Paul said. *Some people feel that more than others. Anyway, listen, love is real, I love Beatrice very much, I love her because I am a damaged person, not in spite of it— damage opens your heart, you know, if you allow it to—and, oh, that's all I have for you. Good luck with the rest of your life. I wanted to give you the bookstore.*

For Real? Like I Can Have It?

Yeah, take it. We're done. We're retiring. We don't need any-thing, I mean we've got enough food in the house for the rest of time—we're not expending very much energy sleeping so we don't need a lot. We're just going to sleep as much as we can until the world ends.

What About Joey? Michelle asked. Shouldn't He Inherit It? I Just Started Working Here.

Oh, Joey picked up his heroin habit again, Paul said with a shrug. *I don't think he'll be around much. I made sure he had food, but junkies don't eat a lot.*

That's Not Good, Michelle said.

It's fine, Paul said. *The worst thing that can happen is he dies a few months before he dies. It makes him happy. It gives him better dreams, he told me.* Paul clapped his hand on the counter, done. *So, do what you like.* He gestured around the store. *There's a safe under that patch of peeling linoleum in the back room. The key for it is on that key ring, one of those. Buy yourself some food, canned stuff, that's all you're going to need. If Joey comes by, you know, share it all with him, but it's yours I'd say. Nice knowing you, Melissa.* He smiled through the web of his beard. *Who would've known when you got hired here that I'd end up giving you the place? That you'd be the last human I spoke to, huh?* He shook his tangles. *You gotta love life, just for things like that. Gotta love it. Listen.* His sleepy, bloodshot eyes widened with a sense of seriousness and bore into Michelle's like they were seeking out her soul. *There's not enough time on the planet for you to get over your heartache, but you should just trust that if things hadn't all gone to shit you would've gotten over it. You would have been in love a bunch more, I can feel it. You're one of those people. I bet you fall in love easy, don't you?*

Michelle shrugged. I Suppose.

Nothing to be ashamed of. Doesn't make the love less real. It's just your state. It's a gift. Anyway, you'll probably never love again, but just know that you would have. Just know that. Sayonara. The man lumbered out the door, exiting with the familiar chime. He was no longer her boss. Michelle looked around her workplace, the bookstore. She was a business owner. She owned a bookstore. It had ceased being a functional bookstore, of course, and was more of a strange library, a place for addicts and fragile people to come out of the killing sun and find some peace, maybe leave with a book or a dollar in their pocket. Michelle supposed it was becoming a sort of social service agency, which was not the worst thing.

She locked the door and grabbed the ring of keys from beneath the register. There were about fifty keys on it, all sort of grimy, stinking of metal. She rattled them in her hand as she walked to the back room, that corner of linoleum. She'd kicked it idly during lunch breaks, listening to the *flick flick flick* of it beneath her combat boot as she heated up leftover pasta in the microwave. She pulled it back and saw the cubby that had been created beneath it, found the solid safe, heaved it out with some difficulty.

On the twelfth key the top came off. Lots of money was inside. Michelle could imagine an earlier moment, maybe even last week, when finding such booty would have filled her with adrenaline, such joy, that she would have had to lie her body down on the floor and wait till the feelings passed into something functional. But the money looked oddly like any collection of anything. A box of seashells, a jar of marbles, a store full of books. Paul was right, all she really needed was food. She'd stopped paying rent and that seemed fine. She'd stopped drinking and cigarettes didn't work without alcohol to both feed the compulsion and numb her of its grossness—the stink, her moist and yellowy fingers, the swamp in her lungs. Michelle needed hardly anything and now had more than enough to secure it for her. She took out a small bundle of cash and sunk the safe back into its cache beneath the floor.

22 Michelle had stopped drinking—because it was killing her. This story isn't bound by what really happened, but Michelle's sobriety in this book and in life is a rare moment of narrative resolution. She'd be a fool not to exploit it.

But telling it, really telling it, would be too much. Michelle tried to encapsulate it in a sort of montage, like Rocky Balboa training for his big fight. *Flash,* Michelle meditates. *Flash,* she overcomes a moment of craving. *Flash,* she learns how to pray. *Flash flash flash* she goes to a bunch of AA meetings and gets a sponsor, someone she can't write about because of the anonymity thing. Actually, Michelle worries that writing about AA violates the anonymity thing.

Michelle could make Michelle get sober without AA, but that would encourage any alcoholics who deeply want to believe they can do it on their own. I mean, who wants to go to meetings in churches and listen to weird strangers who've ruined their life talk about God? Michelle didn't. She, too, tried to get sober without AA and found that her twisted life minus the familiar coping tool of alcohol was more hellish than a hangover. She hadn't known then that people went to AA to learn how to live. She thought it was a support group for losers who needed help with the fact that their life would never be fun ever again.

Michelle didn't want it to seem like she was the rare person who could get sober and achieve actual sanity without AA. And Michelle thought it was weird that she could write a bunch of stories about being wasted all the time but then couldn't write honestly about how she had become sober. But from here on out, Michelle doesn't drink anymore.

23 *I haven't talked to you,* Wendy said, her tone a bit hurt. *You know they're shutting down the telephone services. I wondered if you would even say goodbye to me. And your brother. I worry about you two, especially now with the world ending. You don't know what it's like to be a mother worrying about her children. It's its own thing. You'll never know. You'll never know such worry, now.* Michelle could hear her mom exhale smoke.

I Wouldn't Have Known Anyway, Michelle said. I Never Wanted A Kid.

You say that, but I had a dream. One of those dreams everyone's having. You had a baby, your brother had a baby, it was like we were all a real family.

Michelle hadn't recalled seeing anything about a baby in Ashley's files. But Ashley's files, she realized, stopped at the end of her and Ashley's relationship.

You really haven't dreamed about the baby? Oh, it's a cute thing.

Boy Or A Girl? Michelle asked.

Wendy snorted. *You won't say. In the dream. You give it some weird name so no one knows if it's a boy or a girl and you say you're going to just let the baby figure out what it is. Good thing the world is ending, huh? You'd have some kind of confused person on your hands if you did that.*

It sounded like something Michelle would do, actually. Am I Alone, she asked, With The Baby?

No, no, you have some person, you know. She looks like a boy but she's a girl. She's good, I like her. She gives people a good feeling. You're happy.

Really?

Yeah, really, you're in love. You really haven't dreamed about this?

No.

Well, you're older in the dream. Kind of old to be having a baby. Maybe it hasn't come yet.

I Was Thirty-Seven In My Last Dream, Michelle said.

Oh, no, you're older than that in the baby dream.

Jesus, Michelle said. That Sounds Grotesque.

Well, how are you doing in the real world, huh?

In truth, Michelle was doing fine. Every morning she woke up in a different part of the bookstore. She dragged a pile of cushions onto a pile of books and slept there, like a child surrounded by toys. She slept upstairs in the stacks of cassette tapes, she slept in the break room above her hidden pile of money. Michelle opened and closed the bookstore depending on how she felt about humanity that day. She had to have an open heart to open the door. One afternoon a woman, batshit crazy, began hurling books at the wall, emitting a shrill keen. Michelle joined her. It felt fucking fantastic. *Eeeeeeeeeeeeee!* she trilled, the sound coming from deep in her throat. She chucked book after book at the wall, where they collided with other books, the lot of them tumbling to the floor to land in a pile of still more books. The woman stopped, just briefly, to see if Michelle was mocking her, but feeling safe in her insanity resumed her cries and hurls. She cackled and Michelle cackled back. Almost every day had a moment like that to open into, something totally apocalypse.

In the break room she made a lousy cup of coffee, regretting that she would probably never taste real quality coffee again, but grateful nonetheless for the caffeine. She would select a book and read it. She'd read in her pile of cushions, sneezing at the dust. She'd read behind the counter as if she were a normal girl at a normal workplace during a normal era, slacking off in a normal manner. She'd sit on the counter. She'd sit on the ladder or a chair. She selected books at random, ones she'd never heard of. *Glory Goes and Gets Some. Car. The Speed Queen.* She grabbed ones that made her think of San Francisco: Kevin Killian, Dodie Bellamy. She read the entire *Tales of the City* saga. She read books about Los Angeles: Kate Braverman and Mike Davis.

The hours of operation were ruled by insomnia, anxiety, boredom. On many nights Michelle stayed open through till sunrise, closing up shop in the morning to sleep like a vampire in the windowless back room. The novelty of living like this, like the kids in *From the Mixed-Up Files of Mrs. Basil E. Frankweiler*, was not lost on her. Michelle imagined that it would take a while for the odd romance of it to wear off, and Michelle didn't have a while.

With the exception of Matt Dillon, Michelle spent time

with hardly anyone. His visits were infrequent, but when he came he brought Michelle cigarettes, which she began to enjoy again. He liked spending the night on her cushions. *Like camping*, he'd laugh, enjoying the weirdness of it, reading out loud to her from books strewn across the floor, playing a divination game where he picked a sentence at random to forecast their next day, or explain the nature of their erratic coupling, or detail what they could expect in the moment the earth exploded. Together they remembered the places they'd longed to sleep as a child—inside refrigerator boxes, in a play structure at a park, behind the couch, beneath the Christmas tree, beneath a stairwell in the library. They agreed that the bookstore was as good as all such places rolled together, though Matt was quick to return to his own home, which Michelle imagined was quite lovely and probably home to a quite lovely woman as well.

I'm Fine, Michelle said to her mother. She had slid into her loneliness and found it oddly comfortable. She felt badly for the years she'd pestered her mother into increased happiness, trying to rouse her into someone else's life. I'm Thinking Of Starting An End-Of-The-World Book Club. Like Where We Read Books About The End Of The World. And Discuss.

Well, you'll never guess what happened at my work, Wendy said, and continued without pause. *We all moved in. We took over.*

Moved In Where? Into The Asylum?

That's right! Wendy exclaimed. *Oh, it's excellent. We play games all night, we've got that big kitchen, we all take turns cooking, all the nurses. I made shepherd's pie last night. It was good. I used that packaged cheese on top, you know the stuff that comes in the mac and cheese boxes?*

The Orange Powder? Michelle asked. You Put That On Your Shepherd's Pie?

It was delicious, Wendy insisted. *We've been eating mostly ramen so it was a treat. Everyone's calling me "Chef" now.*

But Where Are The Patients?

Some are still around, we still take care of them. Some wanted to go, we let them go. Listen, everyone is crazy out on the streets. Who am I to tell someone they got to stay all cooped up when they're gonna be dead so soon?

Are You Going To Get In Trouble?

Nah, Wendy said. *This is happening in a few places. My friend Dolores is a nurse at an old folks' home, she said whenever one of her patients dies a nurse moves into their room. Or a CNA or whatever. It's better than living alone right now, waiting for some gang to rob you.*

Alone? Michelle asked. What About Kym, Is She With You?

Oh, honey, Wendy said. *Kym left me.*

What? Where Did She Go?

She left me for a man.

No! Michelle shrieked.

Oh, yeah. Yeah, she did.

When? Oh My God! Are You Okay?

Wendy laughed. *Yeah, yeah. I'm fine, we're fine. You know, we were more like roommates for a long time. I mean, it was hard, don't get me wrong. But it's good now. It's better. You know, it's a relief not to have to take care of someone all the time.*

Is She Sick, How Is She? Where Is She?

She's living with him, some guy. I don't know, I don't like him, but she does. He's just some guy from the square, you know, a guy who hangs out down there. He's a toughie. Got tattoos and stuff like that.

He's Taking Care Of Her? Michelle asked.

She's fine! Wendy screamed. *She's fine. She's not sick anymore.*

Are You Kidding?

I guess she just needed to get laid. You know?

Oh My God. I Can't Believe This. Does Kyle Know?

I don't talk to you kids. You don't call me, I don't call you two, we don't talk.

I Know, Ma, Michelle said. I'm Sorry.

It is what it is. You know I love you?

Yeah, Michelle said. Of Course I Do. Do You Know I Love You?

Oh yeah, I know it.

Really? Michelle asked. Really? You Really Do? Michelle felt that love rise up inside of her, that scared and frustrated love. She wanted to push it somehow into her mother, make her feel what it felt like to love her. How tremendous and difficult.

You don't have to try so hard, 'Chelle, she said. *Just love me, okay? And I'll love you. Simple. Okay?*

Okay. She was crying.

Are you safe where you are? Wendy asked.

Yeah, Michelle said.

'Cause you know you can come and stay with me if you need to. I could try to find the money to get you here. We all help each other out, it's really nice.

Michelle thought about ending her life in a mental hospital with her mother. It had its appeal. I Don't Think It's Even Possible To Get To You, she said.

Well, I'm glad I got to talk to you, Wendy said. *Before they turn the phones off. And I hope Kym gets it together to call you, you know she loves you, don't you?*

Michelle did. Yeah.

I'd like to speak to your brother too but he doesn't return my calls. You know what that means.

What? Michelle asked.

He's got a boyfriend. He never wants to talk to me when he's got a boyfriend.

24 Michelle called Kyle. Do You Have A Boyfriend? she demanded. I Talked To Ma, She Said You Won't Talk To Her And That You Never Talk To Her When You Have A Boyfriend. Do You Know That Kym Has A Boyfriend? Our Mothers Have Lost Control.

Yes, Kyle affirmed. *I know everything. And yes, I have a boyfriend.*

Kyle! Michelle exclaimed. She recalled the dream of the garden. Is He, Like Does He Have Really Blue Eyes, Dark Hair?

Yes! Kyle shrieked. *Yes! Yes!* This was why he did not call their mothers when he fell in love. He became like a small dog in love, full of yips, chasing his tail, a teenage girl, perhaps, shiny and pink. All the mothers could do was make fun of him.

The One We Dreamed Of, Michelle said.

Yes, Kyle said. *We found each other on Craigslist and went on a date and it was like love at first sight. It was amazing. It is amazing.*

Wow, Michelle said. He's Like How He Was In Your Dream, Like In Real Life? All My Dream Lovers Are Teenagers Right Now.

It's all about timing, Kyle said. *People change, they keep changing. You got to catch them at the right moment or else you can't sync up. I think I would have met Walter really soon anyway. He was redecorating my boss's apartment.*

Kym Left Wendy For A Man And Wendy Is Living At The Mental Hospital And Dreaming She's A Grandmother.

They needed to break up, don't you think?

I Guess. There's No Time To Overthink Anything Anyway.

I know! Kyle cried. *I love it! I'm moving in with Walter. It's so easy. If we were going to keep living we'd never do it! Listen,* he said, *we want to have you over before the end of the world, okay? Will you please come over for dinner next week? I can't believe how quickly time is passing.*

I Know, Michelle said. And I Would Love To.

25 Through the weeks Michelle had many dreams, and then she ceased to have any. The darkness of her slumber was a deep relief, was the most rested she had ever felt. She awoke lit with such energy, coffee was suddenly unnecessary. Which was great, since it had finally become unavailable. Lots of things had become unavailable. The shops were empty, the faucets were dry. There was a sensation that things were shutting down, switch by switch. Instead of this fomenting anxiety, a peacefulness descended on Michelle, on Michelle and on the people around her. On everyone, perhaps. A peek at the computer revealed a total lack of missed dream connections. As the soothing cloak of blackness had been draped over Michelle's dreams, so it seemed that everyone else had lived out their astral lives and could finally get a good night's sleep. Perhaps this is what it will feel like, Michelle wondered, when it all goes away. The moment felt extremely close. Michelle thought it wouldn't be so very bad. All day she looked forward to the velvety blackness of her nights, though her days were sweet as well.

The night before the world ended she visited with Kyle and Walter in Walter's impeccably decorated apartment. He was charming and clearly in love with her brother, and such a wonderful cook he managed to make a scrumptious feast from the sad array of cans stacked in his pantry. The three of them had a banquet. Walter busted open cans of salmon and vegetables and created a dish that made it easy to forget the world had ceased being able to sustain life. With cans of chocolate syrup and condensed milk he made astounding desserts. Cans of fruit were lit on fire with fine brandy poured from hoarded bottles. He filled goblets with the liquor and raised them in a toast.

Michelle, Kyle said. *Are you not going to drink? The fucking world is ending. I'd put my money on tomorrow. I think we're done.* Kyle made a face that suggested his hand was on his hip, even as his hands sat gently on the table. Sometimes the way her brother spoke made her think of bright fishes, wiggling. He put a glass in her hand.

Michelle thought of Joey. He'd come by the store once, to get money, and she'd given him a bunch. He was delighted by her bed of pillows heaped by the art books, and shortly after lying back on them he nodded off, staying that way until nightfall.

I must've been tired, he quipped. He was bony but not much more so than ever. His bandanna was gone and his bald head sprouted random hairs. Michelle missed his sharpness, his jokes and observations. The anxious wheel that pushed him through the world had ceased turning. Joey was beyond relaxed. His body when she hugged him was rickety as an old ladder. The embrace lingered and for a moment Michelle was frightened he'd nodded out on her, but then he pulled back and Michelle saw he was crying. His hand moved slowly toward his head, reaching for the bandanna. He remembered and stopped, laughed, but his hand stayed in the air, wavering.

Joey, Michelle said. You're A Mess.

I love you, he said primly, slowly, like sounding the words phonetically. He dipped his face toward hers for a kiss and Michelle stayed very still so that he wouldn't miss his target. He looked like a strange and ancient bird, pecking curiously at her cheek.

Was it sad that Joey was high for the end of the world? Would it be sad for Michelle to be drunk? She hadn't drunk now for many months. The thick, syrupy perfume of the liquor wafted from the wide glass. It caught at the back of her throat and made it clench. At night, before sleeping, Michelle would select a book from the Self-Help, Psychology, or Religion sections. She was no longer obsessed with drinking, but if the thought of it began to nag her she'd close the store and meditate, her ass on a pillow, feeling the dust sweeping against her face with every inhalation.

She supposed, in a sense, that it would be no big deal if she drank the brandy tonight, or even if she kept on drinking it until the world collapsed tomorrow, she could feel it, too, they were done. But, she just didn't want to. The strength of its smell, a fume rising up her face, reminded her of the choking toxic fog of the sea. She shrugged.

I Don't Like How It Tastes, she said honestly. Kyle laughed at this and Walter took back her goblet, split the drink among the two of them. The remains of the meal were before them, a mess of sauce and chocolate-stained napkins. Walter's plan was to dump the entirety of the table out the window. He giggled like a kid whenever he mentioned it.

What the fuck? he'd ask for affirmation. *Right? What the fuck?*

What the fuck, they'd agreed.

He placed a pack of menthol Nat Shermans before her on the table. *Well, at least smoke!* he exclaimed. It made people nervous, Michelle realized, when you didn't have a vice. Menthol Nat Shermans were her favorite cigarette. She smoked three in a row, stubbing her cigarette out on her plate like she remembered her grandfather doing when she was a child. It was disgusting and decadent and it delighted the men.

She said goodbye to them casually. There didn't seem to be a point to a large farewell, they'd been building up to this moment for so many days, it was nearly a relief. *I want it to be over*, Kyle had said earlier, and the others had nodded solemnly. She kissed Walter's cheek and he pressed the pack of Nat Shermans into her hand.

Keep them. And, wait. He dashed to the kitchen and returned with a little bag of what looked like dirt. *Coffee*, he said. *Good coffee.*

Michelle shoved the fragrant bag in her shorts pocket. She hugged her brother tight and kissed both his cheeks, like Parisians. Are You On Xanax? she asked him.

He brought his thumb and forefinger together and winked. *A little.*

Good. I Don't Want To Worry About You.

Don't worry about me, girl. We're going to drink and fuck all day long and when it all comes down we won't even know what hit us.

I Love That, Michelle said.

Outside Walter's apartment Michelle stepped around the contents of the dining-room table, the smashed china and shattered goblets and silver flatware shining under the moon. The sky was filled with stars now that the lighting had mostly been shut off. Los Angeles was as dark as the countryside. A single candle flickered in a melted lump at the bottom of a metal candleholder. Michelle lifted it to light another Nat Sherman and walked home to the bookstore, lighting one cigarette off another. Smoking was divine, she thought. It really let her know that she had lungs, had a body. Her air passages expanded with the diabolical menthol, it felt almost healthy. Michelle giggled. She'd never felt so safe in a crazed urban place, in the dark, alone. With everyone about to die, who would bother her? And if they did, why should she care? She anticipated running into fellow humans, almost longing for one last possible adventure, even a bad one, on this her last night on earth, but the streets were empty and even the freeway was silent of crashes. Michelle figured anyone who'd made it this far must have wanted to stick it out. It suddenly struck Michelle as very special to be one such person.

26 The last night on earth Michelle dreamed of a person who was a girl and a boy and together they swam in a sea Michelle had never seen. The sea was blue and waves broke upon rocks that were not rocks but something else, something alive, and beneath the clear, sweet water they spied sea fans, the leaves shaped like the tails of whales, webbed and purple, swaying with the suck of the tide. The brightest fish darted around Michelle, with her face in the water she watched a ray lift off from the ocean floor like a great bird in flight, its back scattered with sand, its elegant and deadly tail streaming behind like a ribbon. A turtle lumbered by, the water around it lit blue from the sun, the sort of light that encircles angels in religious paintings. It dove toward a rock and began munching fuzzy scum from the cragged surface. Everything appeared to fly, as if the ocean were another sky, a bluer, truer firmament. Was this how it used to be? Dreaming Michelle wondered at the deep, at the snake of an eel moving with the undulations of a whip cracked.

The person who held her in the salt of it kissed her with an open mouth, passing a golden fish between them. Their kiss was the fish, the fish their love, something wet and sleek and iridescent. Waves pushed their bodies together as if the ocean were a meddling friend, a matchmaker, and when their hips bumped their cunts became luminescent and the glow was visible beneath the waters. Michelle felt the tender fish swim into her mouth and she pushed it back soft through the lips of her lover.

Luciferin, the person whispered to her, tickling her ear with the fish. *Photoprotein.* Jellyfish tentacles unfurled from the depths of their bodies, the venomous lashes loosened and stinging, the fantastic pain of it bringing them beneath the waves where they fucked against the coral.

Tipping on lucidity, Michelle observed their junk with fascination, wondering at the pulsing, transparent lamps they had become. They kept their humid jungle air tucked deep in the balloons of their lungs. It would have been wiser to grow gills. The lovers couldn't stay under the water forever, like the turtles they would have to break the surface for a gulp of oxygen.

In tandem the lovers rose from the deep, spitting water. They kissed in the waves, no fish now, only their mouths, and the person held Michelle gently, floated her like a child. The ocean and her person held and bobbed her. Both gazed up at the sun and felt lucky and content. Michelle could feel the fish of their kiss swimming in her belly.

Are we really here? asked the person.

Yes, Michelle affirmed. The ocean was so warm and so blue, like the person's eyes. Michelle gazed at her. She looked like a sea elf, with mischievous ears and the facial architecture of a model. Her eyes were both oval and slanted, like in anime. Michelle gazed at the face as if it were a planet, and it gazed back at her.

Face! she said in recognition.

Face! Michelle giggled back. Is Love Real?

Oh yes, the person nodded. *Love is very, very real.*

Michelle could feel the love radiate out from the person's heart. It seemed to be the very thing that warmed the sea they swam in, the thing that fed the coral, the source of all life. They wrapped themselves together and found they fit perfectly. Michelle had never felt so soothed and wanted. Inside her surged a desire to do magnificent things for this person. She wanted to lay her on the sand and pet her head forever. She wanted to tell her every truth she'd ever known. She wanted to feel them grow as close as a hermit crab and its shell. She wanted to move inside her with the perfect motion of a sea fan in the water.

The World Is Over, Michelle nearly cried. Why Did This Take So Long?

We weren't ready, the person said. *We're still not.*

Where Are You Right Now? Michelle asked.

In the suburbs. I go to college. I'm a little awkward. I just cut my hair and I still have dreams that I can't get it all into a scrunchie.

Michelle laughed. I Live In A Bookstore, she said. I Sleep On The Floor. I'm Ninety-Seven Days Sober.

Congratulations, the person kissed her nose, leaving a droplet of salt. They kissed some more, their mouths tangy with the ocean. Michelle could feel the fish swimming inside her. She cupped the little wave of her belly.

It's Yours. They both knew it, but Michelle wanted to say it. The person kissed her harder.

Of course.

What Should We Name It?

Luciferin, she said. *Aequorin. Fireflies and jellyfish. Did you know that bioluminescence is the most common form of communication on earth? When the world explodes we'll become light.* She kissed Michelle like it was their last kiss and their first. She kissed Michelle like she was about to wake up. The kiss was the kiss that redeemed their earthly lives, the kiss was what everything was leading up to. Every bad and good thing Michelle had ever done was perfect and right, for it had led her to that kiss. With that kiss Michelle's life would have finally begun, if it hadn't already been over. All of this information was inscribed in the kiss, their story was petroglyphs marking the caves of their mouths and together they read. Together they drank the sea and pulsed with light.

Michelle woke up in a pile of pillows, the ocean streaming from her eyes.

27 On the last day of earth, the morning sun was high and bright. Michelle pulled open the blinds that she normally kept low to keep the LA glare from bleaching the books. The sun blasted the shadows. The bookstore looked lovely, her heap of pillows cozy in the sci-fi corner. Books and books and more books scattered on the floor, hanging from shelves. Michelle hadn't cleaned it one bit since acquiring the place, she liked watching entropy have its way, the accumulation of dust and cobwebs, haze on the glass, the books' journey as they were knocked around the store. Michelle wondered what she would read on the last day on earth. She made the real coffee she'd gotten off Walter, wonderful Walter. She was thrilled that Kyle was leaving the planet in a better style than he'd arrived. Michelle lit a Nat Sherman and let the coffee spring to life inside her.

She thought of everything. She thought of Chelsea and the dirt and the cigarette smoke and the public pools—the tough, mean kids in all their tough, mean glamour. She thought of her mother Wendy, earnestly learning to be a nurse, hunched over books with her pen in one hand and an ashtray, and Kym, a tangle inside, stifled desire making her sensitive to all the earth's vibrations.

She thought about little Kyle, clogging about with his feet in a pair of their moms' heeled boots. She thought of being a teenager and the toxic stink of hair bleach, the burn of it on her head, lining her face with eyeliner, the panic of getting it wrong and having to start over, the deep satisfaction of teasing her hair, combing it backward so that it sat hugely on her head, walking out into the world like that— and so what if the world hadn't responded very positively, Michelle knew she looked awesome and she was grateful for that, there on that day in the bookstore, she was grateful that she always trusted in herself above everyone else, in spite of everything else, she always moved into her destiny with excitement and bravery—yes, she realized, lighting a Nat Sherman off a Nat Sherman. It had been brave of her to be who she was in her life and it had been exciting, even the worst of it. Even the foolishness, the things that hadn't happened and more so the things that she'd allowed to happen, all of it. The eight years with Lu, the utter loss of love and then the rebuilding that happens, the architecture of your heart reconstructed to welcome a very different type of creature.

Michelle remembered the person from her dream last night, could still feel their fish in her belly. She was glad the Internet was gone or else she'd spend the whole last day on earth trying to find her, and it was better this way. She knew the person was loving her somewhere and Michelle was loving her, too. Soon they would be light.

Michelle sat at the kiosk before her laptop. She could, after all, write only the stories she was meant to write. She could write nothing more than that, nothing more or less perfect. As it turned out, time could not be wasted and everything had happened perfectly to deliver her to this moment, alone in her bookstore, lighting cigarettes off cigarettes. She loved only in the way she was built to love, and she had loved the people she had meant to. She hadn't been worthy of Andy, but she had loved her. She had loved Lu, for many years she had loved her. And all the brief people, many of whom hardly deserved it, she had loved them, too. At the end of the world, Michelle regretted none of it. She hoped they had all loved her, too. She wished that she had loved them even more.

Michelle opened a blank document. She imagined a girl whose openness to everything was its own current, pushing her into life. She remembered the feelings of love and drugs sickening her body, and felt tender toward the experience even as she was glad it was over. She felt the same about the doomed world itself, an impossible tenderness that did not blunt her relief that it was all going to end soon. She began to type.

Michelle wasn't sure when everyone started hanging out at the Albion.

She could almost smell the dank, yeasty stink of the old red bar. She typed. The sun arced across the sky, creating an installation of light and shadows as it burned through the store. She kept her motion across the keyboard, like the sun outside the windows, she arced. The sun sank and Michelle kept typing, saying goodbye to the sun and then taking it back because the sun would not be going anywhere. Tomorrow the sun would be here, wherever that was, and its roll and spin would be as it was today. Michelle shed a tear for the sun, the poor demonized sun the humans had run from when it only wanted to shine and bring warmth, she hoped there was another people somewhere feeling its happy glow.

Michelle's story, stanched for so long, came quickly and clearly, page after page it came, the story of Michelle and her tiny life made big, her blunders and foolishness made human, sometimes noble, her struggles redeemed, momentarily, and her love. That Michelle was the kind of person who loved felt good in those moments of writing. Michelle's fingers bounced against the keys like hail. She banged the story of her life into the computer, telling it until the words before her vanished and the very world around her was gone.

Acknowledgments

Much gratitude to the San Francisco Arts Commission and the Center for Cultural Innovation for their support of this project. Many thanks to Ali Liebegott and Beth Pickens for their work in creating the Radar LAB Writing Retreat, where the majority of this book was created. Thanks also to my writer roommates that first year; your excellent creative vibes are in this book: Lucy Corin, Nicole J. Georges, Thomas McBee, Sara Seinberg, and Myriam Gurba. For early reading and support I again thank Ali and Beth as well as Tara Jepsen, Amanda Verwey, Daniel Handler, Eileen Myles, and Emer Martin. The humblest of thanks to Dia Felix, Rocco Kayiatos, Bretton Fosbrook, Cari Campbell, Sash Sunday, and Sini Anderson. Thank you, Laura Mulley. Thanks to Lindsay Edgecombe for her daily wonderful support. And thanks to Jennifer Baumgardner, whose enthusiasm for this project from day one has been incredible. Much thanks to Jennifer, to Kait Heacock, Lauren Hook, Suki Boynton, and the entire Feminist Press team for their amazing vision, care, and work on this. I could not have hoped for a better home for this book.

And the deepest thanks to Dashiell Lippman, for making everything possible, always.

MICHELLE TEA is the author of many works, including the memoirs *Valencia* and *Knocking Myself Up*, the essay collection *Against Memoir*, and the tarot classic *Modern Tarot*. A prolific literary organizer in queer and feminist communities, she co-created the long-running performance tour Sister Spit and conceptualized the global phenomenon Drag Queen Story Hour. Formerly the editor of the Sister Spit series at City Lights and the Amethyst Edition imprint at the Feminist Press, Tea is now the founding publisher at DOPAMINE Books, a collaboration with Semiotext(e). She is the recipient of honors from Lambda Literary, the Rona Jaffe Foundation, PEN/America and the Guggenheim Foundation. She lives in Los Angeles.

The Feminist Press publishes books that ignite movements and social transformation. Celebrating our legacy, we lift up insurgent and marginalized voices from around the world to build a more just future.

See our complete list of books at
feministpress.org

THE FEMINIST PRESS
AT THE CITY UNIVERSITY OF NEW YORK
FEMINISTPRESS.ORG